Devil's Valley

Devil's Valley

A Novel

André Brink

Secker & Warburg
LONDON

Published by Secker & Warburg 1998

1 3 5 7 9 10 8 6 4 2

First published in the United Kingdom in 1998 by
Secker & Warburg,
Random House, 20 Vauxhall Bridge Road,
London SW1V 2SA

Random House Australia (Pty) Limited
20 Alfred Street, Milsons Point, Sydney,
New South Wales 2061, Australia

Random House New Zealand Limited
18 Poland Road, Glenfield,
Auckland 10, New Zealand

Random House South Africa (Pty) Limited
Endulini, 5A Jubilee Road, Parktown 2193, South Africa

Random House UK Limited Reg. No. 954009

A CIP catalogue record for this book is available from the British Library

ISBN 0-436-20461-4
ISBN 0-436-27503-1 (South Africa only)

Printed and bound in Great Britain
by Mackays of Chatham PLC

In Memoriam
JOHN BLACKWELL

When a man dies a library burns down
African proverb

Author's Note

I could not have imagined the Devil's Valley in this novel without thinking of the Gamkas Kloof, known as The Hell, in the Swartberg range of the Little Karoo. Yet there is nothing straight-forward about the relation between the two. The Hell might have turned out like my Devil's Valley had its isolation from the out-side world never been disturbed. But the difference goes beyond such comparison, since, when all is said and done, The Hell can be visited, albeit with some difficulty, deep in its mountain range, while the Devil's Valley, its inhabitants and its history exist only on the pages of this book.

For the diary passages in Part 4 I have (once again) made use of the journal of the Boer woman Susanna Smit as transcribed in Carli Coetzee's *Writing the South African Landscape*.

Several of the stories set in the Devil's Valley are based on old Khoisan and Boer narratives. A few of the episodes from Hans Magic's life are used with permission of Katinka Heyns.

The universe is made of stories, not of atoms.
– Muriel Rukeyser

Most journalists are restless voyeurs who see the warts
on the world, the imperfections in people and places . . .
Gloom is their game, the spectacle their passion,
normality their nemesis.
– Gay Talese

One

Come A Long Way

'I BEEN SITTING here, waiting for you,' said the old man, not bothering to look at me.

My fucking heart missed a fucking beat. Cautiously, as if I had reason to feel guilty, I shifted the rucksack on my back. I'd noticed the old dude from quite a distance, perched on the rocky outcrop, as grey as the grass. Without dislodging a stone or missing a step I'd come down all the bloody way from the top where the four-by-four had dropped me, heading straight for the small herd of mottled goats; and what with the sun coming at an angle from the front there was no shadow either to warn him; yet there he was on the ridge, in his stupid old-fashioned skin trousers and waistcoat and floppy wide-brimmed hat, his back to me, staring out across the deep ravine, and saying in that level voice, as if he'd bloody well been watching me all the way, 'I been sitting here, waiting for you.'

I put out my hand. 'Flip Lochner, Oom.'

'Ja, I know mos.' The crusty old customer was still gazing into the distance, so I had to drop my hand. 'You come a long way in this snow.'

Around us the mountains were shimmering in the late-summer heat. Bloody baking-oven. I wiped the sweat from my face with my sleeve. 'Snow, Oom?' I enquired cautiously.

'Ja, didn't you see? The mountains are white.'

I decided on the diplomatic approach. 'I can imagine it must be pretty cold here in winter.'

'Man, woman, child and beast, they all died of exposure.'

He drew the skin waistcoat tight on his sinewy body, shivering briefly as if he could actually feel the cold. He looked fucking ancient, but very straight, kind of patriarchal, his angry grey beard stained with tobacco juice like a tuft of dry grass pissed on many times, the mouth caved in, chewing on his gums. Something left on a shelf well past its sell-by date.

Devil's Valley

'I suppose that's the Devil's Valley down there?' I asked sort of unnecessarily after a while.

'What's it look like to you?'

'More like Paradise.'

A reluctant grunt made his Adam's apple jump. Then, a touch more affable, he said, 'We always believed Adam and Eve must have lived down here. I mean, before God got angry with them.' Adding as an afterthought, still without bothering to look at me, 'Name's Lermiet. Lukas Lermiet.'

It wasn't the sort of name one comes across every day or forgets once you've heard it. I could barely hide my surprise. 'But that's the family name, isn't it?'

'Well, what did you expect?' he asked in a huff. His voice was like old bloody dry grass rustling, and with a Dutch accent to it.

'I'm sorry, but it just struck me . . .' I tried to collect my thoughts. 'I mean, the first man who trekked into this valley – when was that? In the 1830s – was also a Lukas Lermiet, wasn't he? Lukas Seer, they called him. And then almost nothing more was heard of them for well over a century and a half. It was only the other day, in Stellenbosch, that I heard the name again . . .'

'Is that what you come for? To nose around? We minding our own business here.' For the first time the old fucker looked at me. The kind of look that unsettles one even in broad daylight: colourless eyes peering through a tangle of grey eyebrows, dulled by cataracts, with a remoteness about them, an absence. What was uncanny about it was this: on the one hand it seemed to miss nothing, picking up all the shit that had ever happened to me, all the hidden agendas behind it, even those I hadn't resolved for myself yet. On the other hand he seemed to be staring right through me, in one way and out the other, as if I was a bloody sheet of glass through which he could see everything in the landscape that had been there before us and would outlive us: the cliffs and ridges folding away, layer upon layer under the fucking endless sky, the slopes reaching down, all steep and forbidding like, to the long narrow valley at the bottom, as bloody void and whatever as it must have been in the time of God and Genesis.

'It's a piece of history that's never been written up properly,' I tried to justify myself.

'With good reason, if you ask me. Why would anyone want to write it up?'

'So that people will know.'

'What for?'

I had to calm his suspicions. 'Oom, I promise you I won't offend anyone.'

The old number scraped his throat and spat a green gob mere inches past my face.

So Very Sudden

'I met Little-Lukas Lermiet in Stellenbosch,' I began again.

No answer. He was sitting there like a dumb piece of rock.

'The day he died I was on my way to see him,' I went on. This might be the only bait he'd swallow.

But he still didn't bother to answer; I couldn't even be sure that he'd heard me.

'You might say I owe him one,' I explained. 'To come here, I mean. To look up his people. It was all so very sudden.'

'Little-Lukas had no business to go where he went. He had no right to flap out about us,' snarled the old man. 'He got what he deserved.'

'Oom?' I asked, taken aback.

Silence.

'I take it he was a relation? The same name and all.'

'None of your business,' he growled.

'Well . . .' I knew when there was nothing more to squeeze from a stone. 'At least I thought I'd come and see for myself.'

Open Eyes

'You can still go back,' said Oom Lukas in his raspy voice, so gruffly I wasn't quite sure if he'd spoken or just cleared his throat. 'And if you want my advice you'll turn back while you still can. Once you put your two feet down there it may soon be too late.'

'No, Oom, I can't let such a chance go by. I've been waiting for this for years. And after I spoke to Little-Lukas . . .'

'Then you going into it with open eyes.'

Words I was to remember only too fucking well, much later, too late.

'If you don't mind, I can go down with you when you go home,' I proposed.

'You'll be waiting a long time.'

'Don't you live down there in the valley, then?'

'Says who?'

'I'm afraid I don't understand.'

'That's your worry.' He sat mumbling to himself for a while before he spoke up again: 'You want to go down, you do it on your own.'

'Then can you show me the way?'

He sniffed, and for a while he seemed to have switched off. Then he raised his hand-carved kierie. 'Go down this little slope to the break in the cliff, and past the two big boulders of the Gate. You can wait down there, someone will come. And down in the kloof Lukas Death will take over. You can stay with Poppie Fullmoon. I already told them to expect you.'

'But how could you have known? I haven't discussed this with anyone.'

Ignoring the question he said, 'That's to say if your mind is really set on it.'

'It is.'

'All right, then get going. But mind the snow, it's very slippery. We'll talk again.'

Hooking my thumbs under the straps of the rucksack that was giving me hell, I began to go down the slope, my heart in my throat. I'd been warned that it could take days to find one's way down to the valley. If you make it. More than one climber had fallen to his death down these cliffs – and they were experienced mountaineers, not people whose systems had been fucked up by years of smoking and drinking and whatever, especially whatever. And could I really rely on the word of an old dodderer whose head had clearly taken a knock?

God's Grandmother

Down below me stretched the Devil's Valley, much as it must have been when it was first torn into the earth's crust. Ungodly cliffs on either side, with ridges and bands in reds and oranges and browns, greys and blacks, thrown up from their original horizontal layers by bloody unimaginable forces. Some had been shoved into diagonal or even perpendicular positions, others were rippling like petrified waves. The kind of landscape that turns a man into a fucking ant. As if the earth itself had turned and tossed in a pre-dawn slumber before it sort of sat up, all bleary-eyed. And down at the very bottom lay the deep slit of the valley, half-hidden behind dark thickets of natural forest. The kind of view that turns on a dirty mind.

It was like being the first man ever to set foot in this place. I could imagine the sensation the first Lukas Lermiet must have felt looking down here, the kind of randiness that marks every first man: seeing the earth unfolding ahead, just waiting to be conquered. With my tape-recorder and my camera, here we go.

In the motherfucking cliff-face ahead of me was a single breach. That must be the 'Gate' the old man had spoken about. The two huge boulders he'd pointed out were speckled grey on the outside, but where the crust had eroded the rock was flame-red. I stopped for a moment to look back. A hundred yards higher up I could see the old dried-up turd still perched on his rock surrounded by his grazing goats, motionless like a stone carving, and worn away by wind and sun, water, lightning. Brittle and fragile, a mere twig of a man, older than God's grandmother.

Infamous Fruit

MY TIME IS running out. From where I'm sitting now, just out of sight of the sprinkling of whitewashed houses and the squat stone church, I can look out over the scorched slopes. It is hard to believe how much has happened in the time I've been here. From deep inside the Devil's Valley, like Jonah from the belly of the whale, I've got to cry out or something. But who will hear? No matter, I've just got to try, there's nothing else I can do. The day I came down here, when I passed through old Oom Lukas's high gate, the rocks mottled with lichen, bird shit, dassie piss, the crap of baboons, pollen blown by the wind, all this was still waiting to happen. Yet in a way it was already there. Sure, the old number had given me due warning, but how could I have known what he meant? These things always come too late. One prepares to face the threats one knows, not the fucking unknown. And at that moment all was still unknown.

Would I have turned back, that afternoon, if I'd then seen what still lay ahead? Jesus, it would have spared so much. For me, for Emma, for everybody in the Devil's Valley. All the violence of suffering, suspicion, intrigue, jealousy, memory, blood, betrayal, scorched earth. All these things which today converge to spell 'knowledge' – or, more pretentiously, 'wisdom'. Yet I have a hunch I would have pressed on regardless. I mean, would Adam have turned down his woman's infamous fruit – apple or apricot, mango or fig – if *he*'d been wise before the event? No way.

Tall Tales

The problem is that I have no bloody way of making sure what I have to show for my efforts. Statements, testimonies, accounts, or just a damn handful of ravings? A man who spent his whole life trying to fly. A woman who drove a stake through her husband's head. A savage who fathered seventeen children on the grave of his enemy. A witch who turned into a white goat when the moon was full. A girl who gave her own body as ransom for her father's life. The dead and the living celebrating New Year together. And a hell of a lot more, plumes in the wind, lightning on the horizon. But with no substance at all, just bloody inventions and tall tales. How can I get this to make sense? This is what bugs me. Especially now, with my time running out.

When I first came here I was still cocksure that it would all work out. And when the old fart up there told me his name was Lukas Lermiet it was like a sign that I was on the right way. Okay, I was ready to see almost anything as a good sign. For what I had behind me didn't bear much thinking of: fifty-nine years old, a wife gone off with someone else, two children who'd kicked me under the arse, the job at the newspaper where all my juniors had long been promoted past me, a fuck-up of a life. With only one thought in my mind: now it was all or nothing, now I was going for broke, to feed the rat that had begun to gnaw again, the old dream I'd thought I'd given up. Another man, I suppose, could shit on a dream like this, but for me it was ambitious enough. Perhaps I still had it in me. I mean, for Christ's sake, it wasn't as if I meant to move heaven and earth, or change the world. Have a heart. All I planned to do was to write a little tract of history, something to hold its own, something different from the daily news. From our crime reporter. Jesus, at fifty-nine. Starting each day in front of the cracked mirror: the nicotine-stained fingers, the purple spiderweb across nose and cheeks, eyes bloodshot, liver spots, the man who passes for me. Flip Lochner, pleased to meet you. A sight for sore eyes. But I haven't always been like this, God is my witness. And this may be just about my last fucking chance to prove it, right?

Crawling So Deep

IT WAS THIRTY years ago that I first found out about the Devil's Valley. Those were my days of innocence when there were still so many things waiting to be done for the first time. I had a touch of style then, even if I say so myself. In my life, and in what I put on paper. There were people who actually believed I was going to make it as a writer. I was still teaching, fired by ambition and great illusions, and planning my thesis. History, what else? Always my favourite subject. And I was in no mind to produce something that would gather fucking dust on a fucking shelf, no way. Unlike the themes some of my contemporaries at varsity built their reputations on: *Electrolysis in the Gut of the Earthworm, The Diet of German Sailors on Ships in the VOC in the Second Half of the Seventeenth Century, Criteria of Taste and Succulence in the Grading of Beef at the Cape Town Abbattoir*. Not for me, thank you very much. Mine was bloody well going to be different. I was set on Making a Contribution. Among other things, finally to shit on Twinkletoes van Tonder who'd regularly taken first place in History right through our university years. I'd always had to work my arse off to get somewhere, he just took it in his athletic stride. His father a professor, mine a shunter on the railways. Their house filled with the bric-à-brac of annual trips to Europe; our only showpiece a ball-and-claw radiogram on which over weekends Pa would play his seventy-eights of old Boer music, Chris Blignaut and the Briel Family.

Twinkletoes van Tonder was what Pa would have called a dainty-fart; I grew up barefoot in the shitty little village in the Free State, where the snot froze on one's upper lip in winter. I'm not complaining, mind. And I don't want to go off on a side-spin either. I can take whatever comes my way like a man, right? All I'm trying to say is that Twinkletoes van Tonder was a haemorrhoid in the arsehole of my life. He got his name from sucking up to lecturers, crawling so far up their backsides that only his toes stuck out. With MA wrapped up, the two of us were neck-and-neck for the vacant assistantship in the department. But Twinkletoes, in that ringing bloody phrase from the Bible, was a smooth man and I was an hairy man. And ever since the time of Jacob and Esau the dice have been loaded against us hairy ones. He got the job; I turned to teaching.

Wild Oats

Then one day I stumbled across a reference to a small party during the Great Trek who'd turned away from the other prospective emigrants and wandered into the Swartberg range. Scouting around and reading whatever I could lay my hands on, even spending one summer vacation in the Archives, I finally came up with some hard evidence on Lukas (Seer) Lermiet who'd trekked from Graaff-Reinet in the company of the well-known leader Gerrit Maritz in 1838. What first tickled me was the unusual name. In the Archives I unearthed one Luc l'Hermite who'd come out to the Cape with the Huguenots on the *Voorschoten* in 1688, who might well have been the founder of the family's local branch. But between this Monsieur l'Hermite and my Lukas Lermiet there was many a gap still to be plugged, and all the wrinkles in the line would first have to be ironed out before one could be quite sure. A damn tantalising idea, anyway. In the meantime my early research had suggested that the original Monsieur l'Hermite was not exactly a fucking ancestor to be proud of, as he appeared to have fled La Rochelle to escape a charge of murder, and travelled to the Cape masquerading as a religious refugee. Once arrived, he did a pretty good job covering his tracks while sowing all manner of wild oats, thistles and tumbleweeds well out of sight of the European authorities. And it might well be that a century and a half later the family finally took root among the koppies of the deep interior. All of which was still virgin territory for the researcher.

Anyway, our Lukas Lermiet left Graaff-Reinet in the company of
Gerrit Maritz, but soon ran into trouble with the old sourpuss
preacher of the group, Maritz's brother-in-law Erasmus Smit, and it
seems that, possessed by a vision, and accompanied by a few like-
minded spirits, the Seer turned off course to trek south-east, into the
forbidding Swartberg range. Just as ancient maritime charts of Africa
marked certain parts with the legend *Hic sunt leones*, there were old
maps of the interior on which the Swartberg was superscribed with
the words *Hier zijn duvelen*, or *Here be devils*. Hence, I guess, the name
'Duiwelskloof' – Devil's Valley.

Odd Reference

There was not much more on Lukas Lermiet and his descendants to
be found in the Archives, apart from the odd (sometimes very odd)
reference in minor official documents. In the 1890s an agent of the
Cape government was dispatched to collect taxes or quitrent or
whatever from the people who'd apparently disappeared into the
Devil's Valley without a trace; but he was screwed out of his clothes
and sent back across the mountains like my finger. Whereupon a
whole armed detachment came all the way from Cape Town to
avenge the honour of Her Fucking Majesty. Once again without
result, for no trace of the blasted commando could ever be found;
and soon afterwards the Anglo-Boer War gave the distant government other priorities to care about.

From the time of the 1914 Rebellion came a reference to a
couple of burghers who'd escaped into the valley to hide from
government troops, never to be heard of again. Much later, during
the Second World War, a small band of right-wing extremists from
the Ossewa-Brandwag fled into the valley to get away from Smuts's
officers, and the bodies of two policemen sent after them were later
found in a deep kloof where they'd presumably fallen to their death.
Once again the matter was not followed up.

After the war individuals from the Devil's Valley sporadically
turned up in the outside world, and a legend took root about a
community of physically or mentally handicapped people in the

mountains, the sad outcome of generations of inbreeding. Somewhere in the fifties a team of census agents were sent out to record particulars of the inhabitants, but they never came back; on another occasion an exciseman dispatched to investigate rumours of illicit distilling met with a fatal accident in the mountains. Still later the University of Stellenbosch mounted an expedition of anthropologists and sociologists and God knows what other -ists on a research project, but they returned not only empty-handed but stubbornly mum about the expedition. Then money ran out as the government started cutting down on university budgets, and that was that.

All of which I found promising enough. But my designated supervisor found it too insubstantial. How about the Development of a Christian National Character Among the Voortrekkers, 1836-1843 instead? I might still have pressed my luck, but that was when Sylvia appeared on the scene and began to play me off against Twinkletoes van Tonder; and if I were to abscond for a couple of months to do research in the Devil's Valley I had little doubt that in my absence he'd settle so tightly into her own little devil's valley that once again only his toes would stick out. That was the end of my project. But at the time I thought it would be only a temporary setback. If you ask me, every person has a rat inside, a rat which keeps gnawing away and which you must feed if you hope to survive, otherwise it consumes your fucking guts. And the Devil's Valley was my rat. I was going to feed it. But for thirty years nothing came of it, until there wasn't much left to consume in me.

Comes Out Red

That is, until Little-Lukas Lermiet appeared on my horizon a few months ago. The occasion was a day-long seminar in Stellenbosch on 'History and Reporting', to be introduced by Professor Hardus (Twinkletoes) van Tonder, Head of the Department of History, D.Litt. et Phil., S.H.I.T., Dean of the Faculty of Arts, as well as Vice-President of the South African Academy of Education, Arts and Science. My presence, as member of a panel on Investigative Journalism, was either pure coincidence or fate, depending on the paradigm, I think that is the term, you use. Our editor was called away on an important mission requiring all his attention (something to do with his wife's investments), the news editor was otherwise engaged (he has a friend with a box at Newlands), two others who'd been approached were not available, which was how yours truly, well down the pecking order, came to be delegated at the last minute.

This kind of seminar is not my line at all. Do I still *have* a 'line'? I have no idea any more what I'm doing in journalism. Cynicism stains one like nicotine. There was a time . . . but forget it. Compromise is the name of the game, until you swallow your last lump of self-respect like the vomit of a bad hangover. Right up to the eighties there were moments when in a flush of misplaced romanticism or something I still thought I had a 'role' to play. You go out on a story to Old Crossroads or the KTC squatter camp, you look on while police set fire to the shacks of people who refuse to move elsewhere; you see a child, sent by his mother to the corner shop for a half-loaf of bread, run down by the cops in the yellow van, who then jump out to shoot him execution-style. Then you go back to the office and file your story with the news editor, a shithead ten years younger than yourself, who draws red lines through most of it and tells you to rewrite the piece. Anything you give to that cunt is like a fucking tampon: it goes in clean and comes out red. And when you object, he blows his top and tears up the sheets. You try to protest. He looks you in the eye and asks, 'What are you trying to do, Lochner?' You tell him, 'I was there, sir.' He says, 'For your information, this never happened.' And after the incident has been repeated three times you give up trying. You cannot resign either, because jobs are scarce and you have a wife who has Joneses to compete with and two kids at varsity, so don't rock the boat, buddy. When you shave in the morning, you look past your own image in the mirror, pretending you're not there. You feel like a whore on the point of retiring, but she's already got AIDS and all she can still hope for is to infect a few more fuckers before she croaks.

Fucking Symposium

And then they have the bloody cheek, on a Saturday you planned to spend working on your Cortina and watching rugby on TV, to pack you off to a fucking symposium on Investigative Journalism. Look, if you have to, ask me about crime statistics, and I'll be happy to oblige. Last year: an average of three murders an hour, a rape every twelve minutes (or, considering that only one out of every thirty-five is reported, one every twenty seconds), an armed robbery every five minutes, a case of child abuse every ten minutes (but of course even fewer of these are reported than rapes), and this happens twenty-four hours a day, seven days a week, fifty-two weeks a year, right? As Alan Paton said, 'Ah but your fucking land is beautiful.' And we still have Mandela. But all I'm trying to say is, ask me a thing like that and I'm your man. But don't come to me with symposiums and conferences and shit. So what does a man do? You go. That's what you do.

In a Corner

Crap of a high order, lasting a whole morning and afternoon. Afterwards the big brass decamped to a reception in the rector's house, while I ended up with a few other rejects and off-cuts and a group of rowdy students in a pub.

I landed in a corner, a position I'm no stranger to; and by the fourth or fifth round, when I was comfortably leading on points, I was approached by a spotty youngster. Little-Lukas Lermiet, the name registered after the second or third attempt. As nervous as a fucking puppy not sure whether he's going to be stroked or kicked. Quite an intelligent, narrow face, but his eyes looked like a frog's through those thick glasses, and he had a bit of a st-stammer. The kind of dude that just begs to be screwed out of his senses by a really wild girl to change him into a fucking prince.

He clearly wasn't much of a talker; and I was, not to put too fine a point on it, introspectively inclined. It was a mere week after Sylvia had left me the note (with two typos) and both children had telephoned to make sure I had no doubts about who was to blame; and striking up a conversation with a pimply youth was not high on my list of priorities.

'Sir, there was s-something you said this morning . . .' began Little-Lukas.

Few people call me sir; and my contribution to the morning's discussion, I knew perfectly well, had been a load of shit. So there was much bleary-eyed suspicion mixed with my feigned curiosity.

'. . . about the D-Devil's Valley in the Swartberg.'

I could vaguely remember the reference, yes. Some stray off-the-cuff remark about topics still waiting to be investigated.

'I-I live there.'

Deep in my guts I felt something stirring; the old rat was gnawing again.

He was the first inhabitant of the Devil's Valley I'd every come across in the flesh. It would seem that an old pedlar, a smous, had plied him with books in the Valley, until much pleading and effort and bargaining at long last landed him permission to study outside. Before his time the odd bright youngster had from time to time been allowed to go to school in one of the towns outside the Devil's Valley, but Little-Lukas was the first and only one ever to go to university. As far as I could gather, however, more and more young ones in the past few decades had simply left the place for good. Then why did one never run into them? Perhaps no one thought of asking; also, most of the exiles presumably chose not to broadcast the matter. It sounded as if the valley had become practically deserted, in spite of a tradition of large families. 'There's only the old ones and the very young ones left,' he said, 'and of course the h-handicapped ones.'

Had I met the little nerd thirty years earlier it might have made a difference, but when I first became interested in the history he'd not even been an itch in his father's balls yet. Now it was a bit late in the day. Still, we started talking. In fact we got so carried away that after the pub closed we went off to his digs where he produced, of all things, a bottle of Old Brown. Now I pack a mean slug, and I take my Scotch as it comes from its mother, it's part of the job description, but OB plugs my arsehole.

Godforsaken Place

The first part of the conversation I could still follow. Little-Lukas spilled whatever beans the Devil's Valley could muster about its founding father, the Seer. His first arrival at the deep valley in the Swartberg. The perilous descent, for which the rear wheels had to be removed and the wagons propped up on bundles of wood to brake the pace. After the first day the oxen refused to budge, whereupon Lukas Lermiet first used his heavy hippopotamus whip on them and when that didn't work, gouged out their eyes with a knife. Instead of solving the problem, it made everything worse. One wagon after the other, drawn by the crazed and blinded oxen, fell to fucking smithereens down the steep cliffs. Lermiet's fellow trekkers turned back in small demoralised groups to retrace their own trail through the mountains, all their possessions lost. Not one of them ever reached the outside world again. It was winter, the weather was bloody awful, the snow lay knee-deep on the slopes. What happened to them was never recorded: they must have frozen in that desolate landscape, or fallen to their deaths down any of a hundred precipices.

Seer Lermiet grimly persisted. The heavier the odds the more clearly he saw their glorious future down below in the Devil's Valley. In the end only his own family remained to trek ever more deeply into the mountains in the drifting snow. One of his sons rebelled, but was hit over the head with a length of wood and died after a day or two. Then three of his other sons ran off after tying him up in his sleep. They, too, must have died in the mountains; their bones were never found. All that was left were Lermiet's wife Mina and a daughter and two small sons. Mina pleaded with him to turn back: couldn't he see the whole thing was doomed? This valley was worse than hell itself. Lukas knew only one response. He gave her a thrashing that left her close to death. She never fully recovered. Abject with terror she and the remaining children went with the Seer into the valley of death where he'd seen the Promised Land in a fucking vision.

That was still only the beginning. The worst of the winter lay ahead. The two younger children died of pneumonia. Mina was still bedridden from the flogging. Only then, Little-Lukas said, God appeared to the old shithead and advised him to turn back. All right then, the Seer announced, at the first signs of spring they would leave for Graaff-Reinet. For about a month they enjoyed a spot of peace and quiet, preparing for the return journey.

But on the day before they were to leave, Lukas Lermiet went into the mountains in search of a white gazelle he'd seen in another of his dreams. High up on the slopes he stumbled over a loose stone, fell down a cliff and shattered his bloody leg. He would never again be able to walk properly. Which meant he was doomed to spend the rest of his fucking natural life in that godforsaken place, and his family with him.

Shards and Tatters

This tale was followed, throughout the long night in Little-Lukas's digs, with the bottle of OB between us, by countless others. But of the rest of our conversation I had only a seriously pissed recollection when I woke up again some time the next day in the dank suburban house in Gardens where I'd spent most of my married life with Sylvia. I couldn't even remember how I'd got back. Also, there was other urgent and unpleasant business to attend to. The house had to be sold. Sylvia was demanding action. For the time being I still tried to stall, reluctant to face a battery of agents and house-seekers with snotty comments about damp patches on the walls, structural cracks, loose tiles, hazardous wiring. But through the ruins of my screwed-up world and the heavy hangover I continued to chase random memories of my night with Little-Lukas. The fucking shards and tatters and loose ends of stories. A smous returning with exotic wares from the farthest corners of the world. A girl with four tits. A child with goat's feet. A large naked woman on a bed crawling with cats. And something about a magician who could track you down to the very end of the earth? Yes, I quite vividly remembered this yarn: someone had broken into a house in the Devil's Valley, leaving a shoe behind; the magician clamped it in a vice – and an hour later a man with a shattered foot arrived crawling on all fours and howling with pain. And much more. But all of it mixed up and rather crazy, with no bloody head or tail to it.

Commotion

I did recall that at some stage during the night I'd scribbled the chappie's address on the back of a cigarette box, and after much searching I managed to retrieve it among dirty underpants and gluey handkerchiefs in the laundry basket. A couple of times when I telephoned there was no reply, but at last one afternoon I heard Little-Lukas's st stammering voice in my ear. He sounded embarrassed, apologising for having wasted my time like that and shooting off his mouth. The inhabitants of Devil's Valley were not supposed to confide in outsiders, he explained breathlessly. If his people were to find out . . .

I pulled out all the stops. For the first time in years something had caught me by the balls again. Little-Lukas remained diffident, stammering more and more as I waxed eloquent, like in the old days when I'd still dreamed about an academic career, long before the world had up-ended its shit-bucket on my head. At last Little-Lukas, still far from convinced, relented: all right then, I c-could come back some time and bring my tape-recorder. But 'some time' was too vague for my liking. What about tomorrow? No, sorry, he had a t-test or something. The day after? A history assignment, for Professor van T-Tonder. Fuck the man gently but thoroughly. The day after that? And so I drove him back day by day until the following Wednesday. Time? Let's make it three. Place? At his d-digs.

When I arrived, there was a commotion in front of the sprawling Victorian house where Little-Lukas had his rented room. A crowd in the street, two yellow police vans, an ambulance. Dead on the spot, an elderly woman told me at the garden gate when I enquired. She had wispy hair drawn into an untidy grey bun like a fucking merkin. Little-Lukas was just crossing the street on his way home from lectures, she said with what I can only describe as funereal glee, when the car came charging over the stop street, driving off without even slowing down. Shame, such a nice boy, one doesn't even know if he had relatives. She'd been like a mother to him, even if she had to say so herself. And what about the last month's rent? But the Lord giveth, the Lord taketh away, and who were we to complain?

Smooth and Blunt

JUST BEYOND THE two massive boulders that must have broken away from the highest cliffs in prehistoric times to come to rest at this spot above the Devil's Valley, I noticed a movement in the fynbos. Something was coming my way. For a moment I was unsure whether it was man or beast, but it turned out to be the former. Benefit of the doubt. Not much more than a metre tall, and totally hairless as far as one could see, the face ageless and expressionless, smooth and blunt like a prick. His misshapen legs were too short for his body. He was barefoot. Two large flat feet that seemed to have no bloody bones in them, like a fucking duck's. In one hand he carried a catapult, with the other he was scratching his groin.

Involuntarily I stepped back, glancing round in the direction of the old dude who'd shown me the way, but he was no longer to be seen.

'I'm looking for the road down to the valley,' I explained. 'The old man up there told me . . . perhaps you could . . .'

He grimaced with open mouth, made a vague gesture with the hand holding the catapult, and waddled off into the fynbos. I wasn't quite sure what to do. But after a moment he came stumbling back and waved at me again, making an unmistakable gesture with his obscene blunt head. I began to follow him. Abandon ye all hope.

It was dead quiet among the high cliffs, and all the way along the great slope as we went on, a silence which made me feel totally fucking alien: not the usual kind of silence one expects in the mountains, which is at least broken from time to time by a rustling of wind or the shrill of a cicada or whatever; but the silence of something missing, something lost. I couldn't explain it. And it was only much later, at least a week, before I realised what it was: in this godforsaken valley there were no birds, not a bateleur or a grey partridge, not a weaver or a sparrow or a swallow of any description, sweet fuck-all. But by that time it was like already too late.

Of The Soul

There was something haphazard about our progress down the mountains, as the garden gnome didn't seem to be following any known route. From time to time he would stop to fit a small pebble into the skin of his catapult, close his eyes and let fly. Zen and the art of whatever. Then he'd grin in my direction, mumble something, grab at his fly, and start waddling off along the trajectory traced by the pebble. Until we'd get to the spot where it fell, when the whole process would be repeated.

In this way we zigzagged crazily down ever more arid slopes, among what is usually described as towering cliffs, ranging from yellow through orange to deep red, across huge carbuncles which at a distance appeared fucking unscalable. Once we seemed to head straight for a blank rock-face, but at the last moment the little runt swerved into a small thicket, and motioned towards a hole through which it was just possible to crawl on all fours.

In passing I glimpsed a series of rock paintings in various pigments, white and black and sienna and ochre, on the sloping ceiling right above my head: eland, elephant, little men with bows and arrows and spiky hard-ons. Right across the scene was a name chiselled into the rock in large uneven capitals: STRONG-LUKAS. But there was no time to look more closely or ask the odd question, otherwise I'm sure my waddling guide would have buggered off without me.

Beyond the breach in the cliff the path became easier for a while. Until we reached the next damn obstacle. Then the next, and the next. Every now and then I made a hurried smoke-break. In my fucked condition it's all that helps. Then off we'd go again. One hour, two, four. My chest was rattling like an old-fashioned bellows, my lungs were burning. If only I'd been one of the fitness freaks who regularly climb Table Mountain over a weekend, but apart from raising my right arm or the occasional short series of pushups with something female poised below, I take no exercise. Perhaps this trip would bring on the inevitable coronary, which might at long last get home to Sylvia what she'd lost. Fat chance, though, thinking of her parting shot: 'You've got syphilis of the soul, Flip Lochner.' The filthiest and truest thing she ever said to me. ('Fuck you,' I answered. 'What makes you such a sad case is that you can't even swear properly,' she said. 'You have no imagination.' 'Fuck you,' I told her again.)

As we went down, the kloof grew more and more bloody impossible. And more parched. What from above appeared fertile, even lush, turned out to be screwed by green drought. Even shrubs and bushes that still put up a green face crumbled to dust as one brushed against them. The ravine was becoming narrower too. Overhead the cliffs were closing up. The remaining sliver of sky turned the deep blue of a bloody bruise.

Stopping for another life-saving draw, I asked through the smoke, 'You sure you know the way?'

Prickhead uttered another sound which might mean anything, his fingers working frantically in his groin. But that was as much as I could get from him.

'Where are we going?' I tried again.

He seemed to find that very funny, for he convulsed in laughter, so violently that I began to fear epilepsy. But after a while he placed another goddamn pebble in his catapult and let fly. And off we went again.

Some way down the next slope I was forced to take off my rucksack as our ledge was shrinking to a pencil track. My guide continued to move along surprisingly bloody light-footed on his padded feet, but I stepped on a loose stone, staggered in panic, let go of the rucksack to regain my balance, and just made it. The bag went tumbling down the fucking precipice until it was finally stopped, fifty or sixty metres down, by a grotesquely distorted wagon-tree. Shit. This was all I needed.

Splinters

I cautiously picked my way down after the rucksack, managed to get hold of it and struggled back to the ledge. There I squatted down for a while to catch my breath, feverishly undoing the bloody thing to check the contents. Prickhead stood watching in fucking fascination as I rummaged. Thank God the tape-recorder was packed deep inside, wrapped in clothing; at a glance it seemed okay, but I would have to examine it more carefully later. But the camera was fucked. The broken lens came tinkling from the bag as I undid it. All I could do in a kind of impotent rage was to throw the useless thing into the void that gaped below, as the phrase goes.

Still shaken, I turned to the precious cardboard box in the side-bag. From outside it still seemed all right. Then my heart sputtered as I saw a moist stain spreading through the cardboard. With clumsy fingers I tore the box open, prepared for the worst. My fucking bottle of fucking White Horse down the drain. Everything in the box in which I'd so lovingly cradled it was soggy, and riddled with sharp splinters. Inevitably I cut a bloody finger in the process. Under the gnome's beady eyes I sucked my finger, then began to remove the splinters one by one from the soggy mess in the box. The way an army doctor might pick shrapnel from a wound, except I'm not sure the doctor would so lovingly suck each piece of shrapnel clean. Even the grainy substance of the contents of the box didn't put me off. Although what was left after I'd cleared away the worst looked pretty unappetising. I grimly replaced the box in the bag.

It was some time before I scrambled up again to resume our journey. Just in time, it seemed, as Prickhead had started working away so furiously at his groin that his eyes were beginning to get a glassy stare. Worked up into a proper lather of another kind, I stumbled on after him, following the latest pebble from his catapult.

Until, at bloody last, we crossed a rockfall to the bottom of the valley where a dried-up riverbed ran along a line of withered trees.

Old wisps of beard-moss and lianas studded with ferocious thorns hung scraggily from the highest branches. One of the largest trees, an ancient wild fig, had been split from top to bottom, scorched by lightning in some forgotten time. It must have been the mother of all bolts. Presumably the whole valley bed became one churning flood after a bad storm, but right now it was as bleached as bone. The trees were still alive, but only just; their roots must reach half-way down to bloody China.

We followed the dry riverbed, Prickhead waddling on his weird bow-legs, the catapult now draped across a sloping shoulder. It still seemed improbable for him to move with so much ease.

And then, just as I was beginning to think I'd run right out of steam, we came through a last thicket of trees and saw the valley opening up ahead, with signs of fields, and vineyards, orchards, all bleached by drought, but still bearing the unmistakable imprint of civilisation. There were houses too, few and far between, some of them in a parlous state but all of them apparently inhabited. Four, five, six, followed by a hulking whitewashed church, much larger than one would expect in such a wild place, with a square, squat tower. For a moment I couldn't make out anything more, as the valley swerved to the left.

When I turned back, Prickhead had disappeared. In a sudden panic I looked round: would I ever, if I had to, find my way out again?

Rucksack

Right now the fucking rucksack required more urgent attention. I lowered it on a large flat rock in the middle of the dry riverbed and removed the tape recorder from its womb of odds and ends of clothing. It was one of those nifty little jobs that can fit into a shirt pocket. The red light went on when I pressed the button, but the tape was stuck. So much for technology. A journalist's fate worse than death. I pressed it to my ear but there was no sign of the familiar reassuring hiss. Even a few vigorous shakes made no difference. I'd shaken other things with more success in my life. Furious with frustration I gave it a slap, my stock solution for hitches in anything from a PC to a parking meter; and for once it actually worked. The little wheel was turning again, its whisper music to my ears. I pressed Record, went through my alphabetised repertoire of synonyms for the female pudenda (more satisfactory than the standard one-two-three-four-five), rewound, then pressed Play, and listened approvingly to the recitation, in my own voice, of what years ago had still been within my range of the accessible; just after the letter 'p' I switched off.

Kitsch

Now follows an event that gets my knickers in a knot. It doesn't reflect well on me, but what the hell. I've hit rock-bottom anyway, as Sylvia or the kids or any of my colleagues would be only too happy to testify. A hairy turd is worse than any second-hand car dealer. So here goes, and devil take the hindmost.

Just as I'm bending over to do up the clasp of the rucksack again there is a splash. I straighten my back to look. On the far side of a small thicket of withered underbrush and reeds I discover a long deep pool that somehow escaped my notice earlier. A movement in the pool catches my eye. Now for the kitsch part. I know it sounds like overdoing it, but I swear by my mother's corns that this was how it happened. Crime reporter signing on. A naked girl comes scrambling from the pool, her back to me. She bends over to wring the water from her hair, then sweeps it back over her shoulders. A long black mane that ripples in shiny wet waves all the way down to the bulge of her buttocks. In the interests of truth I must specify that her body is a bit on the thin side to my taste. If this had been my fantasy I'd have filled her out a bit, more curves, more moulded kind of thing. But this is the point: it's not a dream, she is real. So I have to take her as she comes.

Then, like an obliging model, she turns to face me. She throws her head back, both arms raised, her feet wide apart to steady her on the slippery surface of the wet rock. Long legs, if kind of sinewy. The thing about legs is this: no matter how thick or thin they are, how short or long, they meet somewhere. And there's nothing wrong with the bush that marks this meeting point. Black tufts sprout abundantly from the armpits too, something I've always had a weakness for. Altogether, it's the total wet-dream image. Except, as I said, the girl's not exactly the Birth of Venus. I did my stint of Art History at varsity, don't underestimate me, and Botticelli clearly had no hand in this one. Even so, beggars can't be choosers.

Gentlemanly Thing

I just stand there, kind of dumbstruck, like Lot's wife. After a while she lowers her head again, but remains standing with her hands stuck in her thick dark hair, the points of her elbows raised to the late light, looking straight at me.

Jesus, now I'm really flexing the old purple-veined stylistic muscles. I'll soon be the man I used to be. Watch this spot. But I can't keep the girl waiting: she's still standing there at the edge of the pool, looking straight at me. Yet there isn't the slightest hint of embarrassment or shock in her gaze; nothing exhibitionist either, I should add. She simply stands there, looking at me, right into my face as far as I can make out through the threadbare screen of brittle twigs and reeds and stuff between us. I can see the late sun glistening in the droplets on her skin, touching like brush-strokes the elevations of her nose and cheekbones, her collarbones and shoulders, et cetera.

The one who feels caught out and embarrassed is me. As if I have no fucking right to be there. And that's saying something, because there isn't much I haven't seen in my line of work, the whole range from the shit-smelling awful to the bloody beautiful. Take my word. Feeling trapped like a schoolboy in a girls' locker room, I bend over to start fiddling with the straps of the rucksack again. Then it occurs to me that I might do the gentlemanly think and offer an apology. I straighten up. But it's too late. The lady has vanished.

And not only the lady. The bloody pool too.

I broke through the underbrush and tangled weeds to where it had been a minute ago, but there was no sign of water. The hole was there, a rough rectangle among the rocks, but it was empty and quite dried up. So obviously there was no sign of wet footprints either.

Quite Normal

Now don't tell me it was a mirage, a hallucination prompted by a too rampant urge and too little occasion. *She was there.* I can recall every damn detail. Not only the mane of tumbling hair, the straight black eyebrows, the cheekbones, the wide mouth, but something else I'd like to add for future reference, as it is of some importance. The girl had four tits. One pair quite normal, of the size and shape one would expect, the nipples perched like two bees (who said it first?) exactly where one would look for them. And then, a narrow hand's breadth below them, like small smudges on an artist's paper, something first drawn, then erased, but not quite, not altogether, another pair. Not proper-sized boobs, these, only a suggestion of two mild swellings, stings of the aforementioned bees; but no doubt about the nipples. You think this is the kind of thing I could have imagined?

I can remember telling myself: Now this is something I wouldn't mind having a closer look at. Investigative journalism. But the thought also brought a tinge of guilt, as if with that candid gaze she could read my mind (the lingering stain of fucking Calvinism, like a dirty rim in the bath); and that may well have been the reason why I bent down over the rucksack again. The truth, almost the whole truth, and nothing but.

While I was still scouting among the sparse dry reeds fringing the edge of the dried-up rock pool, in search of some trace of her, a voice behind me said:

'So there you are.'

Story of My Life

MY FIRST THOUGHT, when I returned home after Little-Lukas's death, was that the bloody accident had once again put paid to all hope of doing something on the Devil's Valley. Story of my life. But the boy kept haunting me. A few days after the accident I phoned his landlady to find out whether she'd heard anything from his relatives; and about funeral arrangements, that kind of thing. (From our crime reporter.) No, to both questions. There had been no news from family and friends, and unless someone turned up to claim the body the municipality would probably have him buried. The rent, she reminded me, was still outstanding too.

I usually put on a tough-guy act, but in the end I'm a soft touch. I mean, I shout at the fucking bergies who squat on the stoep, then slip them the odd rand, even though I know bloody well it will go straight into a bottle of blue-train. As a result, every month I'd screw up my budget, and Sylvia would have her field day. At least that is now over and done with. Anyway, in an unguarded moment I undertook to pay the landlady her blasted rent, as well as the funeral costs if no relatives pitched up during the next week. Three thousand two hundred and thirty-one rand for a simple cremation, no service, no coffin, no nothing; only a nondescript little brown cardboard box with Little-Lukas's ashes, delivered on my doorstep by a tall man who looked like Groucho Marx.

Abandoned Notes
What was to be done with the box? I considered arranging a burial,

but the picture of Groucho, the landlady and myself in the cemetery on a wet winter's day in Cape Town was too much for me; besides, I couldn't afford any further expense. That was how I started thinking about taking the ashes to the Devil's Valley. Kind of pilgrimage. Also, it was as good an excuse as any.

I dug up my notes abandoned thirty years ago, on the Seer's trek into the Swartberg, stowed in a dilapidated old box in the dust and cobwebs and mouse shit and silver moths and cockroaches in my garage. I added to it the cigarette box from my night of cheerless carousing with Little-Lukas, and then began to sort out the confused memories of our meandering conversation.

There wasn't much sense to be made of it; and most of what returned to me through the remembered fearful swell of OB was hedged in by question marks. Any report slapped up out of that whore's crotch of notes and recollections would have seen me fired on the spot. But frustrating as they were the memories kept haunting me. In the messy business of my life it became a single constant spot of reference. The reassurance of a few small hard facts: this and this and that I knew, this and this and that was certain, unshakeable by wind or weather, adversity or time.

I went to see my editor on the question of accumulated leave; he seemed singularly happy to let me go. From an adventurous colleague I borrowed a rucksack, purchased what was necessary in the line of provisions, added my tape recorder and my camera, plus flash and tapes and film, and set off for the Little Karoo to feed the long-starved rat. In Oudtshoorn I spent a day on enquiries until I found a helpful garage man who agreed to take me into the mountains in his four-by-four, as far as the beacon from which I would have to strike out on foot. That was the Wednesday, a tranquil day in late April, in the afterglow of summer.

Or For Worse

I'd counted on a week, but the garage man persuaded me to stretch it to ten days.

'Saturday suits me better, you see,' he said. His name was Koot

Joubert, a solid block of a man, as heavy as a Bedford truck, if one can imagine such a vehicle with sideburns. 'I'll be coming back from Prince Albert next Saturday. Round about noon, I think.'

High up in the mountains where he dropped me we confirmed the time.

'I'll be right here at the beacon,' I said. 'If I'm not here, don't wait for me. That'll mean that I decided to stay longer.'

'Don't think you will.' With a rumbling laugh like an old engine starting up. 'The people down there is a strange lot. Judging from the ones who sometimes turn up in town for shopping, that kind of thing. They're a wild bunch, man.'

'See you next Saturday, Koot.'

'No, right, okay.' He offered me a hand the size of a gearbox. 'Hope you come back alive.'

I could think of several questions I'd still have liked to ask, but decided to wait and see for myself. I refused to be discouraged in any way. I'd bloody well waited long enough to get to the brink of this tract of history that had tantalised me for so long. For better or for worse, so help me God.

At the side of the gravel road I remained standing until Koot Joubert's dust had settled among the rocks. Then I turned towards the Devil's Valley, with a huge curving slope straight ahead; I felt like a mole on a woman's tit.

One last time I checked the contents of my rucksack. The provisions. The tape recorder and notebooks and ball-point pens. The two cartons of Camel, four hundred, plus a few loose packets stowed in my pockets. Enough for ten days, if I rationed myself carefully. The White Horse safely ensconced in the box containing Little-Lukas's pinkish-grey ashes.

Now here I was at last, and behind me a voice was saying, 'So there you are.'

Usual Places

IT'S DAMN HOT here in the dry riverbed where I'm crouched waiting. There is still time, but not much. If she doesn't come soon, I've had it. And there's such a lot still to untangle in my mind.

The others are about their business among the ruins. In my mind I fit them into their usual places, the way things were before the bloody catastrophes began. Grandpa Lukas, as they call him here, among his mottled goats on the mountainside, chewing or sniffing his strong tobacco. Brother Holy pacing up and down his rows of vegetables, hands behind his back, preparing his sermon of fire and brimstone for next Sunday, while Smith-the-Smith furiously hammers a white-hot horseshoe of pure gold into shape on his anvil for a horse he'll never see. The sprinkling of old people in the cemetery, sweeping the aisles and dusting the headstones and cleaning the little beds of succulents on the graves as they chat to the dead and pass on all the news from the living in exchange for tidings from the other side. Tant Poppie Fullmoon with her bag of herbs, waddling on her small round feet to bring a new baby into the world or strangle another. Jos Joseph planing boards for coffin or bed or doorpost, his mouth bristling with wild-olive nails, one of which he occasionally swallows when he becomes excited. Jurg Water loping behind the forked stick he uses as a divining rod, up and down the dried-up slopes where no drop of subterranean water remains to set the stick twirling in his huge paws. Henta Peach and her gaggle of barely nubile furies twittering among bright shafts of light in some dark shed, ample warning that at moonrise tonight they will be cavorting naked among the bluegum trees again. Hans Magic accompanied by his perennial cloud of flies like a fucking halo around his filthy head. Gert Brush among the paintings never finished because he keeps on adding new faces to the ones hovering in the layers of paint below. Isak Smous counting the money he'll never spend. Job Raisin at his stands of drying tobacco and raisins, branch in one hand to chase away the birds that disappeared from the Devil's Valley a century ago. Tall-Fransina bent over the tip of the coil from her still, surrounded by her innumerable cats as she awaits the blessed moment when the heart of the run can be cut from the heads. Peet Flatfoot, the dwarf I'd christened Prickhead on my arrival, hiding in the thickets beside the dried-up water-holes to spy on the naked girls who have long stopped swimming there. Ouma Liesbet Prune huddled with her small tin trunk on the roof of her little house, waiting for the skies to open so that the Lord can sweep her up to heaven, while her distant nephew Ben Owl lies snoring down below until nightfall when he will get up to prowl in the dark on his club-foot. Bettie Teat and her brood in the sun on the doorstep of the church, a child at each bare breast, waiting for Brother Holy to descend from the cabbage patch to castigate her for the sins of her voluptuous flesh. Also Lukas Death, somehow appointed as my guide and mentor during this stay which is now over and not yet over: he occupies the biblical position of Judge in the Devil's Valley, a combination of justice of the peace, and mayor, and field cornet, besides doing his job as teacher and undertaker.

And then Emma, Emma in church, Emma here in the dried-up riverbed, Emma at the Devil's Hole, Emma in the cemetery at night, Emma's laughter and her silences. Emma bearing the mark of the Devil on her breast, Emma.

She is the one I'm waiting for now. But the one who showed up that late afternoon, among the tangled bushes beside the dried-up pool, was Lukas Death, saying 'So there you are.'

Screwed Up

I swung round quickly: one can only take so much on any given day.

In front of me stood a thin man in a quaint black linen suit, with a wispy ringbeard resembling old photographs of Paul Kruger. Undertaker, was my first thought, which turned out to be not so wrong after all. But on closer inspection he appeared too scruffy for the job: collarless shirt, the sleeves of his jacket frayed and much too short, so that his hands protruded like gnarled, brown sweet potatoes; and barefoot, carrying two heavy veldskoens over one shoulder. In this place, I was to discover, people tend to save their shoes as much as possible. A pretty seedy sight, all told, and rather peed-upon. Judging from the way he screwed up his eyes below the unkempt eyebrows as he stared at me, he was short-sighted too.

'You look as if you've just seen a ghost,' he said.

'For all I know I have,' I was still too fazed by what had just happened. 'I saw a girl in that hole a moment ago. Clear as daylight.'

'It must have been that Emma,' he said with what looked like suppressed rage. 'There's no stopping her when she gets the urge.'

'But the hole was full of water.'

'That one will squeeze water from a stone,' he said, his lips white with disapproval. 'And I'm afraid Little-Lukas backed her up.'

The name hit me in the guts. 'I knew Little-Lukas,' I blurted out.

He nodded as if he knew all about it.

'Little-Lukas died,' I announced.

'Indeed, yes.'

'I wasn't sure you'd heard the news.' I felt quite out of my depth. 'I brought his ashes with me.'

He shrugged, his face closed like a mussel.

'Well, that's that then. I wasn't sure if he still had relatives around here.'

'I'm his father.'

This was getting a bit too much. I put out a shaky hand, what else could I do? 'Mr Lermiet . . .'

'They call me Lukas Death. We all have private handles here.'

'I guess the old man up there on the mountain, Lukas Lermiet, is also a relation?'

'All of us in Devil's Valley are related. When we go abroad we're all Lermiets, but down here it's just the private handles. And you must be Flip Lochner. A pleasure to make your acquaintance.'

Tampan-Ticks or Whatever

Just like when I faced the old man of the mountain, only more so, I stood gawking like the chickens my mother used to dose with fat-and-pepper pills against tampan-ticks or whatever.

'I hope I'm not putting you out in any way?' I asked. For the time being, I thought, the ashes should remain in my rucksack; they were clearly not welcome here.

He didn't sound very encouraging: 'That is as may be. I suppose if you've come all this way you may as well stay.' Adding, as if it were relevant, 'It's a bad year for man and beast, what with this drought and all. Look at this riverbed. Even the wells are drying up. It must be because of Little-Lukas. God has lost patience with us.'

'Isn't it almost time for the winter rains?'

'Last winter God skipped a season,' he said, making it sound like a death report. 'And he'll keep on chastising us until he's had enough.' He sighed. 'We can only hope that he had some hidden purpose sending you here. His ways are higher than ours, you know.' Like the old man up there he spoke with an antiquated Dutch accent. I interposed some apposite grunts from time to time, but he paid scant attention to me. Once again I tried to steer the conversation to Little-Lukas, finding it imbloodypossible to understand how the boy's own father could so stubbornly avoid all discussion of his death; but he ignored it as pointedly as before. It was obvious that in some obscure fucking way they'd already learned about the event; and the gloomy man made it clear that as far as he was concerned the matter was closed. So to hell with it. If necessary, I would scatter the whisky-soaked ashes myself when the time came, in some hidden spot when no one was looking. So rest in peace, poor Little Lukas L-Lermiet.

Lukas Death soon ran out of conversation. For a while we simply stood there; it was as if he felt I needed time to adjust, while I decided to keep my questions to myself for the moment. He waited patiently.

I suppose a man who makes a living from the death of others has no need to move his arse.

At last he said, almost apologetically, 'Well, if you're ready we can go.' And I followed him, stepping out to meet my history.

Settlement

As we proceeded further into the valley the settlement unfolded in front of us. Probably thirty or forty houses altogether, arranged in two uneven rows, all of them whitewashed and built to the same basic plan: long and narrow, with a stoep in front, a hump-backed hearth at the rear, and on one side an outside staircase leading up to an attic under a steep thatched roof. Some were more dilapidated than others, as I'd noticed before, but they were all pretty solid, with thick walls built to withstand the ravages of time and perhaps even the odd earthquake. Every backyard had its shed and its haystack and a longdrop, while most sported an old-fashioned stone well. Among the houses were small thickets of trees, presumably brought in as saplings from outside, as none were indigenous: bluegum and willow, even a few oaks. Some distance above the top row of houses was a whole bluegum forest. On the opposite slope stretched a patch of prickly pears, some late fruit still blazing red or yellow among the bluish leaves.

The two rows of houses were interrupted, on the near side, by a large open space surrounded by a low white wall, enclosing the church with its squat tower topped with a wooden scaffolding which presumably housed the bell. At the back stretched the cemetery in which I noticed two old people in black working among the graves.

Against the back of the churchyard wall was a large pile of stones as if at some stage a monument had been planned and then abandoned; unless the stones had simply been cleared from the fields beyond. I tried to ask Lukas Death about it, but he turned a deaf ear.

The plots were large, unmarked by hedges or fences or boundary walls, each running unhindered into the next. There were chickens and geese and muscovy ducks everywhere, even turkeys. In several yards I noticed large trays and scaffoldings on which raisins and peaches and stuff were being dried. Higher up lay the patchwork of fields and gardens I'd noticed before: vines and tobacco and pumpkins and beans, and peach and apple orchards, and a sizeable stretch of citrus, everything visibly afflicted by drought. Most of the plots had pigsties at the back, and small flocks of goats; but I could see no sign of sheep or cattle. One could hear the chattering and screeching of children among the fruit trees or behind haystacks and sheds.

On one roof sat an old woman in a long black dress, her back pressed against the chimney.

Here and there in the fields and orchards bearded men were going about their work, but as we approached they stretched their backs to watch our passing. Higher up on the slope a bulky farmer stood with a forked stick in his hands, keeping an eye peeled on us. And in the doorways of the various sheds and lean-tos others appeared to stare at us, each clutching an instrument or a tool of his trade: a top-heavy man with short bandy legs was holding a horseshoe in a pair of tongs; presumably the smith. A man with narrow shoulders emerged with a bundle of planks under one arm. Another held a pitchfork, yet another a wooden spade or a hatchet – like the emblems of bloody medieval guilds. There was something outlandish about the scene, although it took some time to register. Only much later, like the sight of a star that reaches the eye long after it's already expired, did I discover what it was: nowhere in the Devil's Valley was there any sign of a black or brown labourer. It might have been somewhere in Central Europe, or on the moon, anywhere but in the South Africa in which I'd been living all my life.

Faces

On some stoeps clusters of women stood talking, all in black dresses and large bonnets, and all of them barefoot; as we came past, they too fell silent to stare at us. The noise of the children dried up as dirty faces peeped through doors and from behind haystacks and through the withered creepers of beans. And behind the small windows of most houses one could make out the blurred movement of human figures. Faces everywhere, eyes, eyes, following us every bloody step of the way. If the silence had weighed on me up in the mountains, it was much worse here. Even the poultry stopped scratching, and on the thresholds of front doors chickens appeared to gaze suspiciously at us, with puffed-up feathers and accusing red-rimmed eyes and necks stretched out.

What little wind there was had died down. Now it was just the two of us, and all the eyes staring with unsettling knowing looks that lay heavily on me, as if all except me knew exactly where we were heading, and why. The only sound I could hear was that of my own footsteps, because the man beside me moved soundlessly on his two bare feet, like a stick-insect. And so we made our way past all those staring houses, each window bearing its collection of eyes like talismans strung up against the panes.

In front of the stoep of the very last house my companion announced, 'This is Tant Poppie Fullmoon's place.' He offered me one of his gnarled sweet-potato hands. 'Well, goodbye for now.'

Coffins

THE FLOOR OF Tant Poppie Fullmoon's voorhuis, where it was visible through all the chests and boxes and jugs and bags and other containers, was of peach stones, with a patina of many years. Here and there the skin of a buck served as a mat. There were no curtains in front of the windows. The small thick panes were bare, and the windows could not be opened as they were built into the wall. The furniture was sparse but serviceable, clearly handmade: a long riempiesbank, a dining table with legs as solid as Tant Poppie's, some chairs, two kists. And no fewer than three coffins covered with embroidered cloths.

'Handsome, aren't they?' she asked when she saw me looking at them. 'Especially this one. It was a wedding present from my first husband. In those days it was still a narrow, dainty little thing, but over the years I've asked Jos Joseph to make it bigger and wider. I had my last fitting only a month ago.'

'A wedding present?' I asked, incredulous.

'Ja, it's our custom. When you get married, the groom gets a handsewn suit and the bride a coffin. Why are you staring at me like that?'

'It sounds eerie.'

'We have other customs with the coffin too,' she said with a chuckle, causing the many bulges of her enormous body to tremble like a pink church-fête pudding. 'The first night, after the guests have gone out to dance outside, the bride and groom try it out. If you get my meaning?'

'I think so,' I said uneasily. 'But isn't it rather uncomfortable?'

'Oh no.' Trembling indignation. 'It's stuffed like a feather mattress. After all, it's meant to make you sleep in comfort for all eternity.'

'And the other two coffins?'

'I was married three times. But these two are rather ordinary, like the men who gave them to me. I'm just keeping them for in case. The first one is by far the best.' A naughty grin. 'It also gave me far more pleasure than the others.'

It was the first hint I had of what I think was to become the most disturbing discovery of my stay in the Devil's Valley: the way the pious, even the macabre, co-existed with the outrageous. And that was still quite mild compared to some of the things that happened later. But I mustn't get ahead of my story. There's a fucking time and a fucking place for everything, as the nun said when she met the priest with the five pricks.

What was quite out of place in that house was the assortment of containers that took up most of the voorhuis, all of them as far as I could make out filled with sticks and twigs and dried leaves and roots and ground powders, a veritable witches' sabbath of herbs and doepa. The mixture of smells and odours that wafted through that house was enough to make a strong man wobbly in the knees.

She must have noticed how the stuff affected me.

'Medicine,' she explained, covering the whole room with the kind of gesture God must have used to divide land and water. 'It's the will of the Almighty that I must look after the people. In my own way.' She stressed the last point, and rightly so. God might provide the blueprint, but what happened in this place was clearly up to Tant Poppie.

It was important for my immediate future to gain her confidence, and preferably her support and approval. I can't say that she was overly friendly. There was something diffident about her attitude, a kind of brooding, ominous goodwill, which warned me to watch my step. The problem was that I had no idea of what was right and wrong in her two button-spider eyes, set black and beady and seriously out of alignment among the folds and lobes of her huge face. *Mene mene tekel*.

To the left of the narrow voorhuis, and opposite her own bed-room, my room was already waiting: an old-worldly Boer bedroom with a solid bedstead of polished dark wood and a low wash-stand with pitcher and ewer; also, below the small curtainless window with its uneven hand-rolled panes, a sturdy little table with a wax candle and a tinder-box – 'For your writing', she explained, as if it had been agreed upon before I came.

Apostle

After I'd unloaded my rucksack, she made me sit down at one end of the huge dining table.

'An apostle?' It was a statement, not a question. And the tot she poured from an earthenware jug into a sizeable tin mug filled it to the rim. It was as clear as rainwater. Her own was just as big. She sat down opposite me, with the large dusky space between us. The place was still heavy with the ungodly odours from her home pharmacy.

Tant Poppie raised her mug and said with great solemnity, 'God Almighty.'

I mumbled something and took a swallow. I staggered back. And never spared another thought for my dear departed White Horse. For if whisky weighs in at 43% alcohol, Tant Poppie's so-called apos-tle must have been close to 80%. It seared down my throat like a fucking naked flame.

'Jesus Christ!' I spluttered.

She nodded approvingly, as if it was the expected response to her toast. 'To drink this witblits it helps to be a child of the Lord, other-wise the Devil will steal your soul from right under your eyes,' she said, smacking her lips, before raising her mug to empty it in another draught. I followed at a more cautious pace, but did nothing to stop her when she offered to refill my mug. By which time she was already on her third.

'This is Tall-Fransina's best,' Tant Poppie said. 'She always saves the heart of the heart for me. I tell you this stuff is so clear, if you put it right next to an empty bottle, you won't see the difference.'

In the Soup

What followed was, if truth be told, much worse than my fucking night with Little-Lukas. At some stage I burst into song, offering my hostess a rendering of all the hymns and psalms I could recall from my green youth, before plunging into a medley of rugby songs, and then a selection of compositions I'd never heard before in my damn life. Tant Poppie lit some candles (I still remember the heavy smell of grease) and came and went between the table and the kitchen like a great ship sailing on dark waters. I can feel the purple poetry welling up again.

She did everything herself. Here, too, there was no sign of black or brown servants. For a moment the discovery threatened to sober me up, but another gulp from the latest apostle Tant Poppie had placed before me settled the problem and inspired me to new heights of improvisation.

Some time during the next few hours a large bowl of steaming soup was placed before me, and a chunk of bread beside it on the bare table. Tant Poppie called me to order by rapping loudly on the table with her spoon to intone a long and complicated prayer in High Dutch. After which I ate and sang, and choked, and at one stage landed with my face in the soup, but Tant Poppie promptly saved my life, wiped my face with a very dirty cloth, and after that I think I sang some more.

We were interrupted by a knock on the front door. Tant Poppie opened it, and there was some urgent conversation in the doorway by the light of a lantern; as far as I could make out, some woman had gone into labour and Tant Poppie was urgently summoned. She bustled about for a while, fetched a bag from her room to fill it with bits of this and that from her pharmacy, then sat down opposite me again to offer a prayer of thanks, after which she went off into the night with the stranger. In her absence I topped up my mug several times as I continued my performance. In the course of the night many people turned up just to stare at me. No one came inside, but every time I raised my fucking head there were new faces at the windows, pushing and shoving as they took turns to gape and gawk. I waved at them, and sang to them, but all they did was throng and stare.

Among them, and this I remember quite clearly because for a moment I was shocked as sober as a man who'd just survived a bloody accident, I saw a face I recognised as if in a flash of lightning, the face of a woman pressed against the panes, like a large pale moth in the night, surrounded by long black hair, the face of the young woman at the pool.

I stumbled to my feet to take a closer look, but my legs gave way under me and by the time I woke up again the candles were flickering low in their saucers, and the windows were drained of faces.

Small Black Window

One way or another, presumably on all fours, I got back to my room and scrambled into bed, nearly suffocating in the fucking feather mattress. But during the night I must have woken up again, because I remember seeing the stars through the small black window, stars so large and so close that they seemed like the white flowers of some exotic bloody night cactus right against my eyes. I'd never seen such stars before. Except when I was a child, on the plains of the Free State, summer nights, winter nights, but that was a time when everything was still possible and stars like those were not only seen but heard.

First Morning

OVER THE NEXT few days the going was tough. I seemed to be both there and not there. Wherever I came or went, I was stared at by the inhabitants as if I'd just arrived from the bloody moon, which in their eyes may well have been the case. To get through to them was out of the question. Tant Poppie was more approachable than the others, but even she appeared to be doing no more than was imposed on her by the obligations of fucking hospitality.

Be that as it may, on that first morning, the Thursday, she saved my life. I woke up well into the dazzling day, with the most blinding headache I'd ever had in my damn life, which is saying something. With a great effort I struggled to sit up, groped for the packet of Camels on the floor, nearly tumbling from the bed in the process, and with the fourth or fifth match managed to light one. It's the only sure remedy, I know from bitter experience, even though more people than just Sylvia held it against me. But this morning even my Camels were useless. Thick black waves of pain and nausea kept breaking over me. If only I would die quickly and with as little mess as possible, Lukas Death could box me in a coffin, with or without a stuffing of feathers, and dispatch me straight to the other side, COD. But no such mercy was afforded me. And then Tant Poppie entered. Tant Poppie who'd had at least as many apostles as myself the previous evening, before working steadily right through the night to coax a stroppy new life into the world. She gave me one look and promptly went to fetch a concoction of her medicines. Pressing my nostrils shut with one hand as if I was a child, she emptied a large spoon down my throat. It tasted like something straight from the deepest recesses of hell. I remember shaking myself like a wet dog coming from the water. And the next moment I was healed.

My one desire was to have a bath. But this was quickly ruled out. In this place water was a luxury. Like Lukas Death, Tant Poppie mentioned the wells drying up. The only remedy was a drop of water from my pitcher, which was my ration for a week. I could still do without shaving – whether I shave or not I always look in need of a razor, and all the men in this place have beards anyway – but how the hell was I to cope with the rest?

Of the Lord

Tant Poppie's only comment was predictable: 'It's no use complaining, Neef Flip, it's the will of the Lord.'

I felt like taking her up on that one, but after she'd just saved my life it seemed a heathen thing to do.

'His ways are inscrutable,' I said smartly. Which she took as a commendable sign of resignation; and I had the impression that it somewhat improved my standing in her eyes.

One could measure my recovery by the fact that after my paltry ablutions – up as far as possible, down ditto – I could actually face the breakfast Tant Poppie had prepared for me: wholewheat bread with lard and fig jam, eggs, a length of sausage, and the bitter brew that passes for coffee in the valley. I set upon it like a vulture, but was checked emphatically when she hammered on the table with her spoon, shut her eyes, and plunged into her customary High Dutch invocation of the blessing of the Lord upon this our meal. I realised anew that in this house I would have to step very carefully.

Devils Dance

After breakfast Tant Poppie instructed me to take out the bread she'd been baking since well before dawn. Large and round and risen high, the loaves came from the tins. But she hastily stepped in before I could do anything further. First, she scolded me, one never touches a fresh loaf with a cloth: you use your naked hands. And one look at her hands made me realise that I'd never be a match for her: her palms looked like the footsoles of a Brahmin after his stint on the hot coals. Secondly, she impressed upon me never to turn a loaf from the pan upside-down. 'Because then the devils dance on it.'

'Where did you pick up such superstition?' I asked in surprise.

'It's because I'm a Godfearing person that I watch my step,' she replied curtly. 'Where the Lord is near, the Devil is never far away.'

I thought it prudent to change the subject, and Tant Poppie needed little prodding to acquaint me with the names and daily business of all the settlers. 'Just so you can be prepared, Neef Flip,' she explained.

'Where should I go,' I asked after her lengthy introduction, 'to look up the history of the place? Where are the documents kept?'

'Documents?' asked Tant Poppie, eyeing me suspiciously.

I explained: 'Baptism certificates, letters of transport, tax papers, church registers, anything. Just as a starting point.'

'You don't understand.' She chuckled briefly and shook her head. 'It was to get away from all those things in the Colony that our Seer first brought us here. You won't find anything like that in this place.'

'But if I want to write up your history, where do I get the facts?'

'I suppose you'll just have to talk to the people.'

'What about private papers, old journals, diaries, letters?'

'We don't hold with such things, Neef Flip,' she said very firmly. 'Ever since the time of the Seer no one around here has had any need to write to the outside world, and nothing comes in either. It'll just be asking for trouble. And what happens among us we all know anyway, so there's no need to write it down.'

I could feel my courage leaking like an old man's bladder. Yet I suppose there was something exciting about the discovery too. Twinkletoes van Tonder, I said under my breath, you've never stumbled across a fallow field like this one where no historian has yet set a fucking foot. Every word spoken in this place is a bloody new invention. This is how the writer of Genesis must have felt. *Let there be light*. So here goes.

Smudge Of

On the stoep outside, where the glare of the sun momentarily
brought back an afterthought of migraine, I stopped for a while to
consider my options for the day. It was slowly getting through to me
just how unprepared I was, how fucking daunting the task.

Before I could come up with a proper plan I became aware of a
small boy spying on me from behind the nearest pillar. All I could
make out at first was a shock of red hair, two green eyes and a
smudge of snot on the upper lip. When he realised that he'd been
seen he quickly disappeared behind the pillar. But a moment later he
was peeping out again.

In general I find children, including my own, among God's more
unfortunate mistakes (which says a lot, given the general balls-up he
made of the world, trying to polish off in six days what a more cir-
cumspect housewife would have spread across several millennia).
But mindful of my recovery after my encounter with Tant Poppie's
witblits, I was ready to express some goodwill with a smile. Which
turned out unsuccessful as the boy got such a fright that he just broke
into tears and ran away. Next time, I decided, he could go and shit
himself.

Eager Whispers

That more or less set the tone for the next few days. Wherever I
went, there were people going about their usual business; but the
moment I arrived, they would freeze and pretend they were stones
or shrubs or something. As if I was a fart which everybody knew
about but no one would admit to. Yet the moment I turned my back
they would break out in eager whispers.

On all my jaunts the little snot-bug followed me — at a safe distance, true, but unfailingly there. From time to time I would stop to
threaten him with all manner of dire actions, but it made no impression. Later I tried to cajole him, I even offered him handfuls of raisins
and droëwors filched from Tant Poppie's pantry, but no go. After
that I simply pretended not to see him any more.

Carpentry Shed

When I managed to corner them singly, in shed or workplace or shel-
tered back garden – and by the Saturday I'd become quite adept at
stalking the unwary – the people turned out to be a touch more
approachable, if still far from communicative. It wasn't that I didn't
try my best, armed with the bits of background information from
Tant Poppie (and in due course from Lukas Death as well) and all the
wiles and thick-skinnedness a hairy crime reporter accumulates in a
lifetime: but even so I was making practically no headway. And in the
process I discovered, to my alarm, that my daily ration of fags was
being exceeded at an alarming rate, not only through my own smoking but by offering them as bribes.

'Cigarette?' to the reed-thin Jos Joseph in his carpentry shed,
teeth clenched on a mouthful of wild-olive nails. He was planing a
new plank for a coffin belonging to someone who, like Tant Poppie,
had increased in size and girth since some long-ago day when the con-
tainer in question had first served as wedding gift cum nuptial bed.

'Ja, thank you.' Stopping briefly to light it, then resuming the
relentless planing, his head and shoulders so sprinkled with wood-
shavings that he looked as if he'd been shaken from a flour-bag.

'Do you people have a good life here?'

'What's a good life?' Blowing out smoke, planing, planing.

'I came to find out more about the history of the Devil's Valley.'

Fucking smoke, fucking plane.

'It was Little-Lukas Lermiet who first told me about the place.'

Smoke.

'I came to know him reasonably well.'

A hammer-blow to the side of the coffin. Fumes of smoke.

'It came as a terrible shock when he died.'

'This plank is warped,' he said.

'What can you tell me about the first Lukas Lermiet, the Seer?'

He spat out the nails and stalked out.

Question Mark

Next stop, the graveyard, where a few old dodderers were weeding and hoeing the parched flower-beds. They ignored me flat, so I returned the compliment by browsing among the graves and reading the hand-carved inscriptions. There were more High Dutch verses from the Bible than names, with no date anywhere in sight. Some of the oldest stones, judging by their weatherbeaten appearance, bore surnames like Portier, Koen, or Nel; all the others were inscribed with the Lermiet name. One stone was totally blank, except for a large question mark.

From the size of the graves I gathered that children were in the vast majority, some stones bearing as many as five or six names. Then came something unexpected: one headstone, considerably larger and more ornate than the rest, decorated with naïve carvings of angels and devils rather indecorously intertwined, was simply marked LUKAS LERMIET, with a second line proclaiming: ZIENER GODS or 'Seer of God'. But the surprising part was that the grave looked empty, a simple rectangular hole covered with boards. I lifted one and peered inside. It was indeed empty. This sent me to a bent old man raking gravel on a grave.

'Excuse me, but could you possibly tell me something about Seer Lermiet's grave over there?'

'I'm busy,' he muttered without looking up.

Windblown Black Stork

Frustrated, I beat a retreat. Past the little house where Ouma Liesbet Prune was perched on the roof, as always, like a windblown black stork.

'Good morning, Tante.'

'Satan, be gone. I'm waiting upon the Lord.'

Lewdness of Thy Youth

On to Brother Holy, striding stiff-legged like a secretary bird along his rows of withered cabbages, hands behind his back, perorating at the top of his voice.

'Good morning, Brother, and how are you this fine morning?'

'Terrible, terrible. It's a weary life on this wretched earth.'

'Lovely weather we're having.'

'We'll pay for it, don't worry.'

'Big vegetable patch, this.'

'But dry.'

'The cabbages seem to be doing well.'

'A good harvest ruins the soil,' he commented morosely. Then, without warning, he intoned, 'The word of the Lord came again to me saying: Thus saith the Lord God, Thou hast defiled thy sanctuaries by the multitude of thine iniquities; therefore will I bring forth a fire from the midst of thee, it shall devour thee, and I will bring thee to ashes upon the earth in the sight of all them that behold thee. All they that know thee among the people shall be astonished at thee: thou shalt be a terror, and never shalt thou be any more.' Under the onslaught the cabbages were wilting visibly.

'Cigarette?' I proffered.

'A sin, Neef, a venal sin.' He glanced round quickly to make sure there was nobody near. 'But if you insist.' He hastily thrust it into his inside pocket, preparing in a spray of spittle to lunge into the next passage: 'Thus thou callest to remembrance the lewdness of thy youth, in bruising thy teats by the Egyptians for the paps of thy youth.' The cabbages began to look up again, but he suddenly interrupted his sermon to ask, 'Did you know we had a man here who travelled through the whole world, including Egypt and the Great Karoo? And he brought back wondrous things from far places.' I thought it was merely his way of speaking. Only much later did I discover how literally he'd meant it. At any rate he gave me no opening to put any questions, as without pausing for breath he broke into a new tirade on paramours whose flesh is as the flesh of asses, and whose issue is like the issue of horses. By that time I was already out of reach both of his showers of blessings and his lecherous imprecations.

Milk

In the main doorway of the church, propped up against the massive doorpost, legs languidly outstretched, I found Bettie Teat with her brood, looking for all the world like a complacent pink sow with a litter of piglets. God knows how many of them there were, as they were squirming and wriggling and climbing all over her, squealing and shrilling and grunting as they jostled and elbowed their way to her ample dugs. Dishevelled hair covered her eyes, her belly looked nine months pregnant, and her face was a study of utter contentment. Intrigued, if a bit apprehensive, I stopped. If I'd heard Tant Poppie correctly, Bettie's offspring had been fathered indiscriminately by the men of the settlement, since she couldn't find it in her heart to say no. And apparently it didn't take much to impregnate her. 'She's like a flower,' Tant Poppie had said with what might or might not have been disapproval. 'If you ask me, she gets pollinated by the wind.'

'What are you looking at?' asked Bettie, shifting a child from her left breast, a trickle of milk dripping from its chin.

'I'm trying to meet the people in the settlement,' I explained. 'And how are you?'

'I'm in a bad way,' she answered with a broad smile. 'They say mos everybody around here is in a bad way.' She gave a generous, inviting wink.

'What are their names?' I asked, gesturing at her litter.

'I get all mixed up,' she confessed with disarming frankness. 'So now I've started calling all of them Brother. He talks to me so beautifully about sin.'

Involuntarily I cast mine eyes up to the mountain where the preacher was standing, staring fixedly at us with an expression that seemed disconcertingly possessive to me. And indeed, after a minute or two he began to amble down in our direction.

'Oh my God,' said Bettie in a fluster, beginning to collect her brood and tuck away her breasts. 'Here he comes. It was only yesterday he told me it was time I got more careful and here I'm sitting in the sun again.'

Before I could reply she scrambled round the corner, followed by a squeal of little pigs. In the background, I noticed, Brother Holy had resumed his sermon among the vegetable beds.

Just As Well

I'd noticed Jurg Water from a distance, strutting as always behind his weathered forked stick. Usually he moved out of sight the moment he noticed me, a thunderstorm brewing on his large face; but this time I came upon him from behind.

'Any hope of finding water?' I asked, feigning interest.

'There's no hope for nothing or nobody,' he snarled, glaring at me. 'This stick is no bloody use. I might as well have used my dong.'

'You may still find something where you least expect it.'

'What do you know about water?' he grumbled. 'What do you know about anything?'

'I'm just saying.'

'You can shove your saying up your arse.'

And he stalked off after his fruitless rod.

Raisins and Figs

For a while I wasn't sure what to do next. But just as I started off again, I became aware of sounds from the shed behind his house and decided to investigate. The moment I appeared in the doorway the giggling and whispering and scurrying among the wheat-bags and the piles of dried quinces and raisins and figs abruptly stopped like a gust of wind suddenly dying down. Once my eyes had grown accustomed to the fragrant darkness inside I could see dishevelled girls' heads popping up from everywhere, with blushing cheeks and hay-stalks in their hair.

'What are you doing here?' I enquired expansively.

'Nothing, Oom.'

Embarrassingly unconcerned about the much too tight dark frock that clung to the precocious curves of her buxom body, a redhead appeared from behind a pile of tobacco leaves.

'And what's your name?'

'Henta, Oom.'

A chorus chanted, 'Henta Peach, Oom.'

'Why aren't you in school?'

A wave of giggles and whispers from which I couldn't glean anything.

'What do you think I've come here for?'

With shocking directness, Henta said, 'Cunt, Oom?'

It came so fucking unexpectedly, it must have been the first time in thirty years that I'd blushed. Then, in a stern teacher's tone, I said, 'I've come to find out about your history.'

They stared at me blankly.

On the spur of the moment I asked the question that had been prickling on my tongue ever since Lukas Death had spoken the name: 'Does anybody here know a girl called Emma?'

An urgent whisper did the rounds, but they gave no answer.

'I believe she used to swim down there in the river, when there was still water in the rock-pool.'

This time one of them ventured, 'Ma told us to tell you nothing.' And ten others took up the refrain. 'Tell you nothing . . . tell you nothing . . . tell you nothing.'

'I've heard that she and Little-Lukas were close friends.'

This provoked some giggling, followed by, 'nothing . . . nothing . . . nothing.'

End of conversation. Outside, my little private pest was waiting again, at a safe distance, the usual green patina on his upper lip. I said something, but he pretended not to hear. Pissed off, I moved on to try my luck elsewhere. Petrus Tatters, large and angular, with flapping jacket, the shoemaker who wouldn't stay home at night. Job Raisin like a dried fruit among his trays. Tall-Fransina in a man's shirt and trousers beside her still, her hair chopped short. But nowhere could I find an opening. And my supply of smokes was dwindling fast.

Bloody Glass Darkly

Gert Brush, too, was happy to accept a cigarette. With his sloping head, hair over his eyes, a loner by nature, and blessed with a perpetual grin, his appearance seemed to have been fixed by a clock striking six at the wrong moment. In his long tunic which looked more like an outsized shift, one could find him sweeping the street with a broom of branches every morning. But in the afternoons he withdrew into his voorhuis to work on the paintings which I was told were his real passion. His paints and brushes and oil, I'd heard from Lukas Death, were brought in by Isak Smous when he came back from his bartering trips; and like all the other men in the settlement he'd taken over the job from his father. On the floor, with their faces to the wall, stood a dozen or so canvases on which, Lukas Death had told me, Gert Brush had painted, over the years, the portraits of all the inhabitants of the Devil's Valley. As soon as he'd completed a round of canvases he would start again at the beginning, overpainting the previous portraits. It was his habit, as it had been his father's and grandfather's, to dilute his paint quite excessively with linseed oil, for reasons of parsimony rather than aesthetics, as a result of which all the earlier faces remained vaguely and disconcertingly visible, staring up at one as if through a bloody glass darkly. The first time I met Gert Brush, Lukas Death had brought me round, if somewhat reluctantly and only at the price of an extra cigarette. The potential historical importance of the collection excited me, but I soon discovered that in spite of his chronic grin Gert Brush was as pigheaded as the rest.

'Who's this one, Gert?' I asked in front of a man with an unusually ruddy face.

'It's Little-Lukas's grandfather, Lukas Devil. He was mos born with two goat feet.'

'And the face looking over his left shoulder?'

'Our first predikant, Doep Dropsy.'

'Tell me more about the Lermiet family.'

'The people wouldn't like it.'

'They needn't know about it.'

'They'll know.'

'Another cigarette?'

He had no qualms about accepting, but he stuck to his guns. And the mere thought of all those images with their faces to the wall, beyond my reach, stuck in my gullet.

No Dearth

The only person I found more or less approachable was Lukas Death, yet by no stretch of the bloody imagination could even he be called forthcoming; and like Tant Poppie Fullmoon he gave the impression of tolerating my presence only because for some reason he had to. I could, however, exploit his weakness for cigarettes. There were few questions he gave straight answers to, but at least he was prepared to give me an idea of how the settlement functioned. How occupations were handed down from father to son, or mother to daughter; how he conducted his lessons, which were more or less restricted to the three Rs, a smattering of geography and whatever passed for history in this place; how Brother Holy ruled his congregation through the fear of God; how Isak Smous left for the outside world every three or four months, accompanied by a safari of helpers, with the products of the valley to be exchanged in the Little Karoo for whatever the Devil's Valley needed in return.

Most of our conversations were rather patchy, and they never lasted long; sometimes it would be very awkward indeed, as on the Saturday morning when we had to talk over a small child's body he was preparing for burial – a waterhead with shrivelled limbs. It was while working in his morgue that Lukas Death gave me the lowdown on the formal organisation of the settlement: the Council of Justice, the Council of Policy, the Church Council, the Burial Committee, the Water Management, the Missionary Action Committee, the Chamber of Commerce. Each of these bodies was composed around Lukas Death himself, and the same members served on each, with some provision for co-option; and although in theory it was possible to call elections it never happened in practice since whenever anything of importance happened all the inhabitants would automatically flock to the church to discuss it and take action.

What got my goat was the bloody Missionary Action Committee, but Lukas Death was unable to shed much light, apart from conceding that in the absence of heathens to convert this particular committee had never met in living memory. 'But it has to be there,' he insisted, 'just in case, you see.'

He placed old brass pennies on the bulging eyes of the deformed child. Not an appetising sight. And as Lukas Death pointed out, after a century and a half of inbreeding there was no shortage of such as these.

Hit My Father

It was on the same Saturday morning, on my way home from Lukas Death's morgue that my snotty shadow risked for the first time coming a few steps closer. He'd needed several days to rake up the courage. I only realised he was creeping up on me when he was a mere five yards or so behind me. Then, staring far into the distance as if talking to himself, he asked:

'Does Oom come from far away?'

I looked round. 'You talking to me?'

He took a step back, his eyes still avoided me.

Catching on, I continued on my way, but walking more slowly now to give him time to keep up. I said, 'I come from very far away.'

A pause. 'Does Oom come from heaven?'

I made a vague gesture towards the distant peaks. 'From very high up.'

'Is Oom the Lord God?'

I knew I had to play it skilfully. 'Why do you ask, boetie?'

'If Oom is the Lord God, won't Oom please hit my father with a thunderbolt?'

'Why?'

'He's too hard on us, Oom.'

'What does he do then?'

'Is Oom really the Lord God?'

'Not actually.' I stopped to light a cigarette. 'But I'm a close friend. I can always put in a word for you.'

'No, jus' give me then a smoke-stick.' He pointed to my packet of Camels.

'You're too small to smoke.'

'It's not to smoke,' he mumbled, on his face an I-didn't-ask-to-be-here kind of expression.

For the hell of it I took out a cigarette and held it out to him, meaning to snatch it away if he made a grab for it. But he was much too fast for me. Swift as a vervet monkey he zapped it from my hand and scuttled off. At a safe distance he sat down on a rock and, keeping a furtive eye on me, tore the paper from the cigarette, shook the tobacco into a cupped hand and greedily gobbled it up. When he'd finished the last bit, he got up again, chucked his bubble of snot in reverse, and darted off. Another dead end. Yet this time I felt that some kind of progress had been made.

Something Improper

ONLY OVER THE weekend did things begin to change. It was on the Sunday, to be exact, which was devoted to their version of Holy Communion. Nagmaal. As early as Friday I became aware of a barely repressed excitement building up like some sort of bloody fever in the settlement. Tant Poppie started baking like mad, and from what I could discover on my regular walks the same thing happened in all the other kitchens. Tall-Fransina was getting so fucking agitated beside her pot-still one could swear she had turps under her tail. The old folk in the cemetery were throwing up clouds of dust as they dug and weeded like fucking ants, especially around old Lukas Lermiet's empty grave. At ever shorter intervals Henta Peach and her gang came charging through the streets and into the bluegum forest or up the dry riverbed, chattering like a fucking swarm of weaverbirds that had seen a snake. Jurg Water broke into a near-gallop as he moved about from bloody dawn to dusk in search of unseen waters.

The most visible sign of something unusual was the increase in the numbers of mentally and physically handicapped breaking out from the dark hideouts in the houses where they were usually kept out of sight: the dim-witted and the maimed and the retarded, the waterheads, the mongols, the spastic, the blind, the cross-eyed, the crippled, the dribblers and babblers, the eaters of earth and grass and shit, some of them on foot if not on all fours, others pushed on wooden carts and wheelbarrows. They'd been around in the settlement every day, here and there, usually tended by a mother or an older sister or an aunt; but since the Friday morning they were com-

ing out in fucking droves, like flying ants before a storm. It was getting on my bloody nerves, an all-too blatant exhibition of sins better
kept secret.

Smothered Cry

Towards nightfall on the Friday I was beginning to feel like a fucking
bee in a bottle. I'm sure Tant Poppie's customary series of toasts to
Father, Son and Holy Ghost made it worse, but even without them I
just had to get out, especially as it was such a fucking beautiful night,
with a kind of late-summer balminess in the air; and full moon too.
But as it happened, I wasn't allowed out, because over supper Tant
Poppie announced that she was expecting a 'patient' and wanted me
to stay in my room.

'Something serious?' I asked, not just from curiosity but to show
some goodwill.

She pursed her lips in a chicken-arse kind of pout, and her two
quick eyes looked past me on either side. 'It's just something that's
got to be done before Nagmaal.'

It was too early to go to bed, so I tried to get on with one of
the porn paperbacks I'd brought along in my rucksack, even if the
candlelight made reading heavy going. Soon after dark – a sliver of
the full moon was just showing above the slope at the back of the
house – I heard Tant Poppie's visitor arrive. Two, as far as I could
gather when I went to listen at the door: an older woman and a girl.
They spoke in whispers, which made it impossible to discover more;
but from time to time a voice broke through, allowing me to draw
my own conclusions. A journalist with my experience needs little
more than a wink and a nudge. For about an hour there was a bustle
of activity in the voorhuis: the shuffle of bare feet, a rustling and fidgeting about, once or twice the sound of a pitcher put down heavily
on table or floor, sometimes a more audible cryptic word from Tant
Poppie: 'Hold her tight' – 'Open up' – 'Come on, it's not so bad' –
'Just press my arm' . . . And once there was a smothered cry from
the girl, followed by Tant Poppie's contented voice. 'Good. Now
just lie quietly for a while.' But the girl kept on whimpering softly.

If it was what I thought was happening under this damn godfearing roof, the Devil's Valley was an even tougher nut to crack than I'd believed before.

I drifted into sleep while the girl was still moaning away in the voorhuis; and so I never saw the bloody full moon rise – as, with frustrating pigheadedness it followed the curve of the mountain slope all the way to the top, always remaining just out of sight, showing no more than a thin luminous edge. Every time I got up to look, I'd think: just five more minutes – two – now! But it never happened. And in the end, its full fucking glory still denied me, I fell asleep.

Woke Up

In my sleep I had a totally screwy dream. Now I really have a shit in people who tell their dreams to others, as if these things could be of the slightest interest to anyone but the damn dreamer. But I must make an exception of this one, with good reason.

I dreamt I woke up from the moon flooding the room like a wash of white water spilling right across my bed on the floor. Jesus, here comes the poetry again. I remember getting up in my dream, half-blinded by the light, to look through the window. Detached from the black side of the mountain, the moon was at last drifting free in the dark blue sky like a huge blister. I dreamt I opened the window to climb out – which was of course impossible as no window in the settlement can be opened. But since when is a dream inhibited by the fucking feasible? Outside it was sultry, and very quiet. The mountains naked in the night. No light anywhere, no sign of anything moving. What time it was I couldn't tell, as I'd left my watch behind. I set off towards the bluegum wood which began a little distance above the church, a black stain in the dark, like ink spilled on the mountain slope. Below my bare feet I could feel, even in the dream, the warmth of the day still lingering in the ground.

What lured me to the forest, I couldn't tell. It just seemed the natural thing to do. Among the trees the moon got lost. It was bloody dark, yet I had no trouble at all finding my way through the smooth trunks and the parched underbrush, as if I knew exactly where I was going. After a long time the trees suddenly opened up ahead of me, as I seemed to know they would, and once again I could see the moon, now drifting in a haze. While I'd been in the forest a heavy white mist had come down from the mountain.

Unmelodious Chant

For the first time I could hear sounds. Voices, girls' voices, like some kind of chanting, punctuated by sharper, shriller cries, and a sound of moaning, like that of the girl in Tant Poppie's voorhuis. But the noise was muffled, either because of the mist, or because they didn't want it to be heard. Which would make sense, for when I got to the edge of the clearing I saw a sight that would surely have turned some of the older settlers in the valley belly-up with shock. A throng of young naked girls dancing among the trees. Except that dancing is not the right word: they were simply rushing about wildly, blindly, to and fro among the trees and through the clearing, arms and legs flailing. It was like a flock of night birds flapping about, crashing into the shrubbery or flying headlong into one another. But there was nothing exuberant about it: in fact, there was a kind of mute panic in their frenzy, which made it more unsettling than erotic.

Because of the heavy fog and the unreliable moonlight, it took some time before I could make out what they were actually doing. This was no fucking kids' game, but more of a mass flagellation. Only then could I understand the flailing arms: the girls had an assortment of thongs and switches and canes and freshly plucked branches with clusters of leaves still attached to them, with which they lambasted one another. As some of them came thrashing past me, close enough to distinguish details in the mist, I could see dark weals and streaks of blood on their limbs. And what from a distance had sounded like some unmelodious chant, was now much closer to a bloody half-hysterical wailing.

It was Henta and her gaggle once again. Of course I couldn't be entirely sure in that screwed-up light, what with the frantic nature of their goings-on, but from time to time I thought I recognised some of the faces from the shed; and Henta herself was unmistakable, with her wild red mane, her body smeared with blood or filth.

For how long it went on, I couldn't tell. But gradually the pace began to wind down, and I realised that fewer and fewer of the naked bodies were coming past me, until at last the clearing lay all empty and abandoned in front of me; and slowly the mist began to lift, and everything slipped into silence once again.

Wilted Little Bunch

I remember that in my dream I spent some time just wandering about the clearing, dazed, trying to find signs of what had just happened. But all that remained was broken switches and branches and clusters of bluegum leaves that had come off in the frenzy. I stopped to pick up one of the bunches, pressed it to my nose and inhaled the sharp tang of bruised eucalyptus. With the smell still stinging in my nostrils I became aware of another presence and looked round. Prickhead was hovering among the trees, a lecherous leer on his boneless face, both hands furiously burrowing between his bandy legs. Only for a moment, then he was gone again.

Still carrying the bunch of leaves, I returned to Tant Poppie's house in a dwaal, climbed back through the window, undressed, and lay down. Only now, retroactively, the memory began to stir up sexual feelings in me. In my dream I tried to wank off, but gave up before I came, and dropped off into a restless sleep.

The following morning the turbid memories of the dream remained with me. I felt like another drop of Tant Poppie's terrible herbs, only this time I wasn't sure it would do the trick. This struck home in full force when at last I stumbled to my feet with heavy limbs, and put on my clothes, and discovered as I half-heartedly straightened the bed a wilted little bunch of bluegum leaves under the pillow.

The Goddamn Dead

ON SATURDAY IT felt as if the tempo of life in the settlement was moved up another gear: the baking in the kitchens, the slaughtering of goats at the slaughter-tree, the processions of the variously afflicted in the streets, the bustling in the churchyard; and from early morning a team of women invaded the church to sweep and dust, to polish pews and pulpit and windowsills with beeswax. I came as far as the threshold before their pointed glances drove me off. More passionately than ever Brother Holy marched up and down the vegetable patch to call down fire and brimstone on the long-suffering cabbages. At regular intervals the bell rang out across the valley from the scaffolding that topped the blunt tower. 'Bell', I suppose, is too fancy a word for the heavy sheet of iron suspended like a gong from a crossbeam and struck, in the manner of J. Arthur Rank, by Smith-the-Smith; but the sound that came from it was enough to wake the goddamn dead.

The Nagmaal weekend was clearly not taken lightly. I was beginning to look forward to the event, kicking off with the preparatory service on Saturday night. Not out of any residual piety, but as part of my research project (I could see Twinkletoes van Tonder's twat-face in the background, the turd). But when I broached the subject between the second and third apostles that evening, Tant Poppie firmly put down a small round foot, and I realised that she spoke with the voice of Medes and Persians.

I must have worn my disappointment on my sleeve, for she tried to explain in a soothing tone of voice, 'Look, it's not that the people won't want you there, Neef Flip. But they haven't had time to get used to you yet and it may upset them to see a stranger at Nagmaal. They need time.'

God and Man

I had no choice. From the front door I watched her go into the deep dusk. In a weird way there was something quite touching about all the people coming from their homes with lanterns in their hands, and the groups merging as they went, clusters of lights growing larger and larger as they converged on the louring hull of the church. Then darkness took over and I was left alone, forsaken by God and man. After a while I heard the mournful sounds of their evensong. It made me feel so fucking melancholy my heart went out to people I didn't even know.

I never thought the day would come when I'd envy a bunch of churchgoers. Even as a child I'd found church a shit place. Pa used to insist that Ma and I attend two services every damn Sunday. He rarely went himself, except for Nagmaal, but I guess that was his prerogative as head of the house. For me, no excuse would do, and it didn't take much for his brass-studded belt to tear strips from my bare arse. Church and thrashings went hand in hand, like yellow rice and raisins, or pumpkin bredie and beetroot salad. The only time in my life I can remember when Sunday church was not a chore but some sort of adventure was in the early days with Sylvia. But that was because Twinkletoes van Tonder was a deacon, which spurred me on to accompany her so I could keep an eye on the claim I'd staked out for myself. From time to time she hinted that it mightn't be a bad idea for me to aspire to a deaconship too, but the very thought made my arse-hairs stand on end. To begin with, I was too hairy, I sweated, and that is totally fucking unacceptable among the washed and brushed and dusted brigade of the Lord, enveloped in a cloud of cologne and pink-smelling powder and aftershave. It took some time before I realised she was just using religion to further her own designs on social climbing, and since then I've been to church only for one wedding, two christenings, and perhaps four funerals, including those of Pa and Ma.

Rummage Through

In the distance the hymn died away in a final heart-rending melodic sob. I turned back into the house, now even stuffier than before, to feed my frustration by refilling my mug once more from Tant Poppie's bottomless stone jug; and inspired by the fire-water I began to look through the bags and bundles and boxes of doepa and muti in the voorhuis. Most of the stuff was herbs and roots, some of which I could identify through appearance, taste or smell — buchu, wild wormwood, rue, dried aloe, cat's tail, dog-piss weed, khaki bush, bluegum, ginger, and two large bags of dagga — but there were less savoury items which called for another top-up of my mug. The skins of meerkats and dassies, the horns of small antelope (steenbok? duiker? oribi? klipspringer?), tufts of hair tied together with thongs, the talons and teeth of predators like lynxes or servals and possibly even the odd leopard, the paws of monkeys and baboons, strips of snakeskin, empty tortoise shells. And also, tied up separately in filthy rags or skin-bags a collection of shrivelled black objects which seemed like dried organs: hearts or kidneys, bladders, tendons; even a few small skulls with bits of smelly skin or flesh still attached to them (mouse, rat, otter, leguan, skunk?). What curled the hair on my scrotum, even after bracing myself with another dose of witblits, was the suspicion that not all those dried organs were of animal origin. A crumpled ear, something resembling a dried and shrunken child's foot, one badly decayed and blackened object like a span of rolled tobacco or dried sausage which my dirty mind took to be a mummified prick. Some of these objects were not even quite dried out yet. One, in particular, nearly made me puke: a long sinewy slither which still felt damp to the touch. I pulled back as if a mother-fucking snake had bitten me, but my fingers were already stained with a dark and oozing substance. Something like an umbilical cord.

By now I'd had enough, right? I started closing up everything I'd been prying in. By this time I was much the worse for wear. And I had no way of telling how long the little number had been standing in the door watching me before I became aware of his presence. Perhaps he wasn't even there.

Black Shadow

But at last I did notice him, a black shadow in the blue-black rectangle of the open door. Perhaps I'd smelled him rather than seen him, for even among the heavy odours of the voorhuis the stench he gave off was something else: a smell of woodfire and rancid sweat and tobacco and vomit and piss and shit, you name it. Reeling like a headless chicken I steadied myself with a hand against the frame of the kitchen door and muttered,

'Good evening. Can I help you?'

'No,' he said. 'I thought *you* might be needing *me*.'

A small man, as thin as a kierie, with a wild bush of hair and beard in which eyes, nose and mouth seemed to be stuck on at random. No teeth to talk of: when he opened his mouth it was simply a red hole gaping in the underbrush.

'Who are you?' I asked.

'They call me Hans Magic.'

Something came back to me through the mist. 'Are you the man Little-Lukas spoke about?'

'What did he say?'

'I'm afraid I can't remember.'

'Just as well.' He gestured with a hand so shrivelled and knobbly that it wouldn't have been out of place among Tant Poppie's muti. 'I think you'd better leave that stuff alone.'

'I was just curious.'

'Curiosity filled the graveyard.'

'Would you like some coffee?' I asked to change the topic.

'No.'

'There's a pot on the stove.' I staggered to the kitchen. Even if he didn't want any, I needed the antidote. I poured two mugs. When I looked up he was gone. Only the pungent reminder of his smell still lingered among Tant Poppie's many odours.

I gulped down the black liquid that goes by the name of coffee in this place, but it made no difference to the state my head was in. At a loss for something else to do I helped myself to another drink and went to bed. The next morning it took another dose of Tant Poppie's herbs (Jesus, if only I could be sure that's what they were) to pluck me out of purgatory. By that time I'd already missed the early morning service which had begun at bloody sunrise.

When Tant Poppie started preparing for the mid-morning service, I was feeling like an orphan at a church bazaar.

Someone Similar

But God or someone similar had something different in store for me.

Seated on the biggest of the three coffins in the voorhuis, Tant Poppie was huffing and puffing to wiggle her two tiny round feet into her tie-up boots when the front door darkened. I looked up from where I'd been watching Tant Poppie's preparations and saw something like a large harvester cricket appearing on the stoep. It was a very thin, very angular, very bearded, very dirty old man, propelling himself on two homemade crutches. Old Lukas Lermiet, the man who had welcomed me, if that's the word, on the day of my arrival in the mountains.

'Grandpa Lukas,' said Tant Poppie, struggling to her feet with one boot still in her hand. Had she been a Catholic I have no doubt she'd have crossed herself.

He steadied himself between his crutches. Only now did I notice what I'd missed the first day: one of his legs was missing. From the hip the empty leg of his skin trousers dangled down floppily like a windbag on a still day.

'Poppie,' he said, brown tobacco juice dribbling down his beard. 'I've come to take the two of you to church.'

'The two of us, Grandpa Lukas?' she asked in a shrill voice, sounding almost coquettish, like one of Henta Peach's precocious Lolitas.

'You and the stranger within our gates.'

She gave me an accusing look and started hobbling about on one foot as she tried to put on the other boot; after a while she was forced to sit down and catch her breath before she could do up the laces. Bared up to her round white knees, her legs were planted wide apart like the two columns in the temple of Dagon between which Samson had taken up his stance. The sight from where Grandpa Lukas was standing in the front door must have been enough to strike a strong man blind.

I hurried to put on my windbreaker, which was the closest thing to a jacket I'd brought with me, and joined them on the stoep. Tant Poppie's black eyes, busy as fleas, darted over me and I didn't miss the prune-like pursing of her mouth, but she made no comment. Together the three of us set out, Grandpa Lukas swinging like a bloody bell between us.

Home-made

In front of the church the brethren and sisters were assembled in righteous conversation as they waited for the final bell, all of them in fucking solemn black from head to toe, and all of them shod for a change. When they saw us coming they parted to either side, and like the Israelites trekking through the Red Sea we passed on dry feet. A murmur rippled through the crowd. Grandpa Lukas's appearance was clearly making an impression. He bloody well deserved it too, coming all the way down those goddamn mountains on two crutches to attend the Nagmaal.

They filed in after us. Grandpa Lukas steered me to one side, as Tant Poppie went to the other: men and women were seated separately, primly divided by the centre aisle. Soon the pews were crammed to capacity, like loaves and buns and things in a bloody bakery. There was something home-made about the scene: the pews were homemade, the shoes, the jackets and trousers and dresses, even the children had a fucking home-made look.

As unobtrusively as possible, while they sat waiting in decorous silence I allowed my eyes to wander across the congregation. A lugubrious spectacle if ever there was one, like a crowd gathered at the scene of a crime. There seemed in all of them a kind of grim dedication. Not for the first time, and not by any means the last, I struggled to equate this great show of piety with the excesses I'd witnessed in the dark. Perhaps, I thought, the way they flocked to church was fired by the expectation of learning about new sins to be committed, new limits to transgress.

I tried to pick out from the crowd the handful of more familiar faces. But most were strangers to me. There was one face to which I kept returning: a young woman, in black like all the rest, but curiously striking, perhaps because of the whiteness of her face, the large dark eyes staring straight ahead, the black hair plaited and piled on her head. She seemed disturbingly familiar, but at first I couldn't place her. She must have become conscious of my stare, because she suddenly turned her head to look at me. And now I recognised her, or thought I did: the kitsch girl from the rock pool. A gaze which hit me in the scrotum. Then she turned her eyes away again. Confused as hell, I tried to contain my thoughts. If she was here, then she was real after all, and then the scene at the pool must have happened. But why had I not seen any footprints? One moment the pool had been filled with water, the next it was dry. This was all too bloody much. Again I looked at her, my eyes unashamedly fixed on the swelling of her chest contained in the black chintz, or whatever material it was. Underneath, I sculpted the four tits I'd seen with my own two eyes. But below that severely sober dress no one would suspect such a thing.

I started up when Grandpa Lukas poked me in the ribs. The others were already rising. I scrambled to my feet. A thundering male voice gave up the note, and all the others joined in, off-key but with great gusto.

Body and Blood

The rest of the service passed in something of a daze, which I'd have liked to ascribe to the previous night's apostles if I hadn't suspected other reasons. Song, prayer, song, prayer, song. Passion and conviction had to make up for a piteous lack of musicality. Then came the sermon for which Brother Holy had been practising all week. His voice moved up and down precipitous Jacob's ladders, up to the heavens and down to earth again, then into the lowest depths of hell where it dwelled with relish. Followed by more singing, more praying. Jesus Christ, we'd been at it for almost two hours now. These people had stamina.

Only when it was time for communion to be served did I catch up again. And with good reason, because when it came to the part about this is my body, this is my blood, there was a startling deviation from what I remembered from my youth and my early times with Sylvia. At the critical moment Lukas Death and Jos Joseph came from the vestry behind the pulpit, carrying a newborn white goat. It was placed, bleating loudly, on the sturdy communion table covered with a starched white cloth. Then, while Jurg Water held the kid in position, Jos Joseph stretched back the thin neck as far as it would go, produced a ferocious-looking knife, and with a single stroke cut the little creature's throat. Blood spurted across the tablecloth. The congregation murmured approval. In a few deft movements the white skin was stripped from the carcass and small chunks of flesh were cut from leg and shoulder. Brother Holy was already waiting with a platter the size of a ploughshare.

'Take, eat, this is my body.'

The pale pink flesh was still lukewarm when it landed on my tongue. It was practically still pulsating, and I felt my throat contract. But I'd be damned if I was going to disgrace myself. The effort sent tears into my eyes, but I swallowed the lump down.

I could only pray, for what it was worth, that the blood wouldn't be fucking goat's blood too. But praise the Lord, the dark red stuff on the pewter cup passed from row to row, from one beard to the next, turned out to be wine after all; presumably the produce of the Devil's Valley, judging by the fierce acidity and the potent kick, although it was nothing compared to Tall-Fransina's witblits. I took a small, polite sip, only to discover too late that most of the other members of the congregation gulped down several large mouthfuls before passing on the cup; and afterwards the men spent a considerable time sucking the moisture from their well-soaked beards and moustaches.

Bladder or Kidneys

More prayer, more song, more song, more prayer. And at long last we could return to God's own good sun outside. Tant Poppie joined up with us again, and together we shuffled from group to group to exchange comments on the sermon and enquire about our joint and several states of health. This took an unconscionable time, as I soon discovered that no short answer could do the job, particularly if Tant Poppie was in the offing. What was expected was a fucking catalogue of one's entire medical history, from corns to gout to water on the knee to rheumatism to stiff joints to haemorrhoids to kink-in-the-gut to kidney stones to dislodged vertebrae to flatulence to toothache to earache to headache to blocked nose and postnasal dripping to God-knows-what; and when finally one thought the inventory was complete, there would be an afterthought like, 'And then my lower back is also giving me hell.'

In the course of the next hour, before we could return to Tant Poppie's house, I began to conjure up aches and diseases in my body which I'd never suspected before. Because I, too, was asked penetratingly about my health. This was the most surprising, and in many respects the most revealing, experience of that Nagmaal day: that instead of ignoring me as before, everybody began to show an almost indecent interest in me. Where I came from, who my parents were, what work I did, what I was doing here . . . and those were only the preliminaries.

Among the people Grandpa Lukas introduced me to was Isak Smous with his shiny bald head. I'd wanted to meet him for some time now, as his connection with Little-Lukas and his regular trips to the outside world made him a key witness. But there was little time for conversation on this hectic day. Also, he looked rather sat-upon among the members of his family: his wife Alie, with a face like a meat-grinder, and her two identical sisters, Ralie and Malie, a threesome whom even that fucking old Greek, Perseus or Theseus or whatever, would not have dared to tackle without gloves; and a clamour of kids in tow. But before we had time to go beyond an exchange of greetings, Grandpa Lukas brought on somebody else for me to meet.

Proper Meal

In between I tried to keep my eyes open for another glimpse of the young woman with the dark hair. But she was nowhere to be seen. Perhaps, I began to think with a sort of resignation, she hadn't been in the church after all; or otherwise she was just making a bloody habit of disappearing before she could be pinned down in any spot — at the pool, at my night window, wherever.

Another person I lost in the throng was Grandpa Lukas himself. One moment he was still beside me, talking, introducing me, waving new people in our direction; the next he was gone. And in the end Tant Poppie and I went home alone, where a massive meal was waiting: she had hung everything over the fire in the hearth before church, obviously knowing from a lifetime of experience exactly how to go about it. Goat's head baked in its skin, yellow rice with raisins from the Devil's Valley, stewed quinces, sweet potatoes, pumpkin, a fucking gargantuan meal for just the two of us.

'Pity Grandpa Lukas couldn't join us for dinner,' I said when we were half-way through.

She looked surprised. 'What makes you think he would?'

'He's so thin,' I said. 'One can almost see right through him. I'm sure he could do with a proper meal.'

'Grandpa Lukas stopped eating a long time ago.' She wiped her mouth with a large serviette. There was finality in the gesture.

'But why?' I asked.

'Because the man is dead,' she said. 'More than a hundred years ago already.'

With the Children

AFTER THAT MEAL I succumbed to a sleep of death. What Tant Poppie had said about Grandpa Lukas should have been enough to keep me awake for the rest of my goddamn life, but in retrospect I think the shock was simply too much to handle. Perhaps I didn't *want* to believe it. And when my head hit the pillow I was gone. It was four o'clock before I came round again, dumb and thick with sleep. Tant Poppie wasn't there, presumably out on a 'case' or visiting. Unable to stomach the heavy smell of the house I stumbled outside, although I didn't quite know where to go.

That was when the change in the settlement's attitude towards me really started coming home to me. It began with the children.

As I came out on the stoep there was a young boy waiting for me, with a wooden pail of water.

'Is this for Tant Poppie?' I asked.

'No, Oom, I brought it for Oom.'

'What for?'

'Water is scarce, Oom. So I asked Pa, Oom, because we still got some in our well, Oom, and he said it was all right, Oom.'

'Who's your father?'

'It's Isak Smous, Oom.'

I was rather touched by the gesture, all the more so after the standoffishness in the place over the last few days. 'You must please thank him for me. And thank you, too.'

'Yes, Oom.'

I carried the pail to my room and very carefully, without spilling a drop, emptied it into the pitcher. When I returned outside he took the pail from me and ran off, kicking up small clouds of dry dust.

I followed one of my usual routes through the settlement. At the heap of stones behind the churchyard my personal little pest popped up again, streaked with his trademark mucus.

'Afternoon, Oom,' he said. It was the first time he'd greeted me of his own accord.

For a moment I looked at his suspiciously. 'Yes, good afternoon. What do you want?'

'Brought Oom this.'

He approached, whisked the scum from his upper lip with a deft flick of his tongue, and held out something between his cupped hands.

'What's this?'

'Chameleon, Oom. It's for Oom.' Adding, as I still hesitated, 'For good luck, Oom.'

'I see.' Somewhat reluctantly I accepted the little green creature. It swivelled its eyes in my direction. After a while it started creeping up my shirt sleeve, very slowly, reflecting on every trembling step.

'Thanks, boetie. What's your name?'

'Piet Snot, Oom.' I should have expected as much.

He followed me for some distance before running off on his own. I went on alone, with my small green charm.

Smell of Eucalyptus

Up along the nearest slope, past the long ostrich pen where the grey females were brooding on the nests while the flamboyant males stood guard at the hedge, fluttering their long transvestite lashes. From there I entered the bluegum wood. It was the first time I'd set foot there, but after the dream of two nights before there was something on my mind I wanted to clear up. The undergrowth among the trees was very dense, and in some spots it was tough going. I actually found it reassuring, as it confirmed beyond all doubt that only in a bloody dream could I have found my way so easily through the wood on the night of the full moon.

After the day's heat there was a heavy smell of eucalyptus in the air. It was as quiet as hell. Not a mouse or a rat scuttling in the shrubbery, not an insect among the trees. Only the crackling of twigs underfoot as I walked.

At last the trees began to open up. I must be approaching the top edge of the forest, I thought. But it turned out to be a large clearing among the bluegums. I recognised the spot immediately. No doubt at all. Something long and thin, like girl's fingers, clutched at my heart. This was fucking impossible.

It was still very quiet. Only the heavy eucalyptus smell settled on me like a headache. I started looking around in the clearing. Here and there were broken branches and bunches of leaves, some dry, others merely wilted. But it proved nothing. Of course not.

As I reached the far edge of the clearing I saw something moving among the trees, like a flitting shadow.

It was Henta. Still wearing her church dress, buttoned up right to her chin. But now she was barefoot, and her long dark-red hair freed from the two tight plaits which that morning had drawn her eyes into slits.

'Afternoon, Oom.' Something seductive in her voice. This child was much too knowing for her years.

'Hello, Henta. What are you doing in the wood?'

'It's where we come to play, Oom.'

I swallowed, hoping she wouldn't notice. 'What kind of play?'

'Oom saw us mos, the night before last.'

'Henta, don't talk shit to me.' Not the kind of language to use in front of a bloody child, but she'd asked for it.

Below Her Chin

She gave a little smile. And she came a step closer. Her cheeks were very red, her eyes unnervingly bright.

'What do you want now?' I asked cautiously. One could never be sure with this one.

'I got something to show you.'

'Yes?' Now I was really getting worried.

Without warning she leaned forward, clasped the hem of her dress in both hands, and raised it to right below her chin. Under the dress she was naked.

On my forearm I could feel the chameleon raise a foot. I glanced down. One of its round eyes was fixed, expressionless, on me, the other on her.

I've never thought twice about taking my chances: God knows, there have been few enough over the years; and I don't easily refuse what comes for free. But that Sunday afternoon I suppose I was down to my last scruple. And in a way I feel perversely proud that I managed to keep my cool. It was almost with a kind of wryness, even sadness, that I said, 'No, my child, I don't think this is such a good idea.'

For a moment she didn't move. Then dropped the hem of her dress. It's hard to describe the expression on her face. Angry, crestfallen, embarrassed? But there was something else as well, something that fell through the gaps in my vocabulary, something darker, of which for all I know I understood as little as she did.

Terrible Innocence

Back in my room I placed the chameleon on one of Tant Poppie's medicinal twigs and stood it in a tall thin castor oil bottle on the wash-stand beside the ewer. I lit a cigarette but stubbed it out after a pull or two. Then I lay down on my bed, aware only of a feeling of emptiness.

From far back I remembered the first girl who'd played Henta's game with me. Maureen. The terrible innocence of it all. And how the next day her parents had arrived at our house with their church faces, and how Pa had belted me that evening so that for three nights I had to sleep on my fucking stomach. In a way everything that happened afterwards was somehow second-hand.

Hairy Shoulder

And later my thoughts inevitably turned to Sylvia, to the fuck-up we'd made of our life together. Where had it all begun? Surely we'd had good times too, once. Perhaps she got pregnant too soon. Six months after the wedding, just weeks before we were to leave for Europe to paint the place red. I still remember the farewell party. Jesus, the look in her eyes when she danced with Twinkletoes van Tonder. But I wasn't going to show the chip on the hairy shoulder. God forbid. Pity I had a bit too much to drink though, she too, for different reasons, and when we tumbled into bed at home at three or four in the morning, we fucked like dogs and slept like hogs, and only in the morning realised we hadn't used anything. The atmosphere was as acid as the vinegar she recklessly used to douche herself, blistering the inside of her cunt, and too late anyway, the harm had been done. Three weeks later the testing strip proved what it wasn't supposed to.

All plans suspended, she cancelled her scholarship, I dropped my registration for Ph.D. and took the fucking job at the newspaper, we needed the measly few rand a month extra. After Louise's birth sex was no longer an escape, except when we were either too mad or too drunk to care. How various the ways of saying, 'I love you', once you've mastered the fucking grammar of perversity. Like any kind of torture it's just a matter of refinement. Marius was the final, unforeseen, product of our years of open warfare. Sylvia moved into the spare bedroom and began to spend her days, with Louise in tow, in malls and things, running up bills for clothes and shit I couldn't pay for. I turned to whores and the odd little sordid fling with secretaries and cub reporters until I got slapped with a warning for sexual harassment. And Sylvia laid on her own affairs, more or less discreet to start with, except she made damn sure I'd find out when it would hurt most exquisitely. It was worse when she bedded my chief editor. The cherry, no pun intended, was bringing one of my juniors home. God, I can still hear the caterwauling of her orgasm, real or faked (did I ever learn the difference, did she?). After that I couldn't care a fuck any more. Syphilis of the soul, right?

What's left is just this stupid sense of betrayal all the way. But who by whom? Each time you kiss a little bit of yourself goodbye.

All I know is that I've never had a way with women. Who was to blame? Okay, I'm not trying to duck anything. But I mean, who ever prepared me for it? Ma with the ciggie stuck to her lower lip, the curlers in her hair, the candlewick gown? And who never intervened when Pa came home pissed beyond description on Saturday nights to pluck Dolf and me from our bed for a thrashing? Don't get me wrong. I'm not complaining. An Esau with hair on his body is supposed to take it on the chin. But I just don't know. Woman, woman: a fucking wilderness for me.

Cakes and Tarts

IN A WAY this was just the beginning of the events of that weird Sunday. Because after the children it was the women's turn. Tant Poppie was barely home again when they started coming: the women with their cakes and tarts and daughters. The righteous sisters of the congregation, five or six of them in a row (and several more during the following days), each with a special gift from the oven, or a jar of jam, a basket of quinces or pomegranates, a roll of mebos or a bowl of honey, to welcome the stranger from outer space in their midst. And to present their nubile daughters, right, bedecked in fucking frills and embroidery, with ribbons in their hair.

The first mother asked without any beating about the bush, 'Do you have a wife of your own?'

'I live alone,' I said. Had I known what was to follow I'd have sworn with my hand on my heart that I was happily married to an angelic wife to whom I'd pledged eternal devotion before Almighty God. (Whether it would have made any bloody different is a moot point.)

'Well, that's good then. This is Lettie. I hope you like her.'

In one way or another the news must have spread, because the visitors who followed came straight to the point.

'Here's a milk tart and this is my daughter, may your going in and your coming out be blessed of the Lord.'

After the encounter in the bluegum wood these situations were easier to handle. For fear of giving offence I didn't openly turn down any offer. But I explained that I'd come to their valley to write up their history, which would keep me so busy for the foreseeable future that it would be hard to find time for anything else.

They didn't appear to feel rebuffed; but the slumbering look below their half-mast eyelids was worrying, as if they'd coaxed me into an agreement without allowing me to check the fine print.

So much for the women.

Their procession was interrupted by the insistent ringing of the church bell, and in a way the evening service, of which I remember next to nothing, was a welcome escape. The atmosphere was quite special, I must say: the brooding dark space lit only by the lanterns the people had brought with them. But the rest was just a blur. Grandpa Lukas wasn't there. Nor, as far as I could see, was the girl Emma. Unless she was seated too far behind me in the women's block, because I couldn't turn round to stare too openly. Also, I felt tired and headachy. All I needed now was to be left alone in my room with my thoughts.

Blood Sports

But there was no rest for the wicked. As I was undressing in the corner nearest the window — I must say, I found the absence of curtains rather annoying, and I sleep in the buff — there was a knock on the thick panes. Outside I could see a lantern, surrounded by a number of savage male faces with beards and hats, and tufts of hair sprouting from ears and noses. My first thought was that they'd come to drag me out and string me up the nearest tree: for all I knew Henta had given them a different version of our story, or otherwise one of my female visitors had demanded vengeance for an imagined slight. But it turned out to be a hunt, and they had come to take me along.

I've never been a blood sports fan: not from any scruples, but because I'm just too fucking lazy. I'd much rather spend an afternoon in front of the TV with a six-pack at my elbow, or on a special occasion on the railway stand at Newlands. Participation I prefer to leave to others.

But that night's invitation was not to be turned down. I don't think there was a subtext to it ('Come along, or else . . .'); but the faces in front of my window in the blustering light of the lantern, with their ancient rifles and kieries and clubs and knives in their gnarled fists, prompted me to make up my mind pretty quickly.

There were five of them: the carpenter Jos Joseph, whose fragrant dusting of shavings and sawdust appeared to lure gnats at night; the shoemaker Petrus Tatters, gaunt and angular like a scarecrow with flapping coattails; the glowering Jurg Water with his heavy limbs and his purple nose like a misshapen turnip; Isak Smous, small and busy on his short legs, his bald head shining like an ostrich egg in the moonlight; and then the morose Lukas Death in his crumpled suit, black against the black of the night, so that his face appeared like a floating mask. Together, they looked like an exhibition at an agricultural show. And they would not have won first prize.

Man Among Men

Had Lukas Death not been with them I might still have looked for an excuse: but his presence was somehow reassuring. He was at least more congenial than the rest.

The group was clearly fired up by the prospect of a nocturnal hunt. And we'd barely stepped off Tant Poppie's stoep when a large rifle was pressed into my hands. I'm not particularly knowledgeable about firearms, but my father used to have one of those which he occasionally took on a springbok hunt. As far as I know my grandfather had brought it back from the Anglo-Boer War after refusing to give it up when peace was declared (which cost him a year in prison). A Mauser. Strange what a thrill it sent through me. A man among men. The hair on my body stood up like a dog's, and I could feel my balls contract. Onward, Christian soldiers.

As if Jurg Water could sense what I felt, he announced with deep-throated gusto, 'This is how our ancestors used to advance against the enemy.'

I took the gap: 'Did they have many enemies then?'

'Our people were always beset by enemies,' he declared with great conviction. 'One can never relax one's vigilance.'

'What kinds of enemies?'

'Every kind you can think of,' said Jos Joseph through his cloud of gnats. 'Everybody's hand has always been against us.'

'Were there enemies waiting down here in the valley when your people first arrived?'

'This place was as empty as the world before God started working on it,' said Lukas Death. 'But that doesn't mean a man can relax. There were always enemies trying to come in from outside, you see. In the early days the Cape government tried to get us out of here. They once sent a whole commando, hundreds of armed men, many of them heathen coloured pandoers. But that was in the time of Strong-Lukas, and he was a fighter like Gideon in the Bible. With only five men to help him he wiped out that whole army and threw their bodies down the cliffs for the vultures. You can still see his name chiselled on the Bushman Krans. I tell you, there's always the pestilence that walketh in darkness and the destruction that wasteth at noonday.'

Whales Too

'There must have been wild animals too?'

'What do you think?' asked Lukas Death ponderously, as if pronouncing a blessing. 'Lions, crocodiles, tigers, the lot.'

'Elephants, too,' added Isak Smous enthusiastically. 'Rhinoceros, hippopotamus, everything.'

'How on earth did they get in here?'

'God mos made them.'

'And whales too,' topped Jos Joseph, swallowing a gnat, which kept him out of action for a while.

'Quite so,' confirmed Petrus Tatters. 'In the old days that dry riverbed in the kloof was a proper flood. In the time of the Deluge it was all covered by the sea, of course. And when it dried up the whales remained.'

'Lukas Lermiet's oldest son, Lukas Nimrod, was the one who started killing off the wild beasts,' said Lukas Death with what sounded like due respect; they were his direct ancestors, after all.

'So you see,' Jurg Water concluded, 'our people have lived

through hard times here. Every step was taken in blood and suffering. And it still goes on.'

'What are we hunting tonight?' I asked as they fell quiet. We had reached the opposite slope by now, just above the fields, below the patch of prickly pear. I was conjuring up visions of elephants and lions, monsters, dragons, demons.

'Porcupine,' they answered in a chorus. And Lukas Death explained, 'The bastards are destroying the fields. In good times we don't mind too much, but in this drought there's not enough to eat for us and them.'

'Oh.' I couldn't stifle my disappointment. After the impressive build-up I'd been expecting rather more.

Boy's Arse

Jurg Water must have picked up my tone, because he hastened to expand, 'Mind you, a porcupine can be a very dangerous creature. We've buried some of our greatest men with a quill in the heart or the guts. Lukas Nimrod himself was one of them. A terrible quill right through his head, from temple to temple, one night while he was asleep. In those days porcupines were much bigger, of course. Height of a buffalo.'

'They say the one that got Lukas Nimrod was the size of a young elephant,' Petrus Tatters corrected him. 'They found his tracks afterwards.'

'Even the small ones can be dangerous,' added Jos Joseph, just in case I got the wrong idea.

'There's always the quills too,' added Isak Smous, in a more mercenary mood, skipping along on his short legs to keep up with us. 'The women make dainty little boxes out of them and they fetch a good price in Oudtshoorn.'

'All you can think of,' snorted Jurg Water.

'On the last porcupine hunt Little-Lukas was still with us,' said Isak Smous, injecting a more reflective tone into the conversation.

'His heart wasn't in it,' sighed Lukas Death.

'You were too soft on the boy,' snarled Jurg Water. 'I don't spare the rod with *my* children. They won't dare go against my wishes. A boy's arse is made for thrashing.'

Pa would have agreed.

'And a girl's?' asked Isak Smous with a hit of mockery in his voice, but with an undertone that made me wonder.

Jurg Water stopped in his tracks. 'What do you mean?' he said.

'Just teasing, Jurg.' Isak withdrew to a safe distance.

A muffled rumbling came from the others. No one spoke openly, but I was aware of a kind of subterranean resentment.

Lukas Death was the one who took things in hand. 'Now come on, men. Let's not argue in front of a stranger.'

'I want an answer first,' insisted Jurg. He stood with half-raised arms like a wrestler. 'What's Isak trying to tell me?'

'Ag Jurg, calm down, man,' said Lukas Death, with a quick glance in my direction. 'We're all poor sinners.'

'You're talking from experience,' mumbled Jurg Water. 'All the way back to the first Lukas Lermiet.'

'I won't have anything said against Grandpa Lermiet,' warned Lukas Death as if announcing a hymn to be sung. 'He's our common ancestor, his sins are ours.'

'Then tell that little runt to mind his own business.'

Dangerous Beast

For the time being an uneasy peace was restored, and the Christian soldiers could resume their march against the evils lurking in the night. But in the brief flare-up I'd become aware of a darker undercurrent which might have been there all the time, but never quite so clear: something menacing that had to be kept in check like some dangerous beast.

And then the dangerous beast we'd been stalking suddenly appeared in our midst: a half-grown porcupine trying to escape from the lantern light on a trot, then swinging round to face us, cowering, quills up.

There are many stories about our Boer ancestors who were such masters of the battle and the hunt: one bullet, one antelope (or lion, or Englishman, or kaffir, delete whatever is not applicable). But in the Devil's Valley, in spite of the scarcity of ammunition, this rule clearly did not apply. The five men with me immediately started firing at the scared little creature; and I unashamedly joined in. A reckless turmoil of men in the dark, after Jurg Water had dropped the lantern to cock his ancient gun.

It was pure luck that Jos Joseph was the only victim. When he fell down in his tracks with a bellowing sound, surrounded by a startled cloud of gnats, I thought it was the end. But for the moment the battle was too hectic to attend to him. He had to scuttle off on all fours, out of the whirlwind of hunters and hunted, while the rest of us pounced on the spiky creature that had suddenly become a deadly enemy responsible for the death of a true-blooded man. At least, that was what it looked like in the matt light of the moon, for Jos Joseph had collapsed in a heap just beyond the fringe of our cavorting.

Kieries and Clubs

Until that moment the porcupine had not been harmed, even though the shooting was reverberating among the mountains with duller and duller rumbling echoes from a distance, like a thunderstorm raging across the valley. When Jos Joseph fell, the hunters became like men possessed. Throwing away their guns, they moved in with kieries and clubs. Petrus Tatters sank to his knees from a blow to the head. I also received my share of blows, but nothing serious; in fact, it was only much later, back in my bed, that I became conscious of the pains I'd never felt in the frenzy of the battle. I simply grabbed my Mauser by the barrel and began to hit out in all directions – striking here a shoulder, there a shin, and occasionally the porcupine. Until at last, with a curious thin wail, the small animal crumpled into a lifeless lump.

Exhausted, I stumbled to one side. The others were still furiously at it. They kept on hitting the dead animal as if they were in serious danger. The adrenalin was so strong one could smell it. It was the kind of scene I'd witnessed only once or twice before in the course of my work. Once in '86, when the police and their Witdoeke allies attacked the Comrades at Crossroads. Two years later when a funeral in Kayelitsha degenerated into a necklacing. But then I'd been only a bystander. This time I was part of it.

The others were still venting their heroic rage. One or two attacked the carcass with their heavy boots, only to jump back bellowing with pain caused by quills in the shins. It took a long time before silence returned to the Devil's Valley. After the great uproar it was quite unearthly. All that could be heard was the panting, and a sudden outcry from Jos Joseph when someone plucked the quill from his calf – which, as it turned out, was the only damage the poor turd had suffered.

No one spoke on the long way back. Two of the men carried the meagre remains of the porcupine by the legs, triumphantly, like a trophy. We were all smeared with blood, together with the filth and dust of the battle.

Little-Lukas's heart hadn't been in it, I thought. Neither, by God, was mine.

Wet Dream

Some time during the night they dropped me off at Tant Poppie's front door, and I stood in the dark looking after them: the men with blood on their hands and clothes, and porcupine quills stuck triumphantly in their hats; carrying among them the little bundle which had come to the fields in search of food.

In my room I took off all my clothes and half-filled the ewer with some of the precious water the boy had brought. It was cold, I had goose-pimples all over, but I scrubbed myself like a slaughtered pig.

I was still conscious of blowing out the candle, but after that I blacked out. In my sleep a woman came to me. She drew the kaross from me and set to work with the kind of clean, absolute lust a man only dreams about. By the time I became aware of her, I was already far gone. She was as naked as a prick. And she was bloody well everywhere, against me, on me, below me, beside me, all over me. It felt as if I'd got caught in a fucking storm, high above the earth, in masses of black clouds through which lightning streaked and hurricanes swept, tossing me about, this way and that, one moment flinging me down into a vacuum, then hurling me up into space. Inbloody-describable. It was too dark to make out anything – except now and then, in the midst of our contortions, the fleeting silhouette of a head or a shoulder or a breast against the square of the window. Right through it all, not a single goddamn word was spoken. There were only the sounds of our struggle, heavy breathing and deep moanings, and in the end the long high scream of her orgasm. Only then did her prehensile cunt let go of me. She relaxed for a few moments to lie wet and panting against me.

I was totally fucked. In my dazed state I kept moving my hands over her body, blindly, without really knowing why; and it was only much later that I realised what I'd been trying to find: four tits. But there were only two of them. Too slippery to catch, she broke from me and escaped in the dark. In a last wild grab I got hold of a foot, and she fell to the floor, and I tumbled from the bed and landed with my face in the moist hairy thickets of her crotch, but with a laugh she kicked herself free and got away, back into the night from which she'd come. I stumbled back into my bed, and only much later sat up to light the candle. Strangely shaped shadows, like hairy baboons or owls with ruffled feathers, scattered across the walls and huddled in the corners. The hair on my body was knotted with the sticky sub-stance of our secretions. A wet dream like I'd never had in my fuck-ing life.

All I could remember was the foot I'd clutched, a foot with long toes and fleshy webs between them. And, more mundane, a long blue ribbon knotted loosely around my prick.

Ancient Grace

I smoked two cigarettes and blew out the candle again. Dark and heavy like a flood sleep came washing over me. In the swell I saw once again the hunters dancing like madmen round their quarry. But slowly a female figure became visible through the whirl of arms and legs and distorted faces. Once again I saw Henta bend over and stretch up. Her sinful eyes. The sort of ancient grace of that movement. But above the hem of her raised dress her face seemed to dissolve, as if seen through running water, changing into that other, elusive, imagined, young woman's face; and instead of Henta's inconsequential nipples I saw four tits, two grapefruit-sized and two smaller, staring at me like the eyes of a chameleon. And from far away I heard a raspy old voice say, 'I been sitting here waiting for you.'

Two

Everything Except Death

FACTS. FACTS WERE now my passion. When I was young, at the time I was still teaching history, I believed in the possibility of truth. Historical truth, so help me God. Gradually I was shocked out of this certainty, as out of most others. All that remained was my faith — tempered by cynicism, okay, but even so – in facts. I'd dig among the rubble in search of a handful of irreducible facts. I mean, this was what had brought me to the Devil's Valley. But until that Nagmaal Sunday things hadn't gone well for me. Now at last it seemed the tide was turning. About fucking time too, if I still meant to leave on the Saturday. I couldn't just sit back waiting for something to happen. It was time to pull finger, get down to facts.

The obvious place to start was Tant Poppie's breakfast table, the Monday morning. She'd given me bits of information before, but this morning she was suddenly much more co-operative, perhaps because I'd tried to softsoap her by asking about her medicines. She certainly didn't need much coaxing.

'Yes, Neef Flip, even if I say so myself, this place would have gone to maggots without me. What I know I got from my mother, and she from hers, all the way back, past the Great Flu, back to the very first people who came into the Devil's Valley.'

'Do you really have a cure for everything?'

'Almost everything, except death.' A heavy sigh. 'Because I must say, death is hard on us. Particularly the young ones. You'll see many olive plants around every table, but only a few of them grow up. And nowadays you can't mos even depend on those that grow up. Barely ripe, they want to get out into the world. There is fewer and fewer of us living here.' The heavy chair creaked as she shifted her mighty posterior. And then she took the plunge: 'But for all those who stay behind I try to do what I can.' A sweeping gesture across her collection of bags and boxes. 'You can ask me anything, Neef Flip. Try me. Suppose you have a thorn you can't get out. Right, then I catch some flies and fold them in a muslin cloth and mash them, and the mush goes straight on to the thorn. Otherwise I use a paste of dried pig's gall. For snakebite I make a cut in the breast of a black rooster and press the bird against the bite until it stops kicking. After about eight chickens all the poison is out. For spiderbite there's a different cure again. By far the best is burnt pumpkin and calabash seeds. But if it's something more serious, say heart disease, I draw wild thyme or naartjie peels or bitter-leaves or rue on water, dagga is very good too. It also helps for fever, drawing three of the green tips on boiling water.' Now she was unstoppable. 'A tortoise is ideal for a child with croup, it often happens in winter. I chop up the whole thing and press the pulp through a cloth and give it to the sick child. For inflammation I skin a live black cat and press the skin to the place; if it goes on, I give the patient a goat's stomach water to drink while it's still warm. For asthma the best cure is the burnt shell of a scaly anteater, but that's quite scarce, so I maar use the gall of a goat, drawn for three days on linseed oil in the sun. The oil I get from Gert Brush, he gets a regular supply from Isak Smous for his painting. Buchu is wonderful for bile and anything that's to do with the kidneys, from burning piss to old man's gland, and rue for the squitters, while for migraine I draw bluegum leaves and salt on Tall-Fransina's witblits. Mother's milk is a good cure for many complaints too, and luckily Bettie Teat is always available. If a man is going blind, one squirts the milk straight from the teat into the eye, then it's as good as new again. They say it started with old Lukas Seer, not a day went by without a woman milking in his eyes. And I can tell you, it's good for insomnia too, especially if the milking woman can lie right next to you. But the best cure for insomnia is to kill a speckled rooster, and while it's still jumping about you catch its blood and mix it with witblits and stir in some ground goat's bones and bake it in chicken fat. It never fails.'

'Sounds like a long story?' I asked.

Tant Poppie nodded gravely. 'The best cures take time, you see. But there's quick ones too. For heartburn I give them gum from the sweet-thorn tree, or plain raw earth, and for almost any ache under the sun a mixture of goat's droppings and vinegar helps on the spot. You can apply it to the skin or you can drink it. Those droppings are really wonderful stuff. But for some complaints you need more patience. For instance, for gout you have to rub some snake poison into a cut on your skin every Sunday just before church, right through the winter months. Or otherwise you wear a thin riempie cut from the skin of a leguan. Now take something like epilepsy. To cure that I have to cut the person's nails for three Fridays in a row, toes and fingers; then I mix these with a few hairs cut from his crown, and I feed the lot to the runt of a pig litter. The piglet is then buried alive, and by the time he starts rotting the patient is cured.' She shifted on her chair again. Her folded hands could barely reach over her stomach. 'So any time you have a problem, Neef Flip, you know who to come to.'

'I will,' I promised, keeping a straight face, then leaned forward with my elbows on the table. 'But my real problem is not one of health, Tant Poppie. There are so many things in the Devil's Valley I simply don't understand yet, and I wondered whether you could help. You have such a way with people.'

If she was a cat, I'm sure she would have purred. 'What is it you don't understand?'

Small and Precise

In this kind of situation, my job has taught me, one starts with something small and precise, not with the larger issues. I placed my little tape recorder on the table between us and pressed Start.

'What's that thing?' Tant Poppie asked with heavy suspicion in her voice.

'It helps me to remember,' I said cryptically, anxious to avoid details which might put her off.

She kept a wary eye on the recorder as she asked, 'Well, what is it you want to know?'

'Can we start with Little-Lukas?'

'What about him?'

'Why is everybody so set against him? No one seems to care about his death. And if he really was a direct descendant of Grandpa Lermiet's then surely he should have had some standing here.'

'He did. But you must understand that in this place we want to keep our lives to ourselves. He spoke too much.'

'You mean to me?'

'Yes, to you. But of course we didn't think of you then the way we do now.'

'Was it only Grandpa Lermiet who made the difference?'

'We always look up to him.'

'Even though he's been dead for so long?'

'He may be dead but he's still around. You saw him yourself.'

'His grave is empty.'

'Ja.' She uttered something between a sigh and a chuckle. 'You see, some time after his death, this is how the story goes, people started hearing sounds coming from his grave at night. A kind of knocking. Some said a voice crying out. It went on until people got so upset they decided to dig up the grave. When they opened the coffin, it was all filled with hair and nails, no sign of Grandpa Lukas himself. But a few weeks later people started seeing him, here, there, all over the place. It was then they decided to leave the grave open so he could come and go as he wished. It suits him like that. For Nagmaal, or when there's something special happening, he comes down here, otherwise he just looks after the goats on the mountain. It saves hands. And he keeps out strangers when they come too close.'

Heathen Habits

'I've been told,' I said, 'that over the years a number of outsiders tried to come in here: government agents, tax men, police, census people?'

'Ja. Grandpa Lukas could never stand those nose-pokers.'

'What became of them?'

'Depends. Most of the time he just scares them off and they leave. He has his ways. But when they don't listen, he passes it on to Hans Magic or Lukas Death, then they get our Council of Justice to make a decision.'

'And then?'

'Some of them got killed in accidents. In the old days it was sometimes necessary to send out a commando. That was before my time. All I personally know about was when an excise man came in here, I was still a child, the man wanted to confiscate the pot-still that belonged to Tall-Fransina's father. But then old Lukas Devil, he was Lukas Death's father, well, he and a few helpers led the man back up the mountain and somewhere along the way he caused trouble and fell down a cliff. Anyway, that's what we were told.' Her broad face remained blank. 'And years later Jurg Water's father and two of his friends came down here. They were allowed to stay because they were in trouble with their government about a war or something, and they were willing to marry women from the Valley and settle here. There was a bunch of policemen sent after them, but as far as I know they also had some kind of accident in the mountains. And then, still later, there was a whole lot of scribes and pharisees or whatever trying to come in to find out all about us, our history, our customs, everything. Said they came from some place of learning. The same place Little-Lukas went to afterwards. The town is called Stellenbosch.'

'What happened to them?'

'They were just told to go. Our men had guns with them, and they stripped the strangers of all their clothes, so they did as they were told. And that was that. We really don't want outsiders here. One never knows what they can bring in with them. Diseases, heathen habits, idolatry, unrest, all kinds of things.'

'Is is really because the people in the Devil's Valley are scared of strangers, or are they hiding something?' I knew I was pushing it, but

I had to risk it.

'Like what?' she asked.

'I'm just asking.'

'It's the good Lord Himself who brought us here,' she said, flaring up. 'If it wasn't His will, we wouldn't be here today. You seen these mountains for yourself. What's in here is meant to stay here, and what's outside must stay out. It's clear as daylight that God didn't want us to mix with others. We got to keep our blood pure. We're strong on purity in the Devil's Valley. That's why he wanted to keep us from all the evil out there.'

Changed

'What do you people really know about the outside world?' I asked.

'It's a bad place.'

'The country has changed a lot.'

She didn't answer, but her two squinting eyes were watching me like spiders.

'The country went through bad times which lasted for many years,' I said, 'but a while ago we had elections and now there's a new government and everything.' Even if it might be asking for trouble, I couldn't stop myself. 'We even have a black president now. The whole world looks up to him.'

'Well then you can mos see what God wanted to protect us from.'

'One thing I noticed here,' I said, 'is that all the people in the Devil's Valley do their own work. I find it hard to understand, because I know what our people are like. At the time of the Great Trek, of which the Seer was part, each family took their own servants with them. Free slaves and indentured labourers and such like. There were as many of them as Trekkers. Are you telling me there never were any black servants with the Lermiet party?'

'It was God's will that only Boers came in here,' she said with solemn emphasis. 'Kaffirs and Englishmen are enemies. The Bible says they shall bruise our heel and we shall bruise their head. We're very strict on keeping God's law and ordinances. Don't you remember the Israelites in Canaan? – God told them to kill all the Philistines and things, and when they didn't do it properly the place became a hell-hole of heathens and idolaters.'

Vermin

'Did the early settlers in the valley also have to kill strangers?'

'There was no need,' she said. 'I told you mos there was no one else here, this place was set aside for us from the beginning of time, so God kept it clean for us.'

'At least there must have been Bushmen around at some stage,' I pressed the point. 'I saw their paintings up there.'

'So what?' She uttered an angry grunt. 'We're talking of *people*, man. Bushmen are vermin. Anyway, if there was any of them around it must have been long before the Lermiets came in.'

'How lucky to find such a fertile spot just waiting for you,' I bitched.

She didn't seem to catch my sarcasm, but even so it took a while before the heaving of her bosom returned to normal.

I went on: 'We on the outside just had to learn the hard way to get along with others.'

'Ja, so I heard.'

'So you do get news from outside?'

She studied me carefully for a few minutes before she answered, 'From time to time we hear stories. When Isak Smous goes out with his stuff he brings us news. But it only strengthens us in what we know. I told you we live according to the Scriptures here.' She was working herself up again. 'Every Wednesday Brother Holy has a Bible-study session to explain it all to us. There's only one Bible in the valley, you see, the one the Seer brought with him, it's kept on the pulpit now. But thanks to Brother Holy we learned most of it by heart. You people from outside won't understand. You don't know us.'

'That's why I came. To get to know you.'

'It's not just a matter of coming here and getting to know us, man. One must be born here to understand from the inside. Only

God has the right to judge.' I picked up an unexpected edge to her voice: 'You see, not all of us can escape judgement by cheating death the way Grandpa Lukas does.'

'Did he do something that deserved judgement then?'

'Who am I to say? What does one person know about another?'

Another dead-end, like when Prickhead and I came up against the sheet of rock. I had to find another entry.

'What about Grandpa Lukas's wife?' I asked. 'Is she still around too?'

'The dead are always with us. It says so in the Bible.'

I'd have liked to take her on about this, but I'm afraid my knowledge of the Bible wasn't up to it. For the moment I simply persisted: 'I've heard how they came down here. The wagons falling down the cliffs, the eyes of the oxen poked out, the mountains covered in snow, the children dying. And how Grandpa Lukas's wife had to bear it all. Until at last he decided they could go back.'

'He saw a vision,' she corrected me.

'I suppose so. But then he had the accident. How did she cope with it all?'

'God made most women to suffer.' Her little black eyes flashed at me. 'But why do you go on so, gnawing at the past like a dog with a bone? We were never beholden to anyone here. We always got along well with God, we understand each other.'

Is Just Trouble

'God seems to be getting impatient,' I ventured. 'If the drought is anything to go by.'

She sighed. 'I'm afraid this drought will pass without a drop of rain,' she said. 'But we've come through worse than this, and we'll do so again. God chastises those he loves, you see. So when life gets hard we know the Lord is close. And this coming Wednesday we're having a day of prayer. Perhaps he's just waiting for that to open the sluice-gates.'

'Some people say the drought is sent as punishment.'

'If that is so, it can only be because of Little-Lukas.' An angry gesture sent shock-waves through her upper arms. 'He always had ants up his arse.'

'But other children also went to study outside before he did?'

'They just went to school. He was the first to go further. What do you call that place?'

'University.'

'That's right. Little-Lukas was too clever for his own good, man. And he managed to swing them all, including Grandpa Lukas. If you ask me, it was because he had that girl Emma on his side, because I think the old man had a weak spot for her. All the men had. Many years ago there was another one like her. Mooi-Janna. Lovely-Janna. She walked barefoot through all the men's dreams. No one could tame her, she was like a klipspringer in the mountains. But one day she fell down a krans and died. If you ask me, they're all besotted with Emma just because they never got over the sadness the Valley still feels about Mooi-Janna. That's why with Emma everything is on a knife's edge. You always get the feeling that with her it could go this way or that, heaven or hell.'

'I saw Emma in church yesterday.'

'Everybody was in church yesterday.'

'She and Little-Lukas were close.'

'He was all over her,' she grunted.

'Did the people talk about it?'

'Why should they talk about it?'

'They weren't married, were they?'

'What happens in the dark happens mos in the dark.'

I couldn't make out whether she was serious or merely trying to cover up.

'I'd like to meet this Emma,' I said. 'I have the feeling I won't begin to understand Little-Lukas before I know more about her.'

'Emma is just trouble, man,' she snarled, more fiercely than I'd have expected.

'But I've *got* to speak to her, Tant Poppie.'

'You'd do well to stay away from her.'

'Little-Lukas spoke nothing but good of her,' I said, although I couldn't really remember any particulars.

'He was bewitched by her.'

'Surely he knew her better than anyone else?' I asked.

'No one knows Emma the way I do,' she hit back and got up, making it quite clear that as far as she was concerned the conversation was over.

Devil's Handiwork

But I couldn't possibly back off now. 'How can you say so, Tant Poppie?'

She studied me for a moment, then relented. 'Because I brought her up. I took pity on her when everyone else was against her, poor little mite. All orphaned and alone. If it wasn't for me, they'd have —' she checked herself — 'she'd have gone the same way as her mother. But I must have known better. She has the mark of the Devil on her body.'

That made me sit up. 'What's his mark look like?'

'One doesn't talk about the Devil's handiwork.'

She started clearing the table.

'Why isn't Emma living with you any more?'

'Look, for years I protected her. But then she turned Little-Lukas's head. So when Hans Magic decided he must die, I told her to clear out. It doesn't pay to get into Hans Magic's bad books.'

'How did that happen?'

'Emma never watches her mouth, that's what happened.' She went through to the kitchen with clattering plates and bowls.

I stood up to give her a hand with the rest of the dishes, but she quickly stopped me. 'You sit right there, it's woman's work.'

Against my better judgement I sat down again. 'What happened to Emma's mother?'

'Maria died.'

'I gathered that. But how?'

She started wiping the dishes with her dirty apron; there was no water to be wasted. Everything in the kitchen was greasy from long use.

'Maria fell to her death,' she said, blowing on a plate. 'An accident. It was the will of God.'

I took a chance: 'I didn't see her grave in the churchyard.'

'You haven't seen everything in this place yet,' she said curtly. Adding smartly, 'And you better pray that you never get to see it all.'

Rough Tongue

LUKAS DEATH WAS the person I now wanted to talk to. But in the mornings he gave lessons in the schoolroom tacked on to his house. So I had to find another target for the time being. Isak Smous, I thought; he was a direct link with Little-Lukas. And rightly or wrongly I felt that after our nocturnal escapade I'd come closer to my fellow hunters. Just as Emma, in Tant Poppie's eyes, carried the sign of the Devil on her body, I must now be marked by what we'd done together. And talking to Isak might somehow confirm my rites of passage.

But as I set out from Tant Poppie's house, I was waylaid by Tall-Fransina who beckoned me from the lean-to where her still was rigged up. She needed a hand to feed her fire with bluegum faggots from the stack against the far wall. As always, she was surrounded by cats. A few of them immediately began to weave through my legs, stiff-tailed, purring possessively.

'This must be hard work for a woman on her own?' I asked.

'I get help when I need hands,' she answered brusquely.

'Have you been living alone like this for a long time?'

'Of course.' She was watching with falcon eyes the mouth of the snake from her still. Tall and strong, legs planted apart, in her man's shirt and waistcoat and skin trousers, with the broad-brimmed hat on her head and a small calabash pipe stuck in her mouth (I never saw her smoking, but she always had that pipe between her strong white teeth). Only when I came right up to her did I realise how tall she was. It was difficult to guess her age: fifty-five? Sixty? In her youth she must have been a stunner. As if she'd been reading my thoughts she said, 'No, I never married. I can't bear the smell of a man.'

'It must have been a loss to the Devil's Valley.'

She laughed deep from her stomach and showed me how to feed the wood into the oven under the still for the heat to spread evenly.

'You have a deft touch,' I complimented her.

'Takes a lifetime,' she said contentedly. 'My father taught me himself. It's come down a long way in our family. After he became bedridden I took over.' After a while she added, 'In all the years I've been here there was only one man who really understood what it is about, and that was Little-Lukas.'

Surprised, I looked up. 'I didn't realise he knew anything about distilling.'

'I wanted him to take over from me.' She closed up suddenly. 'Now it's too late.'

'Is there no one else you can talk to?'

'I don't have time to sit and talk. When it's pressing-time I work night and day. I distil other kinds of fruit too – peaches, prickly pears, whatever. For the rest I have my cats.'

'You seem to have a whole house full of them.'

'Twenty-four. There isn't place on my bed for more.'

I bent over and held out my hand to a large black tomcat with smooth pelt and green eyes that was rubbing itself voluptuously against my leg. A small rough tongue licked the hair on the back of my hand.

I looked up at her. 'I'd like to know more about Little-Lukas.'

'Little-Lukas had his chance, but he wasted it on a bowl of lentils.'

'You can't blame a young man for being ambitious, Fransina.'

'It had nothing to do with ambition, it was his prick.'

'Emma?' I asked pointedly.

'What was there Emma could teach him that I couldn't?' she snapped. Then, brusquely: 'You must go now, I've got work to do.' She picked up a leaf from an overhanging branch of the lemon tree next to the lean-to and held it under the mouth of the thin copper tube from which the first drops were just beginning to pearl.

Ugly Too

Still thinking about what Tall-Fransina had said, I came past Ouma Liesbet Prune's little house, one of the more dilapidated dwellings in the settlement. She was too old to care, and her distant nephew Ben Owl too fucking hopeless. As always, she was perched on her rooftop, her tin trunk clutched to her chest, staring up into the sky as if she could see what was hidden from ordinary mortals. But I was distracted by Jurg Water coming round the corner, rod in hand. He stopped when he saw me.

I greeted him with a show of camaraderie. 'Hello, Jurg. How's the great hunter this morning?'

'What's it to you?' He glared at me as if I was something caught by one of Tall-Fransina's cats.

'I'm all aches and pains myself,' I confessed. 'Suppose I'm not yet used to your kind of nightly jaunts.'

'What's this shit you're talking, man?'

'We gave that porcupine hell, didn't we?'

'Look, I haven't got time for crap.' And off he went.

A funny feeling settled in my gut, but I tried to keep it down. Jurg was a screwed-up bastard, there was no point in letting him upset me. But to tell the truth, I wasn't feeling all that sure of myself any more.

Just then I heard Ouma Liesbet calling in a high-pitched voice, 'Boetie, I want to talk to you.'

It was a hell of a long time since anyone had called me Boetie; but given her age it was perhaps her good right.

'Ouma?'

'Come and talk to me.'

Well, it wasn't as if I was in any hurry. But it meant climbing up to the attic landing, hoisting myself up to the roof from there and following the parapet to the chimney. God knows how that little wisp of a creature managed to get up and down.

It took me several minutes on the roof to catch my breath. From close by she looked fucking ancient, the thin skin on her face like the crinkled skin on a cup of boiled milk. Her eyes were watery and ringed with red. She gave off a sour smell.

From up there one could see the whole tract of the Devil's Valley, running all the way from the dry riverbed in a long gentle curve to Tant Poppie's house at the far end. The two rows of houses past the solid church which stood there like Luther of old, so-help-me-God-I-can-do-no-other. Some distance away in the bushes, well beyond Tant Poppie's house, I noticed another dwelling, more a hut than a house, which I hadn't seen before.

The little sparrow beside me must have followed my gaze, because she said in her tiny insect-buzz of a voice, 'That's Hans Magic's place.'

'Why does he live so far apart from everybody else?'

'That's how he wants it.' A dry chuckle. 'Just as well. No one can stand it too close to him. It's years since he last had water on his skin. And then he's ugly too.'

'I've seen other ugly people around the Devil's Valley, Ouma Liesbet.'

She sniffed. There was a bright drop at the end of her bony nose. 'Boetie, when I say ugly I mean *ugly*. You see, there's a dull kind of ugly, which is the ordinary kind. And then there's an ugliness that's all bright and bold. That's the way God himself meant ugly to be. And that is Hans Magic.'

Lightning Bird

I would have liked to find out more about the man, but by the set of her sunken mouth it was obvious that she wasn't so inclined. I continued my survey of the settlement. The sheds and backyards and haystacks. The long line of common fields, vegetable gardens, vineyards and orchards on the opposite slope; and on the near side, the ostrich pen with its hedge of aloes and stacked thorn-branches, and the bluegum wood beyond. From here one could look unhindered into all those lives.

'How did the ostriches get here?' I asked.

'Isak Smous's grandfather brought in a few eggs many years ago. That was in the time of the feather-boom.' A tinny chuckle. 'I hatched them myself.'

'How did you do that?'

'It was easy. I was still young. I had a good body. And let me tell you, you won't find such fine feathers anywhere else.' A dry laugh. 'In my youth, when we celebrated New Year, I used to dance for them, I'd wear nothing but feathers. And then the menfolk plucked me.'

'How come that you're spending your days all alone up here?'

'I'm waiting for the Lord, didn't you know? No one can tell the day or the hour. When the time comes His judgement will fall on all of us, that's what we were brought up with.' Suddenly inspired, she continued with a tone of deep satisfaction. 'This is only a temporary abode, says the Bible. Sooner or later God will send His thunder and lightning to raze the whole world to the ground. If you read Revelations you'll see there will be nothing left.' She made a pause, then added quietly, 'But there's another kind of lightning too, and I sometimes ask myself if that isn't worse. It's the one inside us, the one laid by the lightning bird the old people spoke about, you know, they had so many stories.

'How does it go?'

'It comes from far back. They used to say that if God gets angry with the world He sends a storm, and in the storm a lightning bird comes down from the clouds to lay her eggs deep inside an antheap, like coals of fire that go on smouldering in the dark. And there they stay, sometimes for years and years, no one knows they're there. It's like a fever in the blood. When their time comes, they hatch; and then their fire destroys everything.'

'It must be tough if you never know when they're going to hatch.'

'That's just how it is,' she said resigned. 'All we know is that sooner or later it is going to end. One day will be the last. That's why I'm waiting up here. Only at night it's not so easy, the stars make such a racket.'

'You need someone to look after you.'

'There's my distant nephew, he's three or four times removed, Ben Owl. He sleeps in the daytime because his eyes are too weak for the light. But in the dark he misses nothing. He looks after me as well as anyone could, every night he brings me food and drink and spends some time with me. Even if it's a bit of a nuisance, what with all those voices in his head talking so loudly, and all at the same time, I can hardly hear myself.'

Chameleon

Before I could answer, and without any transition, she asked, 'What are you doing with that thing?' She pointed at the chameleon on my shoulder.

'Oh, he's quite harmless.'

'It's his kind that brought death into the world, did you know?'

'How can you say so?'

'That's what the old people used to tell us.' She leaned back against the chimney. 'They said that in the time of Adam and Eve God sent a chameleon to Paradise with a message: Just as the moon wanes and dies and then grows full again, you mortals will die and always rise again. But the chameleon is a slow creature, as you know, and it took its time. One day, when it was resting on a twig, a hare came past and asked about his business. The chameleon told him about the message and from the goodness of his heart the hare offered to run ahead and spread the news. But he was in such a hurry that he forgot half the message. And when he arrived in Paradise he told Adam and Eve that God wanted them to know: Just as the moon wanes and dies, you mortals will also die.' The laugh she gave sounded almost cheerful. 'Well, that was that. The harm was done, and by the time the chameleon arrived in Paradise the people had already received the message of death. Which is why, the old people said, Adam and Eve maar turned to eating figs.'

I tried to sort through all the irrelevant shit in my mind. 'If I'm not mistaken, Ouma,' I said, 'that story was first told by the Khoikhoi people.'

'And who might they be?'

'The Hottentots.'

'We've never had those in the Devil's Valley,' said Ouma Liesbet with comic indignation. 'It's a story handed down by our own people.' Without waiting for an answer she asked, 'What are you going to do with the little dragon?'

'Piet Snot gave it to me to bring me luck.'

'What would he know about luck?' She clicked her tongue. 'Poor little turd. He hasn't got it easy with that father of his.'

'Who is his father?'

'Jurg Water of course.'

I added two and two together and arrived at rather more than four.

'Can you tell me more about the Valley?'

'Of course I can, but why should I? Life is too short to waste on gossip.' And then she seemed to forget all about me and started mumbling to herself, something that sounded like a counting-out chant. 'Lukas Seer begat Lukas Nimrod, and Lukas Nimrod begat Lukas Up-Above, and Lukas Up-Above begat Strong-Lukas, and Strong-Lukas begat Lukas Bigballs, and Lukas Bigballs begat Lukas Devil, and Lukas Devil begat Lukas Death, and Lukas Death begat Little-Lukas.' Another dry chuckle. 'And that's only one of the lines. Because you must know, the old Seer had seventeen children, nine sons and eight daughters. And with each of the eight daughters he had a few more. And just before he died he even had a child with one of his granddaughters. All scriptural, of course. You know, like Lot and his daughters. Today evil is sprouting like weeds in the valley. That's why I prefer to sit up here until the Lord comes to fetch me.'

'How can you be so sure that He'll come?'

'He came for Elijah, didn't He? And He came for Enoch. And He came for Lukas Up-Above. He told me Himself I'm next.'

'What exactly happened to this Lukas Up-Above?'

Single Bird

'He spent his whole life trying to get out of here,' she said. 'If you ask me, it's because he had such a shrew for a wife, no one could stand it with her. But poor Lukas was so fat, he could barely walk. They say he was twice as double as Jurg Water, and high on his legs. That put him on the idea of flying. He first made wings of all kinds. Feathers, branches, wood, bags filled with tumbleweed and thistles and reed-plumes. But every time he nearly killed himself. Then he tried wind. First he got all the children together to rake up a wind with branches. When that didn't work he started eating anything that would blow up his stomach, so that he could fart himself across the mountains. That time he very nearly died.'

'And then he gave up?'

'Not a hope. No, next thing was, he tried fire. He stuffed big bags with dry grass and set fire to them. But one day the whole mountain caught fire and just about everything burned down, the fields, the orchards, the roofs of the houses. And he too. Scorched off all his tailfeathers. He fell from high up in the sky on his own roof, it was just flames all over, his own wife burnt to death, which was her just deserts.'

'That must have set him back.'

'Never. For a while he gave himself up to drink. He thought if only he could get drunk enough flying would come by itself. But it didn't work either. Then, after he'd been cured of the drinking he made himself a little cart. His heaven-cart, he called it. A little square box of a thing, like the basket of rushes the mother of Moses wove to put her child in. And when it was finished he built a huge cage and sent out the children to catch all the birds in the Devil's Valley. With traps, and cages, and lime, everything you can imagine. For weeks and months on end the children brought back birds. And when they'd caught every single bird in the mountains he hitched them to his heaven-cart and there they went, over the mountains, to hell and gone. He was never seen again. Up to heaven he must have gone. And now it's my turn.'

'But it must be very uncomfortable up here.'

'Here on the roof I don't bother anybody and they don't bother me either. Also, I don't have a coffin like the others, so it's better to wait up here.'

'Weren't you married then? I thought every woman in the valley gets a coffin as a wedding present?'

'That's so. And I got mine too. All measured and everything. And my groom and I gave it a proper lie-in, I can tell you. But then I gave it away. That poor young girl Maria needed it more than I did.'

'Would that be the mother of the girl Emma?'

'Yes, that's the one.'

'Please tell me about her.'

Fertile Place

She sucked the inside of her toothless cheeks. Perhaps there was a story coming, I thought, but in the end she only shook her head, which looked like a frayed stocking drawn over a darning shell.

'The least said the better. All I know is that life in our valley has been going downhill ever since Maria died. That was a sign. These are the Last Days, Boetie. The sun shall be turned into darkness, and the moon into blood. You think you saw blood last night? But there's more coming.'

'How do you know about last night?'

'I saw you, of course.'

Mad as a fucking coot. Yet it brought a brief sense of relief too, after Jurg Water's rebuff. At least I had a witness, so for once it hadn't been a dream. If her word was anything to go by.

'So you saw the hunt?' I asked eagerly.

But her mind was wandering. 'Ag, poor Maria. And what's going to become of Emma now with Little-Lukas dead and all?'

Trying to get the conversation back on track, I prodded her: 'Tell me about Emma, Ouma Liesbet.'

'Why do you want to know?'

'The day I came here I saw her swimming in the rock pool over there. And then she just disappeared again.'

'Perhaps it was better for you that way. Remember what happened to Little-Lukas.'

'Emma couldn't have had anything to do with his death.'

'It was to get away from her that he left. All I know is that Little-Lukas was perfectly happy here, but he was so scared of her he'd have done anything to get away from her.'

'I thought he loved Emma.'

'He loved her, yes. But he was scared as a hare.'

'Tant Poppie Fullmoon said this morning that Emma has the mark of the Devil on her body.'

'Poppie knows what she knows.'

'What kind of mark would it be?'

'If there is a mark she must have got it from her mother. Ben Owl always said Maria caused trouble and Ben had reason to know. A thing like that is passed from mother to daughter. One doesn't talk about it. You either see it or you don't, and what you don't see isn't meant for you. Now go on, I must prepare to meet my Bridegroom.'

Squawking

Inside, Isak Smous's house looked just like all the others, except that it had more rooms – a workroom and a store for his wares, space for his offspring, and bedrooms for himself and Alie, and Malie and Ralie.

One of the three meat-grinder women made us coffee. I should add that it was the only household in the settlement where I got offered proper coffee. Most of the other families were quite happy with a poison brewed from some bloody local root. I'd tried witgat once when I was on an assignment for my paper in the Northwest, but that was like ambrosia compared to the concoction of the Devil's Valley. The wife (or sister, or sister) served the coffee in the store where we sat, and then rejoined the others in their rounds of feeding babies, kneading dough, churning goat's milk, swatting flies with a bluegum branch, sweeping floors with a brushwood broom, chasing poultry from under chairs or tables, or whatever their chafed red hands found to do. It was an interior like those described by Burchell in his *Travels*, in the early nineteenth century: or even earlier by John Barrow, whose accounts of Boer life in the deep interior so upset the colonists.

At one stage a din broke out when one of the three sisters climbed on the roof to throw a hen down the chimney. All hell broke loose as the squawking, flapping chicken came fluttering down, and I was on the point of jumping up when Isak calmly looked up through his stained and dusty half-moon reading glasses and explained, 'They always clean the chimney on Mondays.'

Closing the Door

He returned to the much-thumbed exercise book in which he'd been adding up rows of scribbled figures when I came in. But there was a matter I just had to get out of my system, as pressing as any fart: 'Looking at you right now, Isak, no one would guess you'd been on a hunt last night.'

Half-surprised, half-annoyed at being interrupted in his calculations, he stared at me. 'What funny questions you ask,' he mumbled.

'I've got to know, Isak. You were there after all.'

He just shrugged his sloping castor-oil bottle shoulders and stuck his nose back into his work.

Sucking in my arsehole I went for broke: 'Or are you telling me we weren't there?'

'There are things better not talked about, Neef Flip.'

And that was bloody well it. I was left to my frustration while he finished his bookkeeping.

All around him stood boxes and chests and bags filled with merchandise. It was a mystery how he'd lugged all that stuff across the mountains and down the precipices of the Devil's Valley. But when I asked him about it, he just laughed, stroking his hand across his bald pate as if to flatten an unruly mop of hair.

As restless as a fly he jumped up to show me the contents of his containers. Against one wall, the produce of the Devil's Valley: honey and rolled tobacco, raisins and ostrich eggs and dried fruit and prickly-pear beer and calabash pipes, as well as Tant Poppie's herbs, Jos Joseph's miniature wagon chests, Sias Sjambok's plaited whips, Petrus Tatters's veldskoens. And piled up against the opposite wall the merchandise picked up in Oudtshoorn and Calitzdorp, or as far afield as Uniondale and Ladismith: sugar and salt and ammunition, needles and bolts of chintz, paraffin for when the lard ran out, here a hatchet head, there a ploughshare or a spade – only the most indispensable stuff, for in the course of time the Valley had become quite surprisingly self-sufficient.

At a given moment he grabbed me by the arm and took me to the master bedroom, carefully closing the door behind us so the women couldn't see us, and removed from under the bed a battered old tin trunk which he unlocked with an ancient key to show, with all the pride of a new father, what clearly was his treasure: the trunk was half-filled with banknotes, which he scraped away to reveal a sizeable molehill of golden pounds.

'Where does this come from?'

'It's from all the buying and selling over the years.'

'But what can you do with money in the Devil's Valley?'

'It's not a matter of doing but of having,' he laughed.

I grubbed in the coins with my hands, shaking my head.

'There used to be much more,' he said in a flush of anger. 'But these people were a lot of scoundrels. It's hard on an honest man to live among such sinners.'

'What happened then?'

'In my father's time a bunch of good-for-nothings – Lukas Death's father, old Lukas Devil, was the gangleader – waited until he'd gone over the mountains, then they stole all his money. They melted the gold and made a billy goat out of it and put it on the pulpit in the church, calling on all the people to worship it, can you imagine a thing like that, just like the Israelites in the desert.'

'Sounds a bit far-fetched to me,' I said curiously.

'It's the honest truth I'm telling you, Neef Flip. And if you ask me why they did it, I'll tell you it from was pure spite, spite and jealousy, because they couldn't stand somebody else making a success of his life.'

He ceremoniously closed and locked the trunk again, and pushed it back under the bed. Then he steered me back to his store.

Every Word

What caught my eye this time was a small box filled with books. He wanted to shove it aside but I stopped him.

'And these books, Isak?'

'I picked them up outside too, at auctions and things.'

'Do you read them?'

'No, I'm not a reader.' It took him a while to open up. 'There's one or two people around here who sometimes ask for a book. Lukas Death of course. And Brother Holy, when I have something religious' – a sly wink – 'or something with pictures, you know what I mean?' He cupped a hand over his crotch, then grew serious again. 'But mostly I brought them in for Little-Lukas.'

'How did he get started?'

'He often went into town with me, you see, when he was a little boy. That's how it began. First newspapers, then books from the library. But it was actually Emma who pushed him. And as they grew up the two of them would spend whole afternoons reading here in my store.'

I kneeled beside the box and started unpacking. A curious mix. Several were by older Afrikaans authors: a few volumes from Langenhoven's collected works, ghost stories by Leipoldt, some poetry, an early grammar. A couple of Dutch titles, even some English ones, like *The Jungle Book*, and *Alice in Wonderland*, and *The Story of an African Farm*. And then Oscar Wilde's collected works, and textbooks on biology and geography, history. The most unexpected was Immanuel Kant.

'And this one?' I asked, both amused and amazed.

He looked at the Kant and grinned. 'That one had Little-Lukas stumped. He tried his damnedest, I can tell you. He went so far as to copy every word of it into his exercise books, and when his hand got numb then Emma took over. They thought that would help them understand. They never made it so far, but I tell you, they never gave up trying. And from then on Emma kept up with him, book after book. There was a kind of fever in those two.'

'You aided and abetted them?' I joked.

But Isak remained deadly serious. 'There was no way I could stop them, Neef Flip. We had a few children before them who also liked to read, but they never had it so bad as these two. And the others always came back after Standard Eight or Matric. People from here don't transplant easily. But Little-Lukas and Emma . . . If anything, she was worse than him.'

'Then why didn't she go to university too?'

'How could she? What is the use of education for a woman if she can't bake a loaf of bread for her husband?'

'And so he went off on his own?'

'He promised to bring her books every vacation. And then the two of them would work together for hours here in this room, all out of sight. Quite a touching thing to see. You can imagine how it was for her when he died.'

'I must talk to her, but no one gets to see her.'

'She's still in mourning,' he said gruffly, closing up like a bloody clam, as if I'd trespassed on private property.

'There's a lot about Emma I simply don't understand, Isak.'

'It's better to let her be,' he said, just as reluctant to pursue the subject as Tant Poppie and Ouma Liesbet Prune had been. 'She carries bad luck with her.'

One Never Knows

'Because of her mother?' I asked.

He began to burrow in his merchandise again and didn't answer.

'What happened to her mother?' I insisted.

'Sometimes I wondered if I could perhaps smuggle Emma out of here,' he said as if he hadn't heard me. 'But one never knows with Hans Magic. He won't let Emma go just like that.'

'What has he got against her then?'

'Hans Magic is a dark horse. All I know is that he's got a grudge against her. They say she insulted him. But Hans Magic gets affronted so easily, it's hard to say.'

'Little-Lukas told me about him, but I was stone drunk, so I can't remember much. But there was something about a thief whose shoe he'd caught in a vice . . .?'

'So he told you. Yes. And then he died.'

I was waiting to hear more, but he was clearly not prepared to help me out. I decided to take the bloody bull by the horns: 'What I don't understand is how the news of Little-Lukas's death reached the valley?'

He shrugged.

'And everybody seemed to be expecting me when I came,' I went on. 'Lukas Death, Tant Poppie, Hans Magic, the lot.'

'It was Grandpa Lukas who told them.'

'But how did *he* find out?'

His answer was quite unexpected: 'I told him.'

'You?!'

'Yes,' Isak said casually. 'As it happened, I was in the Little Karoo with a load just after Little-Lukas died. That's where I heard about it, so I went on to Stellenbosch and spoke to his landlady. She told me about you, and that you were going to come here.'

'Why didn't she say anything to me?'

'I told her it was better not to talk about it.'

It took me a while to digest it all. Then, following a new track, I asked, 'For how long have you been in your line of business?'

'It runs in the family.' He seemed relieved to move away from Little-Lukas. As he busied himself with his stocktaking again he started talking in fits and starts. If I hadn't brought my tape recorder I'd have been screwed trying to sort it all out afterwards.

Merchandise

Isak's story began with his first ancestor – inasmuch as anyone in the Devil's Valley could still point to a specific ancestor, except the Lermiets of course, and even with them it seemed mainly hit-or-miss.

This gentleman, Abraham Koen (a Boer variant of Cohen?), first arrived in the Devil's Valley with a load of merchandise some time after Grandpa Lermiet had broken his leg. The loss of the leg was another story: according to Isak the leg became gangrenous, starting at the toes, and to save his life the Seer had to hack it off with his hunting knife in three stages – first at the ankle, then at the knee, and finally in the groin. By that time the family was reeling from all its misfortunes and Abraham Koen/Cohen's appearance was something like the coming of the Lord. Even old Lukas Lermiet, never an easy customer, relented. His wife, especially, couldn't think of enough ways to express her gratitude. As a result of which she was pregnant by the time Abraham Koen quietly fucked off one night – just in case the Seer saw something amiss.

But the amazing thing – or perhaps not so amazing after all, given that Lukas Lermiet was on the verge of death – was that no one except Bilhah realised she was carrying another man's child.

'I thought the wife's name was Mina?' I interrupted.

'Her name was Bilhah.' And without giving me another opening he picked up his thread again.

It was at least three years before Abraham Koen returned. Whether Lukas Seer had just resigned himself to the inevitable by then or whether he'd really never guessed the truth, no one could tell. But Abraham became, in every respect, a member of the family. There were times when Lukas Lermiet still threw one of his legendary tantrums, destroying everything within sight; and then Abraham would quietly take his possessions and bugger off. But he returned every time, at shorter and shorter intervals, invariably loaded with provisions and implements of one kind or another.

The Lermiet clan was beginning to nibble at the bait. I mean, as Father Abraham explained, just look at what the Devil's Valley had to offer. Skins of the game they shot (by that time Lukas Nimrod had already begun to win renown as a hunter). Wild honey from the bees that nested in the high cliffs. Bush tea. Dagga. It was as if the Lord himself had planted a dagga garden in this place, judging from the way the stuff grew in the kloofs. All this produce could be sold abroad, or bartered for necessities. The old Seer kept on protesting, more from habit than conviction, but Abraham had the advantage of mobility; if he wanted to go no one could stop him, nor when he decided to come back. And of course he had Bilhah's support to rely on, expressed in ways both pleasing and practical. She made sure that there was never cause for strife between the men, as she remained fertile for an exceptionally long time, and in due course the older daughters also began to bring their side. Lukas Nimrod and the second son, Hard Hendrik, did what was required of them from an early age. And all this kept the females busy; after all, it wasn't as if they had so many other things to do.

Bloodline

In this way Father Abraham's comings and goings began to shape into a useful and predictable pattern, making life ever more manageable in the growing settlement. From time to time he also brought other men with him for jobs he regarded as indispensable – regularly provoking angry protests from Lukas, and energetic support from Bilhah and her daughters, as well as, eventually, her granddaughters.

Among the arrivals who won approval was a preacher, Doep Dropsy. There were whispers that he'd fallen into disgrace in his Cape congregation, for minor misdemeanours involving communion wine, and more serious ones that included manslaughter; but Isak Smous's memory was not very clear on these points. And in the Devil's Valley they didn't seem to matter so much anyway. Most of the people who'd moved in here over the years needed to cover up some dirty tracks behind them. Doep Dropsy's history could readily be left behind the mountains; all that was necessary was the offices he could perform. If you think of it, the place was in bloody dire need of a man who could tend to the spirit, surrounding the rituals of burial, baptism, communion, and marriage; and Doep Dropsy was like an answer from heaven. Testimonials weren't necessary, the readiness was all. And Doep Dropsy was ready, if nothing else, to look after both the spiritual and physical needs of his new flock. As the Seer's womenfolk could testify.

There was another man Abraham brought in, a man whose hands could take on anything from stonecutting to carpentry, an artisan by training and an artist by nature. His name was Ruben Portier, soon changed to Ruben Tabernacle; and judging by the solid and secure masonry and woodwork of the houses, and most particularly of the church, he had been an inspired choice. In addition he, too, was not found wanting in doing his bit towards the multiplication of souls in the Valley.

In later years the bloodline was presumably renewed a few more times (thank God for small mercies), the last time being the arrival of Jurg Water's father and his two fellow firebrands from the Ossewa-Brandwag during the Second World War; but Isak didn't have much to say about those. Understandably, he was more interested in talking about his own position in the community. What mattered to him was that in every generation there was at least one man who could follow in the footsteps of that first entrepreneur called Cohen or Koen and ensure a measure of prosperity for the settlement while amassing a sizeable personal fortune on the side.

Under One Roof

Among these predecessors was a great wanderer known as Jacob Horizon, Isak's grand- or great-grandfather. On one of his early journeys he'd met a young woman the likes of which one usually finds only in a dream. According to Jacob he'd found her in the Vale of Sharon, but it might just as well have been in the Little Karoo. Her name was Katarina, Katarina Sweetmeat. She had not come cheaply. To begin with, Jacob Horizon had had to put up with three years of fucking hard labour with her father, and then he still had to pay a lobola comprising most of his earthly possessions. But he thought it worth while. And it was the most wonderful day of his life when he could finally bring her back into the Devil's Valley as his intended. He'd specially hired a black servant, bedecked in bloody white livery, to carry her down the mountains.

The problem was that all the other men in the valley, young and old, became besotted with her. Most stricken were the seven sons of Strong-Lukas, that is to say, the grandfather and great-uncles of Lukas Death. Those seven were used to running amok among the mountains and there were few brave enough to stand up to them.

They were a shrewd bunch too, it wasn't just a matter of bedding and wedding the woman. Oh no, Katarina's heart had to be won properly. Now as you know, explained Isak Smous, there's a bad spot in every pretty girl. And they soon discovered that Katarina Sweetmeat was as vain as Salome in the Bible. She could never get enough of looking at herself. But in Jacob Horizon's home there was only one small mirror, not nearly enough for a woman who liked to see herself from all sides at the same time. Some say Jacob was too stingy to buy more mirrors, but the more charitable view is that after paying so much for his bride he simply had no bloody money left. Be that as it may, the seven brothers saw their chance. They covered one whole room in their home with mirrors — walls, ceiling, even the floor. In one sweeping glance Katarina could see all of herself from top to pretty toes, and all the sweetmeats in between.

She dropped Jacob Horizon like a turd and moved in with the seven brothers.

The brother designated to marry her was Lukas Bigballs, for rather obvious reasons. But God doesn't sleep, said Isak Smous deeply satisfied. Lukas Bigballs was allowed no more liberties than any of his brothers, as Katarina was much too infatuated with herself.

'How did your grandfather get over it?' I asked.

Isak Smous gave an embarrassed chuckle. Jacob Horizon was broken, he said, and yet not broken either. Remember he had his ancestors' entrepreneurial blood in his veins. He knew that in the long run there's only one approach that works with a woman and that is patience. After Katarina had married Lukas Bigballs, Jacob Horizon went off on another trip and stayed away for three whole years. And just as he'd calculated, Katarina Sweetmeat began to miss him in his absence. So much so, that his return became a real cele-bration, and nine months later Katarina gave birth to her first child.

Like most things in the Devil's Kloof, it became routine. Jacob Horizon would go off, stay away for a year or two, come back, and Katarina would fall pregnant. How it happened remained a mystery, because Lukas Bigballs and his brothers kept watch on her like fuck-ing falcons, day and night. She never set foot outside the mirror room, which was the outroom where Lukas Death now has his mortuary. Only once a week was she let out for a walk up the kloof, accompanied by all seven brothers; yet every time Jacob Horizon came back from his wanderings it was the same story.

The Lermiet brothers decided that the only solution was to get rid of Jacob. One night all seven of them surrounded his house to dis-patch him from this world with picks and shovels. What they didn't know was that his loyal black servant, the one who'd accompanied him on all his journeys, the only black person ever allowed into the

Devil's Valley, had warned him beforehand, and Jacob got away. This time he stayed away for seven years, until everybody thought it was for good. But then he returned after all, and Katarina Sweetmeat fell pregnant again, even though she was no longer young. She was still beautiful, though, especially when she looked at herself in the mirror.

'What hold did Jacob have on her then?' I asked, intrigued.

Isak Smous shook his bald head. 'He was Katarina's first love, remember.'

'But she left him.'

'Does anyone know what moves a woman? The man she leaves, she keeps for life. The one she picks loses the lot.' Isak smiled again, slowly, as if he knew what I did not.

'But you said the brothers never gave her a chance, they watched over her day and night.'

'Love mos finds a way, man. The story has it that on full-moon nights Katarina changed into a little white nanny goat and flew from the chimney. And as it happened, the moon was always full when Jacob returned from a journey.'

'But that's nonsense, Isak.'

'Love is never nonsense,' he said as if I'd insulted him personally.

'What became of them?'

'Katarina died at the birth of her last child, the one who came after the seven years. The Lermiets broke all the mirrors in the outroom to get rid of every trace of Katarina. But they still had her child to look after. He was the one who became known as Lukas Devil, born with two goat's feet.'

'What happened to Jacob Horizon?'

'He never went on another trip. Decided to stay on permanently to keep an eye on the baby. And in the process he got over the itch. But anyway, he'd brought home enough stuff from that last trip to keep the Devil's Valley happy for a long time. After his death it all went to the church.'

'What's become of it now?'

'Come with me,' said Isak Smous. 'Let me show you. Then you

can see with your own eyes.'

Facts, Facts

Facts, facts, I thought. Here they come, and not a bloody moment too soon.

We went down the rough road to the church, past the heap of stones piled up against the cemetery wall. Was I imagining things or did Isak give it a wide berth? Heavy and solid the church rose before us, a huge hulking thing, the blunt tower like a hump between its shoulders. On the front doorstep Bettie Teat was reclining as usual, crawling with children. High up on the massive door, as we came past, I noticed a large ring, presumably of brass because it had turned green; quite artistic in its way, decorated with vine-leaves and acorns and the faces of the little angels and devils. What its bloody function was, I had no way of guessing; probably purely ornamental, as it was much too high for a knocker. Before I could ask Isak, he hurried on, perhaps to get out of Bettie's reach.

He led me round the building to the vestry door, which wasn't locked. Nothing in this settlement is ever locked. Perhaps it isn't necessary, there's always someone looking after all. That morning too. I could see Brother Holy standing among his vegetables, solemn as a marabou, to keep an eye on us, and for some reason that look was enough to make me feel guilty.

Isak told me to wait below the pulpit while he scuttled up the steps on his short legs. There he dived in behind the gleaming dark wood that smelled of beeswax. The massive structure, I soon realised, had been carved by an inspired hand. Ruben Tabernacle's, undoubtedly. Given the primitive tools he must have used, presumably no more than a knife and a chisel and something to smooth the surfaces, this was a fucking amazing piece of work. The greater part of the pulpit had been cut from a single block. It must have been some tree – yellowwood, with the deep, almost-orange shine one finds only in the oldest wood. But what most surprised me, this being the first time I had the chance to look at it up close, was the carving along the top edge of the pulpit. Funny business. From a distance one couldn't make out any details, and from close up it just looked like a weave of abstract shapes. Yet the moment I turned away they appeared to regroup into identifiable figures. Pretty fucking startling figures at that, a proper kama sutra of men and women caught up in the clinches of sex; and the couples were not all human either. There were men with goats, with chickens, with tortoises; women with peacocks, with snakes, with ostriches, take your pick. The moment I tried to focus on any given couple, they would promptly dissolve again into the general blur of unrecognisable shapes. Was it my bloody imagination? Hallucination? Shades of my night with the succubus? The first sign of DTs provoked by Tant Poppie's apostles? Time to pull myself together. There was something seriously wrong here.

But before I had time to sort it out, Isak Smous came scampering down the pulpit steps again, bald head gleaming, a triumphant smile on his face.

'Here you are.' He placed a much-used little tin trunk on the long Communion table. 'This is what Jacob Horizon brought back to convince the doubting Thomases.'

Darkness

He started unpacking the trunk. Some of the objects didn't exactly impress me. A pair of battered binoculars as an example of the advances of science in the world outside. A porcelain doll with one arm missing, which he made out to be a child somehow petrified after Herod's massacre. An object that looked like a large salt crystal, apparently broken from the remains of Lot's wife in the bloody Jordan valley, but resembling quite suspiciously a stalactite from the Cango caves at Oudtshoorn. A conch shell one could press against one's ear to hear – cross my heart – the sea of Galilee. A cheap oriental shawl of the kind one can pick up in any oriental bazaar, covered with sequins and gold thread and dragons, which turned out to be nothing less than Joseph's fucking amazing technicolour dreamcoat.

'And now for the real magic,' said Isak, removing a small carved box from the trunk. The kind of trinket box one finds at a flea-market and puts down again. 'How do you like this?'

'Not bad,' I said noncommittally.

'What matters is what's *inside*, Neef Flip,' he said, his voice down to a whisper as he reverently placed the little box in my irreverent hands. 'In this box,' he said, 'is the Darkness of Egypt.'

'May I look?' I asked.

He snatched the box from me in horror. 'Never! The Darkness will escape,' he said. 'Don't you realise what my great-grandfather suffered to carry this box over the hills and dales of the wide world? He was pursued by enemies all the way. Egyptians, Turks, Philistines, Moors, Jews, Indians, everything. And now it is right here in our church. Can you believe it? One thing I can tell you: as long as it is here no evil can befall us.'

Flies

MUCH OF THE afternoon I spent in my room sorting through my tapes. But I was disturbed by the clanging of the sheet of iron that served as church bell. On a Monday afternoon? Surprised, I sat up. The sound continued to reverberate through the narrow valley, thrown back by the most distant cliffs. It called for closer investigation.

But when I got outside I found little Piet Snot waiting for me on the edge of the stoep.

'Hello, Piet. What's up with that bell?'

He was too absorbed in his two cupped hands to answer.

'What have you got there?'

He opened a chink between his fingers. A dazed fly tried to crawl out, but he quickly trapped it again. 'Flies, Oom. For the chameleon, Oom.'

Lower down in the valley the bell was still clanging away.

'You sure you don't know what's going on at the church?'

'No, Oom.' But he wasn't looking at me.

With a sigh I invited him in and sat down on my bed to watch impatiently as he fed the chameleon a few half-crushed flies. By the time it was done the bloody bell had stopped.

'Right,' I said, getting up. 'He won't look another fly in the eye for days. Off you go.'

He shook his head stubbornly. 'I want to stay with Oom.'

More irritably than I'd meant to, I said, 'No, you can't stay here. I want to go and see what's going on.'

Without warning the boy broke into tears. Not loudly, just a whimpering, snot-drenched wail as if life had become too much for him. It grated my nerves.

'Now come on, man, it's okay.'

'I'm sorry, Oom.'

'Is there anything you want?'

'No, Oom.'

'Just tell me.'

'Yes, Oom. No, Oom.'

I went down on my haunches beside him, but he stepped back as if he was scared I'd hit him; the poor child was in a fucking state.

'You can tell me if there's anything, Piet.'

He moved an anxious hand across his face, with predictable results. Not knowing how to show my damn sympathy, I pressed my half-soiled handkerchief in his hand. 'Take this. Clean yourself.'

'Yes, Oom.' He withdrew a few more steps and started wiping his face energetically, which only worsened matters. At last he ventured, 'Oom . . .?'

Scabs and Bruises

'What's the matter, Piet?'

'The other day when I thought Oom was the Lord God.'

'What about it?'

'Oom mustn't tell Pa what I said, Oom.'

'Of course I won't. It's between you and me.' I tried to comfort him, gain his confidence: 'What's up with your father?'

'He beats me, Oom.' Unasked, he suddenly turned his back and pulled down his floppy short pants. His thin buttocks were criss-crossed with scabs and bruises.

I just stared in shock.

'Oom mustn't tell him, please.'

'What if he does it again?'

He just shook his head, sniffing.

'Does this happen often?'

He made a movement with his head, but I couldn't make out

what it meant. Then he mumbled, 'I can take it, Oom. But what he does to my sister isn't right, Oom.'

'What does he do?'

'No, Oom, I must go now, Oom.' With that he turned tail and fled.

Pig

It was some time before I could face going outside, and down to the church. The dirt road was deserted. Not a soul in sight, except for the odd afflicted individual slobbering or twitching in silent agony; but I didn't trust the silence. And as I drew nearer I could see the whole community gathered on the square in front of the church. So something momentous was happening after all. But what could it be? Fire? Bad news? Some kind of political meeting? The first few people I tried to speak to were concentrating so eagerly on whatever was happening at the church door that they never even heard me.

It was only when a few deep male voices started shouting from the front and the throng moved back from the door that I caught a glimpse, through and over the heads, of what was going on. At first it seemed like a fucking wrestling match. After a while I could make out that it was a youngish man tugged this way and that by five or six of the others. They were tying his hands to the brass ring on the door, pulling his arms so far above his head that his feet barely touched the ground. A small opening had cleared in front of him. I saw Lukas Death step forward with a knife in his hand. In a few quick slashes he cut the man's clothes clean from his body: a single stroke caused his shirt to fall back in two halves over his shoulder-blades, another severed his belt, so that his skin trousers slipped down to his ankles.

A wave of sound moved through the assembly, the rumbling and growling of men's voices, the shrill cries of women. From the crowd Jurg Water stepped forward with a whip in his hands. It looked fucking ferocious. He raised his massive arm and brought it down with a stroke which I'm sure could fell an ox. A welt of blood broke out across the man's back and he screamed like a pig being slaughtered.

'One!' shouted the crowd.

Jurg handed the whip to someone else, I couldn't see who it was. All I saw was the arm raised high, followed by the smacking sound of the blow, another scream, and the yodelling of the mob: 'Two!'

Once again I tried to find out what was going on, but no one was interested in talking to me. There was a kind of frenzy in them which made me think of the hunt the night before.

'Nine!'

'Ten!'

'Eleven!'

My God, when was it going to end? The man hanging against the church door was bellowing like a bloody animal, while the spectators cheered in exultation, like a rugby crowd during the last ten minutes of a game, with the score equal. It was the same mood I'd witnessed at the necklacing, years before. And these people were not mere spectators: they were trampling each other to get to the front, to be part of it, to take turns with the whip.

'Twenty-one!'

'Twenty-two!'

'Twenty-three!'

Dog

On what looked like a box beside the church door stood Lukas Death, that meek, pissed-upon person, keeping an eye on the proceedings and waving his arm at every stroke like a conductor. The naked man suspended against the door was no longer so loud as before, and the jerking, swaying movements following each blow were beginning to weaken. Yet each new flogger was still lashing out with every grain of strength he could muster.

'Thirty-three!'

'Thirty-four!'

'Thirty-five!'

'He's never going to get out of this alive,' I protested to a large woman in front of me. 'Someone should stop them.'

'You stay out of this!' she yelled at me, elbowing me out of the way.

I tried to push through the crowd but was blocked by a solid mass of bodies.

'Forty!'

'Forty-one!'

'Forty-two!'

The man in front was now hanging with his full weight from his tethered wrists, no longer trying either to resist or to dodge the blows. Each new stroke caused a mere shudder to run down his bleeding body, like a dog twitching in its sleep.

'Forty-six!'

After Action

The people were getting more and more frantic in their efforts to grab the whip. It was like a fucking orgy. One young woman close to me was screaming uncontrollably, plucking out her hair, tearing her clothes. Unexpectedly, she swung round and got hold of me, her eyes wide open in a blank stare, but clearly unaware of me, as she began to weep convulsively. Even at her bloody worst Sylvia had never been like this.

'Forty-nine!'

And then, in a long, last breathless scream, 'Fifty!'

There is stopped. Suddenly it was quiet. And in the silence Lukas Death stepped from his podium with quiet dignity, took out his knife once again and cut the thongs from the man's wrists. He crumpled in a small bundle on the threshold. Brother Holy opened the door. Three or four men picked up the body by the arms and legs and dragged it into the gloomy darkness inside. The man's legs were streaked with blood and piss and shit. He was still uttering small whimpering sounds, like a young puppy. Brother Holy closed the door after them.

The crowd began to disperse. No one spoke. After action satisfaction.

Shamgar and Deborah

I felt like throwing up (Jesus, I thought, what's our crime reporter coming to?) My face was cold. Must have been the sweat drying. In a dwaal I went across the open square to where Lukas Death was still standing, pensively stroking the wrinkles from his black suit.

'Lukas!'

He looked up with an almost apologetic smile, on his face a shy expression that unexpectedly made him look like Little-Lukas. 'So you came too?'

'What's going on?' I asked, furious. 'Why for fuck's sake didn't you stop them?'

'Stop them?' He clearly didn't get it at all. 'I'm doing my job, Neef Flip.' He stooped to pick up the object he'd been using as a podium; only now did I notice that it wasn't a box at all but the great leatherbound copy of the High Dutch State Bible which usually sat on Brother Holy's damn pulpit.

'What do you mean?' I asked.

'Well, the Water Council met. And then the Council of Justice met. My duty is to see that their decisions are carried out. I'm their Judge, as surely as Othniel, Ehud, Shamgar and Deborah were Judges of the people of Israel.'

'That man could have died.'

'He deserves no less.' Nothing ruthless in his voice, a simple statement of fact. 'Without law and order we will be nothing.'

'But what in God's name did he do to deserve such punishment?'

'He stole water.'

I gaped at him in disbelief.

'In a drought like this it's the worst of all crimes,' he explained. 'Don't you understand?'

I felt like I'd been kicked in the bloody stomach. 'And what's going to happen to him now?'

'Three days.'

'In the church?'

'In jail.' He pointed. 'It's up there in the tower. Very secure. No windows a man can escape from.'

'But Lukas, Jesus, surely . . .'

'Don't worry, Neef Flip. We know what we're doing. I told you mos the Lord rejoices in law and order. Also, that man needs time to think about his sins. When he comes out Brother Holy will work on him. Three days in the dark, without the distractions of food and water, does wonders for the soul.'

'You can't do that to a human being.'

'Did he think about other people when he stole that water? It's life or death for all of us here.' He sighed. 'If Wednesday's prayer meeting doesn't work things will be getting even worse.'

'But the man needs help.'

'What he needs is redemption, not help. You just stay out of this, Neef Flip.' He was still talking in his hesitant, apologetic way, but there was an unmistakable undertone of warning.

Not Yet Out

Soon after supper with Tant Poppie – the usual pious toasts over the apostles, the blessing, the soup and bread, the thanksgiving – I went out on the stoep again as my room was too bloody stuffy and the fumes in the house made my head spin. God knows what this place must be like at the height of summer. It was almost May, but the heat still pressed down on the valley like a heavy blanket. But outside it was better. Very dark, as the moon was not yet out, but the stars were bright enough to see by. After the day's violent sun the mountains were giving off their fragrance in the dark. Buchu and rosemary, goats, dassie-piss, mimosa flowers, all the nameless smells of the night. Through it all, the smell of dust, the smell of drought. But in the dark even that was no longer quite so bad. Whatever had happened during the day now felt remote and unreal.

Most of the houses were dark already, as the people didn't like wasting candles. All the naked windows staring into the night and exposing themselves to stares from outside. Perhaps others had stared through my own window like this before, while I was reading, or washing myself in a spoonful of water, or beating my meat, brushing my teeth, making my notes. A sudden little shiver ran down my spine. In the end, no matter how tough you may be, you remain bloody vulnerable.

The Oldest Form

As I came past one of the dark, quiet houses on my way I saw an angular shadow slipping from the front stoep and dissolving in the night like a lump of sugar in a large cup of black coffee. From the flapping coattails I knew it was the shoemaker, Petrus Tatters. My first impulse was to call out a greeting, but I changed my mind. It wasn't his house and his stealthy manner made me think that he might not wish to be recognised. If I remembered correctly, Tant Poppie had once mentioned that the widow of the late Giel Eyes was living there. In his lifetime Giel had been a difficult customer and no one had mourned his loss. So who could blame her for having her fucking cat pinched in the dark?

Ouma Liesbet was still up on her roof, but she had someone with her. Probably Ben Owl. They were chatting quietly, outlined against the stars splashed across the sky like spilt milk over which it was useless to cry. On some of the other stoeps there were also small clusters of people. Smith-the-Smith was in the lean-to behind his house working at his furnace. I greeted him in passing but he didn't seem to hear me; perhaps he didn't want to. He was working with such dedication that I stopped to watch.

After a while I went on my way. The valley was invaded by an almost unearthly bloody tranquillity. And yet I had the distinct feeling of not being alone, as if the whole night was filled with invisible marauders. And with sound as well, sound impossible to locate or define, but which might be the smothered cries and moans and writhings of the oldest form of human congress in the world. It was particularly noticeable near the graveyard, but only when I was walking, with the dull thudding of my footsteps and my heartbeat in my ears; because the moment I stopped to listen it would be quiet again, with not even the rustling of a leaf.

As I moved beyond the thin line of houses up the slope, the hint of sound went on all around me, but always just out of reach. In and behind sheds. On and under haystacks, among cabbages and withered pumpkin shoots, even behind the hedges of aloes and branches; and later in the bluegum wood. The moon was just coming out as I walked in among the trees, but as usual the white disc remained behind the edge of the mountain; it would be well past midnight before it drifted free. In the meantime I was alone in the forest, among the black trees and even blacker shadows. Everywhere the suggestion of a fucking murmuring, fumbling human presence persisted. Every few yards I stumbled over something, and I'd swear it must be a couple fucking, but whenever I tried to go nearer on all fours it would turn out to be only the stump of a tree, or a rock, or a heap of earth, or a bloody bag of manure.

Then back again down the decline, past the ostrich pen. There I was stopped by an unearthly muted roar. Must be the booming of a male ostrich, I tried to convince myself, but no matter how I pricked up my ears the sound was not repeated. I started to walk on, but stopped again. This time it was unmistakable, but it was a different kind of sound altogether, like a muted clamour of voices. They were heading towards me. I ducked behind a tree.

A single black shadow with a pronounced limp came moving up the incline towards me. Only when it passed right beside me did I recognise the man. It was Ouma Liesbet Prune's distant nephew Ben Owl. But what about the talking voices then? As I looked after him, I heard them again, now growing fainter as he went on, surprisingly agile on his club foot. It must have been the voices in his head Ouma Liesbet had spoken about.

Back

I came past the church again. No suggestion of life at all. Now the settlement was invaded by fucking irredeemable silence, even in the cemetery.

A single window shone in the dark. At the back of Isak Smous's house. Perhaps he was still working on his book? But his store was in the front, where we'd spent the morning together.

I went closer. That single bright rectangle caught me in its bloody thrall. I had to find out who was still doing what at this ungodly hour. Taking care not to make any noise I approached to the edge of the patch of light in the backyard.

It was she. I swear to Almighty God. Emma.

It was her bedroom. She was standing in front of the window brushing her dark hair. My first impulse was to step back, but then I realised she was using the pane as a mirror to look at her reflection; beyond the window she wouldn't see a thing. I was part of the night's blank darkness. Even so, it felt as if she was looking straight at me, like the day I arrived. Because this time it really was her. No two ways about it. The other night outside my window might have been hallucination. Even at Nagmaal in church I could have been mistaken, what with her hair piled on top of her head. But now it was loose again, a dark flood cascading down her shoulders, pure goddamn poetry.

My first reaction was rage. So this was why that cocksucking, motherfucking bastard Isak Smous had become so cagey the moment I mentioned her name. But what was he covering up for?

Emma's arm had stopped its long stroking movements. She put down the old-fashioned brush with its ornate handle — a gift from Isak? I could wring the little shit's neck — on the bedside table. I crept closer to see what she was going to do next. There were two books on the table, one blue, the other brown. Behind her against the inside wall stood a narrow bed, the kaross covering it already folded back. There was a garment draped over the edge, it looked like a long white nightdress. She came back to the window. I stepped out of the patch of light.

From a distant past a memory came back. My last year at school when I'd gone on similar night walks to haunt like a poltergeist the home of the girl I was in love with, waiting for hours on end to stare through a chink in two floral curtains at the segment of the bedroom beyond, in the hope of a glimpse of Belinda. She was the magistrate's daughter, I was I; and I'd never dared to speak a word to her. A railway line ran between us.

Only once in all my solitary vigils had I caught more than a hint of movement between the curtains. It was a month before the school-leaving dance and I'd decided, come hell or high water, I was going to ask her. I mean, Jesus, the worst she could say was no. And then, the night before I was to take the plunge, I saw Belinda. She must have come from her bath for her hair was still wet and she stood between her curtains drying it with a red-striped towel. Even if God had decided to strike me there and then with a fucking thunderbolt, I would have died singing His everlasting praises. But He has better ways to avenge Himself, mark my words. I mean, after seeing her like that I couldn't possibly invite her to the dance, could I now? I'd missed my chance. I was only bloody seventeen, remember.

Front

Emma began to undo the buttons down the front of her dark dress. I was a Peeping Tom, lower than shark-shit on the bottom of the sea. I knew I should fuck off, I had no bloody right to stay. But it was impossible to turn away. I just had to see what there was to see. I had to know, for sure, once and for all.

Emma undid two buttons, each one took an eternity. I could see the small hollow where her collarbones met. The paleness of her skin.

On the third button her thin white fingers lingered. Then she turned away, leaned over, and blew out the candle.

If she came back to the window now she was sure to see me in the moonlight.

Like a damned sleepwalker I went home, past the night-still houses of the settlement.

Same Thing

AFTER MY WANDERINGS through the rank recesses of the night I suppose it was only to be expected, but when it overcame me in the small hours I was still caught unawares. I was struggling through a thicket of lustful dreams when like the previous night I was surprised by a woman. A sound woke me up. Two sounds: something like the hoot of a barn owl, something like the barking of a baboon. But there was no time for wondering, because by then I was already engulfed in female flesh. It was the same thing all over again. My first thought was that it must be the same woman, but it wasn't. Even in the dark all bodies are not similar. This one was stronger, harder, tougher, the hair in which she tied us up and sometimes nearly strangled us was longer, her limbs more muscular, her smells and taste sharper on the tongue; but she was just as fucking uninhibited as her predecessor. This time, to turn on the purple stuff again, it was like a wave that dragged me into unfathomable green tides and swells and undertows. The joy of this kind of dream is that you can give free rein to everything you usually repress or contain, your most exorbitant imaginings. Also, I was better prepared for it this time, and I remember consciously groping for what I'd been looking for so long: but once again there were only two of them, not four.

What I did find out was that her feet were not webbed. But there was something else. She had a harelip. Which might have been fucking repulsive in daylight, or in anything other than a dream, but in that encounter it opened up new dimensions of caressing and sucking that left me exhausted when at last she abandoned me like a fucking kelp washed up on the moist beach of the night.

I still had enough sense to jump up and flick on my lighter as she left. But the draught caused by her dash to the door instantly blew out the flame. All I could make out in the brief flare was a whirl of long limbs, the pale gleam of a body half-covered in a tangle of hair, a bundle of clothes under her arm. And that kept me awake, because a succubus is not supposed to be visible in the light.

Erotic Dreams

IT WAS HELL to get going in the morning, but no matter how stiff and exhausted I felt, I was anxious not to waste another bloody minute before returning to Isak Smous's house to speak to Emma personally. But on the way I had to pass Tall-Fransina's shed again and how could I refuse when she called me to give her a hand with the firing once more? Half-amused, she stood watching me from the snake, her man's hat pushed back on her short-cropped hair which hardly showed any sign of grey. Her skin was surprisingly fine for someone working outside so much of the time. Leathery, okay, but fine-tanned leather. The fucking cats were all over the place again.

'I was wondering if you'd be coming back,' she said with a knowing laugh.

'I can give you a hand if you need one.'

'Did you come to help or to ask more questions?'

'You're very suspicious.'

'I'm not a child, Neef Flip. And I know you've been asking around.' Without warning, she said, 'Old Hans Magic came round early this morning to find out what you were here for yesterday.'

'What's it to him?'

'He wanted to know if you'd seen Emma yet.' Busy as she was, shifting the large stone jugs in which she captured her spirit, I could see she was watching me intently.

'He can come to me if he wants to find out,' I said, annoyed.

'I think he wants you to come to him.'

'He can wait,' I said. But actually I felt quite smug; it allowed me some space to manoeuvre in. I squatted down to caress one of the cats, a beautiful ginger tabby. I'm not particularly partial to cats but somehow they always seek me out. Must be my smell, my hairiness, whatever. And Tall-Fransina's collection fascinated me; they were like erotic dreams emerging from some secret dark place. Their eyes, amber or jade, suggested a kind of arch-female wisdom.

So Filthy

'You have a way with cats,' she said approvingly.

'They're less suspicious than their madam.'

'I have reason,' she said. 'Not because of you, but people in general. If you lived here you'd have known. How one is always being watched, by everyone. How each one of them is always on the lookout for a chance to get at the others. You can't take anyone at their word. Cats are different. Once they decide to let you into their lives it's for ever.'

'What's Hans Magic got on me?'

'He doesn't know what to make of you. He's always had some hold on everybody here, because they're so scared of him. Now you're moving in between them and him.'

'What's he trying to hide?'

'It's not a matter of secrets. It's the way everybody here stands together. You must remember, we lot all know one another, but you came in from outside. People are curious, you're a mystery to them, and now that Grandpa Lukas has opened the gate they want to talk to you. But of course they're scared too. They don't know what you're going to do with what they tell you.' Unexpectedly, she said, 'You mustn't be too hard on poor old Hans. He doesn't mean bad.'

'There's no need for you to defend him.'

'He's a terribly lonely man,' she said. 'And there was a time when he was very different. Before he became so bitter and filthy.'

'What happened?'

'Ag, let bygones maar be bygones.'

'Why did he want to know about Emma?'

'Have you spoken to her?'

'I'm on my way to her right now.'

'You'll have to wait for the afternoon. In the mornings she helps Lukas Death in the schoolroom.' She must have noticed how the news upset me. 'What is it you want from her?'

'I can't tell before I've seen her. It's just that one way or another every single conversation in this place seems to point to her.'

'It's because they're all feeling guilty about Little-Lukas.'

'I rather got the impression that they're blaming him. Yesterday you said something like that yourself.'

'It's not that I'm blaming him. It just makes me sad. He spent so much time here with me, you know. Playing with the cats, like you. I was the only person he could really open his heart to. When he was small his mother was too sickly to look after him, so I more or less brought him up.'

'And then he left you for Emma?'

'You mustn't take literally what I said yesterday. It wasn't like that at all.' Fucking formidable in her silence, her dignity, her loneliness, she stood opposite me.

'It's over now,' I said, with a kind of sympathy that caught myself by surprise.

'One still tries to hold on. Especially after it's all slipped through your fingers. Like sand. Like water.'

'Little-Lukas is dead,' I said, 'and it doesn't seem right to me that the Devil's Valley should begrudge Emma the fact that she's still alive.'

'Is that what it looks like to you?'

'Isn't it true?'

She turned back to her work. 'Better ask her yourself.'

On His Easel

The school was still on, so Emma wouldn't be home yet. But as I came past Gert Brush's house he appeared in the doorway and called me to bum a cigarette.

There was a painting on his easel in the voorhuis, but when I came in he hastily put another in front of it. In spite of the wooden,

naïve style, I immediately recognised the features of Lukas Death.
But like most of Gert Brush's work it had been overpainted many
times: on the top layer was Lukas Death as one saw him today, thin
and righteous, with his hang-dog face. But clearly visible underneath
was another portrait of the same face, only much younger. More
shadowy in the background, in deeper half-obscured layers, loomed
the ghost of yet another, a quite frightening face with two red glowing eyes. And behind this one still more shadows.

What struck me, like on the other paintings by Gert Brush I'd
glimpsed before, was the weird use of colour: everything was done
in whites and pinks, like fucking marshmallows, so that all the portraits looked seriously sick to the point of unworldliness. I didn't
want to offend the artist, but I was curious to know more.

Gert came up with a very practical explanation: 'Well, you see,
I never had any lessons, it was just my father who taught me. And he
also had trouble with the colours. I tried everything, man, once I
even went to the Little Karoo with Isak Smous to see if I could find
better colours there, but they don't seem to make skin-colour.' He
placed his hand on the canvas next to Lukas Death's face. 'See? It's
just not the same.'

I bent over the messy table on which his brushes and paints and
oil and turps were spread. 'This is not really my line, Gert,' I said,
'but I'm sure with only white and red you're never going to get it
right. Shouldn't you mix in something darker? Brown, perhaps?'

'Brown?' he asked, shocked. 'But I'm painting *white* people, Neef
Flip.'

'Why don't you give it a try?'

'They'll skin me alive, man.'

He was so upset that I decided not to meddle with his aesthetics
any further. I returned to the painting on the easel to study the pink
images.

'Why are there two portraits of Lukas Death?'

Gert turned his head to the side. 'The earlier one I did at least
twenty years ago. It was time to bring him up to date.'

'The younger face looks like Little-Lukas.'

'Could be.'

'Are you going to paint over the first one now?'

'Ag man, the more I try to paint out the old ones the more they come back. Yesterday, for example, you couldn't see young Lukas Death at all. Nor his father, old Lukas Devil, looking over his shoulder there. But you can see for yourself, today they're back.' He stroked a finger lightly across the ghostly face; a smear of paint came off.

Golden Billy Goat

'How did Lukas Devil get his name?'

'He must have been the most unruly of all the Lermiets. He was born with two goat's feet, you know,' said Gert Brush, touching again with a possessive gesture the vague image lurking behind the layers of paint on his canvas. 'No one dared to cross him. About forty years ago, they say, he took on a couple of census officials sent to get the particulars of all the people in the Devil's Valley. We didn't want them here, but they stood their ground and of course they had the government behind them. But Lukas Devil said the hell with that thing they call the government. He found a way to get the two of them into the church, told them he wanted to introduce them to some of the oldest inhabitants, and when they got to the tower he closed the door behind them, and there they stayed until they were skeletons.'

'The man sounds like a real terror.'

'You can say that again,' said Gert Brush, picking up steam. 'And there was something else he did which caused quite a stir. The way I heard it, Isak Smous's father, old Jeremiah Smous, cheated Lukas Devil out of a billy goat. The Smouses have always been a crooked lot. Well, Lukas Devil wasn't a man to trifle with. So one day when Jeremiah Smous was over the mountains on a trip, Lukas Devil took a tin trunk full of coins from under the old swindler's bed and then he and Smith-the-Smith's father smelted the whole lot and made a golden billy goat out of it. Anyway, just before church the following Sunday they put the goat on the pulpit to shame the Smous family in front of God and the whole congregation.'

'What happened?'

'One thing I can tell you, and that is that Jeremiah Smous never tried to swindle anyone again. He'd learned his lesson. But he bore a grudge to the day of his death, and he got old Hans Magic's father to cast a spell on Lukas Devil and Smith-the-Smith's father to plague the two of them with nightmares for the rest of their lives. It didn't work with Lukas Devil, they say his goat's feet made him immune to spells. But Smith-the-Smith's father never had a proper night's sleep again. He died with his eyes open. And Smith himself is so scared of nightmares that every evening he makes four new golden horseshoes to shoe that mare if it shows up. They say it's the only cure for a nightmare, to corner it and put a new golden shoe on each of its hooves.'

'And the gold comes from that billy goat they made out of Jeremiah Smous's coins?'

'That's right. And every morning Smith-the-Smith smelts the shoes again, because they have to be fresh every night, or else they won't work.'

'Do you believe it?'

'I'm not saying it's true. I'm just telling you what the people say. Not all of them either, because you'll hear so many stories in this place you can never be sure what really happened.'

'I was beginning to wonder whether they're trying to pull a fast one on me.'

'They're dead serious about it,' he ticked me off. 'And you'll be making the mistake of your life if you don't believe them.'

I shook my head. 'If you're here for only a few days like me, it's enough to make your head turn.'

'It just depends on how long you can go on.'

'You think I'll get to the truth in the end?'

He grinned. 'I suppose it just depends on what you call the truth, Neef Flip.'

Perhaps Both

Leaning over to inspect the painting more closely I accidentally pushed against it. I managed to catch it, but in the process I couldn't help noticing the painting behind it, the one he'd been working on when I came in. And once again I found myself looking at the face of the girl at the rock pool. No doubt about the likeness, even though it had only been blocked in large, preliminary strokes. The face showed some detail, but the rest of the figure was little more than a smear, as if he hadn't decided yet whether it should be a nude or a woman in a full-length dress. Perhaps both. Once again there was a hint of earlier figures lurking in the layers of paint.

'So you know her?' I asked, more accusingly than I'd meant to.

'Everybody knows everybody in the Devil's Valley.'

'Did she sit for you?'

'You must be mad,' he said, and burst out laughing.

I couldn't understand his reaction; to flatter him, I commented, 'You have a good eye.'

'I always paint from memory,' he said. While he was chewing pensively on the back of a brush, I kept on gazing at the painting. The figures in the deeper layers appeared to become restless. Gert Brush put out a hand and turned the canvas back to front. 'I'm sorry, Neef Flip, but this wasn't meant to be seen. It's not finished yet, and I always feel it's a bad sign if people look at something unfinished. Please don't talk about it. One never knows what people will do. You see, I've never painted a woman from the Devil's Valley before.'

Little Railway Track

AT LAST, IN the late afternoon, having caught up with my notes, I took the path to Isak Smous's house on the far side of the church. He came out on the stoep when I knocked; behind him Alie-Malie-Ralie went about their energetic bustling in voorhuis and kitchen.

'I'm looking for Emma.' No need to beat about the bush.

'Why?'

'Why didn't you tell me she lived here in your house?'

'You never asked.'

I restrained the urge to throttle him. 'I'm asking now.'

'Emma isn't here right now.'

'Where is she?'

'No idea. She comes and goes as she pleases.'

I was in no mood to argue. Why did the bloody little man annoy me so? Without saying goodbye I stomped off.

Almost by themselves my feet took me out of the settlement, in the direction from which I'd come that first day, hard on Prickhead's fleshy heels. Everything seemed exactly like before. Only drier, if it was possible to imagine such a thing. The reeds parched as bones, the withered undergrowth, the long rock pool with a flaking black rim of old algae at the bottom where the last moisture had dried away: it was all still there.

As was the girl with the black hair. The girl who had by now acquired a name. Emma.

There was only one difference. This time she was really there. At least I think so. And properly dressed, buttoned up to her chin in a little railway track.

At the last moment I nearly turned tail, but she'd already seen me. So I had to put on a casual air.

'Am I disturbing you?'

She shrugged. 'Oom can stay if Oom wants to.'

The form of address hit me between the eyes. 'For heaven's sake don't call me "Oom".'

'What else can I call you?'

'My name is Flip Lochner.'

'I know.' And then, 'Oom Flip.'

'Emma, please.'

She repeated the shrug, whatever that might mean.

'I saw you in church on Sunday morning,' I persisted. 'At least I think it was you.'

'And last Wednesday here at the waterhole,' she added.

I gasped like a fish on dry ground.

And then she was the one to look embarrassed. 'Oh I'm sorry,' she said, 'but you won't know about it of course. I dreamed I came here for a swim and then Oom found me here.'

'You dreamed?'

'I don't usually sleep in the day, but I wasn't feeling too well, it was that time, so Alie-of-Isak sent me to bed. And then I dreamed.'

'But I *was* here. And I saw you.'

She opened her mouth. I could see she wanted to say something. But then she started to blush, a deep, old-fashioned blush which I thought no longer happened in the young. Red as a birthmark it spread from her face down her neck. I'd have given anything to be that blush. She seemed totally bewildered. Be my guest, I thought. It wasn't as if *I* could make head or tail out of it.

'Oom really saw me?'

I know what goes for what in the world. And the expression in her eyes gave me no choice.

'Yes, I'm sorry.' In spite of myself I gave a crooked grin. 'Or not all that sorry, to tell you the truth. I mean, I'm sorry if it embarrassed you, but not that I saw you.'

Desperate Romantic

Her eyes narrowed slightly. Contempt? Annoyance? I preferred not to know. Almost-black eyes, under thick eyebrows which met in the middle. Seeing her in close-up like this for the first time, I can honestly say that she wasn't beautiful. But then, I mean, what is 'beautiful'? In the eye of this beholder there was something else about her, something that spoke directly to the lower spine, which they say is the seat of the sense you use to recognise what really matters. And she looked even younger than before. More vulnerable too, if the bloody desperate romantic lurking inside the crime reporter may say so. But her eyes were dark with a kind of knowledge that came from far beyond her years, if this doesn't sound too fucking precious.

'What is Oom doing here?' she asked.

'I thought everybody knew. I felt I owed it to Little-Lukas.'

A brief nod, as if she wanted to think about it before she answered.

'You were close to him,' I said.

'What did he tell Oom?'

'Emma, don't call me Oom".'

'What did Little-Lukas tell you?'

'Not much.' I changed my mind. 'No, that's not quite true. We spoke for a whole night. He'd heard that I was interested in the Devil's Valley, it's something that goes very far back, but which I'd never followed up. And I got the impression he was just dying to talk to somebody. But I'm afraid we drank too much, and afterwards I was in something of a mess. So I set up another meeting, but on that very day he was killed.'

'I want to know everything,' she said with sudden urgency.

'That's about all I can tell you.'

'I'm not just talking about Little-Lukas. I want to hear everything Oom can tell me about the world outside. I spent three years there at school with Little-Lukas, but then I had to come back. No one ever comes here. If only Oom knew how terrible it is to be trapped in here and *know* there's a world outside, a world you once saw and where you want to go back to but which you'll never ever be allowed to see again. Can Oom understand that?'

'A bit, I think.'

'*Please* try to understand!' She grabbed me by the arm. Her eyes were burning. 'From the first day Oom came here I tried to find an excuse to come to you. I even went to Tant Poppie's that first night, and looked through the window, but there were too many people.'

'I've also been looking for you since I saw you here the first time.'

'Why?' Her voice was tense. All of a sudden, I sensed, there was a hell of a lot at stake. 'To talk about Little-Lukas?'

'No. To find out more about you.'

Once again she was the one to be embarrassed. Nervously, she started playing with a piece of dry bark between her fingers. She didn't look at me again. Yet when she spoke it was about the boy after all: 'They never wanted him to go away.' An angry little muscle flickered beside her mouth.

No, I thought again: no, she isn't pretty at all. Yet the more I tried to deny it the more of a hold she got on me.

'Were you against it too?' I asked.

'I was the one who made him go.'

'Why?'

'Because I was the one who really wanted to go. But I couldn't.'

I reached back to what Isak Smous had said: 'Because you're a girl?'

'Of course,' she said, her voice heavy with resentment. 'The old men have all the say in this place.'

'I believe they all have the hots for you.'

'I suppose they all think I'm available. And I don't dare offend them, otherwise . . .'

Her voice trailed off. A heavy silence lay between us. At last I tried to jump-start the conversation again. 'Tell me about Little-Lukas.'

'He wasn't all that keen to go away, but I went on and on. I told him it was for both of us. I mean, he was bright enough. It wasn't easy for him either but at least he was a boy. All the old men . . .'

'Why are they so dead against it?'

'They think it'll be the end of the Valley if people start coming and going as they want to. It's a bit easier for the men. From time to time one of them even goes out to get married, and brings his wife back here. The women never, it's out of the question. No outsider may lay a hand on their womenfolk. They're jealous of their possessions.' She gestured with her head in the direction of the settlement. 'Can you imagine anyone being jealous in a place like this?'

'Have you never thought of running away?'

'Of course,' she said with pent-up anger. 'I tried. But Hans Magic fetched me back and Tant Poppie gave me such a hiding I couldn't sit for days. She has a heavy hand.'

I tried not to think of what lay behind her simple words.

'And then?'

The large black eyes in her pale face looked straight back at me. 'I just had to accept what I never wanted to. They can't forgive me for not really being one of them.'

'But you were born here.'

'Yes. But my mother brought me in from outside.'

'I don't understand.'

Equally Naked

'It's not necessary to understand.' She swung out her legs and got up. Without looking at me she began to walk away. But she didn't go far. She bent over and broke off a dry reed, and remained standing with her back to me, stripping away the papery leaves. Then, with an angry gesture, she threw the reed into the rock pool which had been full of water once, where she'd used to swim, the pool she'd dreamed; then turned round slowly and came back to me. 'Why do you want to know?'

I looked at her strong, narrow, naked feet, then up at her face, equally strong, equally naked. The too-much in her eyes.

'I don't know why, so don't ask me. And if you find it bloody impertinent of me, then please forgive me. But I do want to know more about you.'

'What makes you think I want to be known about?'

'Because a moment ago you wanted to leave, but then you came back.'

'I only came back because I saw you in my dream.' Her eyes looked into mine as if I was the one being tested.

'Is that reason enough?' I asked.

'It couldn't have been an ordinary dream. Not if you saw it too. Something like that happens for a reason.'

'And that's why you came back?'

An unexpectedly light, defiant laugh. 'No. It's because of the chameleon on your shoulder.'

'What difference could that make?'

'I can see he isn't scared of you. So perhaps one can trust you.'

'Little Piet Snot gave him to me,' I said reflectively.

'Poor little chap.' She sounded relieved to change the subject. Our real conversation, I thought, was happening behind the words we used.

'I got the idea his father is very hard on him.'

'Not just on him. Oom Jurg Water is a pig.'

'Piet said something about a sister too.'

'What chance does a girl like Henta have?'

The name struck me like a blow from a whip. 'Henta?'

'Didn't you know?'

Curse On It

'There's something terribly wrong with this place.' I was really too upset to talk.

'I know. It got my mother too.'

'Who was your mother? What exactly happened to her?'

She came to sit down beside me, but still looked past me, up the mountain. 'My mother was Isak Smous's sister. Half-sister, really, for she had a different father. In this place they don't keep strictly to husband-and-wife.'

'I've noticed. And I'd like to find out more about that too. All these bloody righteous people, and yet . . .'

A brief gesture. 'That's not important now.' She went on, 'I was told that my own grandfather came in from outside, he and my grandmother got to know each other' – she twisted her lip – 'and then he left. But on the way out he fell to his death. The sort of thing that often happens here. Perhaps he was the one who planted the bug in my mother's blood, because when she was just eighteen she left with Isak Smous on one of his trips and stayed there for a year. Then Lukas Death fetched her back. Not many of our people survive out there.'

'And was there trouble when she came back?'

'What do you think? She was pregnant.'

I nodded slowly. 'I think I'm beginning to understand.'

'You don't understand anything!' she stormed. 'If a girl in the Valley falls pregnant it needn't be the end of the world. Tant Poppie gets rid of just as many babies as she brings into the world. As long as it happens in the dark and no one sees, that is the only rule. But my mother wanted to keep me, and so here I am.'

Impertinent

'And your mother?'

'After she died Tant Poppie brought me up. Deep down she has a soft heart, and she never had children of her own.'

'What about your mother?' I asked again.

'Tant Poppie was like a mother to me.'

'What I want to know is . . .'

'What happened to my mother.'

'Yes.'

'Why do you want to know?'

The directness of the question, and her quiet way of asking it, unsettled me. 'I'm sorry. I know I had no right to ask. In my work . . .'

'What do you do?'

'I work for a newspaper.'

'Tell me about it.'

'There isn't much to tell.'

'Tell me anyway, tell me everything.'

I was hesitant at first. What was there in my life that could possibly interest her? Sylvia never listened, it bored her to death; and the children got irritated, I'd never been much of a role model, as Marius made only too fucking clear. But Emma seemed set on it, so I started raking up randomly whatever I could. Small episodes, anecdotes, things I didn't even realise I had remembered, began to come back to me. She listened intently, a few times she even laughed. A laugh so dark and so bloody beautiful that I went out of my way to dramatise incidents and invent new ones, just to hear it again. Jesus, I hadn't spoken about my work to anyone in this way for years. But in the end that was also what made me stop.

'You can't possibly want to hear more,' I said, suddenly self-conscious. 'How can it mean anything to you?'

'Do you know what it's like to live in the Devil's Valley?' she asked as before.

'There's nothing special about my life, Emma. It all turned out so different from the dreams I had when I was young. In those days I still had ambition, there was nothing too big to attempt. Most of all I wanted to be a writer, a historian.'

'Why didn't you?'

'Never had the chance.' I reconsidered. 'Perhaps I simply wasn't good enough.'

'Don't say that!'

'One sheds one's illusions. Then it becomes easier.'

'I also thought I wasn't good enough to go out and study,' Emma said tensely. 'But that's not true, you know. One mustn't believe what others try to tell you.'

In different circumstances her seriousness might have amused me, but the restrained passion with which she spoke scorched each separate word into my mind.

'It's too late for me now,' I said, as evenly as I could. 'But not for you.'

'You don't know what you're talking about. I'll never get out of this place alive.'

'Now please don't turn on the drama.'

'You won't ever understand. You're a stranger.'

I could feel something momentous building up in her. I'd give anything to help her open up, but I didn't know how to. I've never been able to handle that kind of situation. Out of sheer bloody clumsiness I put an arm round her shoulders. 'Emma,' I heard myself say, 'don't you want to tell me?'

She just shook her head. No, no, no. After a long time she said almost inaudibly. 'There is a curse on me.'

To Her Throat

From way back something returned to me. At first I hesitated to say it out loud, but then decided to risk it. 'Tant Poppie says you have the mark of the Devil on you.'

Once again the unsettling straight gaze of her eyes below the thick straight eyebrows.

'What kind of mark is it?'

It was an improbable moment, a moment outside of time, with something that tautened and pulled between us, a moment that could bloody well decide everything for us.

With a small, slow gesture, as if she was barely conscious of it herself – and yet she was, I could see it – she raised her hands to her throat, to the top button of the long, long row, just like the night before: but then she hadn't been aware of me, and now she was.

Would she really – dared she – undo those buttons? I still don't know, here where I'm crouching at the rock pool waiting; nor did I know then, as I sat on this same spot opposite her. All I could do was to place my hand on hers to restrain her.

'There's no need,' I said. 'I've seen it already.'

I could see the question rising in her eyes, like a moon or something.

'I saw you when you came to swim here in your dream, remember?'

'Are you sure of what you saw?'

'Absolutely sure.' My hand remained on hers for an unbearably long time, on the spot where her collarbones formed their little hollow and where I would have been able to see her heart throbbing if I hadn't stopped her.

'If they find out about the mark, if Tant Poppie ever says anything, it will be the end,' she said. 'Because she's the only one who has ever seen it.'

'Except Little-Lukas.'

'He never saw it.'

'But I thought the two of you . . .'

'That's what they all think,' she said calmly. 'But that doesn't mean it's so.'

'But Tant Poppie said . . .'

A little wryly she said, 'I am still whole. He was too shy.'

'You loved him though,' I said clumsily.

No Birds

Just as directly as before she said, 'What does "love" mean? The way I see it now, I only held on to him because he stood between me and them, it made me feel safe. Since he died I'm not sure of anything any more.'

'What makes you think they'll turn against you?'

'They're already against me. They've been against me from the very beginning, because of my mother, and now it's even worse. Before the time they held back, first on account of Tant Poppie, then on account of Little-Lukas, because he was Lukas Death's child after all and that counted for something, even if Lukas Death always tried to keep us apart. But now it's changed. That dirty old Hans Magic has been waiting for a long time to get at me. He says I humiliated him. And there's Ben Owl too, all the way from my mother's time. Because she humiliated *him*. Now the hunt is open. For the moment I can still keep them off while I'm in mourning. But it won't last long.'

'When all is said and done, what can they really *do*?'

She looked away and said nothing.

'Tell me,' I demanded. 'What can they do to you?'

'They stoned my mother.'

I felt the blood throbbing in my temples.

'She lies under the heap of stones against the churchyard wall.'

There was no sound around us, not even the wind. A silence louder than a scream. That was when for the first time I realised what was missing in the Devil's Valley: there were no birds, nowhere, none at all.

Three

Got Pregnant

'HOW CAN YOU be sure?' I asked Emma.

'I just know.' Her eyes did not waver. 'Tant Poppie told me, from the time I was little. Everybody knows it.'

'When did it happen?'

'The day after my birth. They were just waiting for it. If it wasn't for Tant Poppie they'd have killed me with my mother.' For the first time she showed signs of bitterness. 'When my mother got pregnant outside, I'm sure she could have chosen to get rid of me before she came back. Or even afterwards. No one would ever have known. But she decided to keep me, even when she knew they were going to kill her. It's hard to live with a thing like that on your conscience.

'But it wasn't your doing, Emma. Blaming yourself won't get you anywhere.'

'It's easy to talk if you're not the one.'

'Only a very special woman would have done what your mother did.'

Once again that ambiguous shrug.

'I'm going to help you find out exactly what happened to her,' I said.

In her eyes I could see that she didn't believe me, and why should she?

But I insisted: 'I'm going to find her for you. I promise.'

She nodded, but said nothing.

There wasn't much time left. In my mind, on the way back to Tant Poppie's place, I calculated: Wednesday, Thursday, Friday.

Only three more days, because at dawn on Saturday I'd have to set out to keep my appointment with Koot Joubert at the beacon up on the mountain. There was so little I'd achieved so far. For each step ahead, it seemed I was sliding back two.

Soft Fleece

Or three, I thought, that night. Because nothing could complicate an already pretty screwed-up situation more than what happened next. Heaven knows, there was enough to keep me awake as it was. But I barely had time to sort through my thoughts. Because for the third time in as many nights a female visitor came to my room. It started with a sound outside, like the hooting of a barn owl, only more eerie. I sat up. There was a shadow at my window. I got up to look. Outside everything was deserted. But as I stood at the window I saw a figure skulking across the backyard on four legs. Its slanting gait and bent tail were unmistakably those of a baboon. But since when did baboons venture abroad at night? Something caused the hair on my body to stand up. But by that time the creature had gone and I returned to my bed. I had barely settled in under the kaross again when I heard the door open. In the dull shimmering of the moon I distinguished a woman. Even if I hadn't seen her I would have smelled her. And some atavistic signal beyond my control immediately caused my prick to jump to attention.

Like the others before her she deftly pulled the kaross from me; like them, she was naked. What set her apart was the soft fleece that covered her whole body. Her back and buttocks, her stomach, her arms and legs, even her two breasts: not a thick coir mat like mine, but a fine down. Which made me stand like a fucking pick-handle. And yet I tried to fend her off. Don't ask me why. I mean, Emma had no fucking claim on me, nor I on her. Jesus, I was there for a few days only, any possibility of getting involved was out of the question. If I felt anything for her, it was more like compassion, how shall I put it, a kind of paternal concern to care for her, nothing sensual at all. Or was there? I simply didn't know. I don't want to know. All I knew then was that this woman complicated my life no end. But hell, I'm flesh and blood. And she was, like her sisters, a female animal that stopped at nothing.

Right, so I didn't want to. But at the same time I tell you I wanted nothing else. And when at last she'd wrestled me to the ground – quite literally, as we'd taken a tumble from the bed and did the rest of our cavorting on the floor – she broke away from me and, with a deep, dark, laugh, scrambled to her feet and fled. And when I tried to light the candle, still panting and trembling, the bloody lighter packed up. By the time I produced a spark from the primitive tinderbox Tant Poppie had provided it was already too late. Or not quite. For in her hurry to get away she'd not had time to grab her clothes.

But my first feelings of triumph soon evaporated, because all I was left with was a dress like any other in the Devil's Valley: black chintz, with a row of buttons down the front. No frill or fold to set it apart, everything severe and sober, fit for church. And there was nothing else, nothing personal to suggest a private identity, no bra or panties. With my face buried in the dark cloth I drew her smell deep into my lungs. But I could put no name to it. It might even have been Emma's. Except that it wasn't; and that weighed me down with all kinds of feelings that kept me wide awake for the rest of the night.

Heap of Stones

So I was feeling rather the worse for wear when I got to the heap of stones beside the churchyard wall in the early dawn on Wednesday morning. Following my meeting with Emma the day before, this was the obvious place to start. And in a way the events of the night had made it even more urgent, driven as I was by the Calvinistic urge to atone for my sins through some kind of punishment.

I'd meant to come early so that I could work as undisturbed as possible. But I'd misjudged the settlers. Already there was life everywhere. Any number of simpletons wobbling about. Smith-the-Smith in his shed, going at it hammer and tongs since well before dawn to melt down his unused horseshoes. Ouma Liesbet on her rooftop, waiting and ready for the Lord who seemed to have forgotten all about her. Jurg Water glowering through the fork of his divining rod. Bettie Teat lolling against the stained church door, abandoned to a caress by the early rays of the sun. Men and women at work in the parched fields. The old people among the graves, and Brother Holy observing me from his shrivelled vegetable patch. As if they all knew exactly what I was going to do.

Surrounded by so much life, visible and invisible, I felt paralysed before I'd even started. But I had no choice, after those frightening words Emma had spoken so calmly: *They stoned my mother. She lies under the heap of stones against the churchyard wall.* I was supposed to remain disinterested, an objective observer, non-judgmental, concerned only by what could be proved, by the truth. Facts, facts with which to feed the gnawing rat. But where is the boundary between observation and engagement?

Even these thoughts were irrelevant. All that mattered was that I'd made a promise and had to keep it.

So fuck them all, I thought. Let them look if they want to. This was the least I could do, this insignificant little archaeological dig. To see what lay buried here. *If* there was anything.

I bent over to pick up the first stone from the heap, and threw it aside. Then the second. Then the third. Somewhere in the Bible there's the bit about the one without sin having the right to cast the first stone. Perhaps, I thought with a touch of whimsy, the one who's sinned most may cast away the first.

Under These Stones

My own little heap was just beginning to take shape when a shadow fell across me. I suppose I should have expected it, but Brother Holy's booming voice still caught me unawares:

'And what might you be doing so early?'

'Good morning, Brother Holy.' I feigned innocence. 'Are you well?'

'No, I am in a bad shape.'

'On such a beautiful day?'

'It's on account of so many beautiful days that we're now smitten with drought.'

'I want to find out what is under these stones.' I picked up another heavy rock from the larger heap and transferred it to mine. Only a very strong man, or a madman, could have handled this one.

'And what do you expect to find?' enquired Brother Holy.

'I have no idea. Perhaps you can make a suggestion?'

'Vanity of vanities, saith the preacher, all is vanity.'

I shifted another heavy stone followed by a few smaller ones.

'Could it be bones?' he suddenly asked.

I straightened my back. 'Maybe. Do you think there are bones here?'

'And suppose you find bones, what would they tell you?'

'We'll just have to see when we find them, won't we?'

'I shouldn't like to be the one who disturbs the sleeping in their rest.' There was a shrill tone breaking through his voice.

'It depends on how they came here.' I moved a few more stones.

His voice climbed the steps of an arpeggio. 'As thou knowest not what is the way of the spirit, nor how the bones do grow in the womb of her that is with child: even so thou knowest not the works of God who maketh all.'

'But what if it was not the work of God but of the Devil, Brother Holy? Then it would be better to find out, don't you agree?'

His colour deepened to a royal purple. His long fingers moved up and down along the buttons of his long black coat, fastening and unfastening them. I pretended not to notice as I went on heaving stones from one heap to the other; but from the corner of my eye I was watching him closely. And I wasn't nearly as calm as it might have looked on the surface.

The explosion I'd expected did not come. Brother Holy managed to control his heaving breath, and buttoned up for the last time. As if pronouncing a final blessing, he said, 'On your head be it, Flip Lochner. Don't say I didn't warn you.' And off he strode, all knees and elbows.

Original Sin

What possessed me, I still don't know, but from sheer contrariness I
called out after him, 'I have reason to believe the woman Maria lies
under these stones.'

He stopped. And turned slowly.

'What do you know about Maria?'

'Just keeping my ears open.'

He reflected. I could see his large Adam's apple moving up and
down a few times. 'If there are bodies down there,' he said after a
while, 'they will belong to people who died a just death ordained by
the God of our fathers. Because they were an abomination in His
eyes. And it does not behove us to question the will of God.'

'So it's true that Maria lies here?'

'I'm not saying yes and I'm not saying no. If there are bones here
they go back to the earliest times of the Devil's Valley, generation
upon generation, all those who were impure.'

'How, impure?'

'Our God brought us into this valley to set us apart from the
iniquities of the world outside. He is the Great Divider, the one who
in the Scriptures is called Hammabdil. He divided light and darkness,
heaven and earth, dry land and sea. He also divided us from the race
of sinners. And from time to time when someone is born among us
who bears the mark of original sin, he has to be removed from the
congregation of the Lord. It is their bones you may find here.'

Almost majestically, before I could respond, he turned to lope
back to his cabbages. What intrigued me was that his legs appeared
to bend backwards like a heron's, but it could have been an optical
illusion.

Shattered

I stood looking after him, then returned to my work. But it was
heavy going in the sun. After a while I took off my shirt and threw it
to one side. Brother Holy's words were still throbbing in my mind.
*Generation upon generation. All those who were impure. The mark of origi-
nal sin.* I felt as if I'd come to the edge of a precipice; but below me

was only fog, one couldn't see down to the bottom. And I wasn't sure that I wanted to see that far.

But for Emma's sake I had to go on.

After another half an hour I decided to take a break and go home for some refreshment, even if it was only a mouthful of the valley's hellishly bitter coffee. It was when I picked up the last big stone I could still manage that I discovered the white bone below. And as I kneeled down to scratch more cautiously, several more. Odd bits and pieces. And then a skull. I felt cold in the full blaze of the sun. I looked up. From far away, among the cabbages, Brother Holy was watching.

I picked up the delicate skull. One side was shattered. But it was impossible to draw any quick conclusions. All I could tell for sure was that it was not the skull of a grown-up. Much too small for that, too frail, too flimsy. It looked like a mere baby's.

To Rub Up

Without any conscious decision, I put on my shirt again and set out for Lukas Death's house, the nearest one to the church, in the lower row. Minutes later I was in his voorhuis, a long gloomy room with a dark peach-stone floor, the centre of which appeared blacker than the rest. I had the little skull in my hand.

From the open kitchen a woman wearing a starched white apron approached. Presumably she was Lukas's wife; I hadn't met her before. There were lines of suffering on her face, but she seemed quite calm and composed, and her eyes looked straight at me.

'You must be looking for Lukas,' she said. 'He's in the back room. Because of this afternoon's prayer-meeting there's no school today.' For a moment I thought she was going to say more, so I stopped to wait for it. But all she said was, 'If you don't mind, go round the outside. I don't like that thing in the house.' Clearly not a woman to rub up the wrong way.

The back room was where I'd found Lukas Death on previous occasions. A euphemism for the mortuary. In some spots the whitewash was peeling from the walls and I wondered absently whether those might be the patches where Katarina Sweetmeat's mirrors had been removed. Lukas Death was standing beside a coffin, working on a corpse, a very old man. I've seen enough corpses in my line of duty, but they still make me feel creepy. It clearly didn't bother Lukas, as he stood with a mug of coffee in his hand looking down at his handiwork. I got the impression that I was interrupting a conversation.

'You're busy,' I said unnecessarily.

Lukas looked up, confirming my worst suspicions. 'I was just having a chat to old Oom Bart Biltong. He was very upset about having to lie still for so long, he's had back trouble for years, you see, but I think he's coming round to the idea.'

'I don't want to interrupt. But your wife said I'd find you here.'

'Dalena always says too much.' With a sigh. 'But have a seat.' He pointed at the foot of the coffin, but I preferred to stay just where I was.

'Death is keeping you busy,' I remarked, just to say something.

'It's in our nature to die,' he said pointedly, then added with some resignation, 'I suppose we must be grateful, for everyone who passes away in this drought saves another pail of water a day. That's how I explained it to old Bart.'

'Sounds heartless,' I protested.

'It's life and death,' he said laconically. 'You might say it's because of the drought that old Bart is lying here today. Not so, Oom Bart?'

To my relief, old Bart didn't respond.

'How did it happen?' I asked.

'It's his own fault,' said Lukas Death. 'He went to clean out his well and he's much too old for that kind of work. He used to ask a neighbour to help him, and give the man a pail of water for his trouble. But then Oom Bart decided water was too scarce to share, so he tried to do it on his own and fell in.' He resumed his esoteric ministrations. 'But I'm sure it's not because of Oom Bart that you came to see me.' He'd been studiously ignoring the skull in my hand. 'So what brings you here?'

Iniquity of the Fathers

'I found this skull under the stones behind the graveyard.'

Lukas Death went on bustling about the coffin for another minute, mumbling either to himself or to the dead man. Then he asked, 'And?'

'Aren't you surprised?'

'Why should I be? If you go on digging you may find more. That's what the heap is there for.'

'Lukas, I must know what is going on here.'

'Why "must"?' he asked gently. He leaned over to mumble something to the body again, straightened old Bart's shroud and moved the lid into position, but without screwing it down just yet. 'Have a good rest,' he said to the old man.

'*Who* is buried under those stones?' I demanded.

Lukas looked even more shat-upon than usual, but he remained endlessly patient. 'We are strictly just in our ways, Neef Flip.'

'That remains to be seen. What about that poor man you locked up in the tower?'

'Alwyn Knees? Brother Holy will let him out tomorrow. There is a time and a place for everything under the sun.'

'Not for the ones buried under the stones.' I pointed at the crushed side of the skull. 'How did this happen?' When he remained silent for too long I insisted, 'Did he get stoned too?'

'You can see for yourself, can't you? We follow very closely the commandments given to the people of Israel.'

'This one was a baby. How could he have deserved such a death?'

'I the Lord thy God am a jealous God, visiting the iniquity of the fathers upon the children unto the third and fourth generation of them that hate me,' he recited.

'What the hell do you call "iniquity of the fathers", Lukas?'

'For that, you will have to know our history.'

'That's what I'm here for.'

Fires of Hell

WHAT LUKAS DEATH offered me that morning was not at all the history I'd been waiting for, but another story. Entertaining enough, to be sure, but what fucking use was it to me? Still, for what it's worth, this is what he told me:

In the beginning of the world there was a great battle between the hosts of God and the legions of hell. Not surprisingly, God got the upper hand, although it cost the lives of many angels. But the enemy was near wiped out. It was just batwings and arrowtails and split hooves wherever you looked. The only one who got away was the Devil himself. He fled across the face of the earth, with God in hot pursuit. And slowly God began to gain on him, He was quite an athlete in his young days. In those times the world around here was still flat, the plains lay level with the tops of the mountains up there. But when the Devil realised he was being overtaken he began to burrow into the earth like a mole, scorching a tunnel all the way down here into the valley, where the fires of hell were still burning. All the cliffs were red-hot. One can see it to this day where the rocks were split: black crusts on the outside where the fire turned to charcoal, but deep inside, in the very kernel, they're still red.

God sent a few angels after the Devil to bring him out, but their wings got scorched and that was the end of them. Whereupon God decided to call it a day before all His best men were lost. And the Devil remained down here in the valley, making sure he always kept below the overhanging cliffs where no unexpected bolt of lightning could strike him.

As Brave As

For many years the Devil lived here undisturbed by man or God, until he began to relax his guard. But God is like an elephant, He never forgets. And one day He sent His servant Lukas Seer Lermiet with a large party of trekkers to fetch the Devil from the valley. It was a hellish journey and along the way most of the wagons were dashed to pieces on the rocks, oxen and all. In the end only Lukas Seer and his family reached the floor of the valley down here.

The first night after they'd arrived at their outspan everything looked so peaceful one couldn't believe the Devil was anywhere near. And Lukas Seer and his family were so exhausted after the trek, they just made a fire to keep the predators away and went straight to sleep. That was when the Devil saw his chance. He knew if he could get rid of the Seer, God would never dare to send another scout after him, for in the whole world there was not another man as brave as Lukas Lermiet.

As soon as the people were asleep the Devil crept to the outspan in the pitch dark — it was a moonless night — and he took a long, burning log from the fire and prepared to hit Lukas Lermiet over the head. But the Seer's wife Mina woke up and in the dull glow of the fire she saw what was happening. She screamed like the last trumpet, Lukas Seer woke up and instinctively rolled to one side, so that the blow only struck him on the hip. Which was enough to cripple him for life, but otherwise he was all right. And he tackled the Devil with his bare hands.

But the Devil was no lightweight. As Lukas Lermiet made a grab for him he stood back and stamped out the fire with one of his hooves so that there was no light to see by. In that darkness Lukas Lermiet had no chance at all. But God looks after His faithful. He took the full moon by the ears and plucked it out from behind the mountains — one slope had to be shoved out of the way, but for those who have faith a thing like that is child's play — and so Lukas could once again see what was happening.

It was a battle like the world has never seen since. For three days and three nights it raged. The two fighters became so tired they could hardly raise an arm, but in a clinch of death they kept on throttling each other, rolling this way and that, from one end of the valley to the other, from the rock pool over there in the kloof to Hans Magic's place. To and fro, to and fro, until the whole place was covered in sulphurous fumes, but they never let go. The Seer's wife and children tried many times to have a go at the enemy with picks and shovels and logs and yokes and whatever came to hand, but the two fighting men were clenched in such a tight bundle that it was impossible to tell one from the other.

But at long last it was all over for the Devil. As he blew out his last breath a ball of fire cartwheeled along the valley, splitting trees and rocks along the way, as if lightning had struck the place, not the usual kind of lightning from the sky but from the heart of the earth. And when at last the noise died down Lukas's family came to bring him round. It took another three days and nights before he woke up. His wife nursed him with herbs and roots they found in the mountains, the kinds Tant Poppie Fullmoon still uses for her remedies, and at last Lukas Lermiet recovered. Except for his leg, which was paralysed and had to be amputated in the end. That was the Lord's punishment because he'd fallen asleep instead of keeping watch.

Lukas Lermiet realised he would never be able to leave the valley again, nor could his wife Mina and his children leave him behind. So he built himself a house, right on the spot where he'd killed the Devil. It is the house in which I still live to this day, and in the voorhuis you will notice a black spot on the floor. If you step on it on a cold day you can feel a dull glow under your feet, coming from deep down where the Devil is still smouldering away.

Unadulterated History

After that the people flourished in the Devil's Valley. But just as in the time of the Israelites in the desert, the people of the settlement began to forget how God had saved them. And now, just to remind them, one or two children in every generation are born with a lame hip. Such children have to be removed from the bosom of the congregation. It is the will of the Lord, His name be praised.

'A nice story,' I said with feigned appreciation, not wanting to antagonise Lukas Death unnecessarily, but feeling rather let down.

'It's no story!' he replied indignantly. 'It is unadulterated history as it has come down to us.'

'But, Lukas, you must admit it could have become distorted as it got passed on from one generation to the next.'

'You forget one thing,' he said smartly. 'The man this history happened to may have died, but he is still in our midst. Grandpa Lukas. He makes sure that we keep to the truth.'

'That still doesn't prove anything,' I said scornfully.

'What is it you don't understand?'

'First of all, the way I heard it, Lukas Lermiet's wife was called Bilhah, not Mina.'

'That's Isak Smous again. He twists everything to suit himself.'

'Why should a name like Bilhah suit him better than Mina?'

'Because his ancestors brought in Jewish blood.'

'But I thought the Lermiets and the Koens and the Portiers and others intermarried so much that it's impossible to tell a circumcised head from an uncircumcised tail?'

He grunted disapprovingly, masticated for a moment, then conceded, 'Mina was the wife he brought into the Devil's Valley with him. But after her death he went in to Bilhah.'

'And where did she so conveniently come from?' I asked with a poker face.

His collarless shirt seemed to become too tight for him; but he wasn't to be cornered so easily. 'Why should that surprise you? The Scriptures themselves do not give us every verse and chapter. For example, they don't tell us about other people made by God at the same time as Adam and Eve, but when Cain arrived in the land of Nod he took himself a wife, so we know there must have been others around.'

'You mean the Devil's Valley was something like the land of Nod to the east of Eden? There were other people living here too?'

Eyelid

'I didn't say that,' he cut me short. 'The way it came down to us, Bilhah was first married to another trekker. Her husband died on the way down and she stayed on with the Lermiets.'

'The Lord truly moves in wonderful ways.'

He looked hard at me but I didn't bat an eyelid. 'That's true,' he said, but I could see he didn't quite trust me.

'Are you sure Bilhah wasn't one of Lukas Lermiet's daughters?'

'Why should he have taken his own daughter to wife?'

'Suppose there was no one else available?' I decided to go for it. 'One thing I've discovered is that in the Devil's Valley things seldom happen the way they do outside.'

'We keep the commandments,' he said. There was a faint glow in his voice.

'What about adultery?' I asked.

'Oh we're very strict on that,' he said emphatically. 'That is, if you understand adultery correctly.'

'I'm open to conviction.'

'We've been fortunate in having some wise men with us who taught us over several generations how to interpret the Scriptures,' he explained, as close to enthusiasm as I suppose he would ever get. 'Adultery happens when a woman from inside the Devil's Valley consorts with a man from outside without the approval of her people.'

'Was that what the woman Maria did – Emma's mother?'

'So you've heard of her.' It was a statement, not a question.

'Yes, I have. And it was her skeleton I was looking for when I found the child's.'

'Why dig up the old bones?'

'It's history,' I said, with what to me sounded like a tone borrowed from Brother Holy. 'I'm trying to find the whole truth. And I won't rest before I've got it.'

'A man can choke on too much truth.'

'Then we'll just have to deal with the choking too. Lukas, I've got to know what happened here. It's important to me.'

'You're so taken with history and truth and everything,' he said, 'but I think deep down you're just curious. What is there still to be said about Maria's death?'

'Everything, as far as I'm concerned. For all you know your son might have married her daughter. Yet I've never heard you speak about Little-Lukas. Don't you find it shocking that he died? I was there –' I knew I was embroidering a bit, but what the hell – 'I was one of the last people he spoke to. Don't you want to know about it?'

He flinched as if I'd touched a naked nerve. Then he continued with clenched jaws. 'Little-Lukas gave away our secrets and paid for it. One doesn't kick against the pricks.'

'Perhaps he was trying to find out his own bit of truth.'

'There's a right way and a wrong way.'

'You think he and Maria were both wrong?'

'Why do you always come back to her?' He was breathing very heavily now. 'It's no secret what happened to Maria. She committed adultery and was punished for it, that's all.'

'And that commandment applies only to women?'

'Of course,' he said, sounding surprised that I should ask. 'It is the woman in her weakness who has to be protected. You must realise that we set much store by our women. Their honour is our honour.'

'And the one who steps out of line?' He said nothing; I tried to force an answer from him. 'That's where the stones come in, isn't it?'

A pause. Then he said quietly, 'It is so.'

'And you call that fucking justice?'

'What was right for the chosen people of God cannot be wrong for us.'

Throwback

'Even if it means stoning children?'

He was getting irritable now: 'I already told you how it works.'

'You said every child who is a throwback with a lame hip must be eliminated.' I held the frail little skull out to him. 'But there are cripples all over the place. Why are only some killed and not others?'

He turned away from me to open the lid of the coffin again and busied himself for a few moments. 'Sorry to disturb you, Oom Bart,' he said. 'I just wanted to make sure your back is all right.'

The dead man presumably made some reply which I couldn't hear. Lukas kept himself busy for a while, tugging at the folds in the shroud, rearranging the hands clasped on the sunken chest, all the while keeping his back to me. It was quite some time before he closed the lid to face me again.

'What were you saying?' he asked.

'About the crippled children.'

'Ah yes. You see, it depends on what kind of affliction the child has. It has to be exactly the same as the lameness the Seer suffered from after the Devil struck him on the hip. And it takes a good eye and guidance from above to recognise it.'

'A lot of guidance, I'm sure,' I said caustically.

'I already told you about law and order,' he reminded me.

'Yes, indeed.' It was time for the gloves to come off. 'But I must confess I don't understand the kind of law and order that kills babies and allows a man like Jurg Water to go about unchallenged.'

By Any man

'Jurg is one of the most respected men in our settlement.'

'That is what troubles me. Do you know what he does to his children?'

'He chastises them in the fear of the Lord, if that is what you mean.'

'Chastise doesn't mean to half-kill them. And I don't think it means what he's doing to Henta either.'

His eyes flickered in their myopic way, but he didn't answer.

'Do you know about it?' I demanded.

'Surely what happens inside the four walls of a home is between them and God.'

'And if Henta is fucked in the bluegum wood by any man with an itchy cock?'

'Tsk, tsk,' he clicked his tongue. 'A mere child.' For a moment I thought he was going to say more, but then he obviously decided to cut it short. 'How can anyone know for sure what happens in the wood in the dark? Judge not, that ye be not judged.'

For some reason it sounded more like a bloody threat than a warning.

Possible Damage

STILL HOLDING ON to the baby skull I returned to the heap of stones behind the cemetery. I placed the fragile little thing in the shade, took off my shirt and set to work again. Perhaps the effort would help to settle my thoughts: I needed a bloody spring-cleaning to get rid of all the shit in my head.

But the work was no use. The events of the night before still lay heavily on me, and added to it was the shock of my discovery and the talk with Lukas Death. By eleven o'clock my hands were chafed and covered in blisters and my whole body aching from the effort. Enough for one day, I decided. My own pile of stones was growing steadily, even though I'd hardly made a dent in the original heap. In the process I'd unearthed half of another child's skull and a few loose bones, but nothing resembling the skeleton of a grown person. Well, it must have happened almost twenty years ago, which might mean several layers deep. I rolled the little skulls into my shirt and walked away. There was only one person I wanted to see right now and that was Emma; but we'd already agreed never to be seen together before dark. In this fucking place it might be useless anyway, but even so we didn't want to tempt fate.

As I passed in front of Ouma Liesbet Prune's dilapidated house she called me in her mosquito voice.

'Boetie, I want to talk to you.'

'I'm busy today, Ouma,' I tried to get out of it, but she was waving so eagerly that I feared she might lose her balance, and I couldn't afford to have that on my bloody conscience too.

Skindering

It meant climbing up to the attic landing once again and hoisting myself up to the roof from there.

'I see you started digging,' she said as if we'd already discussed the plan. 'You'll find many more bones further down. But it won't help you one bit.'

'I'm looking for Maria's skeleton.'

'Yes, so I noticed. But you won't find Maria there.'

'I spoke to Emma. She told me herself.' This was one person I felt I could trust.

'What does Emma know about it? She was a day-old chick, barely hatched, when they killed Maria. But God doesn't sleep, you can take that from me.'

'Well, if Maria isn't buried under the stones, then where is she?'

'I told you mos. I laid her to rest in my own coffin. The night after they killed her Ben Owl and I dug her up from under the stones and gave her a proper burial in one of the old graves. No one else knew about it.'

'But surely people would have got suspicious if they saw the grave had been dug up?'

'The soil is turned over every week for weeding, so no one noticed.'

'Why would you do such a thing?'

'Because Maria was my great-grandchild.'

'Emma said she was Isak Smous's sister.'

'Half-sister. They had different fathers.'

'So I was told. But if Maria was such close family, why didn't she live here with you?'

'Because Ben Owl wouldn't leave her alone. I told him to let her be, but he only listens to the voices in his head. And he said they told him he could have Maria.'

This was something else for me to follow up. How would I ever tie all the fucking threads together? What I was trying to find was a network; all I'd found so far was a damn crow's nest.

Before I could enquire further I heard voices approaching, and the next moment Ben Owl's sleepy face appeared above the ladder at the edge of the roof.

'Were you skindering about me?' he asked, blinking his weak eyes.

I jumped at the opportunity to ask him a few questions, but Ouma Liesbet was too quick for me. 'Ben, go back to bed,' she said sharply. 'This is not your time.'

He yawned and obediently turned to go down the ladder again.

The Fig Instead

She waited for him to disappear before she said with a rasping chuckle. 'You can't blame poor Ben. Maria was a pretty young thing and he was head over heels in love. That's how it goes once a man has looked up into the tree.'

'What tree are you talking about now?'

'Our grandparents used to say mos that after God made Eve from Adam's rib the two of them lived together very happily in the Garden. The only problem was that Adam never knew what to do with a woman, no one had ever taught him, know what I mean? But on the day of the apple, Eve was standing with her legs wide apart on a branch high up in the tree, and as Adam looked up he saw for the first time what there was to see. And when she offered him the apple he chose the fig instead.'

I grinned, but my thoughts were burrowing elsewhere. 'I'm sure I've heard that story before, Ouma Liesbet. But didn't it start with the Hottentots again?'

'Why are you always going on about the Hottentots? It's a story first told by our own people and they knew what they were talking about. Because Paradise was right here in the Devil's Valley, you see. The tree the woman stood in grew at the very end of the dry riverbed that comes down from the mountains. When God chased Adam and Eve out of here, He sent an angel with a flaming sword to split the tree in two. But before that happened it must have been a sight to see. They say the branches were spread right over the rock pool where ever since Mooi-Janna's time the girls of the valley used to swim naked. Which is why the hole is still taboo to the menfolk. I often swam there myself. If you saw me when I was young you'd have worked up an appetite for fruit too.'

Far and Wide

'It was forbidden fruit you and Ben buried in the graveyard, Ouma Liesbet.'

'How could we leave that poor young woman under a heap of stones?'

'In which grave did you put her then?'

'It lies a bit to one side. There's no name on the headstone, only a question mark.'

I pricked up my ears: 'Who was it first dug for?'

'That stone stands for many people.'

'How do you mean?'

'Well, you see,' she said, 'many of our people couldn't be buried here, for one reason or another. They're far and wide in the world. So this grave is here for all of them. If they happen to visit, and it's only natural for the dead to wander, then at least they have a place to stay over.'

'And who would they be?'

'Oh all kinds.' She was silent for a while. 'Lukas Nimrod for one. After he was killed by that peg or quill or whatever he got in his head his old hunting friends decided to bury him far away in the mountains. Some say it was because of his wife. A nasty woman she was who never liked to have him at home. She got just what she deserved when they put him away elsewhere. A woman like that is a disgrace to all of us who keep the commandments.'

'And who else was the grave meant for?'

'Ag, you won't know them.'

'What about Little-Lukas?'

'I wouldn't mind that. But the people can be difficult, you know. These last few years more and more of the young ones have gone away to settle outside the Valley. You can see for yourself how few are left. There are more people living in the graveyard than in the houses. So the ones who leave are written off, and people won't want to make an exception of Little-Lukas.'

'I wish you'd tell me more about the place.'

'By rights I shouldn't share the Lord's time with you,' she said. 'But if you really want to know, all right, then I'll tell you so you can know once and for all how it all fits together.'

It was like a sun coming up. 'I'll bring along my tape recorder tomorrow and record it all,' I proposed enthusiastically.

'Your what?'

I tried to explain, but soon realised it was no use. 'I'll show you tomorrow. Then you can tell me the whole history.'

Had I known then what I know today I'd have stayed right there and tried to memorise it all instead.

Toothless Grin

Ben Owl was fast asleep downstairs in the pigsty of a house when I came down from the roof, so I had no choice but to go home. Tant Poppie was working on her doepa. The smell was earsplitting. She stood up when I came in, pressing one hand to her lower back. Her inquisitive eyes scurried across my hairy body like ants.

'And how are you?' I asked dutifully.

'Terrible, thank you,' she said, and proceeded, as usual, to give me a rundown on all her aches and pains.

I pretended to listen with great interest and then turned to my room, but stopped on the doorstep. 'Why is everybody in the Devil's Valley always telling me things are going badly?'

'It's because the Devil is watching day and night,' she answered like she was giving me an ordinary, practical piece of information. 'If he finds out that things are going well he turns on you in a flash, because he can't stand that.' She wiped her hands on her filthy apron. 'Let's say I'm going to give a hand with a birth, then I mos always take a dirty rag with me, just in case it turns out to be a good-looking baby. If it is, I tie the rag round the child's arm there and then, so that if anybody happens to say what a lovely baby it is, the parents can answer, "Ah but look at that filthy old rag." That keeps the Evil One away.'

'So what you're saying is that you're feeling fine?'

'I'm not saying anything.' She turned back to her medicines and I went to my room.

There, a hopeless task, I tried to dab the worst smell of sweat from my body with a cupful of water and pulled my crumpled shirt on again. The two skulls, one whole and one half, I placed on the wash-stand beside the almost empty pitcher. With small toothless grimaces they stared at me while I dutifully fed the fucking chameleon a few more of the maimed flies Piet Snot had brought and which I'd been keeping in a jar.

Only after that, as I settled on the bed to catch up with my notes, did I discover that something was missing. The fucking black dress I'd hidden under my pillow when I'd made the bed. I got up to investigate. The ribbon my first visitor had left behind and which I'd stowed inside my rucksack was also gone.

I was the hell in. Not so much about the loss, I'd never set much store by collecting sexual trophies, but about the mere fact that someone had mucked about in my private stuff behind my back.

I went to the door again. Tant Poppie was still busily at work, her huge posterior turned to me.

'Tant Poppie.'

She straightened up with a groan, her face red and streaked with sweat.

'Was there somebody in my room this morning?'

'Didn't see anyone.' Her squinting eyes were moving in such a way that I couldn't pin either of them down. 'Is something wrong then?'

'There's some of my stuff missing.'

'Ja?' She wobbled across the floor to the dining table to fill a calabash pipe with dagga. It took an unconscionable time.

'From under my pillow.' I was beginning to wonder whether it was wise to have broached the subject at all. What would she do if she found out that I'd been fornicating under her roof – even if it had been more or less forced on me?

Tant Poppie clearly was in no mind to make things easier for me.

'What exactly is it you're missing?'

I hesitated. 'Some clothing.'

'Now who on earth would want to take your clothes?'

All right, I thought: if that was how she wanted to play it, two could tango. 'A black dress.'

The shiny full moon of her face remained blank. 'How did a black dress land under your pillow?'

'Tant Poppie, you were here on Sunday when those women came visiting and brought me gifts.' I made a deliberate pause. 'And presented their daughters to me.'

'What about it?'

'These last few nights there were women coming to my room.'

'I'm a light sleeper and I didn't hear anything.'

'That's too bad. All I'm saying is that they were here. One of them left her dress behind, another a ribbon. Now they're gone.'

'I suppose they just came to fetch them back. The people who live here don't have clothes to spare. This morning I was out for a long time with Sarie Cucumber.'

'Will you recognise the women if I describe them to you?'

'What did they look like?'

'Well, I didn't see any of them very clearly. But the first one had webbed toes and the second a harelip. The third was covered in hair, all over her body.'

For once her eyes were staring very straight, but whether she was focusing on me or on something behind me was still difficult to make out.

'The hairy one could have been Magda. Her father is old Petrus Tatters. But there's no telling, because her late mother was just the same.' She folded her arms and said with some amusement, 'Birds of a feather, hey?' Then she tugged at her dirty apron and took another pull from her pipe. 'As for the others, I'm not so sure. We've always had lots of harelips around here, so it's hard to say. And Jos Joseph had a daughter with webbed feet, Truida Duck, but she died years ago.'

'You're not suggesting . . .?'

Nightwalkers

'Neef Flip.' She came to stand right in front of me, one hand on a hip, talking through a cloud of smoke. 'Who says your visitors were real women?' She knew exactly how to stretch a pause. 'They could have been nightwalkers.'

'What's nightwalkers?'

'That's what the old people called them. There are males and females, and they usually come out in times of trouble. If a male finds a woman on her own he jumps her. And the females go for men. They suck you dry leaving only a husk behind.'

'You can say that again,' I said wryly. 'But that still doesn't mean that my visitors were nightwalkers. I know a woman's body.'

'Nightwalkers have bodies too, and very lusty ones besides.'

'What are you trying to tell me?'

'One knows a nightwalker by the company it keeps. It's usually an owl and a baboon.'

Once again the feeling of my body hair standing up. But I tried to suppress it. 'That's pure superstition,' I said, irritable.

'Don't talk about things you know nothing about.' In splendid indignation she returned to her work. But after a moment she looked over her shoulder. 'Look, if you expect another visitor like that, you just take a jug of Tall-Fransina's witblits to the room with you and put it next to your bed, with a candle. When that nightwalker comes you quietly take a big mouthful and light the candle, and then blow your loaded breath right through the flame. I can assure you that'll be the end of the nightwalker.'

'Will it really work?'

'If it doesn't work,' she said without batting an eyelid, 'then you take five more mouthfuls and close your eyes tight. After five minutes you will have forgotten all about her.'

She turned back to her bags and boxes, making it clear that the conversation was over.

But I couldn't put it out of my mind. The dress and the ribbon, Tant Poppie's hints about dead women, the nightwalkers clearly appropriated from some old Khoisan belief, just like Ouma Liesbet

Prune's stories. How many times had I come across these traces in the Devil's Valley? Below these quiet waters ran fucking dark currents indeed.

Prayer-Meeting in the Devil's Valley

From Our Crime Reporter

THE COMMUNITY OF the Devil's Valley gathered this Wednesday afternoon in the stone church erected generations ago by their ancestors to confirm their dedication to the cause of the Lord. According to the spokesman of the settlement, Mr Lukas (Death) Lermiet, there has seldom been such a demonstration of unity in the valley, a place which in the past was often characterised by strong divisions.

The occasion was a prayer-meeting for rain, first called a considerable time ago but apparently postponed several times as it was felt that such measures should be resorted to only in the most dire circumstances. In the words of one of the most respected inhabitants of the Devil's Valley, Mrs Poppie (Fullmoon) Lermiet, 'God is a busy man, He can't be bothered with trifles.'

The pews were crammed to capacity, not only by the living but, as far as we could establish, by all the dead of the community as well. Conspicuous among these was the patriarch and founder of the settlement, Mr Lukas (Seer) Lermiet, generally known as Grandpa. Asked whether he had a special message for the occasion, Mr Lermiet said, 'What I have to say I shall discuss man-to-man with God, not with the newspapers. Ever since the *Commercial Advertiser* in the time of the Great Trek we have lost faith in the press. It is all a plot of the English to take us over.'

The meeting, which lasted for several hours, was led by the unofficial preacher of the congregation, Mr Brother (Holy) Lermiet, who opened the prayers. It was noteworthy that the entire service was conducted in High Dutch, and that even the members of the congregation not fluent in it tried their best to express themselves in that tongue. 'One must have the decency to address the Lord in his own language,' declared Mr Petrus (Tatters) Lermiet. Another member of the congregation, who preferred to remain anonymous, explained, 'It is to make sure that God can't say afterwards, as he usually does, that he misunderstood.'

Following the opening prayer, Mr Brother (Holy) Lermiet gave an extensive account of the critical circumstances in which the settlement found itself. 'It pleased God our Almighty Father more than a century and a half ago to lead a handful of whites from the wilderness of the outside world to this haven,' he said. 'Under his guidance we have laboured to maintain the purity of Christianity and civilisation in the face of all onslaughts. Today we find ourselves before an ordeal which may bring about our end. Because where can we turn to? We have taken root in this place, we have bought this small tract of earth with the sweat of our brow and the blood of our bodies, and here we shall die if we must. For it is better to perish in the land the Lord has granted us than to live abroad among the fleshpots of Egypt. Therefore, if God should summon us to die, then let us say Thy will be done. But if there is mercy and forgiveness of sins still to be found, so that we may survive and thrive in the blessings of His rain, let us avail ourselves of the opportunity to set things right between us and him.'

After that the prayer-meeting was opened to the floor. Here follow extracts from some of the more striking prayers. Out of respect for the sensitivity of our readers expletives have been deleted where necessary.

The Late Mr Lukas (Seer) Lermiet

'God, yes, look, we didn't mean to bother You today, but these are bad times and a man can't just lie smelling his own (expletive deleted). I don't know how well You know Jurg Water, but we kept on hoping he would find something with his divining rod. But now any tick can see he's (expletive deleted) useless, which is why we're talking to You under four eyes today. You know me as a man who doesn't beat about the bush. I'm not like that great-great-great-great-grandchild of mine, Lukas Death, who shies away when you corner him. Nor like Petrus Tatters who's such a liar one never knows what to believe, especially when he starts tearing up cloths with the widow of old Giel Eyes. Nor like Brother Holy who picks his words from the Tree of Knowledge when they're still green, while everybody knows all he really thinks about is (expletive deleted). I go straight to the fountain's eye. So You'd better listen if I tell You about the (expletive deleted) this drought has already caused us. If You would take the trouble to walk from where I usually sit up there at the Gateway with the goats, and You follow the route I staked out when I first came down here with my family, along the Bird Krans and below the Honey Krans, past the Bushman pictures where Strong-Lukas's name was written to honour his memory, You can go and look for Yourself if You don't believe me, and then You cut down past Accident Bend, across Breakneck Heights and Hard-Times Hollow and Breakyoke, then down Jacob's Ladder to Griet's Hole, past Snow Neck and Give-up, through the straits of So-help-me-God and Crynot and Tightballs, and then right past Great-Sorrow to Nebo's Point, and from there to Breathless towards Mina's Pisshole, all along the riverbed to the Tree-of-Knowledge and Mooi-Janna's Pool, I hope You're still with me: I'm saying that if You follow that road, right through our valley from Rotgut to Hans Magic's hut, which he should really start cleaning up, the place smells like (expletive deleted), then all You see is just drought and desolation. If I were You, God, I'd be (expletive deleted) ashamed of myself. No one among us would let his house go to ruin like that, excepting Ouma Liesbet Prune who is past the age of accountability and Ben Owl who is too (expletive deleted) hopeless to do anything about it, then he'd have had his (expletive deleted) kicked well and proper. Have You no pride in Your handiwork any more? No father I know of, apart from that (expletive deleted) Jurg Water, treats his children so badly, but he's only second-generation so he doesn't know any better and there's no excuse for Yourself. You think You can get away with murder. You're very quick to claim the honour if things go well, but now that the world is (expletive deleted) You think You can wipe Your (expletive deleted) on us. So all I want to say, God, is that it's time to pull finger. And we don't want a little (expletive deleted) rain that's like an old woman's (expletive deleted). It's life and death now, and what we need is a flood of blessings. You remember what old Ezekiel said about their issue like the issue of horses, well, that's the kind of rain we need today. Anything less than that You can turn sideways and push up Your (expletive deleted). Amen.'

Mr Isak (Smous) Lermiet a.k.a. Koen

'Well, God, You have heard what Grandpa Lukas had to say, and I hope You know how to separate the wheat from the chaff, because the devil in him has never come to rest and for a man of his age he still talks a lot of (expletive deleted). Please forgive him for talking about himself all the time, You will remember that my late father always said pride comes before a fall, but I suppose he can't help it, it runs in the Lermiet blood, and I thank You that in Your wisdom You allowed a trickle of Koen blood to be mixed into it, otherwise You alone would know where we'd be today, as it is we already have our hands full with all Your mistakes running around in the streets, it's because this lot can't stop (expletive deleted), but like Your servant Joshua said, As for me and my house, we will serve the Lord. Now where was I? We all know it is the sin of the Lermiets that is still visited upon us, but if You can find it in Your heart to show this (expletive deleted) lot some mercy, I beseech You to let it rain, otherwise we shall have to consider packing up our belongings and trekking away. Don't You have eyes in Your head, Lord, to see the wretched state we're in? If our hearts must be cleansed first, then I propose You start with Petrus Tatters and Job Raisin and Smith-the-Smith and Peet Flatfoot and all those who are so (expletive deleted) in sin, and eradicate it from them. And for those of us who know the weakness of the flesh, please preserve us from Bettie Teat and Henta Peach and all the other (expletive deleted) who cavort among us and cause our (expletive deleted) to plague us by day and by night. And please tell the members of this congregation that I still have a few pounds of sugar and some Mauser bullets at the old price, and enough chintz for three women's dresses and one for a girl, provided she's not too big in the (expletive deleted). I thank you humbly, God, and you can take that as Amen too.'

The Late Mr Giel (Eyes) Lermiet

'God Almighty, I won't be long, but I've got to tell You something. You have heard what the (expletive deleted) Isak Smous just said. Now if he was the only one, You could have treated it with the contempt it deserves. But as it happens, over the past few weeks we have heard that a number of other people in the valley are also beginning to talk about trekking away to get out of this dry place. Now on behalf of all the dead I just want to say this: they know (expletive deleted) well that they can't go away without taking us with them, because no self-respecting, godfearing person can leave the dead behind to decay among the weeds of the wilderness. But there are so many of us that it is simply impossible to dig us all up, and furthermore we don't want to have our bones disturbed. If Petrus Tatters thinks he can move away just to (expletive deleted) my wife at night when no one sees he's got another thing coming. So the sooner they forget about trying to slink away and dishonour the dead, the better. And the easiest way to put an end to all this nonsense is just to bring some rain. If You did Your duty in the first place, none of this would have happened. Thank You and Amen.'

Mr Jurg (Water) Lermiet

'Lord, this bunch of (expletive deleted) have been talking so much (expletive deleted) that Your ears must be burning. I'd rather greet a puff-adder by hand than have to put up with their (expletive deleted). But by this time I'm sure You know them for the (expletive deleted) they are, so all I can say is (several expletives deleted). You know I've always said it's no (expletive deleted) use to keep the (expletive deleted) kaffirs and the (expletive deleted) English out of the valley while among ourselves we are worse than (expletive deleted). So I'm asking You today to look into their (expletive deleted) hearts, otherwise they'll (expletive deleted) You round every corner. I mean, take Tall-Fransina. Last Tuesday she sold me a jar of witblits for a basket of dried apricots and a basket of raisins, and half of it was heads and tails. If that (expletive deleted) can't tell where heads end and hearts begin, it's time she shoved her (expletive deleted) still into her (expletive deleted) and started (expletive deleted) her cats. And don't forget about Grandpa Lermiet. Just because he's dead and unable to (expletive deleted) he begrudges the rest of us a bit of (expletive deleted). These are the people who have a lot to say about another man's (expletive deleted). Meantime this place is going to (expletive deleted). There is no drop of water left in this valley or I would have found it, trust me. I know this place better than You do and I've been scouring the kloofs without a twitch in my rod, the thing is as useless as a (two expletives deleted). If You don't start raining on us You shouldn't blame us if we (several expletives deleted). Amen.

Mrs Poppie (Fullmoon) Lermiet

'Father, You've heard enough from the menfolk for a while, so let me tell You a few home truths as a woman. They're quick when it comes to talking, but when action is needed there isn't much (expletive deleted) in their (expletive deleted), You can take my word for it. I've known most of them since the time they first (expletive deleted), and I can tell You they're useless. It takes a woman like me to get things done. I'm used to fetching and carrying and keeping body and soul together from dawn to dusk, and You better believe me there isn't much gratitude around. But all I'm asking, Father, is that You should do unto us as you did to Sodom and Gomorrah. I mean, if there are two or three women in this place who are worth their salt, like Lot's wife, then please save the place for our sakes. And don't just save it, Father, because too much saving can lead to (expletive deleted). What we need is for You to start doing Your bit. You created heaven and earth, as You keep telling us in Genesis, and

You brought Your chosen people here, but then You just abandoned us. That's not the way to do it. If You'll forgive my saying so, it's just like a man, never cleans up after himself and always expects others to do his dirty work for him. But we can't make it rain, so now it's up to You. It is fast becoming an embarrassment and a disgrace. There are some people around here, I've seen it with my own eyes, I visit all the houses, who have taken to washing their faces in their own (expletive deleted). And I'm afraid You have to take the blame for it. In the early days our people could still say, Whatever happens is the will of God; and if it is no longer his will, then let us trek. But here we are stuck, on account of Grandpa Lukas's (expletive deleted) leg, and on account of what old Giel Eyes told You, so we can't get out and we can't trek away, we're caught in this narrow place, and You are the one who must now save us. So please start doing something about it and don't let us have to tell You again. Amen.'

Mr Hans (Magic) Lermiet

'Lord, I have no wish to add my little stream of (expletive deleted) to the flood of (expletive deleted) You have already heard. I told them to keep their mouths clear of the weather, that way it stays whole. But they won't listen. And all this praying won't help either, because it won't rain unless the wind is right. But this is another bucket of coals, and since they refuse to listen and keep on sowing suspicion, I just want to ask You: please take that wind and turn it right and let it rain. I thank You in anticipation. Amen.'

Dragged Her Out

IF ALL THE words wasted in prayer that afternoon had been water, the Devil's Valley would have been flooded by nightfall. And as it was, I didn't hear half of it, because I left long before it was over.

Just as Hans Magic was winding up his prayer someone in one of the front benches in the women's block fainted. It came as no surprise, what with all the doors and windows being closed and the late-summer sun blazing outside; and with the heavy odour of a crowd of bodies that hadn't seen water for some time, Hans Magic's worst of all, it was hard to breathe. I was beginning to feel dizzy myself. And the depressing memories of my childhood stirred up by the service didn't help either.

The commotion in the women's block put a spoke in the fucking wheel. It took several minutes before one could make out what was happening in that throng of bustling bodies. As it turned out, it was Henta. Tant Poppie and a few of the other women dragged her out from under the pew where she'd fallen, and surrounded by rather more helpers than were called for she was carried to the vestry behind the pulpit.

Among them I recognised Dalena, Lukas Death's wife, efficient and no-nonsense; but it was someone else who really made me shake off the heavy drowsiness that was paralysing me. Emma. Her narrow body in the long dark dress that flared around her legs; the attitude of her head, the dark hair once again piled high. By this time the next person to offer prayers was already on his feet. All the eyes dutifully turned to him. Except mine. That was why I noticed Emma hesitating just below the pulpit stairs, so briefly that no one not alert to it would have noticed. Her eyes moved quickly along the pews. It could have been my imagination, but I was sure she was looking for me. And the moment she found me among the potatoes and cabbages in the male block she made just the slightest gesture with her head before she walked on. A last swing of her dress, like a curtain moving in front of a window, and then she was gone.

Rely on Intuition

I was tempted to follow immediately. But I wasn't born yesterday, so I stayed on for a while. The new speaker was already swept away by the tide of his communion with Our Lord and Heavenly Father, Creator of Heaven and Earth, who will come to judge the quick and the dead; but my attention soon wandered while I waited for the best moment to leave. As it happened, the speaker was just beginning to rev up the old engine for the inevitable descent into hell when Prickhead in front of me developed a nosebleed and stumbled from the overcrowded pew in search of fresh air. I gave him a handicap of two paragraphs and three expletives deleted before an uncontrollable cough sent me off after him.

Outside I quickly checked that no one was watching. The place was deserted. In the far distance, from the direction of Jurg Water's house, I could hear the voices of the women who had left with Henta. Poor girl. But for once my thoughts did not dwell on her.

How could I have known so precisely where to go? Let it not be said that only women rely on intuition. Deliberately dragging my feet so as not to raise any suspicion in whatever visible spies might be abroad, I casually sauntered round to the back of the church, stopping from time to time to pick up a twig or a small stone, study it with feigned interest, throw it away, and leisurely walk on. Following the wide curve of the churchyard wall, all the way to the heap of stones at the back.

You Too

She was waiting for me, sitting on the smaller heap of stones I'd begun to pile up that morning, and across which the shadow of the wall was beginning to lengthen. She had undone her hair and there were moist strands clinging to her forehead.

Without looking up as my shadow touched her, she said, 'I'm glad you came.'

'You asked me to.'

'Did I?'

'You'll know that better than I do.'

I gazed at her for a while, but she didn't look up. Absently, she played with a small stone.

I asked, 'What's up with Henta?'

A brief laugh. 'Nothing at all. She pretended to faint. She often does that.'

'Why?'

'Church has a way of working up her father. The only way to keep him off is to pretend that she's ill.'

'Why would church have that effect on him?'

'You've heard them yourself, haven't you? Every time they go to church to pray or study the Bible or whatever, it's like pigs wallowing in mud. It stirs up the worst in them.'

'It certainly didn't seem to have much effect on the weather,' I said wryly and looked up. The sky was drained of colour, an expanse of blackness. Except for a single small wisp of cloud behind the blunt church tower, no bigger than a man's hand.

'If there really is a God He'd have destroyed them long ago.'

'You're not much of a believer, are you?'

'Could you believe in a God like theirs?'

She picked up another stone, repeated the same procedure as before: weighing, reflecting, rejecting.

'Why did you come here to wait for me?'

'Because of these stones.' I couldn't read her eyes. Without emotion she said, 'They're the only mother I know.'

'Ouma Liesbet Prune told me about your mother,' I said quietly.

'And you believed her?'

'Why should she lie?'

'Everybody here lies.'

'You too?'

She looked at me for a long time, then gave a small crooked smile. 'Of course.'

'Why?'

'If you're scared, what choice do you have? You just lie.'

'What are these people really afraid of?'

'You come in here from the outside, you start digging up every-thing. They can't face it. They thought they could do without remembering. You're making it difficult for them.'

'Still, over the last few days they've been only too eager to talk to me.'

'Of course. Because you listen to them. But I don't think you can rely on that.'

'I suppose that's why all I can show for my efforts is a handful of stories.'

'That doesn't mean that nothing happened.'

'How can I get through to that?'

'I don't know. Perhaps they don't know either. All they have is their stories. The rest is up to you.'

Uncharted Territory

She was forcing me towards uncharted territory, a pool in which my feet no longer touched the bottom. I don't think I've ever had this kind of conversation with a woman before. I'd always thought of women in a different way, and talking didn't come into it. And unable to face her seriousness, I tried to sidestep it with a limp riposte: 'You're very clever, aren't you?'

Even as I said it I knew it was the last fucking thing I should say. And the expression on her face confirmed it.

'For someone like me, you mean?' she flared up. 'I know I'm not supposed to think. But when one is cornered . . . what else can you do?' She stood up abruptly and started dusting her dress, her back to me. 'What's the use of being clever? What's the use of anything?'

She swung round; once again the flaring of her skirt made me conscious of her body, the sharp angles of hips and shoulders, the sinewy strength of legs. A consciousness I could have done without, just here, just now.

'Can you understand that?' she asked. 'I want everything, but I have nothing. And there's nothing I can do about it.' She looked up at the church; I could see her flinch. 'We mustn't stay here,' she said nervously. 'I don't want to be seen here.'

'But where can we go?'

She looked round anxiously. Then said, 'Let's go up to the bluegum wood. There's a clearing among the trees.'

Yes, I remembered. Henta; her dress pulled up to her chin. Suddenly it all came back to me. But why now, after I'd kept it in check for so long? It was like the infallible recipe to have whatever woman in the world you want, as long as for one hour you don't think of her navel. And I suppose that was how I came to think of Henta at this wholly inopportune moment. The extraordinary paleness of her skin, the bluish whiteness of skimmed milk. Her little nipples like the pink snouts of rabbits. The curve of her belly with the deep inverted comma of her navel, and below it the small patch of reddish curls, too sparse to camouflage the cleft of her pussy. The mere act of dwelling so fondly on these details shamed me: the need for it, the hangups behind it. If there was any difference between myself and Jurg Water, I thought, full of sudden disgust, it was only in degree, not in kind. There was something in the Bible about this. Whosoever shall offend these little ones, it is better for him that something something. If any of thy limbs offend thee, cut it off and cast it into the sea. The sea must be pretty well clogged up with cast-off limbs by now.

'What are you thinking about?' asked Emma.

'You,' I lied, and yet in a way I knew it was, unnervingly, the truth.

'I'll take the path past the ostrich camp,' she said. 'You go round the other side.'

On a Naked

She waited for me among the trees, at the edge of the clearing in the wood, exactly where Henta had appeared the last time. Her sudden eyes as she looked at me.

'I thought you weren't coming any more.'

'I wouldn't stay away for all the world.'

'It can't mean anything to you. I'm just bad news.'

'Emma.' All the urgency in me surged up. 'There's only one thing that has made it worth my while to come to this place and that is you.'

She sat down on a naked fallen trunk with most of the bark peeled off, and plucked a leaf from a branch overhead. She started chewing it. I could smell the eucalyptus. All the time she looked at me. 'How come?' she asked at last.

'You're different from the other people here.'

'Does that mean anything?'

'I don't know. All I know is that it means a lot to me.'

She spat out a small green wad of chewed leaf. 'To me too,' she said in her frank, intense, unsettling way. 'And it scares me. Because I know you'll be going away soon. What will become of us then? What will become of *me*? You know, ever since I came back from school you're the only person who has ever listened to me. I wish we could just stay here and talk and talk and talk for ever. It doesn't even matter what we say. As long as it doesn't ever stop. Because I don't know what is going to happen after.' Without looking up she asked, 'When are you leaving?'

'Saturday.'

'So it's only tomorrow and Friday. Then you'll shake our dust from your feet again.'

'There's still so much to be done.'

She looked up unexpectedly. 'I suppose you want to fuck me before you go,' she said with brutal directness, her voice shallow, almost harsh.

'I won't lay a hand on you.'

'Am I so awful then?'

'Now you're twisting my words. That's not fair.'

'Do you *want* to fuck me?'

I looked down at my hands. My nails were dirty. Everything about me was dirty.

Then I looked up. 'Yes,' I said. 'Right now there's nothing I could think of that I want more.' I swallowed deeply. 'But I promise you I won't.'

'Why not?'

'I don't know how to put it. I suppose I don't want to take the easy way out.'

She didn't react. Perhaps she was waiting for something else, something to hold on to, to give her hope . . . but of what? The fuck knows, we were beyond hope as it was.

Probably a Bird

From under her dark eyebrows she gazed at me. Without any obvious connection she said, 'I never thought you'd really go looking for my mother this morning.'

'I said I would. We've got to make sure.' Did I dare go on? I had no choice. 'But then Ouma Liesbet told me she was buried in the graveyard.'

To my surprise it didn't seem to upset her. 'I could have told you,' she said.

'So you knew?'

She gave a little smile.

'Why did you lie to me then?'

'I wanted to see if you believed me.'

'I promise to believe all your lies.'

'You know nothing about me yet.'

'I know enough to want to know more.'

'There's nothing more to know.'

'What do you *do*?'

'I teach the children when Lukas Death needs help. One or two of them I help with extra reading lessons. There are a few bright ones. Poor little bastards, what'll become of them? Otherwise I help Isak Smous with his books. Or his women with their housework. I help with sewing. Always just helping here, helping there. Other people. But what about *me*?' She got up, her whole body taut as a string. 'Can you imagine how it is?'

'You've got to get out of this place, Emma.'

'Show me how,' she said softly, with no hint of cynicism. Then sat down again.

Something rustled among the leaves. Probably a bird.

'Surely,' I said, 'if they don't need you here it would suit them if you left.'

'They're scared of what I could tell.'

'About your mother?'

'About her, about them, about everything.'

'And yet they're helping me with my history,' I reminded her.

'For the moment.' She looked straight at me. 'They let you come in, Flip. That doesn't mean they'll let you out again.'

Improbable Story

It was cool in the wood, where the fierceness of the sun didn't penetrate. Something rustled again. And suddenly I remembered that there were no bloody birds in the Devil's Valley. I jumped up. She was watching me. It was quiet again. I picked up a stone and flung it to where the sound had come from. There was a smothered cry and something began to scamper off through the underbrush. I ran after it. In a small opening among the trees I saw a stunted figure scurrying away. With a mixture of irritation and relief I recognised him. It was Prickhead.

Just to made sure he got the message I threw another stone after him. It hit him between the shoulderblades and he uttered a long whimpering cry, stumbled to the ground, scrambled to his feet again and ran off. The blundering sounds of his flight continued for some time.

Emma was still waiting at the edge of the clearing when I came back, a fist pressed to her mouth.

'Don't worry,' I tried to comfort her. 'It's just that poor idiot, Peet Flatfoot.'

'They're' everywhere,' she said. She dropped her arm to her side again. 'There's only one place no one ever goes to. If you want to, I'll take you there.'

Surprised and curious, I followed her. She led me out of the wood and up a gentle slope towards a kloof overgrown with virgin forest, reaching in deeply among the knuckles of the mountain. It looked greener than the rest of the valley. I'd never been so far before. Without talking, Emma forced a way through the underbrush, and I followed close on her heels. There was a hint of a footpath, but barely visible. Between her shoulders I saw sweat staining her dress an even blacker black.

After a long time she stopped to wipe her face. I was panting, but her breath still sounded calm and even. She pushed a branch out of the way and stood back to let me pass. Against a wall of rock, among dry driftwood, I saw a badly weathered white skeleton, enormous in size, like an ancient ship stuck on a reef.

Amazed, I went to have a closer look. 'What on earth is this, Emma?'

'Look.'

I touched what looked like a rib. It crumbled under my fingers. I inspected the whole length of the skeleton. My first wild guess was that it must be a dinosaur, but of course that was preposterous. Though no more preposterous than what it turned out to be. A fucking whale. I couldn't believe it, but the baleen plates, and the shape of head and body, were unmistakable.

She came up from behind and put her hand on my arm. 'Seeing is believing?' she asked.

I shook my head. 'I can see it all right, but it's bloody hard to believe.'

Like an improbable story in a world of facts it sat there.

'How did you find it?' I asked.

'Everybody knows about it, but most of the others are afraid to come close. When I was small they used to scare us with it. They said if you see that thing you die.'

'It didn't put you off.'

'I thought it was just a scary story. But you can see for yourself.'

I touched another bony protuberance and studied the powdery deposit it left on my finger.

'This isn't all,' she said, curiously lighthearted.

'Nothing can be stranger than this.'

'Come and see.'

Uneven Oval

A short distance beyond the skeleton she went down on her haunches against the rock face, scraped away some old branches and beckoned me to follow her. It looked like a cave, but really was no more than a narrow passage between two cliffs. Here were more of the drawings and engravings I'd noticed on my way down into the valley: stick-men, eland, even a figure resembling a woman in a long dress and a bonnet, which must have been painted after the first settlers moved in here. High above us I could see a narrow segment of sky. About fifty or a hundred metres further the back wall broke away and in the opening, like a natural arena, lay the uneven oval of a rock pool. The water was so black it seemed bottomless.

'This is the Devil's Hole,' she said.

'It must have water enough for the whole valley.'

'Yes, I'm sure, but no one dares to come here. They say this is where the Devil plunged in after he lost the fight against Grandpa Lukas.'

'I thought he died on the spot where they fought.'

'There are many endings to the story,' she said casually. 'Does it really make any difference? All that matters is that people think this place is evil, and they'd rather die of thirst than come here.'

'But you're not afraid?'

'I have nothing to lose.' In spite of the lightness of her words I found something terrifying in them.

'Have you been coming here for a long time?'

'Yes, but not all that often. I suppose I'm a bit scared too, after all. They say the hole goes on for ever. And in some spots there's a kind of eddy, you can barely see it, but it's like a funnel that sucks you down.'

'Do you ever swim here?'

She took a minute to answer. 'From time to time, yes. Especially these last few months. It's been so hot, one gets all sweaty.'

'I'd give my kingdom for a swim.'

'Then why don't you?'

'What about you?' It wasn't so much a proposal as a challenge.

From the way she looked at me I could see it wasn't a simple matter of yes or no either.

After a while she said, 'I think I'm too scared.'

'You needn't be scared of me.'

'Not of you. Of the water.'

That'll teach me, I thought. But I couldn't back out now, I'd already committed myself. She was watching me quite openly, as I started to unbutton my shirt. Her closeness made me feel self-conscious about my hairiness. But it was too late to chicken out. I threw my shirt on a rock. 'My father was a gorilla,' I said, but it hardly sounded funny.

Out of the blue she asked, 'Do you think you'd like to be with a hairy woman?'

I cringed with guilt. Jesus, could she possibly know something? Perversely, the very idea caused my body to react. It was all too fucking embarrassing to handle.

'What makes you ask such a stupid question?' I asked gruffly.

'Just something I dreamt. It made me terribly jealous. I wanted to pull her away from you, but I couldn't move.'

'You dream too much,' I snapped.

Drag You Down

I turned my back to her to undress further, only too aware of my old man's dugs, my paunch, my fucking prick sticking out like a very sore thumb. Much faster than I'd meant to, I started scrambling across the rocks, stumbling into the most undignified bloody postures, cursing under my breath, then hurling myself into the black water, a resounding belly-flop.

The ferocious cold promptly took my breath away. And my sore thumb.

There was no easy gradient in the bottom: below me the rocks simply dropped away, and I had to kick and thrash with all my might to stay afloat and get my circulation going again.

Once I'd caught my breath I started swimming away from the edge in a wide loop, then turned on my back, taking care that nothing was visible above the surface.

'You coming?' I called.

'I first want to finish here.' I swear by my mother's curlers she was washing my fucking dirty clothes. But when I shouted at her she only laughed, and being in no fit state to engage in a tug o'war right now I had to give up. Spluttering, I dived under and started flailing my arms, but made little progress. I was much too out of shape, and the water too cold.

After only a few minutes I turned round. She had finished her washing and was spreading my clothes on the rocks to dry. I saw her standing up. The next moment, without any warning, she jumped in, clothes and all. Bloody fool, I thought, unless she was a very good swimmer that dress was going to drag her down.

'Emma, you're looking for shit!' I shouted across the black water, but she paid no attention.

I started splashing in her direction, but she swam away with a mocking laugh. Still annoyed, as much with myself as with her, I struggled back to the edge and dragged myself out on the warm rocks. The next moment I heard a smothered cry, and when I turned to look I could see that she was in trouble. It could be the eddy that had grabbed hold of her, or the sheer weight of the clinging dress that was hampering her movements, or both; whatever it was, there was no time to waste. Fortunately the rocks around the pool were littered with dried branches, bleached white in the sun, like the bones of extinct mammoths. I grabbed the longest one I could handle and swung it out towards her. She tried to come closer.

'Emma, can you reach it?'

Sorely Missed

On the black surface of the water around her I become aware of motion, a slow, lazy ripple, almost imperceptible to the eye, but there nevertheless, ominous, relentless, deadly. This is serious.

Crime reporter risks life to save drowning woman, dies in attempt.

'Emma, come out!'

For another thirty seconds, stricken by panic, I remain where I am, stretched forward as far as I possibly can. If she doesn't grasp that fucking branch right *now*, I'll have to dive back in. She tries to lunge forward and upward, the tips of her fingers touch the branch, slip loose, let go. She tries again, coughs up water, sinks away. I no longer even think of danger. Still clutching the unwieldy branch I jump back into the black pool and start rowing in her direction with one hand, my feet churning. It may be hopeless, but what the hell else can I do?

'Emma!'

Then, thank God, she manages to grab hold of the branch. I roll over on my back and start kicking, moving away from her. A frightening, invisible force is tugging me back. My breath is coming in deep gasps. I feel like a fish caught on a hook and dangling in the air, suffocating. But I swear to God and all his devils that I'll get out of here. And not without her either.

Sorely missed by his estranged wife Sylvia (57) and his two children, Louise (32) and Marius (23).

That'll be the fucking day.

I keep on struggling and kicking and thrashing about, sending up huge sprays of water. I hear her calling out, see her splashing. The eddy has her in its grip and won't let go. My arms cannot take this for much longer. Blood is booming in my ears.

A young reporter has recently been appointed in the place of Mr Flip Lochner who tragically drowned.

With all my remaining force I pluck at the branch. And now I can feel her breaking from the grasp of the water. I manage to cover the last few yards back to the edge, pull myself out over it, stumble to my feet, still reeling, then lean far over and stretch out to grab her hands. Panting heavily, she reaches for my grasp. The next moment I drag her from the pool across the rocks, like a dark, heavy, drenched rag.

President Mandela this morning awarded a medal for bravery to our crime reporter, Mr Flip Lochner, who has been promoted to news editor.

Dangerous

For a long time I just lay there, spreadeagled on my back, heaving and trembling, unable to think of anything beyond the primitive knowledge that I'd survived. Then, slowly, I became aware again of the warmth of the rock creeping through my frozen body, although I still found it hard to grasp what had happened. Through the warmth, the ease, the relaxation, the flood of relief, I felt a hand touching me. Emma must have recovered before me. She was sitting beside me in her clinging wet dress, dragging her fingers through the hair of my chest. But I was feeling so remote from everything, that I still wasn't actively conscious of being naked.

'Are you dead?' I heard her ask.

'Yes, I think so,' I said. 'But don't let that upset you. It was worth it.'

'You gave me a fright.'

'You could have drowned.' As my consciousness of the here and now slowly came back, I sat up. 'Why didn't you take off that bloody dress?'

'I never thought it would be so heavy.' She shivered. 'It was like something grabbing me. If you weren't there . . .'

'For every damsel in distress there's always a knight at hand, some more hairy than others. Stories work like that.'

'This isn't a story, Flip.'

I pressed her hand.

Her fingers went on combing through the hair on my chest. 'I feel safe with you,' she said.

It was unfair comment; I was naked, damn it, and I was stiffening again. Flustered, I scrambled to my feet and picked my way across the rocks to where she'd spread my clothes. And at the same time I felt sad about doing it, I didn't want to. Putting on clothes was closing off something, a confidentiality, a closeness, a frankness, something perhaps I needed more than she. I kept my back to her.

'I like your hairiness,' she said.

Women had said many things to me, mostly of an uncomplimentary nature; never something like this.

'It's just because the Devil's Valley doesn't have much to choose from,' I muttered, trying to force-feed my legs down the clinging wet jeans. It was heavy going, not made any easier by the hard-on that nearly got caught in the zip.

She sniffed. I looked round. She was sitting with her arms folded around her drawn-up legs, her chin resting on her knees, watching every move I made. But she said nothing.

No Illusions

At last the unwieldy jeans were on; I could turn to face her again. 'You deserve better than anyone here can offer you,' I said. 'And that includes me.'

'Why are you always so hard on yourself?'

'I've known myself for long enough to have no illusions left.'

'I don't believe you.'

The urge to unburden became too much for me. I started spilling it all to her. Everything that had gone sour, my shame, my sins. Sylvia. My children. Louise, whose birth I missed because she came two weeks early. I was up the West Coast on a fucking story, a pretty major one which could land me a sub-editorship, and having finished my field work earlier than anyone expected I stopped to celebrate at Paternoster. There, never one to miss a dare, I got myself into a drinking contest amid the lurid girlie posters in the pub and urged on by a great scrum of boisterous Saturday men. It was fully three days later before I staggered out again, the worse for wear, having missed both my deadline and my daughter's birth. And nine years later, another accident, Marius. Sylvia tried to bring him up as Mummy's little fairy, I wanted him to be a he-man a father could be proud of. Between the two of us he was sunk. Neither of us realised, or wanted to realise, what was happening. The little thefts at school, the missed rugby practices, the failed tests; the interviews with the principal, which I was usually too bloody busy to attend; the shock of the first expulsion. The drop-out, the drugs, the probation following the first appearance in court. Driven to our first real man-to-man, I lost my temper and tried to beat sense into him. 'What do you expect of me?' he sobbed in rage, 'To become like *you*?'

In a perverse way I hoped it would scare Emma off, give her a proper shit in me, which would make it easier when I had to leave in a few days' time.

But all she did was to press her forehead against my shoulder. And she said, 'You're being very unfair to yourself, Flip.'

'Don't tempt me.' I had no choice but to be honest. 'I want you, Emma, and I bloody well need you. What I told you in the bluegum wood was true. But there's nothing we can do about it.'

'Why not?'

'I told you it's impossible. Don't make it more difficult than it is already.'

I pulled the wet shirt over my head and struggled to tuck it in.

She watched while I put on my shoes.

'Must we really go back?' she asked.

'I suppose the people will wonder about our wet clothes.'

'If it rains, they won't notice.'

I looked up. There were indeed clouds overhead. Not many, but it was the first time in the week I'd been there. I couldn't believe it. But perhaps God had decided to relent after all.

'I wish we could stay here,' said Emma.

Something was tugging at us, something that would keep us there, more insidious than the clutch of the whirlpool in the dark water, something that could suck us in very deeply.

'We're dangerous to each other,' I said bluntly.

'If it's not dangerous,' she said, 'it means nothing.' It slapped me in the face like a wet fish: just how young she was; how she could still afford to be absolute.

At the same time, in a way I couldn't explain, her words had sent me back to darknesses within myself. Stay away from me, I thought. And yet I knew I couldn't bear it if she were really to let go of me.

She began to stroke the wrinkles from her soaked dress. 'Let's go,' she said.

'Because it is too dangerous here?'

With what might be a smile in her serious eyes she said, 'Perhaps it's more dangerous down there.'

Terrifying

WE PARTED IN the bluegum wood. When could we meet again? What with the storm coming up, we'd have to wait at least until the next evening.

'Then we'll try to find your mother's coffin,' I said.

'Are you really going to risk it?'

'The sooner we find out the better. There's already been too much loose talk. What we need now is proof.'

'I don't want to cause you trouble.'

'It's worse for you, Emma.'

'I can take it.'

'Tomorrow night then.'

I waited until she had disappeared through the trees, and then went off in the opposite direction, to the far end of the valley. By the time I emerged from the wood heavy clouds were already charging across the sky overhead. It was almost unbelievable, but I saw it with my own eyes. Even so, my thoughts were so screwed up that I registered very little of what was going on around me.

As I started going down the last steep slope to Tant Poppie's house, the wind sprang up from below, so violent and so sudden that it nearly swept me off my feet. It was all I could do to jog down the incline, stagger round the house and tumble through the front door.

The wind was rapidly building up into a gale. Where I took up position in front of my bedroom window – Tant Poppie was out – all kinds of things came blowing past outside: pitchforks, wheelbarrows, chickens, seven ostriches, two pigs, eleven drying-trays and one whole haystack. Funny in a way, but not really. It was fucking terrifying.

I have no idea how long it went on, as I stood there in a kind of daze, even when I could no longer see anything. The dark had swooped down like a large bird descending on the valley with widespread black wings. And all the time the wind was raging, tugging at the roofs, at the walls. There were moments when I feared the whole place was going to be blown to hell and gone. But after a very long time the violence began to abate. There were a few last brief gusts, tearing something down here, smashing something else there. But at last it died down. The clouds were blown away. The stars came out again. And through all of it not a drop of rain had fallen.

To Talk To

I remained at the window, as if waiting for something to be completed, but nothing happened. At least not anything I could have expected. I thought I saw something moving outside and pressed my face against the panes, but it was just about impossible to distinguish anything in the dark. Yet I was convinced there was something. And then, yes, there was – a glimmering of light, a swinging lantern, and a woman in a black shawl carrying it. Another of the sisters of the night? But this one looked middle-aged, quite unlike the others.

With her swinging lantern she went round the house to the front door. She came in without knocking, and only then did I recognise her: Dalena, the wife of Lukas Death. I remembered the piercing way she'd looked at me that morning.

'I've come to talk to you,' she said, out of breath. Behind her calm appearance I could sense other, more turbulent things.

I lit an oil lamp too and we sat down at the long dining table.

'An apostle?' I asked, not expecting her to accept, but she did.

When we were both seated again with our tin mugs, the silence became tangible, inside and out.

Like a Torrent

'I didn't mean to bother you,' she said at last. She held the mug with both hands as she drank, as if to quench a thirst. 'But there are things I need to hear from you. I can't bear this any more.'

'What is it?'

'It's about Little-Lukas.'

'Yes?'

When at last she began to speak it was like a torrent, as if everything she'd been holding back came bursting out all at the same time. She was Little-Lukas's mother, she said, she had a right to know, but no one wanted to tell her anything, she knew what he'd done wasn't right, but that didn't change the fact that he was her child, the only one she'd ever had, and he was never very strong, but such a bright little fellow, and she couldn't take it any longer that his name could not be spoken in decent company.

'Look, one can keep silent for so long and then no more,' she said. 'Even a stone will cry out.' She was clearly beginning to crack up. 'You know, even though I loved him so much Little-Lukas was never really allowed to be mine. When he was small there was often trouble between me and his father, so it was mostly Tall-Fransina who brought the child up. I blamed her a lot, and I suppose in a way I still bear a grudge, but at the same time I don't know what would have become of him without her. And afterwards it was Emma. I was always kept to the edge of his life. But he was my child.' She tightened the shawl over her shoulders. 'And then he went away, over the mountains, out of my hands.'

'There really isn't very much I can tell you, Dalena.'

She was close to breaking point. 'Tell me anything,' she said urgently, 'even if you have to make it up. I want to know everything. I know nothing.'

I started working through my memories; it was like rummaging through an old trunk in an attic. There was so little really, but I tried to stretch it as far as I could. The day of the symposium, the night with the killer bottle of OB, the telephone conversation, the afternoon of Little-Lukas's death. She was soaking it all up like rain.

'They said he was irresponsible, he brought it on himself,' she said. Her eyes stared at me. 'But that's nonsense. It was they who killed him, the old men in the valley. I know them. It's they who fix the limits and the laws, and woe betide the one who steps over. And that is why God is angry with us now, but they are too pig-headed to admit it.'

'It was an accident, Dalena. You must try to understand that.'

'You're the one who cannot understand.' Her colourless eyes briefly flared. 'I'm not accusing you Neef Flip. But you know nothing about us.'

'I've been trying my best to find out, but wherever I turn I run into blank walls.'

Wrong Colour

'It's the old men,' she said, as if she hadn't heard me. 'They wanted Little-Lukas out of here, away from Emma. The whole thing was between them and her. Because she was just about the only girl who would never open her legs to anyone. Not to Jurg Water, not to Isak Smous, not even to Hans Magic.' A brief silence. 'And not to my husband either.'

'You don't mean to tell me that a Godfearing man like Lukas Death would do a thing like that?'

'Why not? This is the Devil's Valley.' Her eyes were glowing now, like embers. 'But for Emma there's never been anyone but Little-Lukas. Which was why they thought if they could send him away she'd forget about him. And he was a clever boy, he'd do any-thing to study. Not even Emma could stop him. But then it didn't work out the way they'd planned it, because Emma just kept on wait-ing for him. They knew if he ever came back he would take her from under their noses. That was why they had to get rid of him, you see.'

'It was Emma who encouraged him most of all to go on with his studies,' I said emphatically, but as gently as I could.

'No, she just wanted him for herself. You can ask Tall-Fransina, she complained about it all the time. All the things Emma did to keep him here.'

'No, Dalena. Emma saw that Little-Lukas had reached a dead-end here, that was why she wanted him to use his chances.'

'I'm not saying anything against Emma,' she interrupted. 'But for Little-Lukas she was nothing but trouble. It would have been better if the two of them never got to know each other, there my husband was right. If she wasn't there they wouldn't have had to kill him.'

'But it was an accident, Dalena,' I repeated. Anxious to persuade her I laid it on thickly. 'Look, I was there. I saw it happen. The car drove across a stop street. It could have happened to anyone.'

'What did *he* ever do wrong?' she asked angrily. 'I mean, he wasn't black or anything.'

'What on earth has black got to do with it?' The crime reporter was pricking up his ears.

She closed up. 'Nothing,' she said curtly. 'I'm just saying. And now I don't even have a grave to look after, no bones, nothing.'

My thoughts tied a quick loop. 'Dalena, I can give you something of Little-Lukas's. If you promise to tell me what you meant when you spoke about not being black.' This was an underhand thing to do, but I just *had* to find out. For the first time I could see a crack in the wall the settlement had been putting up around me.

Her mouth was set in a grim line. At first she refused to speak. But then I suppose the mother in her got the upper hand. 'It just means that all these years we've had children of the wrong colour born among us and then the people had to get rid of them. The throwbacks. But Little-Lukas was no throwback.'

Somewhere, dimly, something was beginning to make sense. But for every answer there were two new questions.

'Throwbacks to *what*?'

'How must I know?' she asked blankly.

'The skulls,' I said, more to myself than to her, getting up quickly to go to my room. But the two little skulls were no longer on the wash-stand where I had left them. For a moment I wondered if I'd imagined them too. But that was too bloody much.

After a while the blind anger subsided. I mean, it wasn't really a loss, it made no difference to what I knew or didn't know. The most annoying part was the discovery that once again someone had fucked about in my things.

'What is it?' asked Dalena-of-Lukas behind me.

I turned round. 'I dug up two little skulls this morning. Under the heap of stones behind the graveyard.'

'Yes, I remember. You brought one round to our house.'

'You saw it?'

'Of course. You came to show it to Lukas.'

Thank God. So this, at least, had not been a hallucination.

Unmistakable Whiff

'Now they're gone.' I came towards her. 'Do you think they belonged to dark children?'

'How must I know? All bones are white. But if you found them under the stones I suppose they must have been the wrong colour.' Her fingers cut into my arm. 'You said you had something to give me from Little-Lukas. Where is it? What is it?'

'There was no one to bury him after he died, so I had him cremated.' I told her about the arrangements, the landlady, the small box of ashes. And then I came out with it, 'I brought his ashes with me. I told Lukas Death about it, but he wasn't interested. So I thought I'd just go and bury it on my own one night.'

'I want my child back,' she said so firmly that I had no choice left.

'Go back to your seat. I'll fetch it for you.'

Unless the box had also disappeared in the meantime. But as I stepped back into the bedroom I stopped. On the foot of the bed, in the faint light coming from the voorhuis, sat a figure I immediately recognised. It was Little-Lukas. No doubt about it, with those thick glasses. He was swaying lightly as he sat, as if he'd had too much to drink. And I caught the unmistakable whiff of White Horse. On his knees, which he held primly together, he clutched the little box.

It lasted only for a minute, then he was gone. But the box was sitting there on the foot of the bed, as if someone had put it out for me.

Feeling quite numb, I returned to the voorhuis with the unprepossessing remains of Little-Lukas Lermiet. Dalena didn't bother to open the box. She just took it from my hands and pressed it against her breast like a baby. Her body remained very straight. A bloody formidable woman indeed. 'There's so little left of him,' she said. She didn't cry, but it was a wrench just to watch her. After a long silence she said, 'If I hadn't come to you tonight they'd have stopped me again. They take everything. They took our whole history.'

'What do you mean?' I asked, intrigued.

'Well, if there were dark children, it must have started with a mother, somewhere,' she said. 'There's always a woman in the background. Not that you'd know if you only listened to Lukas and them.' And at last she gave way to the angry flood I'd seen coming for such a long time. 'What have they been telling you? About Grandpa Lukas who came in here and did just what he wanted? Lukas Nimrod who killed everything that moved? Abraham Koen who bought and sold and lied and cheated? Carpenters and builders and hunters? Jacob Horizon who travelled to the ends of the earth. Strong-Lukas who wiped out the government's commando, and the two handsome rebels we captured to clear our blood, and Lukas Devil who locked up the census men in the church tower. Did they say where the women were in all of this? Do you think those rebels would have agreed to stay here for the rest of their lives if a girl like Talita Lightfoot hadn't bewitched them by dancing naked in the moonlight and lying with them like Ruth with Boaz in the Bible? And why do you think the census men followed Lukas Devil into the church if there hadn't been a girl tied up inside like bait in a trap? She was locked up there with the men and left to rot, we don't even know her name. I can spend a whole night telling you all the stories, and we wouldn't even have dented the surface. But why should you listen to me?

'Please tell me, Dalena. I promise you I'll listen.'

On Her Back

DALENA SPOKE THROUGH much of the night. I dearly wished I could dash out to fetch my tape recorder, but I didn't dare interrupt the flow of her story, as that might put an early end to it. So I'd just have to catch up with my notes afterwards.

She began with Grandpa Lukas, the Seer. Who quietly stole away one night, when his family was in dire straits in the heavy snow of the valley, to pick his way back to the outside world without them. What was to become of his wife and the last remaining children wasn't his concern. They'd become blinkers to his inspired eyes, shackles to his itchy feet. But half-way up the mountain he took a wrong step and fell down a krans and broke his leg. That was where his wife Mina found him three days later and carried him all the way down on her back. Don't ask me how she managed it, she hadn't even fully recovered yet from the beating he'd given her. But she never reproached him with word or look.

And then the gangrene set it, said Dalena, and it was Mina who had no choice but to tie him up with thongs so he couldn't resist, and then she hacked off the leg with a pocket knife. The operation had to be repeated three times as the gangrene crept ever higher. First at the ankle, then above the knee, then in the groin. She'd first tried to knock him out with the infamous Cape Smoke of the time, but even then the pain was so terrible that the cliffs echoed with his roars. He sobbed like a child, begging her to end his misery by killing him there and then. But she swallowed back her own tears and told him not to act like a bloody baby, and then took a chisel and hammer to chop through the marrowbone inside. Afterwards she scoured the mountains for herbs she could use to ease the pain and heal the wounds, and in the end she pulled him through. Lukas Seer did not want to live any more. What was life to a man without a leg? But Mina made sure he would survive with her.

Only after he'd begun to recover, she broke down. What she'd been through had been too much for flesh and blood and she fell seriously ill. But Lukas Lermiet never thought of finding herbs or remedies to save *her* life. Morose and brooding, he spent his days sitting on a rock, staring into the distance, cursing God for striking him such a low blow, and Mina for leaving him to cope on his own; and he only got up again after the vultures had devoured her dead body. We don't even know where her remains were put to rest, if ever they were.

One Must Die

In the second generation, too, a woman played a role. Lukas Nimrod, the Seer's firstborn son with his second wife, spent so much time making the Devil's Valley a safe place to live in that it was relatively late in life before he took a wife. She was Sanna, and nobody was quite sure where she came from. All we know is that she'd been married before, because when Lukas Nimrod took her, she already had two half-grown sons. They were the cross he had to bear in his hectic life. For Lukas Nimrod was a hard man and he had little time for another man's offspring. They were given more beatings than food, and it went from bad to worse after Sanna had begun to give birth to his own children, one every nine months, and sometimes two.

The crisis came when his stepsons were approaching twenty. For all those years they had borne without complaint what their stepfather had made them suffer. But by the time his strength began to wane they were at the height of theirs. And then they rose up against him. Presumably most of the men in the Devil's Valley were involved, as Lukas Nimrod's terror had fallen on them all. So a whole gang of them went with him on a hunt from which he wasn't supposed to return.

Except that it turned out differently. When Lukas Nimrod's two stepsons crept up on him during the hunt, one afternoon when he was peacefully having a smoke, he knocked the first one's feet from under him before he could pull the trigger. The shot fired by the second hit him in the shoulder. But Lukas Nimrod's strength was legendary, and the pain drove him into such a rage that he was even more ferocious than ever. Singlehanded he overpowered both his assailants and tied them up. This so scared the other men on the hunt that they all helped enthusiastically to drag the culprits home.

Right up there in front of the church Lukas Nimrod summoned his wife to witness the fate of the rebel scum. They were to be executed before her eyes.

Sanna fell to the ground and clasped his knees, begging him to save her sons. But he just kicked her off. She refused to give up and at last, for the sake of peace and quiet, he made a decision.

'All right then, for your sake I'll spare one of them. But one must die as an example to everybody here. This is not a place where a man can afford to be soft.'

The problem was that he left it to Sanna to decide which son was to be spared, and which one killed.

'You can't ask such a thing of me, Lukas,' she pleaded.

'The choice is yours,' he said curtly. 'I'll give you time until sunrise tomorrow morning.'

And off he went into the night, one shoulder still drooping, like a large bird with a broken wing. Sanna withdrew with her two sons into the house Ruben Tabernacle had built for them; the door was guarded by a number of heavily armed men to prevent any attempt at escaping.

Right through the night Sanna argued and pleaded with her sons; and in between she prostrated herself on the ground to pray.

When the first sun grazed the mountain-tops Lukas Nimrod came back. From the door his shadow fell right through the house.

'Well, have you made up your mind?'

'I have,' said Sanna.

'Which one?'

She looked him in the eye. 'Neither. Because it is sinful to expect such a thing from a mother. It is not I who must choose, Lukas Nimrod, but you. Show me if you are a man or an animal.'

'I am a man.' Whatever that might mean.

Then he called his men to take both his stepsons out to the clearing in front of the church. Sanna stood in the doorway. Apart from clutching the doorpost so hard that her knuckles showed white through the skin, she didn't show any emotion.

Lukas Nimrod ordered his men to blindfold his sons, but the boys refused. They wanted him to look them in the eyes when he pulled the trigger.

One shot. Two. Lukas Nimrod never missed, especially not at a distance of ten yards.

That night, while he slept, Sanna took the iron peg on which he used to hang the carcasses from the hunt for skinning, and drove it right through his head, into the ground. Just like that woman from the Bible, Jael.

'He bloody well deserved it,' I said. 'But what I find hard to believe is that she did it to her own husband.'

'Any woman, if she's pushed far enough, can do it,' said Dalena.

It was quiet for some time before I asked, 'And then?'

'Sanna refused to have Lukas Nimrod buried in the valley,' said Dalena. 'The body had to be taken into the mountains, out of her sight, to be laid away where no one would ever find the grave.'

Great Consternation

'And then there was Strong-Lukas.' Dalena resumed her long story.

'It's his name that is carved on the Bushman Krans?'

'Ja. That was Strong-Lukas. Who with a small detachment of five men faced a whole commando sent to establish the authority of the Cape government over the Devil's Valley. And this Strong-Lukas really was a daunting man, unlike his fat, useless father, Lukas Up-Above. But the official story says nothing about his daughter, Mooi-Janna. Let me tell you.

'It happened when the first commissioner or sheriff or whatever was sent from the distant Cape to find out what was happening in the Devil's Valley about the registration of inhabitants, grazing rights, taxes and such like. It could well have been Jacob Horizon's wandering that first brought the place to the attention of the authorities.

'The scout never got out of here alive. Whether he met with an accident, as the official version goes, or was executed, or caught by a predator, or simply vanished, no one ever found out. These mountains lend themselves to many stories. All that matters is that a commando was then sent to investigate. Twenty or thirty heavily armed men on horseback. The horses had to be left up there on the mountains, of course, with a couple of agterryers. The rest of the commando found their way down here. It took them three days, and some of them were looking pretty worn-out by the time they arrived in the Devil's Valley.

'Their arrival was rather unexpected and they met with no resistance, because at the time there was a shortage of ammunition and the settlers realised they couldn't take on an armed commando without heavy loss of life. For a few days the men negotiated, and then the commando went off again, taking six of our men with them as hostages. Their leader was Strong-Lukas.

'There was great consternation in the valley on account of our six best men being taken away. Seldom in our history was there so much talking and discussion among the menfolk. Most of them were in favour of going after the enemy and surprising them in the mountains, but that would no doubt have caused a bloodbath.

Daubed With Blood

'It was Mooi-Janna who solved the problem. She was Strong-Lukas's only daughter; all his other children, praise the Lord, were sons. She didn't tell anybody about her plan, because she knew that if the men got wind of it that would set them talking for another three days, and in the end they would most likely forbid her to get mixed up in it, and make a hash of it themselves. What presumption of a girl of seventeen to think she could solve a problem which had proved too much for men of forty or fifty or sixty.

'In those days there were still pretty girls around. But none as beautiful as Mooi-Janna. She went down to the rock pool in the riverbed where she used to swim naked ever since she was a little girl, and where you can still see the imprint of her feet on the rocks. There she washed her hair, and dried it in the sun until it fell down from her shoulders like a dark waterfall, and put on a new long shiny black dress her mother had sewn for her confirmation, from a bolt of pure silk one of Isak Smous's ancestors had brought from a far land; and when she was ready she stole up into the higher kloofs after the commando.

'Mooi-Janna was young and fleet of foot, and she knew the mountains like the inside of her father's hand. So she had no trouble finding a short cut past the commando without their suspecting anything. When she reached the top of the last rise beyond the twin boulders, she sat down to wait for them. For many hours she waited until she could hear the sounds of their coming up from below.

'She was frightened to death. Because it was a hell of a thing she was planning to do, much worse than diving into the Devil's Hole which, as anyone can tell you, means courting death and disaster. But her father's life was at stake and she had always doted on him. As a small girl she'd gone with him wherever he went, far up into the kloofs and ravines where he hunted or went in search of stray goats, perched on his shoulders like a little monkey. Everybody in the valley knew that all this talk about hostages was a cover-up. Those six men would never come back. If they didn't spend the rest of their days rotting in some dark hole of a prison they would be hanged from a gallows where the birds of heaven would pick the flesh from their bones. There was nothing else she could do. And only she could do it.

'When the commando was close enough for her to see the plumes on their hats appearing above the slope, Mooi-Janna got up from the rock where she was waiting. She stripped off her long silk dress and carefully folded it up into a small bundle which she put on the ground at her feet. Her loose hair was shimmering in the setting sun, and the last rays brushed her shoulders as if they were lightly daubed with blood.

'The soldiers, and their six hostages, stopped dead in their tracks when they saw her. The commanding officer came a few steps towards her, his white plume trembling lightly in the wind. Just as lightly as Mooi-Janna was shivering. Her skin came out in goose-pimples. That girl was a sight to behold, believe you me. It wouldn't be proper to tell you everything about her. Enough to say that no man who'd ever seen her — and there were a few who'd spied on her in the swimming hole — would forget that body to the day of his death, if he lived to be as old as Methuselah.

'She came down the slope towards the officer and spoke to him. Her voice was trembling but she stood her ground. If they let her father and his five men go, she said, they could do with her what they desired.

Stood Trembling

'"Let go the hostages," the officer ordered, with a frog in his throat.

'Strong-Lukas uttered a roar when he realised what was going to happen, but one of the soldiers beat him to the ground with the butt of his blunderbuss. There was no further resistance. The six freed hostages ran down the slope as far as their legs could carry them. And the soldiers turned back to attend to Mooi-Janna. By that time it wasn't only the tip of the officer's plume that stood trembling in the wind.

'There were many of them, as I said. Which meant that by the time the last one had had his way with her, the first was ready for more.

'The sun was down. Later the moon came up. Mooi-Janna had lots of time to watch the passing of the stars overhead, how the Southern Cross slowly turned its slow somersault, and how the Milky Way swivelled among the peaks. Except that as the night grew old she couldn't see so clearly any more.

'It was shortly before sunrise that the six freed hostages finally decided to attack. By that time it was child's play to overcome the soldiers, who were strewn about the grass like well-tanned hides. The avengers weren't in any hurry to finish off their quarry either.

Men have their own way of doing these things, and for the soldiers who still had twitches of life in them after the massacre it must have been a strange experience to find themselves choking on their own testicles.

'Only after it was all over Strong-Lukas kneeled beside his daughter and very gently helped her put on the beautiful long black silk dress again, which she was unable to do on her own.

'They went back at the pace of a tortoise. Mooi-Janna couldn't walk. Her father carried her on his broad back as he'd used to do when she was a little girl. Until they reached the place called Jacob's Ladder, just after you've passed Hard-Times Hollow and Breakyoke. There he stopped, and turned his back to the precipice, and shook her off. They all bowed their heads in understanding.

'Strong-Lukas's name was later engraved on the Bushman Krans up there, to commemorate the heroic deed in which, with only five men, he took on a whole commando of fifty soldiers, some reckon a few hundred, and wiped out the lot of them.'

Nanny Goat

'TELL ME MORE,' I said after a long silence, knowing I wouldn't find another occasion like this one soon.

'I must go home.'

'What can you tell me about Katarina Sweetmeat?' I offered her a piece of bait I hoped she couldn't refuse. 'The one who married Lukas Bigballs and who changed into a white nanny goat when the moon was full?'

She clicked her tongue, half-annoyed, half-amused. 'I suppose that is what Isak Smous told you?'

'He said his grandfather or great-grandfather Jacob Horizon brought her in here.'

'That part, I think, is true, yes. But did he tell you that Jacob Horizon stole her from her father's house and brought her here by force?'

'No, he said his grandfather had to work for her father for three years, besides paying him all his possessions.'

'Isak Smous's family have always been too lazy to do an honest day's work. He kidnapped her, that's what he did. And then the seven brothers stole her from him again; he got his just desserts. As if she was a bag of sugar or a goat or something. Whoever got her could keep her. They say she tried to run away many times, but then they beat her black and blue and locked her up in a little room where she never saw the light of day.'

'And the nanny goat?'

'Who can tell? People make up stories that suit them, to hide away their shame. But in the long run one can't hide away lightning, it must show itself. The way I heard it from the old women, Katarina gradually lost all will to live, which was why she accepted to marry a turd like Lukas Bigballs. But she never slept with him, that last bit of pride they couldn't take from her. He never gave her a moment's peace, until one night when he fell asleep too tired to go on trying, she tied a knot in his ball-bag. After that he never was quite the same again. All he could show for it was his name, but I cannot vouch for that. What I do know is that after some time the youngest of the brothers fell in love with her. Soft-in-the-Head Fransie they called him. But apparently he was a nice boy. And as time went on something started up between the two of them.'

'But if the brothers were such savages, how did Fransie ever get a chance with her?'

'He kept bringing her presents. Nothing special, you understand: a bunch of carrots, perhaps, or a mug filled with dew, or a tanned dassie skin, or a fresh honeycomb, things like that. And also a little white nanny goat. She doted on this little creature. And because the brothers knew it, they cared for the nanny goat as if she was the moon itself. Because as long as the nanny was around, they knew, Katarina would stay with them. So she arranged with Fransie that from time to time, when she felt like it, he would let the nanny out. All the brothers would roar off in pursuit, except Soft-in-the-Head Fransie. And by the time they brought the nanny back, he and Katarina would have done their thing.'

'And they lived happily ever after?'

'No. After a long time Lukas Bigballs became suspicious. And one day when the little nanny escaped again he hid in the house. When he saw Soft-in-the-Head Fransie tiptoeing to the back room where Katarina was locked up, he killed his brother with a single blow of a fire-iron, and then went to her in Fransie's place. In the dark she didn't notice the different before it was too late. When her baby was born it had two goat's feet. It was Lukas Death, my husband's father. Katarina died in childbirth.'

Arm Through His

Dalena pushed her chair back and stood up.

'Please stay,' I begged her. 'That can't be all.'

'You haven't heard the half of it.' She picked up the box of ashes and pressed it to her. 'There were many remarkable women among us,' she said. 'But by listening to the men you'll never hear of them.' She went to the door. 'But thank you for bringing me Little-Lukas. It was about time he came home.'

I checked my watch. It was just after three.

'Let me walk you home,' I offered. 'It is pitch-dark outside.'

'I know my way.'

'Just as far as the church then.'

She relented. Her stories told, she closed up again. When we came outside she started walking very fast, so that I had difficulty keeping up with her. There were no signs of clouds at all, the stars were shining with uninhibited brightness.

Less than half-way to the church Dalena stopped.

'This is far enough. Thank you.'

'Are you sure you'll be all right?'

'I have Little-Lukas with me now.' In the dark she was more forthcoming again. 'I hope you don't mind that I came to talk to you. But I just *had* to. Otherwise no one will ever know.' She touched my elbow. 'Look, Lukas needn't know about this. I told him I had to see Tant Poppie about medicine. I'll tell him she was out and I had to wait, and then left without seeing her. You were in bed already.'

Strange, strange woman. All those hidden worlds within her I'd never suspected. But what a loss that they had to be sealed up, and for so long. I looked after her as she disappeared into the night. When she was some distance away something weird happened: I could see Little-Lukas walking beside her, somewhat unsteadily on his feet. She put her arm through his. For a while I could still hear their footsteps, then they fell silent.

It was only a short distance away from Ouma Liesbet's house. Out of curiosity I went nearer. If there was a light on, I could at least check on how she had weathered the storm. But everything was dark.

And then, when I looked up, there she was, fucking honest to God, perched on her rooftop as always, leaning back against the chimney. The pale light of the night reflected dully from her little trunk. The roof itself looked badly damaged, tufts of straw hanging from the edges; it seemed as if part of the chimney had also fallen down. But there she was, as sure as a tombstone.

'Ouma Liesbet?' I called out softly.

She didn't answer, only made a irritable little gesture, clutching her trunk more tightly. It was incredible. All I could think was that she'd gone inside just before the storm and returned to the roof after it had blown over. There was no other way she could have survived that gale.

I realised just how exhausted I was. The day had been too long. I had to get back to my room, and barricade the door, and have an undisturbed sleep for a change.

Up To Heaven

THE NEXT MORNING I first had to work my way through a heavy breakfast while Tant Poppie filled me in on the events of the night. She'd gone to attend to the prisoner, Alwyn Knees, after his release from the tower. Right through the storm she had battled to revive him, trying at the same time to cope with the wife and three small children. It transpired that it was because the woman had fallen pregnant again that Alwyn Knees wanted to surprise her with a pail of stolen water, but then he got caught red-handed; and now the woman was blaming herself for it, and passed out every few minutes. In the last gusts of the storm Alwyn expired and his wife went into convulsions, which ended in a miscarriage. The outcome was that Tant Poppie only came home in the early hours; yet before seven she was already bustling in the kitchen, baking bread.

I was shaken by her news. God, I thought, if only I'd known, I could have offered them the pail of water Isak Smous had sent me with his boy on Sunday afternoon. 'Why didn't the bloody Council of Justice consider the facts?' I stormed. 'Surely there were extenuating circumstances?'

She shook her massive shoulders. 'I know it's hard, Neef Flip. But what will become of us if the law starts making exceptions?'

No way of getting through to her. But what else had I expected?

After breakfast we spent a while over a last mug of coffee. I was dying for a cigarette, but I'd smoked the last one as I got up; what was now to become of me, I preferred not to think about just yet. Depressed about my last Camel, and by Tant Poppie's account of the night's events, I was still staring into the evil brew in my mug when little Piet Snot appeared in the doorway in an even sorrier state than usual.

'Morning, Tant Poppie, morning, Oom. Pa says it's going bad with us too, thank you, and Ouma Liesbet Prune flew up to heaven in the night.'

She must have been blown off the roof, was my first thought; but then I remembered how I'd seen her sitting there well after the wind had died down.

'Where did you hear that?' I asked.

'Everybody says so, Oom. Oom Ben Owl too.' He started choking on a gob of mucus.

'Well, she'd been waiting long enough,' said Tant Poppie, in such a hurry to go that she didn't even bother to remove her soiled apron.

I followed hard on her heels, but Piet Snot plucked me back by the arm. 'Oom?'

'What's up now?'

'Oom forgot the chameleon.'

Cursing under my breath, I hurried back to pick up the chameleon in my room, and then rushed out, followed by the little boy like a streak of snot.

Jesus Christ

A crowd had gathered in the dusty road below Ouma Liesbet's house or what was still left of it. Only now, in the daylight, could I see the full extent of the damage. The back of the roof had blown off, and what remained looked like an old coir mattress someone had ripped open beyond repair.

Ben Owl was addressing the people, but the voices in his head joined in so loudly that it was difficult to distinguish his words from theirs.

Just after midnight, he said, he'd been working behind the house doing some salvaging, when he saw a white cloud approaching from the mountain opposite. It was the kind of shimmering white of a cloud when the full moon shines on it, even though last night there hadn't been much of a moon to speak of. The cloud stopped right above the house, where it began to glow brighter and brighter, until it looked like a brazier filled with flames. As he stood there, fucked out of his mind, the ball of fire began to descend until it was hovering exactly above the chimney where Ouma Liesbet had spent so many years waiting. And when it moved up again, she was gone, except for her little trunk gleaming through the flames, like a white-hot iron in Smith-the-Smith's furnace. For a long time he could still hear her shrill little voice calling out, 'I'm coming, my Lord, I'm coming, oh Jesus Christ!' Afterwards the fire slowly died down and the little white cloud drifted back over the mountains from where it had come.

'Come up and see,' said Ben Owl, turning his large red-rimmed eyes straight to me as if the whole report had been meant for me alone. 'Where the fire picked her up the straw is burnt right through.'

It was true all right. In small groups, to prevent the roof from falling in, we went up the crumbling attic staircase and then along the ridge of the roof to the remains of the chimney. There was a rough black circle burnt through the thatch. One could see the scant furniture in the voorhuis from above: table, chairs, Ben Owl's crumpled bed.

Against that overwhelming evidence there was nothing to bring in. And in the midst of the general amazement I said nothing either.

Shocking White

I thought it prudent to go my own way. I wanted to check on the rest of the storm damage. And it was a fucking depressing sight indeed. Almost no house had escaped unscathed. Several walls had partially collapsed, roofs had fallen in, lean-tos and sheds and chicken-runs had been torn apart and the bits and pieces were strewn all over the place. High up in the bluegum forest I could see a number of bewildered ostriches huddled in the trees. The place looked like the wreck of a fallen plane. It would take bloody weeks to clear up.

Near Jurg Water's shed I heard the familiar chattering of girls' voices and stopped short. I really didn't feel like facing them right now. But before I could get away Henta and her shock of shrikes came bursting through the blown-off door, rushing right past me in a flutter of frocks and arms and legs, like feathers in a poultry-run after a fox had broken in; one could barely distinguish one from the other. Only Henta stood out among them with her ruddy cheeks and wild red hair.

She stopped for a moment as she came past me. Her eyes stared straight at me, frank and impertinent. She gave no sign of remembering what had happened between us before. That first morning here in the shed. The night in the wood. The shocking whiteness of her body under the dress on the Sunday afternoon.

'And how's the world treating you?' I asked with stilted formality, taking a cautious step back, just in case.

'Oh fine.' An uninhibited laugh. 'It's just great.'

The next moment she ran off after the others. She was the only one in this place, I thought, who didn't try to pretend things were going fucking badly. But that wasn't what most preoccupied my thoughts. What struck me, almost like a physical blow, was that she had really not remembered. Yesterday, quite simply, had never happened. For her, *nothing* had yet happened. She existed outside of memory, beyond the reach of history.

Round the corner of the house Jurg Water appeared. He stopped when he recognised me. Made no attempt to greet me, just stood there scowling. He, too, seemed to have no recollection of what we had shared one violent night. This was not the time or the place to confront him. But sooner or later it had to happen. There was a silent appointment between us which would have to be kept.

I walked on again. Now I knew exactly where I was going.

Smoked Ham

IT WAS TIME to seek out a man I'd met only briefly. Without any more delay, tape recorder in my pocket, I took the footpath through the tangle of fynbos in the direction of the hut I'd first seen from Ouma Liesbet's roof.

Hans Magic was sitting on a rickety old paraffin case at his front door, his short legs barely touching the ground, his outlines blurred by a cloud of flies that surrounded him like an aura. A second box had already been set out for me. I could smell him from a distance. Never in my life have I seen such a filthy human being: in full daylight it was even worse than the evening he'd surprised me among Tant Poppie's muti. But he seemed blithely unaware of it himself and welcomed me with a broad grin which revealed all three of his greenish-brown stumps of teeth. The kind of bright-and-clear ugliness Ouma Liesbet Prune had spoken about.

'I was wondering when you were coming to see me,' he said, exhaling a fume of unnameable stenches. 'I was beginning to think you're scared.'

'Should I be scared then?' I challenged him.

He sidestepped me deftly. 'People think all kinds of things. The question is what *you* think.'

'I'm here to find out.'

'You've been putting it off for a long time. But sit down.' He patted the upended box beside him.

I cautiously shifted the box a couple of paces away, out of the worst fumes and the buzzing circle of flies.

Hans Magic had a calabash pipe in his hand. The smell of dagga was unmistakable. He promptly held out the pipe to me. My first reaction was to refuse. My dagga-smoking days were over, and ever since the hassles with Marius I'd been virulently against any form of drugs. Also, if I do have to go to hell one day it'd better be for something really worthwhile, not piddling little sins. Instinctively, my hand moved to my shirt pocket for my packet of Camels, but of course it was empty.

'You have no choice,' grinned Hans Magic, as if he understood my predicament, exhaling a new blue cloud. His face was as weatherbeaten as an old smoked ham.

I hesitated for another moment before accepting the pipe. At least the dagga would camouflage the many other smells.

'What have you got there?' he asked, pointing at my tape recorder.

'This is my own magic,' I joked. 'I catch voices with it.'

'How do you do that?'

'I'll show you.' I'd pressed the Record button just before I arrived; now I wound it back and played him the bit of conversation I'd registered. His colourless eyes flickered when he heard his own voice: *I was wondering when you were coming to see me. I was beginning to think you're scared.* And the rest.

I switched it off.

'You people think you're very clever,' was all he said.

'Do you mind if I use it?'

'Do as you like.' He puffed away, closing his small eyes with pleasure. Then he offered me the pipe again. 'So Ouma Liesbet has left us,' he said.

I inhaled briefly, handed back the pipe and found a comfortable spot for the tape recorder on my lap. As a precaution I kept to the edge of my box. 'How do you know?'

'I just know.'

'Ben Owl says she went to heaven.'

'Who am I to argue with that?' Another puff, before he proffered the pipe again.

'Do you believe it?' I asked, taking care not to inhale too deeply.

'The question is what *you* believe,' he said. 'If you believe she went up, she's there. If not, I suppose she isn't.'

'It can't be so easy, Oom Hans.'

'I didn't say it was easy. Believing may be the most difficult thing of all.'

'I just don't know what to believe.'

His smoke drifted between us like a ghostly presence. I added my own small puff.

Rare Gift

'You didn't come here to talk about Ouma Liesbet, did you?' asked Hans Magic, at peace with the world.

'Did you kill Little-Lukas?' I asked him straight out.

He placed his elbows on his knees, staring into the distance. 'When I was still a little pisser,' he said, 'I discovered a curious thing. I'd be sitting in my ma's kitchen, on the foot-stove, when suddenly a strange feeling would come over me and I'd see somebody's face before me. Then, without knowing what got into me, I'd start to cry and say that person's name. And before nightfall someone would bring news that such and such a one had died.'

'And it still happens?'

'It happens. You see, it's a rare gift. And if you ask me, it comes all the way from old Seer Lermiet himself. But he misused it, and that's a bad thing.' He fell silent for so long that I began to think he'd lost track of his thoughts, but then he resumed. 'At first it scared me. I didn't want to know about it. It's not a pleasant thing to have in you, people start giving you dirty looks, no one wants to have anything to do with you. You can see how far apart I live from them.'

'Were you never married?'

He chuckled. 'Why should I? In my father's family he was the only man who got married and he died young. It doesn't agree with us.'

'It must be a very lonely life.'

'It's really because of my mother,' he said, sucking pensively on the calabash pipe. 'It hit her hard when my father died. She was scared of getting old on her own. And when I was four years old she took me to the church and made me swear an oath on the Bible that I'd never marry but look after her till she died.' A resigned sigh. 'She didn't die before she was in her eighties, and by then my time was over.'

'Did you never regret that oath?'

'Ag.' He cleared his throat. 'When I was younger and before I knew any better, yes, I suppose I did. Once the urge became so great it got as far as the church. But when we stood before the pulpit, my mother got up from her pew and told everybody I took an oath before the Lord, I couldn't break it. And so I came back without my bride.'

'Who was the bride?' I asked.

'It was so long ago it doesn't matter any more.' He began to puff furiously and the flies rose up in a buzzing cloud before coming to rest again.

'Was it Tall-Fransina?' I guessed out loud.

'Leave Fransina out of this.' He narrowed his eyes. 'What did she tell you?'

'I was just asking.'

He sat mumbling to himself for a while. Unsavoury as he was, I couldn't help feeling a tinge of pity for the old fucker. I remembered Tall-Fransina's words, *There was a time when he was very different. Before he became so bitter and so filthy.*

'This loneliness must kill you,' I commiserated.

But his moment of vulnerability had passed. 'I'm well looked after,' he said. 'The women take turns to send me food and things.' He exhaled another godawful whiff over me. 'In the past, when my blood was still warm, they used to send me some tail too, in the evenings. Their way of staying in my good books. Now I'm done with such things. Life gets easier as you grow older.'

He handed me the pipe again. I was beginning to feel more relaxed.

'And the gift has remained with you?'

'All these years, yes.' His eyes gleamed with malicious glee.

'I'd like to know more about it. Little-Lukas told me about a thief you once trapped.'

'Ja. I caught his shoe in Jos Joseph's vice.' He laughed deep in his throat. 'And if you must know, it was Ben Owl who came crawling to me with his shattered foot to claim his shoe and beg for mercy. To this very day he walks with a limp. And I promise you he never tried to steal again. Of course he can't stand the sight of me, but he's shit-scared all the same.'

'Useful gift to have,' I commented. 'You can strike anyone you take a dislike to.'

Heap of Goosefeathers

'It's not for me to decide, man. It either comes over me or it doesn't. That's where Grandpa Lermiet went wrong. You see, he lost interest in his first wife when she became sickly and turned his eye to some-one else. So he told everybody he'd seen a vision that Bilhah was to be his wife and he promptly took her into his bed. No wonder Mina gave up and died. That kind of thing just leads to trouble.' Once again his briny little laugh. But he chose to puff away for a while before he spoke again. 'Now take the widow of old Giel Eyes. She's another one that picked up problems with me. Drieka. One day when old Giel was still alive, she was sitting there on her stoep tear-ing up an old sheet for cloths. I came down from the mountain where I went to have a chat to the old Seer, and I was so thirsty my tongue was like shoe-leather. So I asked her for a drink of water. Now can you imagine, she lost her temper. "Can't you see I'm busy? You bloody old good-for-nothing, you can wait, can't you see I'm tearing cloths?" And right there the feeling came over me. I couldn't help myself. And I said, "All right then, to hell with you, go on tearing cloths, tearing cloths." And off I went.'

'What happened?'

'Drieka has been tearing cloths ever since, I can tell you. She tore up that sheet until it looked like a heap of goose-feathers. And then she started on the curtains. When all her windows were stripped she went on to the next house. That's why you won't see a single curtain in the Devil's Valley. Old Giel got so angry, he was a short-tempered old bastard, he got a stroke and within a week he was dead.'

'And then it stopped?'

'Not a damn. They had to start tying Drieka up in her chair, out of reach of all kinds of cloth. Because if she breaks loose she starts tearing whatever she can lay her hands on. There isn't a single table-cloth or sheet or blanket left in her house. These last few years old Petrus Tatters started calling on her, at first because he felt sorry for the poor thing, so he took her old sheets and stuff to tear up. But one day she got so carried away she tore the clothes from his body and that set them off on new adventures. These days he goes over with or without cloths to tear. Every night, when they think no one sees. That's where he got his name. Petrus Tatters. If he visits Drieka he has to leave all his clothes outside on the stoep, otherwise he goes home bare-arsed.' Through a deeply pleasurable puff he started choking with laughter; I no longer tried to keep up. 'Not that that stops him.'

'Don't you think the poor woman has suffered enough?'

'I told you it's out of my hands. If I get the feeling, I'll make it stop. Otherwise there's nothing I can do. People don't understand, and then they get mad at me. Not that it takes all that much to make them mad.'

'I noticed at yesterday's prayer-meeting,' I said. 'They all had some pretty nasty things to say about the others.'

'That's just the way we are,' he said. 'Everybody knows everything about everybody else, so they can get their teeth into the juiciest bits. At least it keeps life interesting.'

But as he spoke I was wondering: perhaps there was something even worse in the Devil's Valley — the suspicious that *nobody* really knew anything. Because when you know that others are watching all the time, you make sure that they only see what you want to be seen. In the end you reveal nothing at all, and all remain huddled over their own riddles. It's like a pond covered with leaves. Where everything seems so open and exposed, it's easy to miss what lurks below.

Quite Forward

'Are you sure you never misuse your gift, Oom Hans?'

'How do you mean?' He was too far gone from the dagga to become angry, but I did pick up an edge to his voice; and his fumes seemed to give off a more pungent smell than before.

'What have you got against Emma?' I asked him point-blank.

'Is that what she told you?'

'That's what I'm asking you.' I pointed at the tape recorder and reminded him, 'Remember this thing hears everything, and it never forgets.'

He sat staring at the little black gadget for a minute. 'It's Emma who hates me,' he said at last, like a wizened old child trying to pass the buck. 'I never did anything to her. She got a grudge against me because I'm the only man in the Devil's Valley who never fell for her. Not that she hasn't tried. Emma can be quite forward. It was she who kept on asking Poppie to send her over here with food or this and that, a jug of witblits, a jersey or a scarf or a pair of gloves.' He grunted. 'But I don't fall for that.'

I nearly blew a gasket, but the old swine looked so pathetic with indignation that I felt more pity than rage. Also, I knew I should try not to antagonise him, as it could boomerang on Emma. 'All I'm asking, Oom Hans, is that you try to understand. She's been through a rough time.'

'You mustn't believe everything she says.'

His eyes looked at me, a greyish dullness in them, and it took a while for me to remember what they reminded me of: Little-Lukas's ashes in their box, sodden with White Horse. Not a particularly inspiring association.

'Ever since she was a little girl,' he said, 'she got thrashed for the lies she told. Poppie had her hands full with that one.' He began to work himself up. 'She's got this crazy idea that her mother was stoned. Apparently because she got pregnant from a stranger after she ran away from the valley.'

'And it's not true?'

'Not a word of it. That woman, Maria, was much loved in these parts. She made a good marriage and everything, but her husband got killed in an accident when she was six months pregnant. He went on a hunt with some of the other men, and there was some confusion, and he was shot by accident.' After what I'd seen on the porcupine hunt it didn't sound far-fetched at all. 'It sent Maria round the bend and she never fully recovered. Which was why she didn't want to have the child either, so Poppie had to bring Emma up.'

'What became of Maria?'

'She ran away. She was a difficult one, I tell you, and Poppie tried to keep her locked up but every now and then she broke out. They usually went after her and brought her back, but one night she got away. And no one ever found a trace of her again.'

'Even a gifted man like you couldn't find her?'

'Of course I knew what became of her,' he quickly changed tack. 'But by that time she'd already taken her own life, so it was in nobody's interest that I told them. Let her be, that's the way she wanted it.'

I didn't know what to think any more. In a way something felt rounded off; yet it was all still wide open. My thoughts were in the same kind of mess the Devil's Valley had been in that morning, after the storm. It would take a long time to clear up.

Those Children

But I refused to leave it at that. 'Oom Hans, can you swear to God that Maria was not stoned to death?'

'Absolutely.'

'But they do stone people in the settlement? I saw the way they punished Alwyn Knees and I can easily imagine a mob like that stoning somebody.'

'They do indeed.'

'The throwback children: were *they* stoned?'

He just looked at me through a new cloud of dagga smoke. I glanced at the tape recorder. The cassette still had some way to go.

'Were they dark-skinned?'

'You must realise that nothing is as important as the purity of our blood, Neef Flip. In the end you can take away everything from a man, but if his blood is pure you can't touch him.'

'But those children must come from somewhere. Could it be connected in some way with all the old Hottentot stories and super-stitions in the Devil's Valley?'

'Why ask me?'

'Because I have a hunch that you know.'

He grinned, but said nothing.

'Oom Hans, I came here . . .'

'. . . to write up our story. I know.'

'History.'

'One word is as good as another.'

'I must know where those children came from.'

He leaned forward, his chin with its dirty, wispy beard propped up on two cupped hands so encrusted with the filth of a lifetime that one couldn't make out their colour any more. At first it seemed as if he was going to ignore me. But at last he decided to speak.

Dirty Bastards

'All right, I'll tell you. After they survived the hard times in the beginning and the old Seer tamed the Devil's Valley, his family lived untroubled for a few years. Lukas Lermiet and his wife began to prosper.'

'That was Bilhah, I presume?'

'Of course. Don't interrupt. Well, after a few years a tribe of Hottentots moved in here. A heathen lot that stole and plundered and murdered as far as they went. That's mos the way they are. And the Seer couldn't allow such unruliness in his valley. So having seen in a dream that they were coming he called up a commando and went up to meet them. At first the Lermiets tried to negotiate, the Seer was a peaceful man by nature. And in exchange for some beads and a length of copper wire and a couple of half-aums of the witblits they'd already begun to distil in these parts, the Hottentots agreed to bring in a flock of goats, and for a while they all lived together without any trouble. But you can't trust a bunch of heathens like that. Soon there were problems with theft and pilfering and rowdiness, that kind of thing. Lukas Lermiet was a man of law and order, so he had the culprits properly punished. In this manner there was bad feelings building upon both sides, until one of the Seer's grandchildren was murdered in the veld. That was the last straw. He called up his men again to drive the murderers out of this valley for good. And for a while it seemed as if that was that.

'But one night, just as the people were beginning to go back to their old ways, the Hottentots crept back and attacked the settlers in their sleep. Fourteen men, women and children were slaughtered. Lukas Lermiet was tied up by the dirty bastards and forced to watch while they raped his wife. The whole pack of them. And then they scuttled off into the night again.

'Lukas Nimrod was away hunting at the time. He only came back several days after the massacre. Without stopping to rest he rounded up his men again and set out after the Hottentots. They rode on, day and night, until at last they tracked the bastards down and cornered them in a cave. There they visited the judgement of God upon the heathen and only stopped when every man and woman and child and goat and dog was slaughtered. They brought the ears back as trophies, dried like peaches in the sun.

'That was the end of the trouble. Except that Lukas Lermiet's wife turned out to be swelling from the rape, and when the child was born it was black. It was she herself who came forward and asked that the child be killed so that the shame could be wiped out. With her own two hands she put him on that level spot where the church was built in later times, and threw the first stone.'

'But Oom Hans, if that child was killed, how could there have been throwbacks in later generations?'

'The ways of the Lord are inscrutable,' he said firmly. 'It was His way of reminding us of that evil day to warn us against black blood.'

'And it still happens to this day?'

'It happens.'

Too Far Gone

Before he was too far gone I had to get him back to where this whole loop in the conversation had begun. And I asked, as before, 'Oom Hans, did you kill Little-Lukas?'

'You think my power reaches over the mountains?'

'I'm asking *you*. Did you kill Little-Lukas?'

His eyes had a glazed look. 'Do you think it was my doing?'

'I want to know if you got that feeling about Little-Lukas.'

'I can't remember,' he mumbled. His head was drooping.

There was no talk left in him. I got up and pressed Stop on the recorder, and then I left.

When I looked back from some distance away it was just in time to see him sliding from the paraffin case like a doll stuffed with sawdust, covered by the cloud of flies. For a moment I considered going back to check whether he was still alive, but then I heard him snore. And the fucking stench was so powerful that I thought it wise to keep away.

Telling Lies

ALL DAY LONG there was a bustle in the graveyard, what with two new graves being dug for the next day's double funeral: old Bart Biltong, who already lay waiting in Lukas Death's mortuary, and the poor water thief who'd died in the night, Alwyn Knees.

In the afternoon I withdrew to my bedroom to start writing up my tapes. Just as I was working on the conversation with Hans Magic the door unexpectedly opened and Tant Poppie appeared, visibly upset.

'What is going on here?' she asked. 'I thought I heard visitors.'

I pointed at the little tape recorder. 'I showed you this thing before, remember?'

'You didn't tell me it spoke in voices.' She remained at a safe distance. 'This looks like bad magic, Neef Flip.'

'Outside the Devil's Valley it is very common, Tant Poppie.'

'What if it infects us all?'

'It's like Hans Magic's gift,' I said with a straight face. 'There's nothing wrong with it as long as one doesn't misuse it.'

I pressed Start. Hans Magic's voice said, '. . .Emma can be quite forward. It was she who kept on asking Poppie to send her over here with food and this and that, a jug of witblits, a jersey or a scarf she'd knitted. But I don't fall for that.' I pressed Stop.

'Now you're going too far, Hans!' Tant Poppie exploded. She looked at me with deep suspicion in her tiny eyes. 'Where is Hans? Is he in that little box?'

'Only his voice, Tant Poppie.'

'That box is telling lies,' she said aggressively. 'It was Hans Magic who filled Emma's head with nonsense. I told him she was just a child, he already had his chance with Tall-Fransina and missed it, he mustn't expect other people to make his bed for him now. But he started to threaten me in all kinds of ways. So in the end I had to put Emma out of my house, I didn't want trouble like that to hatch under my roof.' She was shaking with indignation. 'You must tell that box to stop spreading these lies, Neef Flip. It'll land us all in trouble.'

It Was Music

It was hard to keep my cool throughout supper, but Tant Poppie was in no hurry and I couldn't afford to show my impatience. After the meal she continued for what seemed like hours preparing her potions (even this stench had became bearable after my visit to Hans Magic). But at long last the house fell quiet and half an hour later I slipped out. In my pocket was the little tape recorder, and from the partly repaired shed I took a spade and a pick I'd set aside earlier.

There was light in Emma's room at the back of Isak Smous's house. Having first checked that there were none of the habitual marauders about – Prickhead, Ben Owl, old Petrus Tatters, or perhaps Henta and her coven – I knocked softly on her window. She jumped up from the table where she'd been sewing: although she must have been expecting me, the sound clearly startled her. She bent over and blew out the candle. Moments later she joined me.

'Emma . . .'

She pressed a finger to my lips and motioned with her head to move away from the houses, in the direction of the graveyard.

Once there, she said, 'You're late. I thought perhaps something happened to you.'

'Tant Poppie wouldn't go to bed.' I took the tape recorder from the back pocket of my jeans and gave it to her.

'Music?' she asked with such genuine excitement in her voice that it made me feel guilty. 'You know, I think that's what I miss most of all.'

'I wish it was music. But it's only old Hans Magic's voice.'

'Don't tell me you went to see him?' She was clearly upset.

'I couldn't put it off any longer. And I want you to hear what he said about your mother.'

'I didn't think you'd discuss it with him.'

'Don't say anything now. First listen.'

Her voice became dark and reproachful. 'Flip, I trusted you.'

For a moment I wished I could undo the whole fucking interview with Hans Magic. But I knew it was vital. And she *had* to listen.

Even in the dark I could feel her deep resentment, but I pushed the Play button.

Mocking Hiss

The tape made a faint hiss. It went on for several minutes.

'When does it start?' she asked irritably.

'Any moment.' But already I became aware of pressure pulsing in my temples. The conversation with Hans Magic should have started well before this. I switched off the instrument, rewound the tape, tried again. The same uncommunicative hiss.

Fast forward. Play. Fuck-all. Fast forward again. And again. But there was only the mocking hiss.

I turned off the recorder. 'It's broken. But this afternoon it was still fine.'

She shrugged impatiently. 'Now you'll just have to tell me what he said.'

I didn't have the courage to confront her. I mean, if Hans Magic had said it in his own voice it would have been different; whatever blame there might be he would have had to take himself. Coming from me it would be like a straight accusation.

Whether it was from irritation or a wish to make it easier for me, I couldn't tell, but she suddenly said, 'I suppose he said I lied to you.'

'He said you didn't know what really happened,' I tried to soften the blow.

'It's nothing new for them to say I'm lying. He most of all. I warned you the first time, didn't I?'

'Emma, you must try to understand.'

'You told him what I said,' she insisted, in that tone of bitter reproach. 'Why? Because you had doubts about me yourself?'

'It's not that. You must understand, if I want to write anything that's worth its salt every fact must be doubled-checked.'

'So Hans Magic told you they never stoned my mother, she ran away and disappeared in the mountains.'

I felt a turd. 'More or less, yes.'

'Why do you think it is so important to him to make a liar out of me?'

'What happened between you and him?'

'Nothing happened. That's why. Because he wanted to. Tant Poppie sent me to him. I thought it was just for the food. I never knew they were in cahoots. I had to throw a whole pot of hot porridge in his face to get away. He shouted after me that Little-Lukas would pay for it.'

Own World

'Are you sure Tant Poppie was in cahoots with him?'

'Why do you think I moved out?'

My head was reeling. 'But she said . . .'

'. . . that she threw me out?' A derisive laugh. 'And you believe them. You believe every one of them. And behind my back you try to find out from them if *I* am lying.'

'That's not so, Emma, I swear.'

'Do you believe Hans Magic, or me?'

'You know what I believe.'

'How can I be sure? Perhaps it's just as well you're going back to your own world on Saturday. There's nothing here for you.'

I couldn't control myself any longer. I grabbed her by the wrists. 'Emma. For God's sake, listen to me!'

'You're hurting me.'

'I just want you to listen. And to believe me, please!'

She turned away. With her back to me she said, 'Believing doesn't come by itself.'

'Jesus, Emma, you *matter* to me. Can't you see that?'

She made no movement, uttered no sound. Perhaps she was crying. Or perhaps it was fucking presumptuous of me even to think so.

Blindly, I stormed on, 'This is not what I wanted, Emma. But you're the first person in God knows how many years I've really cared for. I know it's impossible, I know it fucks up everything for you. But I can't go away from here if you think I betrayed you.'

'You're going away whatever happens.'

'You must go with me,' I blurted out impulsively.

'No.' She turned back to me, her face still invisible in the dark. The moon wasn't yet out. 'You know I can't.'

'There must be a way.'

'There isn't.'

Old and Decayed

I don't know for how long we stood there, struggling against each other, trapped by each other. A jumble of thoughts and memories was tumbling about inside me; I could no longer explain what was happening, what I felt, what I so desperately wanted. All I knew was that I didn't dare let go of her. I felt like we were drowning. And I wanted to save her, the way I'd pulled her from the Devil's Hole the day before; but that had been nothing compared to this night's hell. Without uttering a word we were having the most urgent discussion imaginable, a bloody desperate kind of osmosis.

After a very long time her resistance, as far as I could tell, began to ebb away. But she remained very straight and unyielding. And of course she was right. Without a future I had fuck-all to offer her.

She wanted to go home, but I begged her to stay.

'Let us at least dig up the grave.'

'To check if I lied?'

'Don't ever say that again. I want to give you something to hold on to.'

'And if we find nothing?'

'Then we'll go on looking until we know for sure what happened to her. Even if the whole damned valley tries to cover up.'

She didn't answer. But unexpectedly, and just for a moment, she pressed my hand. Perhaps it was by accident. But I wanted to believe she meant it.

By myself I thought: the one person who would not have lied was Ouma Liesbet Prune. She'd been too close to death for lies to matter any more. And it had been her own coffin she'd given to Maria. If *she* hadn't known, who would?

The moon was not yet visible, but a faint glimmering was appearing behind the mountains. It wasn't difficult to locate the old headstone, even if the question mark was not visible in the dark. But with my fingers I could read it, like Braille.

The earth was surprisingly soft. I didn't even need to use the pick. The doddering old gardeners obviously did a thorough job. Thirty, forty centimetres I went down, then a metre, and still the soil was loose.

'There's something strange going on here,' I said to Emma.

The moonlight was getting stronger.

'Watch out,' she said. 'There's something there.'

'Must be the coffin.'

But it was too soft for a coffin. I kneeled beside the grave and began to burrow with my hands. It was a roll of blankets. There was something inside. A body.

After we'd lifted the roll out of the grave and laid it down beside the heap of earth I'd dug from it, we glanced at each other, but neither said anything.

Inside, when we opened it, we both immediately recognised the face, even in the faint light. It was Ouma Liesbet Prune. One side of her head had been bashed in and it was caked with dried black blood.

Four

Dusty Quinces

THE HEADSTONES WERE faintly luminous in the dark, but it could have been an effect of the moonlight. The dead must be about. But the sounds of invisible fucking thriving in other nights were absent. Out of respect, I could only guess, for Ouma Liesbet cheated out of her ascent to heaven. One could smell the drought in the air, a curious bittersweetness, like dusty quinces, the smell of Africa.

I didn't know for how long we had been sitting there. I'd closed the flap of the blanket again, it was not an appetising sight; but we hadn't moved since then. The moon was sliding downhill to the west, the stars were no longer where they'd been when we found her. Orion had begun to move in behind the mountains, the Southern Cross lay suspended upside down above the farthest peak. The other constellations escaped me. I'm a dud with stars, as I suppose with most things. I'm the product of a difficult birth, my mother always complained. It was as if I refused to let go, and who can bloody well blame me? In the end I was pulled out with fucking forceps. And as he laid me in my mother's arms the doctor, who must have been something of a seer himself, said in a commiserating tone of voice, 'Mrs Lochner, you shouldn't expect too much of this one.' Whenever I disappointed her, which was most of the time, she would repeat the story to me. In the end we grow into the stories laid out for us like clothes for a new day.

'What are we going to do with her?' asked Emma, not for the first time.

We'd already considered everything. Tant Poppie? Even she

couldn't raise the dead. Hans Magic? That might be jumping from the frying pan into the live coals. Or should we call on Lukas Death? In matters of life and death he was the obvious man to make the decisions. Perhaps we should simply carry the body to the church and wait for the reaction when the people gathered in the morning to bury Alwyn Knees and old Bart Biltong. This had been Emma's idea, and there was much going for it. The less we had to do with it the better. But there would be questions asked, I'd argued, and sooner or later, in one way or another, they'd get to us, and then the shit would truly hit the fan.

Nakedness of Her

'We can't leave her here all night, Flip.'

It wasn't cold, but I could feel her shivering lightly against me. I looked at the dark bundle on the ground beside us. For the first time I began to understand something more about the way in which the dead in this place continued to haunt the living. In a sense they are more real than the living, because the living merely pursue their own lives, but we assume the dead. It is only through us they can work through the unfinished business they left behind.

'Why don't we simply fill up the grave and leave her here for someone else to find?' I suggested.

'Then they can get Jurg Water to point out the murderer with his rod,' she said flippantly.

And that gave me an idea. 'Emma, let's bury her again. I'll do the pointing out myself in the morning.'

'But how? And why? It's just asking for trouble.'

'On the contrary. I think it's going to give me just the kind of hold on them I need.'

I briefly explained what I had in mind. She remained sceptical for a while, and even when she understood she still seemed fearful.

'I think it's too dangerous, Flip.'

'I'll protect you,' I assured here. 'No one need ever know that you were here with me.'

'I'm not worried about myself, it's you.'

The nakedness of her words was so disarming that for a moment I couldn't speak. Then I said, 'I promise you I'll be careful.'

'Do you honestly think it will work?'

'It's a chance I just have to take.'

She helped me to slide the roll of blankets back into the shallow grave, then to fill it up again and restore as best we could the little patch of succulents and papery septennials on top.

We had to go, yet we still tried to put it off for as long as possible. It wasn't the shock as such that paralysed us, but something more difficult to explain. A sense, perhaps, of complicity. With death, and with the dead. Even if nothing else had happened between us before, there was now a kind of fatality that bound us. It was frightening, yet curiously and darkly comforting too. Whatever might yet happen, we were in it together. And maybe, in our circumstances, this was already more than we could have hoped for. For a hungry man even a quince that constricts the throat is succulent luxury.

Pestering Her

It was a wrench to turn away from her at Isak Smous's dark house, but we had no choice. She was still frightened, but I made her promise to barricade her door.

Tired as I was, I just couldn't sleep. Everything that had happened continued to haunt me. God knows, we were still no closer to a solution of the goddamn riddle about Emma's mother. The discovery of Ouma Liesbet's death only compounded it. Who could have decided so treacherously to use the old woman's hope of going up to heaven to get rid of her? Why would anybody have wished to do away with such a harmless old soul anyway? She'd never threatened anyone. All she'd done was to perch on her roof like a fucking old cat. And yet it would seem that that had been offence enough for someone to bash in her frail little skull.

Our crime reporter in the role of detective.

One by one I worked through all the inhabitants of the Devil's Valley I'd met. Lukas Death and his wife Dalena. Tant Poppie

Fullmoon, Hans Magic, Jurg Water, Petrus Tatters, Tall-Fransina, Brother Holy, Gert Brush, Smith-the-Smith, Jos Joseph, Job Raisin, the whole bloody caboodle. As far as I knew no one had ever paid much attention to her. They'd hardly mentioned her in all the conversations I'd had with them. I knew everybody seemed to be constantly bad-mouthing everybody else, but in a way Ouma Liesbet had long ago drifted out of the muddy whirlpool of their gossip. And I couldn't remember anything from her own past which could still stir up resentment against her. The only person she saw regularly was Ben Owl who brought her food and drink and spent a few minutes in conversation with her on the roof every night. And I, of course.

Could that have been the reason? But who could possibly have been so upset about my visits as to murder her?

I shook the gravel of our few conversations through the sieve of my memory, but no diamond was left behind; not even a bantom. Except perhaps her promise to tell me 'everything' the next time I came? But surely that had been only between the two of us? The memory made me sit up. I saw once again Ben Owl's head popping up from the edge of the roof as we spoke. Wasn't there something suspicious about that? He was supposed to sleep all day and only come out in the dark.

But even if he had overheard part of our conversation, what was so unusual about it? What were we talking about when he appeared?

I got up and started walking about the room to exercise my thoughts as I tried to edge back, step by step, into our conversation. She'd called me up to the roof, right. I was on my way home with the two little skulls. Right again. It was coming back to me now. It was Maria we'd been talking about. Her death, the headstone with the question mark on it. I'd asked Ouma Liesbet why, if Maria was indeed her relative, she'd been brought up by Tant Poppie rather than by her own family. And then? Then she'd said something like, 'Because Ben Owl was pestering her.' Spurred on by the fucking voices in his head? Yes, that was it. And it must have been at that very moment he'd popped up to ask what we'd been skindering about him.

Afterwards, she'd told me her version of the Hottentot story about the first man who'd looked up from under the tree at his wife. The story Ouma Liesbet had so effortlessly transposed to Adam and Eve. That was when she'd promised to tell me everything the next time she saw me. But in the evening the storm came up and this morning Ben Owl, well past his bedtime, was telling everybody about how she'd gone up to heaven in the night.

Ben Owl, you're my man.

Much Too Much

I was tempted to go out there and then and confront Ben Owl. But I checked myself. My tape recorder was still screwed up and even if I managed to force a confession out of the old nightwalker, who would believe me? It had to be done in public, if at all. And for that I had to wait for the funeral.

But by now I felt bloody claustrophobic. My thoughts needed fresh air.

Deceptively peaceful, the large hand of the night cupped over me. There was no sound, but I knew well enough that there were all sorts of things happening beyond the limits of my hearing, a whole wilderness of life and death that could surely drive one mad if ever it invaded the conscious mind. In spite of my good intentions, I set off towards Ouma Liesbet's house. I mean, how could I stay away?

And there I saw her perched on the roof again, as always.

Clear as daylight. With the fucking little tin trunk on her drawn-up knees, her back leaned against the chimney. Just for a moment. When I looked up again she was gone. Down below, behind one of the black windows, I thought I saw movement.

I hurried away much faster than was necessary, but thank heavens there was no one to see me. At least not as far as I could make out; but the feeling of being observed by invisible eyes everywhere in the night was very strong.

Nowhere in the whole settlement was there any light. Even the back of Isak Smous's house was dark.

One way or another I got to the bluegum forest. I fell over a branch and grazed my palms. I didn't even feel like fucking cursing. As I stumbled to my feet again, dusting my clothes, I had an idea. I retrieved the branch in the dark and held it up against the moonlight. There was a fork in it I could use. My wanderings in the dark had not been fruitless after all.

After stripping the branch of all its twigs and dry leaves, I went home. In my room, by candlelight, I must have spent about an hour trying to carve it into a proper shape: a fork with two short handles and a long tail. Not a very professional job, I've never been a handyman (as Sylvia used to remind me at least once a week for thirty years); but it would do for my purpose. The activity helped me to get my thoughts under some kind of control. There was something familiar about it, which at first I couldn't place. But then I remembered: weekday evenings at home, when I was a child, sitting at a corner of the kitchen table doing my homework, Ma paging through a magazine or laying out patterns on the table to cut out material for the dressmaking she did for a meagre income of her own; while Pa sat whittling away at little bits of wood for catapults, or stakes for his beans and tomatoes, or the occasional whip-handle for which his bywoner father had once been renowned; but as time passed the whittling became an end in itself. He would start by cutting a stick to the right length, then peel away the bark, and simply go on whittling and whittling away until there was fuck-all left; and then he would get up without even looking at the scattered shavings on the floor, and wind up the clock in the passage and go to bed.

Somewhere in the course of my own whittling that night I must have fallen asleep from sheer exhaustion, because when the church bell started tolling on the Friday morning, I woke up on my bed, still fully clothed, beside the white divining rod; and on the chair next to the bed the candle had burnt out in its pool of congealed wax.

Cheer Up the Men

'I CAN DIE FOR a good funeral,' said Tant Poppie over the breakfast table. 'We mustn't be late.' The 'we' made things easier for me.

The church was full to capacity. In a community where this is the most important, if not the only, form of recreation, it came as no surprise. But it took bloody stamina to resist the heat and the heavy smell of armpits, crotches and feet. Fortunately it was still quite early in the morning, so there were no faintings. Under my windbreaker the forked stick was rather uncomfortable, but I had no choice and surely the cause deserved some kind of sacrifice.

My eyes very soon found Emma among the women, but she didn't once look in my direction.

Brother Holy was his eloquent self again. A ringmaster in a fucking circus. And with consummate skill he fused the themes of drought and death.

'Neither of the two brethren who are to be laid to rest today,' he intoned, 'would have been here had it not pleased the Lord to visit us with drought.'

Fucking old hypocrite. Only five days ago he'd joined in, with the same wild relish as the others, in the savage flogging of the very man he was burying today; yet all could be neatly fitted into the Great Plan of God. And without any transition he opened the floor.

This time the prayers were shorter, and the tempers more frayed. Jos Joseph warned God that if things didn't improve they'd be running out of souls soon. And out of wood too, as he couldn't be expected to provide decent coffins at this rate. Which was a gross exaggeration, since Alwyn Knee's coffin was a slap-up job made of off-cuts and boards for which there was no other use, a bloody disgrace. Lukas Death was concerned that the children's education was buggered up by all the interruptions caused by prayer-meetings and the preparation of bodies for burial. Most of the other jobs in the Devil's Valley, God was told in no uncertain terms, were also under threat: Tall-Fransina needed water to cool her witblits as it came from the still; Smith-the-Smith had to have a bucket ready for the irons from his furnace; Gert Brush complained about sweeping the roads without water to sprinkle for the dust to settle; Tant Poppie needed boiling water for births and her concoctions; Jurg Water felt that his authority at home was undermined if his daughter couldn't wash the family's feet before supper at night, and people were beginning to snigger because he could no longer divine the tracery of subterranean courses. And so it went on. Bettie Teat seemed to be the only person who still had some moisture on offer to cheer up the men in the settlement.

Taken Off My Clothes

After Brother Holy had once more reminded the Lord of the trouble they'd had digging two graves in the bone-dry earth, the congregation was invited to proceed to the cemetery. I'd have to make my move quite soon now, but I still didn't know how to find an opening. In this mood there was rather less hope of success than I'd expected. But I didn't have much choice. This place had become to me the threshold between the familiar and the impossible.

On the way out I glanced at Emma again. This time my eyes fleetingly caught hers. But she gave no sign of recognition. She only looked frightened.

In solemn procession the whole settlement filed out through the stained front door of the church, and from there round the building to the cemetery. Near the front, right behind Brother Holy, Lukas Death and the pall-bearers with the two coffins, was the pale, drawn widow of Alwyn Knees, her eyes hollow and feverish. With three wretched little kids clinging to her, she was conspicuously isolated from the rest of the congregation. As we entered through the wide whitewashed gate the woman faltered and had to lean against one of the blunt white pillars to stay on her feet. She seemed on the verge of collapse, yet no one came forward to help her. The little ones clutched her legs and started whimpering.

Even if it turned the mood against me, I couldn't leave the poor woman to her fucking fate like that. Stepping out of my place in the procession, I hurried towards her and put my arm around her. It was shocking to discover how thin she was. Her deadly white face looked up at me in fright, but I refused to let go.

'Let me help you,' I said through my teeth. 'Come on.'

With the three children still holding on to her dress for dear life, we went on. The people kept a safe distance between us and them. We progressed to the two new graves dug side by side against the far-thest wall. By this time the woman was hanging so heavily on my arm that I made her sit down on the nearest tombstone. A few people were muttering under their breath. There was trouble brewing. But then, to my surprise and relief, Tant Poppie broke from the crowd and seated herself beside the widow. The stone tilted into a slightly lopsided position, but it held. She scooped up all three children in one large arm and held them on her broad lap, where they sat too petrified to utter a sound.

Brother Holy was getting ready to practise his scales, but he had to wait until the crowd had calmed down again after the brief distur-bance. I'm not sure that was the most opportune moment, but it was bloody well now or never. Leaving the widow to Tant Poppie's care I stepped forward to the preacher's side.

It felt like the first time I'd taken off my clothes in front of a woman, not knowing how she was going to react to my hairy body. Fucking naked I came into the world, I thought, and fucking naked I stand before you today. Do your damnedest, you bastards. From all the faces swimming in the haze before me I picked out Emma's eyes, large and very black below the straight dark brows in her pale face. And then the bedlam in me subsided into a strange kind of calm.

Message

'Thank you for the opportunity, Brother,' I said solemnly, as if it had all been agreed beforehand. I saw him gasping for breath in indignation, but before he could call on Isaiah, Jeremiah, Ezekiel and their lesser brethren to assist him, I plunged right in: 'It is an honour and a privilege to stand before you today as the guest of Grandpa Lukas Lermiet, even if the message entrusted to me is a sad one indeed.' I fell silent in what I hoped was a pregnant pause. 'Three funerals in one day is a heavy blow for any community.'

If my first pause was equal to a pregnancy of, say, six months, the second one was close to full-term. I allowed the wave of surprise to run through the whole congregation.

'Let me explain,' I said in a tone of great solemnity, 'my brothers and sisters.' Those were words I'd always dreamed of speaking in public. I know Ma had originally cherished ecclesiastical ambitions for me, but after the brief encounter with Maureen behind the sofa they were abandoned. Today I was finally living up to her expectations. Look, Ma, both hands.

'The late Ouma Liesbet Prune appeared to me last night,' I announced. The second wave of reaction was even stronger than the first. I was beginning to relish the kind of power a man like Brother Holy takes for granted. 'I was unable to sleep. My mind was heavy inside me. I went for a walk in the night. And as I passed Ouma Liesbet's house I heard her calling my name. She was sitting on her rooftop as always.' It was not altogether a lie. 'And then she spoke to me.'

Brother Holy began to move beside me: a curious, rhythmic bending and stretching of his knees as if he was preparing to jump. But by now I had the congregation in my hand. The feeling of power was delirious.

'Ouma Liesbet asked me to convey a message to the Devil's Valley on this sad occasion.'

And from there, if I say so myself, I launched into an inspired address about how her lifelong desire to ascend to heaven had been cut short by murder most foul. She had shown me the fatal wound on her head. I had no idea, I told them, of what had become of her, but she had promised to lead me to her grave during today's ceremony. I could not guarantee success, I was a stranger in their midst, but with God's mercy and Ouma Liesbet's help I was prepared to do my best. If they would so permit me. With these words I produced my divining rod from under my windbreaker.

Emma stood staring fixedly at the ground before her as if she meant to look a hole right into it. Tant Poppie had her hands full with the young widow and her children. But the others were agog with excitement.

Brother Holy next to me had finally found his voice again, and a fine voice it was. In a fucking stentorian rage he began, 'Brothers and sisters . . .'

But he was drowned out by the crowd.

'Thank you, Brother,' I said, looking through the assembled people. 'Do I have your consent?'

Whether the clamour signified yes or no, I didn't bother to find out. Like a weathered water-diviner, with the slow, measured steps I'd seen Jurg Water taking on his rounds every day, I started pacing through the cemetery, concentrating like hell. And the whole crowd, except for Tant Poppie and her pathetic little group on the precariously tilted stone, followed me at a safe distance. I stretched the process for as long as I could. Up one row, down the next, then up again, and down again. The white stick, stripped of its bark, pointed straight ahead. I could only hope that the sweat on my brow would be interpreted as a sign of effort, not of trepidation. Because behind all the bravado I knew only too bloody well what was at stake.

Donkey Stallion

Just before I reached the tombstone inscribed with the question mark, the stick actually began to swivel in my hands. I was concentrating so furiously that it began to feel as if the forked stick had a life of its own. Like the dong of a donkey stallion it swung up with such a force that it nearly hit me between the eyes. Then down again. And then it started whirring in circles. With this kind of show I could soon qualify as a drum majorette. The first movement of the rod had caused a collective intake of breath, the second a reverberating groan. By the time the rod was swivelling over the unknown grave the crowd went fucking bonkers.

I stopped dead. 'Here,' I announced, quite unnecessarily. 'Ouma Liesbet wants us to dig right here.'

'But,' interposed Brother Holy.

No one paid any attention to him. The people were totally carried away. They swarmed around the grave, trampling one another for the best view. Right at the back, pale and unmoving, stood Emma.

'Are there any volunteers to do the digging . . .?' I asked respectfully.

The spades with which the men had been slaving away the day before still stood against the wall near the two graves. There was a stampede in that direction. Four or five men started digging furiously, nearly severing whatever feet got in the way. Thank God they were all wearing shoes today.

'Slowly, slowly,' I warned them. 'We can strike something at any moment.'

'Perhaps it's water,' suggested Lukas Death in a hopeful voice.

'This man knows nothing about finding water,' growled Jurg Water. I didn't like the look he gave me.

Dull Thud

In spite of my warnings the digging proceeded furiously. Until, suddenly, there was the sound of a dull thud as the first spade struck the roll of blankets. Everybody fell quiet. The diggers dropped to their knees and began to scrape away the soil with their hands. I remained standing with the forked stick in my hands. As they exposed the blanket, the rod swung up for the last time. The crowd fell back in awe.

I don't know whether he'd been in the throng all along, but I hadn't noticed him before the men raised the dusty bundle from the hole and laid it beside the fresh mound where they folded back the flap. Only now did I see him among them, blinking his weak, watery eyes in the daylight. Ben Owl.

In the stunned silence I said, 'Ben?'

'Why are you talking to me?' he asked aggressively, his voice breaking into falsetto.

'What do you think happened here?' I asked.

'Perhaps the Good Lord dropped her,' he said.

'It doesn't look like a fall to me,' I replied. 'It looks more like a blow to the head.'

'Perhaps she tried to resist when the Lord came to fetch her,' he stammered. 'So he had to whack her with a spade.'

The crowd did not seem impressed. But now they were turning to me for an answer, and I had no wish to be drawn too deeply into it.

'Ouma Liesbet only asked me to find her body,' I said. 'I'm sure we can safely leave the rest to Lukas Death's capable hands.'

He approached hesitantly, looking quite unprepared for the task that lay ahead.

'Don't you think the body should be taken to your place?' I suggested.

He made a helpless gesture. 'Let us not be too hasty,' he said. 'We must first find out what the people think.'

But nobody could come up with a practical suggestion; they were still too stunned.

In my hands the divining rod made another twisting movement. There was an outcry from the front row. I knew I was taking a hell of a risk, but it might be my last chance before I left in the morning.

'I'm not sure at all,' I announced, 'but the rod is still pulling down. Perhaps we should dig deeper.'

There was no shortage of volunteers. And within seconds the digging was resumed.

Delicate Carving

From here the soil was much harder, and it was bloody heavy going. But the men took turns. No one wanted to miss out. Whenever they appeared to slack down I gave another jerk to the stick. It did wonders. The only one to stare at me unflinchingly, his eyes blazing, was Jurg Water. I doubted whether he'd ever forgive me this intrusion on his professional territory. But there was only one more day; after that I needn't worry about him again.

I had no idea myself of what to expect next. At least it was a relief to see someone else do the dirty work.

In the background Emma still stood like a kind of caryatid, both her fists pressed to her mouth, chewing her knuckles. I knew what was at stake for her. If only I could go to her, put an arm around her. But of course that was out of the question.

'Do you really think there's something here?' asked one of the diggers. Their faces were coated with a crust of grime. The hole was about man-deep.

'Ouma Liesbet wasn't very clear on this point,' I said. 'You must remember she was very weak. All I could make out was, "You must dig deep, boetie, you must dig deep."'

At that very moment, as if fucking destiny itself had taken things in hand, one of the spades struck wood. The rod in my hands turned several somersaults.

A coffin became visible through dust and gravel and dry lumps of earth. A very old, very decayed coffin. Even so, the delicate carving on the lid was still visible.

Immediately after the men had lifted the coffin from the hole, Jos Joseph kneeled beside it to trace the pattern with skilled fingers.

'This is my grandfather's handiwork,' he said. 'I'd recognise it anywhere.'

A few of the older men nodded in agreement. Tant Poppie also made her appearance, having temporarily left the widow and her children in Dalena's care.

'Ja, this is Ouma Liesbet's coffin,' she announced without a moment's hesitation. 'It used to stand in her voorhuis. I remember it well. But one night it disappeared, we all thought it was stolen. The whole of the Devil's Valley spoke about it. Nobody ever saw it again, and Ouma Liesbet refused to have a new one made. It was from that moment that she started talking about going up to heaven.

Now, is that true, Ben Owl, or isn't it?'

He shrivelled under the stare from her darting black eyes. 'It's true, Poppie,' he mumbled, and tried to back away, but fell over the mound of earth piled up behind him.

'Ouma Liesbet told me she'd given her coffin to a woman called Maria,' I said sternly.

The name made waves through the crowd. I couldn't look directly at Emma, but from the corner of my eye I could see her coming towards us like a sleepwalker.

'Perhaps we should open it,' I said. My jaws were tight.

The men beside the coffin hesitated.

'This is sacrilege,' exclaimed Brother Holy.

Then Lukas Death spoke up behind me, 'No, open it up.'

Took Some Doing

But the mystery had to remain a mystery for a while longer, because before anything could be done about Lukas Death's order there was an interruption: Tant Poppie jostled the people surrounding the coffin out of her way to demand that Bart Biltong and Alwyn Knees be laid to rest without more ado so that the suffering widow could be taken home.

That gave Brother Holy an opportunity to salvage some of his lost dignity, although Tant Poppie's threatening presence prevented him from opening the taps of his eloquence too widely. Also, his congregation had become so restless in the presence of all the riddles waiting to be solved, that he deemed it wise to cut the rest of the ceremony down to more manageable proportions. From the way he punctuated his oratory with smouldering glances in my direction it was very clear that he held me personally responsible for the disturbance of his sacred duties; but to hell with him.

The last amen still hovered overhead like a cloud of dust when Tant Poppie and Dalena-of-Lukas helped the widow and her wretched family from the half-capsized headstone and escorted them away through the cemetery. Seldom, I was convinced, had two graves in the Devil's Valley been filled up so quickly. Everybody was in a hurry to get back to the third hole. The stone with the question mark on it lay to one side, in silent reproach, next to the insignificant human bundle under the dirty grey blanket. But even Ouma Liesbet Prune was temporarily forgotten in the general excitement to see what was hidden in the half-decayed old coffin.

There was yet another delay when Jos Joseph insisted on first fetching the proper tools from his shed before getting on with the delicate task of removing the lid without damaging his grandfather's carvings. There was something like pride in one's handiwork, he argued.

But in only a few minutes he was back, carrying a long box filled with chisels and wedges and hammers and screwdrivers of various shapes and sizes, and the rest of us stood back in due respect to watch a dedicated artisan go about his business. The man had poetry in his rough hands. The way in which he dislodged those rusty screws and severed the perfect joints that held the mouldering boards together, took some doing.

But in the end it was a bloody wasted effort, because when at last, with endless patience and precision, he removed the lid, the coffin was empty.

Moth and Rust

It said something for the quality of the work done by Jos Joseph's grandfather that the upholstery inside showed almost no sign of decay. Moth and rust had been kept at bay with a dedication that apparently caused even death to think twice. Several of us squatted down for a closer look. The white silk upholstery was stained here and there with faded brownish marks of a kind that made a crime reporter suspect the fucking worst. But I said nothing.

After a long time Lukas Death rose to his feet again, wiping his hands on his sides as if to rid them of invisible stains.

'The coffin,' he announced solemnly, 'is empty.'

It took a while for his finding to sink in.

'But how can this be?' he asked. 'We've dug up graves more than once in the past, and there's always something left behind. Not pleasant to look at, but *something*. And in this coffin there is nothing.'

'But who would bother to bury an empty coffin?' asked Brother Holy.

'There are marks,' I said, pointing at the stains.

'What exactly did Ouma Liesbet tell you?' asked Lukas Death.

'All she said was that the woman called Maria was buried in her coffin.'

'*Who* did the burying?' asked Jurg Water, as if I was the one accused before them.

I preferred to stay out of this post-mortem shit: and to my relief Lukas Death took charge. 'Ben Owl?' he asked.

It Was Dark

Everybody turned towards the unhappy man standing well apart from us, his two wings drooping.

'I must go to bed,' he complained. 'This is not the time to bother me.'

'Did you or didn't you dig this grave?' insisted Lukas Death in a relentless tone of voice I hadn't expected of him. Not a man to be underestimated, I suddenly realised.

'What else could I do?' whined Ben Owl. 'Ouma Liesbet told me to.'

'And did you put a body in the coffin?'

'Ouma Liesbet told me to.'

'Whose body was it?'

'I couldn't see, it was dark.'

'You always see in the dark.'

'No!' protested Ben Owl with unexpected vehemence. 'In those days I was like everybody else. It was only afterwards that I started walking about in the night. Because I couldn't sleep in the dark any more, you see. I was afraid of the ghosts.'

'What did you do then to make you so afraid?' demanded Lukas Death.

'Nothing. I saw nothing.'

'Then why would the ghosts haunt you?'

'I don't know anything,' whimpered Ben Owl. 'I swear.'

'But you did bury somebody in this coffin?'

'Ouma Liesbet told me to.'

'Where did you find the body?'

'In Ouma Liesbet's bedroom. On the floor.'

'How did it get there?'

'I just found it there.'

'And she ordered you to bury it?'

'Yes, she did.'

'Did you always do whatever she said?'

Ben Owl shut his red eyes and didn't answer.

'You were a big strong man,' Lukas Death went on relentlessly. 'She was a frail old woman, at least fifty years older than you. Surely you could have refused if you wanted to.'

'I couldn't. She said there were stories she would tell if I didn't obey.'

'What stories?'

'Stories she made up. Everybody knows what a liar Ouma Liesbet was.' He turned his eyes back to me. 'She lied to this man too.'

'What lies did she tell me, Ben?' I asked.

'She lied to you. That's all I know.'

Mills of Justice

'Was it because she lied that you smashed in her head?' I asked sharply. Our crime reporter as public prosecutor.

I wasn't sure whether the murmur from the crowd signified shock or indignation.

'Now be careful,' warned Lukas Death. 'Nothing has been proved yet.'

'Why should I bash in a poor defenceless old woman's head with a spade?' asked Ben Owl.

'This is the second time you talk about a spade,' I pointed out. 'No one else has mentioned it. Why do you harp on it?'

'Pick or shovel or spade, it's all the same,' he mumbled.

I looked at Lukas Death and shrugged.

Perhaps he was shrewder than I thought; perhaps he was merely helpless. Either way, all he said was, 'Go home, Ben Owl. Go to sleep. We'll discuss it again later.'

'Do you think it's safe . . .?' I began.

'We do things our way,' snapped Lukas Death. 'The mills of justice grind slowly.'

'What about Ouma Liesbet?' I asked.

'Well, she is here, and her coffin is here. We're all of us here. We may just as well bury her.' His eyes wandered across the crowd. 'Will some of the men lend us a hand to place her in the coffin?'

'Shouldn't you examine the body first?' I asked.

'We all saw what she looked like,' he answered. 'What more do we need to know? We owe the dead some respect.' He looked up. 'And there's a storm coming.'

In all the drama I had never noticed, but he was right: there were indeed dark clouds gathering. And gusts of wind. Perhaps God had finally succumbed to the threats.

Heartbroken Widow

ANNIE-OF-ALWYN, as the heartbroken widow was called, was still in Tant Poppie's voorhuis when I came home from the cemetery; but she was preparing to leave. And when she saw me she became even more ill-at-ease.

'There's a storm coming,' she said in panic. 'I must get home.'

'You can lie down on my bed for a while,' proposed Tant Poppie like a clucking old mother hen. 'You need rest.'

But she was adamant. 'I bothered you long enough. You already did too much for me. And I must put the children to bed.'

'I'll walk you home,' I offered. Not for entirely unselfish reasons, I should add; a crime reporter never rests. Fucking swine.

'No, no.' As if I'd made an obscene proposal.

But Tant Poppie unexpectedly supported me. 'Now come on, let Neef Flip go with you. You can't walk out in this wind alone. And he's just in the way here.'

Thanks for nothing, I thought. And with the woman still rigid with fear, perhaps resentment, I picked up two of the children – the smallest clung to Annie-of-Alwyn like a baby baboon to its mother's belly – and stepped out on the stoep.

All the way to her home she didn't say a word. Only when we reached it, in the bottom row and set far back as if shy to be seen with the others, she stopped and glanced at me through her dishevelled hair. 'Thank you for helping me in the graveyard. I nearly passed out.'

'I can't understand why those bastards didn't move a finger to help you.'

'It's every man for himself now,' she said wearily as she opened the door and stood back to let me pass with the two children. 'I think they know that what happened to Alwyn can happen to them next, as the water runs out. They're all scared to die.'

'They were like a pack of wild dogs.'

She shook her head; perhaps it was the memory she was trying to shake off. 'They're not all like that.'

'There aren't many exceptions.'

'Tant Poppie may be difficult, but she's a good person,' she said wearily. 'She already saved my life once.'

'When was that?'

'I had breast cancer,' she said nervously. 'Without her I'd never have made it.'

Almost reluctantly I asked, 'What did she do then?'

She avoided my eyes. 'She does strange things. This time she tied up eight frogs in a cloth and pressed it to my chest. They started sucking, like leeches. But you know, the strange thing was I didn't feel any pain. They just clung on until they got convulsions and fell off. Then she brought new frogs. And so she went on for eight days. After a hundred and twenty frogs — I kept count all the way — the cancer was sucked out.'

'You could have died. If not from the cancer then from the remedy.'

'It would have been better if I did,' she said in a strangled voice. 'That would have spared us all a lot.'

'You shouldn't talk like that, Annie. You're still young.'

She paid no attention. 'Thank you for coming with me,' she said, closing up again. 'I'll be all right now.'

Hysterical Woman

Outside, gusts of wind were tugging at the roof. It was getting dark. Black clouds were gathering at an alarming speed.

'Let me help you put the children to bed.'

'They'll sleep now. Tant Poppie gave them something. For me too.'

'Will you be able to sleep?'

'No.'

I carried the two children to the bedroom. The youngest, already limp with sleep, lay down in the double bed. As I bent over to cover the two with a blanket, something from very far away stirred inside me. Louise. Marius. In the time when, perhaps, they'd still been mine. Jesus.

The wind was getting worse.

'Won't you be scared on your own?' I asked.

'One must just get used to it.'

'I'm not in a hurry. I could have a cup of coffee with you. If you're sure you don't want to lie down.'

'No,' she said. 'The moment I close my eyes Alwyn is there.'

I pulled out a chair and sat down at the dining table. For a long time she remained standing with her back pressed to the jamb of the bedroom door, but at last she came past me to the kitchen to make the coffee.

'Tant Poppie told me you lost your child too,' I said awkwardly.

She kept her back to me as she worked at the hearth. Then, flaring up unexpectedly, she said, 'I suppose I must thank the Lord for it. How could I bring another child up alone?' She swung round to me. 'It's my punishment for not wanting it.'

'Don't say such things. You'll be sorry later.'

'Why?' She pointed at the closed bedroom door. 'There's already three I never wanted.' She trembled. A hysterical woman, I anxiously told myself, is better not contradicted. She came to the table and leaned on her outstretched arms. 'I'm not saying I don't love them. But my God, do you think that's what I wanted? Bringing babies into the world to the end of my fertile years? I'm not Bettie Teat.'

'Annie, you don't know what you're saying.'

'That's right,' she cried through a storm of snot and tears, 'that's what they all say. How can I know? I'm mos just Annie-of-Alwyn. And before he took me I was Annie-of-Job, because my father is Job Raisin. Where was he this morning when I needed him? And where was Alwyn? Is there anybody left to help me, to be with me? Am I just a rag for others to wipe their feet on? Don't I count for something too?' She went on blindly, without check or reason or anything. 'It's always others who take the decisions and give the orders in this place. What must be done, who must do it, why, when, where. Who must live, who must die. And all I'm expected to do is to scrape and bow and praise God, my Lord and Master!'

She was folded double over the table in the rage of her fit of crying. And when I tried to take her by the shoulders she broke loose and swung a blow at me with such violence that she nearly lost her balance. But the action seemed to jolt her back to her senses. She stared at me in horror, her greasy hair in a tangle over her tear-streaked face.

'Oh my God, I'm sorry,' she whispered. 'I don't know what came over me.'

'Let me make the coffee,' I said.

'No. No, it's my work.' But she was too unsteady on her legs to let go of the table. I pulled out a chair and made her sit down, then went through to the kitchen to pour the coffee into the mugs she'd already set out. Atrocious coffee. But it was hot. And we both needed it.

Large Animal

'How was it between you and Alwyn?' I asked. Perhaps it was ill-advised of me; but I got the impression that there was a hell of a lot she just had to get out of her system first.

'Not good, not bad. Do you think the life of a chair is good or bad? As long as someone sits on it, it does what it's supposed to do. That's all.'

'No, Annie.'

'In the beginning one tries to resist,' she said, her eyes in a fixed stare. Outside the wind was like a large animal lowing and straining at its tether; but I doubt whether she was even aware of it. 'You keep thinking it won't go on like this forever, one day something will happen, this can't be all there is.' She slurped at her coffee and gulped it down. 'But then you find out that's just how it is. It's never going to be any different. The few who tried . . .' She closed her eyes as if the memory was too much for her.

'Who were they?' I asked.

'The last one was the girl Emma,' she said. The name made me sit up, but I tried not to let her notice. 'She wanted to go and study. They said no. Dalena-of-Lukas and I and a few others tried to speak up for her. We knew what it's like to want to get out of here. But we missed our chance, so all we could hope for was for Emma to go. Like on our behalf, you might say. The men told us to mind our own business, and when I came home Alwyn beat me up.' She moved her hands up to her bony shoulders. 'He could never understand what was up with me. He said if my father couldn't beat it out of me he would.'

We were silent for a long time.

Then I asked, 'So that was that for Emma?'

Annie nodded. 'She tried to run away, but she was given a terrible hiding. Tant Poppie called in some of the men to help her. Ben Owl. Hans Magic. Lukas Death. She was left for dead. It was a miracle that she survived.' She sighed. 'But that broke her.'

'You think she's broken?'

'She won't ever try again, if that is what you mean. Not ever.'

I sat listening to the raging wind. What hadn't been blown away two days ago, I thought, would be off to fucking hell and gone this time. If only it would bring some rain too, but so far there was no sign of it.

Grew a Moustache

'You said something about "the few who tried",' I said quietly. 'So there were others too?'

She looked past me. 'I suppose they were all mad, one way or another. But at least they tried. Someone like Talita Lightfoot. They said that when she danced it was like she wasn't a woman, she turned into wind, or water, or clouds or something. A wild one. When there was a feast, and in the old days I think there were more feasts than nowadays, she would dance everybody from their feet. But in the end all she was good for was to catch the fancy of the two rebels that came to hide here in the Devil's Valley during some war or other. She had to make sure they stayed, the men said we needed new blood. No one even remembers what became of her afterwards. I suppose she just did her duty and that was that. She probably had twelve children and became as fat as Tant Poppie, perhaps she grew a moustache.' She made a brief pause. 'Only when the moon is full she still gathers all the ghost girls of the valley to dance naked in the bluegum wood.'

A small bunch of leaves brushed lightly down my spine.

But without paying attention to me she went on, 'My great-grandmother also tried to get out. For her it must have been even worse, because she was used to a better life, she came from outside, she had no idea of what was waiting for her here. The men called her Katarina Sweetmeat. In our family she was Katarina-the-Angel. One of Isak Smous's forefathers brought her in and sold her to the Lermiets. They'd sent him to find them a woman, and he got a good price for her.'

I could feel myself breathing faster. 'What was her story?'

'Why do you want to know?'

'I'm trying to write up the history of the Devil's Valley, Annie. But all I've found so far is lies.'

Lies, lies, stories, I thought: and all to feed a rat in need of something more substantial.

'Do you promise you'll write it up exactly as I tell it to you?' she asked with sudden eagerness, as if I'd offered her a long draught of cold water.

'I promise.'

'Then *somebody* will at least know about her, you see. And perhaps about me too. It's terrible never to have been known about.'

A Dog or A Cat

'What happened to Katarina-the-Angel?' I asked.

'She never wanted to have anything to do with the seven brothers who bought her. Because she was so beautiful there were many other men who wanted her. But the Lermiets were a jealous lot. They kept her locked up. If they couldn't have her, they said, then no one else would. So very soon she wasn't allowed to see anybody else, except for the Smous's servant, who was sent in every day to take her food.'

'But she did have children, didn't she?'

'Then you know the story?'

'Not the story, only the lies.'

For a while she looked at me as if she wasn't sure about going on.

'*Did* she have children?' I asked.

'Yes, she did. The first time it was the servant's child.'

'How did they find out?'

'Because the child was black.'

I gaped at her.

'The servant was the only one of his kind ever to come here,' said Annie. 'The people were dead against it, but the Smous needed him, and they needed the Smous, and so they put up with him for a time.'

'And the child?'

'They stoned the child,' she said. 'Because to be black in the Devil's Valley has always been the worst sin of all.'

'But why did they ever allow the servant to get to Katarina?'

She shrugged the thin shoulders. 'He just took in food and brought out the peepot. I mean, he was like a dog or a cat in the household of the Smous. No one thought he'd do a thing like that.'

'And what became of him?'

'He ran off when he saw she was with child, never even waited for it to be born. And later the Smous hired another servant, but this time he was white, one of the boys from the valley.'

'And Katarina?' I asked. 'Did they stone her too?'

She stretched her back and moved a tired hand across her face. 'No, they didn't stone her. They thought up something worse for her.'

'Can there be anything worse?'

'Yes, they began to hire her out. The brothers had her for free, but others had to pay. Usually with nanny goats.'

Moon Was Full

'People are still being stoned,' I said.

She nodded.

'Emma's mother.'

'So far she was the last.'

'But children too? Throwbacks?'

She nodded again.

'But they couldn't have been throwbacks to Katarina. Her child was killed, he had no descendants.'

'No, they must be throwbacks to someone else. But there are all kinds of stories about Katarina's child. Some say the Smous stole him, and swapped him for another child, one he had with an unmarried girl. And then he had the servant's child brought up in the world outside. They say when he was grown up, he started coming back to the Devil's Valley when nobody knew. He always came when the moon was full, and then took his revenge by raping their women. Other say no, he was killed, but then he turned into a nightwalker. How can one ever be sure?'

'How can one even be sure about Katarina?'

'I have something of hers,' Annie said calmly. 'It has been handed down from mother to daughter in our family. Not much, just a small diary. Fifteen or twenty pages, in High Dutch. It says very little, but at least it's something to remember her by.'

I was so excited I had to get up. 'Do you still have it?'

'Yes. But it belongs to me. It's all I have.'

'I won't take it away. Perhaps I could just look at it, copy some of it.'

'You won't want to copy anything if you see it. You'll just think it's boring.'

Copperplate Handwriting

And in a way she was right. What was there really to glean from those cryptic entries in an old-fashioned copperplate handwriting? Except for that one passage in which something momentarily shone through, everything was wrapped in religious meditations, Bible texts, that kind of thing. The odd throwaway reference to herself was like a view from a distance, never a personal confession. There weren't even dates (because, locked up, she'd lost track of time?), only an occasional mention of the day of the week – *Monday,* or *Wednesday*, or *The Day of the Lord* – or a reference to the phases of the moon: full, half, crescent, dark. Or was that the clue? I still don't know. All I have is what I copied that afternoon while the storm raged outside. I was following Little-Lukas's example, I thought wryly, who'd copied Immanuel Kant in his exercise book without ever understanding a word of it.

This World

Friday. O what is this world but a place of unrest & sorrow how much do those who love Jesus Christ have to struggle for this reason the Dear Lord says struggle to go in, some Days have passed during which, waiting for the full moon in a Depressed state of Mind, I have been unable to write. My Lord saw fit to cover his comforting face as if with a Cloud so that my prayers recoiled as if from clouds through which they could not penetrate.

Weak Body

Monday. Full moon. Once again with a Weak Body & Tortured Brain I have to perform all the Labour in the domestic Circle and receive at night like Aholah the Seed of my Lords and Masters like a grateful Servant unworthy to remain in this Life. And this I have to do to give Satisfaction to others, while I would rather hide myself in the lonely Mountain cave behind the Devil's Hole, where no eye except that of God alone could see me. O be still my Soul let it be as it is, try to hold on to your belief that God will also be your Redeemer the world roars, get up, & prepare the Meal O where can I escape to?'

Intestines

The Day of the Lord. I am a Poor Woman confined & Constricted in the intestines of my meagre Home, & the sorrows of life especially at Night oppress the faculties of my Soul I do write on Sheets of Paper ponder the wonders of your Mercy & suppose hereby to provide my Soul with some Solace and thus to Praise you, you my Soul forget not all this Benefits read & reread what the Lord has done to your Soul & ignore what is being done to my body, and praise Him in secret He shall reward thee openly.

Bastard

Dark Moon. Would I call my child a Bastard! I jumped up & called out loudly O no my Father! Chastise me by Flogging me like the others or even by Stoning me but call not my child O Lord! a Bastard! I started screaming & implored the Lord Jesus to intercede for me with God it was as if my Spirit held the Redeemer by His clothes, & I hid my face behind Him, hiding from the Eye of God but soon I was rescued from this Dismay, by the same question (shall I call my child thus) then I thought at least I now shall have a Child that belongs to me for the rest of my Life even if I cannot take it to my Breast, & even though I have to deprive myself for all this time of the Mercy of the Father, for I should rather go to Hell with my child than to Heaven without it, O Lord no rather the dregs, the Scourings, despised & rejected, expelled from the people here on Earth.

Destruction

OUTSIDE THE STORM still howled. I couldn't tell whether the wind was worse than the first time. If the daylight made it slightly less terrifying the black clouds were darker than any eclipse. We were caught in the primitive rage of a fairytale; and it was a miracle that in all that huffing and puffing from some cosmic wolf the bloody house wasn't blown down. Even more so that the children slept through it all. This time not only poultry and goats, pigs, ostriches, wheelbarrows, haystacks and trees came tumbling past, but also Jurg Water's whole shed, as well as a number of few roofs, several longdrop outhouses, and two people: the ever-forging-and-unforging Smith-the-Smith, and another man, Sias Highstep, whom I knew only from sight. Neither of them was ever seen again.

Annie just sat staring ahead of her while the frenzy continued; after I'd copied a few brief passages from her great-grandmother's diary she pressed the much-thumbed little book against her thin chest without speaking another word. And later the clouds were blown away, once again without a drop of rain; and slowly, gustily, with a few furious last flurries, like a child raked by sporadic sobs after a bout of crying, the wind also died down.

At the door, when I left, Annie said, 'Thank you for coming. I'd have been scared in the storm.'

'Thank you for what you told me.' There was something solemn, a strange formality, between us. Like two people, I thought, who'd had sex too soon and now were embarrassed about getting dressed in front of each other.

For an instant her eyes filled with fear again. 'You mustn't tell the people here what I said. Or about the diary. They don't know about it. Not even Alwyn knew. Once you're gone from here it will be all right. But please, not while you're here.'

'I promise.'

With a kind of detached amazement I picked my way back through the storm-wracked settlement to Tant Poppie's house. Outside Tall-Fransina's place a number of cats were wandering about, mewing desolately. There were few people about: a cluster in front of a ruined house, a family beside a heap of thatch that might once have been a roof, a woman carrying a bundle of dead chickens by the legs like a bunch of carrots, Jurg Water on the vacant spot where his shed used to stand. Most of them, I realised, were still too scared to face the destruction. And so most of the doors remained tightly shut, to keep knowledge at bay.

Handful of Feathers

Tant Poppie was indoors too, working at her hearth.

'No rain this time either,' I said as I sat down at the table.

She placed the soup plates before us, poured the apostles with such energy that half of the liquid was spilled, and sat down opposite me.

Her prayer sounded more like a prolonged curse than anything else.

'Did Annie-of-Alwyn calm down a bit?' she asked after slurping down the first spoonful of thick broth.

'It's tough on her,' I said. 'But she's a strong woman.'

She blew into her soup, sending a vigorous spray across the table. 'There's something let loose amongst us,' she said. 'And it's time we got a grip on it. This business you stirred up about Ouma Liesbet isn't going to lie down soon.'

'I only did what she ordered me to do.'

She blew like a hippopotamus again. And I sensed that only her nose and ears were visible above the water: the rest was churning up mud below.

'You reckon it was Ben Owl who killed her?'

'It's in Lukas Death's hands now.'

'No, Neef Flip,' she said. 'It's not so easily said and done. You can't just come in here from outside and stir up things and think you can leave it to us to clear up the mess after you.'

'I have to go back at dawn tomorrow morning, Tant Poppie,' I said. 'What happened to Ouma Liesbet is indeed for the people here to solve.'

'That old bastard Pilate also tried to wash his hands,' she said, draining her apostle and filling up her mug again. After a few moments she asked, 'And did you find what you came for?'

'No,' I said frankly. 'I gathered as much as I could, but it's only a handful of feathers.'

'What else did you expect?'

'I don't know. Facts. History.'

'And don't you think Ouma Liesbet's death is history?'

'It goes further than Ouma Liesbet. It's about the whole Devil's Valley, over more than a hundred and fifty years. I know now it's not so easy.'

'I had visitors this afternoon. They told me that after I brought Annie home you accused Ben Owl about Maria's death too.' Her eyes scuttled across my face.

'I didn't accuse him,' I said emphatically. 'We opened the coffin in which Ouma Liesbet said Maria had been buried. It was empty. From there Lukas Death did the questioning.'

'And did Emma have anything to say?' she asked out of the blue.

'Why should she?' I asked; she must have noticed that she'd upset me.

'She never stopped asking about her mother.'

'It's only to be expected, isn't it? Especially if nobody wants to give a straight answer.'

'You shouldn't have dragged Ben Owl into it.'

'Why not?' I asked. My fuse was getting short.

'Because Ben Owl is Emma's father.'

Off Her Head

I shook my head briskly as if she'd thrown an apostle in my face. 'Come again?'

'I know about the story that her mother ran away from here and came back pregnant. But her mother wasn't that kind of girl. It was just that she didn't want to come back. Lukas Death was the one who went to fetch her. And when she came back all the wildness was gone. She married Ben Owl and settled down with him. He always had a soft spot for her, she grew up before his eyes. But then as she started swelling she went off her head. Some women just get like that, you know. And as soon as the child was born she ran off and drowned herself in the Devil's Hole. They never found her body. From that time no one goes there any more.'

'Why did you bring her up and not Ouma Liesbet who was a blood relative?'

'Because from the time Maria died Ben Owl got funny in the head. It got so bad no one could talk to him any more. And he seemed to blame the child for her mother's death. That's why I brought her up. It was my Christian duty.'

I sat staring at the table, no longer in any mood to eat.

'Why didn't you tell me before?' I asked.

'One doesn't serve one's burnt bread to guests.'

'Then what makes it different tonight?'

'Because you're going away tomorrow, you can't do any more harm.' She got up and cleared away the dishes. 'And I know you can't keep your eyes off Emma.'

'How can you say such a thing?'

'I'm not blind.'

I tried to get up, but sank back on my chair. I wasn't prepared for this.

She started wiping the plates and bowls with a dirty dry cloth, as always. 'Now you see it's just as well you're leaving us. If you stayed, there would have been no end of trouble.'

I didn't wait for her to go to bed, but went out with a mumbled excuse. This was my last night in the Devil's Valley. I had no time to lose. I felt a deep need to be with Emma. But first I had an appointment with Ben Owl.

Bare Yourself

Ouma Liesbet was again huddled on her rooftop in the dark. Unless it was an owl; but I had no time to check, there was no more I could do for her, even though I knew very well that she wouldn't go away again. They accompany us everywhere, the legions of the dead, all of them, mostly invisible, inaudible, but always there, all the voices silenced, all the stories forever unfinished.

Ben Owl was sitting on the steps to his stoep in the dark smoking his pipe as if he'd been expecting me. For once there were no voices from his head to interrupt the conversation.

'Neef Flip.'

I remained at a safe distance just in case there was a pick or a spade within reach.

'You must be a happy man,' he said with heavy, unrestrained bitterness.

'Why did you kill Ouma Liesbet, Ben?'

He sat cracking his knuckles, first one hand, then the other. 'It was for your own good, man. She had no right telling you everything.'

'She hardly told me anything.'

'But I heard her promise that she'd tell you all if you came back.'

'Was that so bad then?'

'Bad or not, those things were not meant for your ears. All these years we've been living here without trouble. When somebody comes in from outside we pull in head and feet like a tortoise. Because you people don't understand.'

Even though I'd heard this so many times before, I protested, 'Perhaps I'd have understood more if the people of the valley had been more forthcoming.'

'One can't bare oneself to the world like that. That's indecent.'

'Indecent?' For a moment my anger boiled over. 'This place is a bloody den of evil and then you talk about decency?'

'It's easy to call something evil if you don't understand, Neef Flip. And you understand nothing. You hear me? Nothing. *Nothing.*'

'Are you Emma's father?' I shot the question at him; it was the only way to catch him off guard.

'Says who?'

'Says Tant Poppie.' There was no need to protect anyone any more. In a place where everybody's hand was against everyone, it might be the only way to reach a grain of truth.

'That old aardvark pokes her nose into every antheap. But she knows nothing.'

'She said Lukas Death went to bring Maria back to you after she ran away. And then you married her?'

'Yes, I married her,' he said unexpectedly frank. 'What else could I do?'

'I don't understand.'

'She was carrying an outsider's child in her. If they found out they'd have killed her.'

'They killed her anyway.'

He pulled at his pipe, but it had long gone out and all he produced was an empty hiss.

Drove Me Crazy

'Then Emma isn't your child?'

'If only she was,' said Ben Owl. 'Don't you understand anything? That girl, Maria, grew up in front of me. I loved her long before she started to grow molehills. But she never wanted to have anything to do with me. Not even after I married her to give the child a name. And that was what drove me crazy. The day the child was born Maria chased me away, said she never wanted to see me again. It was unbearable. I tell you, I was crying like a baby. She started laughing and shouting at me. Said I wasn't a real man, I didn't deserve to have a wife. It was as if the earth just caved in under me. I didn't know what I was saying, it just burst from me. Tant Poppie and the other women who were there for the birth must have heard it. That was how the people found out the child was an outsider's. So they killed

Maria, and it was because of me. I couldn't stop them. But I couldn't leave her under that heap of stones either. So I went to plead with Ouma Liesbet and she said we could use her coffin.'

'And then you buried Maria in the night? But this morning the coffin was empty.'

He stood up. He was trembling. 'The night after that I went back to the graveyard on my own. This time Ouma Liesbet didn't know about it. I carried Maria's body all the way up to the Devil's Hole. I told you mos I was crazy.' And then he began to cry, hideous, muffled little sobbing sounds, like the hooting of an owl. 'All those years Maria never let me lay a hand on her. How many times did I ask Hans Magic to give me a potion to win her love, but he wouldn't. I think he had an eye on her himself, the dirty bastard. Once when he was out I crept into his house to find the right doepa. I knew where he kept his stuff. But then he put his curse on me. Look at my foot, all shrivelled up. After that Maria loathed me even more. For years and years and years. All in vain. Do you know what that does to a man? But now she was dead. For once she couldn't resist.'

I felt the blood drain from my face.

'It was the only time ever,' he said. 'And afterwards I threw her into the Devil's Hole. Where not even Hans Magic would find her. From that day I haven't been able to sleep a wink at night.'

I couldn't move. I couldn't speak.

'Now see what you did,' he sobbed.

Fireflies

THAT NIGHT, I think, was one of the weirdest in my life. Emma was waiting for me in the dark in front of Isak Smous's house, so motionless against a half-broken pillar on the stoep that she looked like a pillar herself. We didn't speak before we were well beyond the last houses. Hand in hand we walked up to the bluegum forest. For the moment there was no need of anything more. If it hadn't been for the warmth of her hand in mine and the movement of her hip against me as we walked, it would have been possible to imagine that it was another fucking dream, like that night of the full moon when I'd met Henta and her sprites up here. Tonight the moon was far from full, yet it wasn't particularly dark, as if the night had a kind of luminosity of its own, like an ancient fire not yet extinguished; and there were fireflies among the trees.

I told her about my visit to Ben Owl. Beforehand I'd decided to keep the worst from her; I mean, Jesus, there was no need to expose her to that final humiliation. But when it came to it, I couldn't restrain myself. It was important for both of us that she know what I knew. Except for Ben's fucking necrophilia. That I had to spare her. And she didn't seem particularly shocked by the rest either. She barely reacted, just pressed my hand more tightly while I told her how Ben had dug up her mother's body to dispose of it in the Devil's Hole.

'You think he told the truth?' she asked at last.

All I could answer, like the last time when we'd spoken about Ouma Liesbet, was 'Emma, when one is on the verge of death lies just don't make sense any more.'

She said, 'I think it's even easier to lie if you know you're going to die.'

Around us was the night, and the wood, once again heavy with near-soundless sound, that low rustle and murmur of voices whispering and moaning and calling out, of bodies writhing and wrestling.

'Can you ever be sure of what happened to her?' I asked.

'I'll just have to learn to live with it.'

'But it's in our nature to look for something to hold on to. Footprints to lead you somewhere.'

But even as I said it I remembered that first time I'd seen her at the rock pool, when she, too, hadn't left any footprints.

Leaves A Scar

'You're like a bird,' I said in another of my embarrassing poetic moments. 'You fly through the air without leaving a scar.'

'It leaves a scar on the eye.'

'There *are* no birds here,' I said.

'Yes, I'm afraid old Lukas Up-Above took them all away with him.'

'Do you think it's true?'

'How will we ever know? Does it matter? All you really need is a story that makes sense to you.'

'I want to know everything about you,' I said.

'No, tell me about *you*,' she said. 'There's so much I still don't know. And I want to remember when you're gone.'

I started telling again, without shape or sequence. Protected by the dark flickering with fireflies, so fucking magical that even while I was there I couldn't believe it, I grasped at whatever came past. The shitty little village where I grew up. Ma and Pa. My little brother Dolf. When I hesitated, or got stuck in a memory, she urged me on: 'You *must* remember.'

'You wouldn't want to hear it all.'

'I do want to. I must.'

'I don't want to remember.'

'Perhaps you've been running away for too long.'

'What makes you think I'm running away?'

'It's the only reason why people come to the Devil's Valley.'

'I think *you* brought me here,' I said lightly.

'Did you think I'd be different from the other women you have known?'

'Yes. And I was right.'

'Don't speak too soon.' With her open palm she stroked across my chest, and down one arm, the back of my hand. 'Why didn't it work out with Sylvia?'

'We were too unprepared. I was too unsure of myself, too suspicious. I couldn't believe she'd really love a man like me.'

'And do you think I can?'

'You shouldn't. But I wish you could.'

'Was it very bad with her?'

'It was hell.'

'For her too?'

I nodded slowly. 'Yes. If I look back now, I think it must have been even worse for her.'

'How come that you lasted so long?'

'I think in the long term you can't go on without the hurt any more. It's the only way to make sure you're still alive.'

'But before that, right in the beginning, it must have been good?'

'It's too far back to remember.'

'I want you to try.'

After a long pause I said, 'Yes, I think it was good. I'm sure it was.'

'And you loved each other?'

'Yes.'

'Tell me about it.'

I told her everything I could remember.

Then she asked, 'And before you met Sylvia?'

I told her whatever random memories came to me. About Maureen behind the sofa, and Belinda at her floral curtains, my first clumsy efforts at university. And all the wasted years that followed. When I'd drained myself, she kept on stroking the back of my hand.

After a long silence she said, 'So these are *your* stories.'

'Don't you believe me?'

'I believe you.'

In the dark her eyes looked at me. I couldn't see them, but I knew them. And in spite of everything that had happened during the day, all the shocks and disillusionments and discoveries, the tracks true and false, the whole fucking whirlpool of events, there was a mysterious sense of joy just in being there with her, even while not knowing, not understanding, not wanting to try any more.

All around us the libidinous sounds continued in the night, but we remained untouched by it all in our small chaste space; because for us desire was excluded, we were beyond it now, for us I think no redemption was possible.

Residue of Reason

We returned through the sweet-smelling wood, past the open space where the ostrich pen had been, around heaps of rubble blown together by the wind, and broken shacks and sheds, to Isak Smous's house.

When we reached the front stoep she said, as if it was the most obvious thing in the world, 'Don't go.'

In silence we tiptoed through the dark voorhuis to her room. There, in absolute darkness, she stood against me for a moment, her head against my shoulder; then she pushed me gently back on the narrow bed. She came to lie against me, fully clothed, her back curved against me.

'Just hold me,' she whispered. 'I don't want to be alone tonight.'

I folded my arms over her. She held one of my hands against her mouth, a small gesture of trust that wholly disarmed me.

And so we remained through the long night, without talking, without sleeping, in a state of grace on the other side of passion. I couldn't deny the body, it was there, yet it was as if I was not really implicated in it. Perhaps there was a residue of reason in it too: I was an outsider here, if she fell pregnant they would kill her – as simple as that. And yet it didn't really have anything to do with practical concerns about pregnancy. It was, rather, a kind of resignation, knowing that this was all we could have, all we could grasp, and perhaps all we bloody well needed.

When in the sad dawn I got up to go, she sat up. She said nothing, but her hand sought mine and held it. Her eyes asked what she did not dare to.

I kissed her on the forehead, committing myself to the mystery of her.

'I'm not going away any more, Emma,' I said. 'For as long as you're here, I'll stay.'

FIVE

A Goddamn Adventure

AS I PASSED the cairn behind the churchyard in the dark grey dawn, I became aware of a figure following me. It was too dark to see much, but even before I recognised him from his swinging walk I knew who it was. I stopped. To tell the truth, I'd been expecting him for a while now. As with Ben Owl the night before, this appointment had been a long time coming.

'Good morning, Oom Lukas,' I said.

'Yes, morning.' The Seer approached, hobbling on his crutches. 'You're early.'

'That's so.'

'Just as well, you have a long road ahead.' He waited for an answer. When it didn't come he prodded me impatiently. 'You going home today, aren't you?'

'No, Oom Lukas.' I looked straight at him, but in the treacherous light he seemed transparent. 'I've decided to stay on for the time being. There's no hurry.' I was surprised by how calm and steady my voice sounded; only I knew what lay behind it. For this time I wasn't blundering into something I didn't know about. This was my choice, not just a goddamn adventure. 'I started something and now I've got to see it through.'

'Have you not dug up enough about us yet?'

'No,' I said.

'Look at the place.' Supporting himself on one crutch he made a sweeping gesture with the other. Most of the destruction was still mercifully hidden in the dark, but I knew what he meant. 'And it's all because of you.'

'It was a storm. I had nothing to do with it.'

'God is angry.'

'Not with me.'

'Every time things go wrong in the Devil's Valley it is brought on by outsiders.'

'If you ask me, the trouble began when the first Lermiets came in here.'

I expected him to be offended, but he just gave a difficult little laugh. As on the first day, it sounded like the rustle of old leaves.

'You're a strange one, Neef Flip.' He shuffled to the heap of stones, where he laboriously lowered himself between the two crutches until he was seated. Then he took a filthy little snuffbox from a tattered pocket. 'Want a sniff?'

The mere thought was repulsive, but to win some goodwill – or time? – I shook out a small quantity of the snuff on my crooked forefinger. It was so strong that my eyes promptly started watering and I sneezed five, six, seven times, enough to expel my guts.

The old Seer grunted with satisfaction and helped himself to a copious sniff.

'So you reckon it was I who started it?' he asked.

'I don't think any one person is to blame, Oom Lukas. It's just something that's been building up over the years, like a bad boil. Now it's ripe. And if it did start somewhere it could only have been with you.'

'Things don't always happen the way one wants them to. You think I would have stayed here if there was a way to get out? But I mos got a leg.' He shook his crutches in a show of impotent anger.

'Your time is long past, Oom Lukas,' I said cautiously. 'Why don't you go to rest?'

'Shall I tell you?' His dull eyes began to glimmer more brightly. 'Because I don't like the idea of facing that devil. He's just waiting for me to come down.'

'What devil, Oom Lukas?'

'Hm.' He took another generous thumbnail of sniff. 'You sure you want to know?'

'I came here to find out. I can't stop half-way.'

'Then on your head be it.'

On Top of the Grave

He looked hard at me. Then he leaned forward on his crutches. Like any old man telling any story.

'When we trekked in here,' he said, 'this whole valley was full of enemies.'

'I was told the Valley was an empty wilderness at the time.'

'They just too scared to tell you, man, don't ask me why. But there were Bushmen and Hottentots all over the place. We had to get rid of them to clear a spot for ourselves. The few who survived agreed to live in peace with us. They damn well knew what was good for them. And for some time things went well. But then my wife died.'

'That was Mina?'

'Who else?' He snorted. 'You know what it does to a man to be burned by desire and have nothing to douse it with?'

'Your second wife was Bilhah?'

'God knows what her real name was,' he said. 'I christened her Bilhah. I mean, how can a man sin with a woman's body if she doesn't have a name from the Bible?'

'She was a Hottentot woman,' I said with a straight face.

'What else could I do?' he asked. 'Abraham and Isaac and Jacob also had to make do with what they could get, didn't they? It's straight from the Word of God. And anyway, a root needs moisture, it's that way inclined.' He scratched his beard. 'And there would have been no problem either, except then her bloody husband mos got difficult. Well, he left me no choice, we had to fight it out. I thought a few quick slaps would do it, but that shit was a real devil in the shape of a man. And underhand too. I tell you, if he'd come to me man to man, I could have killed him with one shot, but he waited till I was asleep. So it was with our bare hands. From morning star to red dusk. Until at last I pushed him down into his own fire. The coals were almost gone, but still hot enough to give him a good roasting while I sat on his head.'

'You killed him?'

'Of course I killed him.' He spat something green past me. 'And shall I tell you what I did next? I am a Lermiet, Neef Flip, I got my pride. Dog-tired as I was, I dug a hole and put the body in it. And then I told his wife to lie down on top of the grave and I gave it to her right there. The next day I built my house on that very spot. Seventeen children I made on that grave. In later years they rebuilt and change the house a bit, but it's still there where I built it, where Lukas Death lives now. Sometimes the heat still comes up from the old grave below where we used to do our thing.'

'And since then you were the baas here?'

'What do you think? No one ever dared raise a hand against me. Some of that devil's children tried to crawl back here and take their revenge, years later, but by that time my sons were already growing up and we were man enough for them.'

'And your sons?' I asked. 'Lukas Nimrod and the others, did they also take their wives from Bilhah's relatives?'

'Lukas Nimrod took Bilhah's daughter, yes. But what's the difference? By that time we were all one family.'

'So the throwbacks from later generations came from Bilhah?'

'They were the exceptions,' he said, pride in his voice. 'We Lermiets are good breeders. We fucked the whole Devil's Valley white.'

Thorn In His Eye

I narrowed my eyes against the first colourless light coming through the mountains. 'Why were they trying so hard to cover it up?'

'One doesn't keep on sucking from a dry teat.'

'Bilhah was your own wife. How could she bring shame over your descendants?'

'I'm not saying anything against Bilhah. She was a good meid. But white is white when it comes to the crunch, goddammit. And God takes pleasure in pure blood. A bastard race is a thorn in his eye.' He leaned further forward to stare me right in the face. 'Look man, there's nothing one can do about tomorrow. It comes as it must. All you can do something about is yesterday. But the problem with yesterday is it never stays down, you got to keep stamping on it.'

The old Seer sat back again. He seemed to have done with me. The light was stronger now. I sat weighing up his story in my mind, testing it against the many other versions I had heard. Was there anything true about it, anything at all? Or was Emma right when she said that it didn't really matter, as long as it made sense? Whatever 'sense' may mean: but I suppose that was her point. In spite of my suspicion and resentment, I felt moved by something in the old fucker, perhaps in all his breed. With the lies of stories — all the lies, all the stories — we shape ourselves the way the first person was shaped from the dust of the earth. *That* is our first and ultimate dust. Who knows, if we understood what was happening to us, we might not have needed stories in the first place. We fabricate yesterdays for ourselves which we can live with, which make the future possible, even if it remains infinitely variable and vulnerable, a whole bloody network of flickerings, an intimate lightning to illuminate the darkness inside. And what lies at the root of it all is not this one's crime or that one's sin, but the involvement of a whole community. And now I, too, had been drawn into it.

How fucking precarious it all was. For them. Above all, for myself. That first afternoon, ten days before, a bloody lifetime ago, this same old man had warned me, up there on the mountain, *You going into it with open eyes.* It wasn't true, I hadn't known. How could I? But now I knew. It was a knowledge for which, for all I knew, I had traded my soul.

From the Rafters

TANT POPPIE, AS I might have expected, was already at work in the kitchen when I came in. I'd have preferred to slip quietly past her to my room, but she stopped to fix such a glare on me that I hesitated. She said nothing, asked nothing; but she stared with her raptor's eyes.

'How are you this morning?' I asked, feigning innocence.

'Awful, thank you. My whole body is racked with pain.'

'I'm very sorry to hear that.'

Her quick eyes darted suspiciously across my face. 'Don't you believe me then?'

'Oh I do, I do. I think you're an incredibly strong woman to bear it all so bravely. It must be a hard life.'

Her eyes narrowed. 'You got a lot to say for someone who has just come in.'

I refused to take the bloody bait. 'I was talking to the Seer,' I said with a poker-face.'

'All night long?'

I shrugged. It wouldn't surprise me if she knew already, the way these people seemed to know everything; but she wasn't going to hear it from me.

'I made you padkos,' she said, pushing across the table a bundle tied in a checkered cloth. 'You have mos a long way to go.'

Trapped. But I tried to handle it as undramatically as possible. 'I decided to stay on a little longer, if it's all right with you. Otherwise I must find another place to stay. I really don't want to put you out.'

'What made you change your mind so suddenly? Only yesterday you were all set to go.'

My right hand made a ball-and-claw in my pocket. But I refused to budge. 'There's just too much unfinished work still to do.'

'And what does Grandpa Lukas have to say about it?'

Now watch your step, Flip. 'I'm sure he understands,' I said non-committally.

'One wonders,' she said, turning back to the oven built into the side of the open hearth, 'one wonders what use it could be.' She plucked open the iron door and grabbed a breadpan with her bare hands. She turned the pan over and suddenly called out in dismay, 'Now look what you made me do. I turned the bread upside-down.'

'Just turn it back.'

'It's too late.'

'It's a silly superstition, that's all.'

'How can you say such a thing?' She was so upset about the bread that she didn't know which way to turn.

At that moment a dirty little figure appeared in the front door. It was Piet Snot.

'Tant Poppie,' he said breathlessly, 'Pa says Tant Poppie must come quickly. Oom Ben Owl is hanging from the rafters.'

Hit the Fan

Tant Poppie waddled right over the poor child. And before he could scramble to his feet I followed her. In front of Ouma Liesbet's house, which looked even tattier than in the dark last night, the settlers stood gathered in the dusty road.

Now, thought the crime reporter, the shit has hit the fan.

The crowd immediately made way for Tant Poppie, but before I could follow the gap had closed up again. Only when a familiar stench approached from behind, followed by Hans Magic and his aura of buzzing flies, did the tightly packed crowd part again, and after taking a deep breath to last me for some time, I stuck to his heels. At the same time a small hand clutched my arm. It was Piet Snot again. He'd brought my chameleon with him – he must have fetched it from my room – and placed it on my wrist with an expression of deep reproach. Fortunately Hans Magic's smelly passage was so overwhelming that the people took a while before they closed their ranks again, which gave me time to work my way inside.

Tant Poppie, Dalena-of-Lukas, and a few other people were at work around Ben Owl's body which lay outstretched on the floor, as stiff as a board and with his tongue protruding, his twisted face a deep purple. The kind of scene I've described in many a filed report. Matter of juggling the adjectives. From one of the rafters overhead a twisted thong still dangled. To one side lay an overturned chair, presumably kicked over by Ben Owl. Jurg Water was hovering in the background, brandishing the long butcher's knife with which he must have cut the thong. But it was clearly too late. Tant Poppie's efforts also proved fruitless.

'God does not sleep,' pronounced Brother Holy from a dark corner, clearing his throat as if preparing to propel himself into a sermon straight away.

'It was all unnecessary,' said Hans Magic in an accusing tone of voice. 'Why didn't he come to talk to me before doing such a stupid thing?'

'You were the one who shrivelled up his foot,' Brother Holy reminded him.

'If he didn't go where he wasn't supposed to go, there would have been nothing wrong with his foot.' He took out his dagga pipe. 'And then, for all we know, Maria would also have been alive.'

'I don't think he ever meant to harm Maria,' I interposed.

'And what do you know about it?' asked Hans Magic through a heavy cloud of smoke which, mercifully, began to dampen his olid fumes. But the flies remained a fucking pestilential presence.

Unable to keep silent any longer, I said, 'I spoke to Ben Owl last night.'

Everybody in the voorhuis turned to me. The people kneeling or squatting beside the body rose to their feet. No one said a goddamn word.

Just One Blow

'After what happened at the graveyard yesterday I wanted to find out more from him,' I explained. 'It was clear for all to see that he knew more than he said. I thought he'd get angry with me, or clam up. But he was very frank. I suppose he already knew he was going to commit suicide.'

'And what did he say?' asked Jurg Water aggressively. 'You're very quick to poke your nose into our affairs. What with your bloody forked stick and all. As if you know anything about finding water.'

'I know nothing about water, Jurg,' I tried to placate him. 'I told you I only did what Ouma Liesbet asked me to. My rod found her body, that's all. When it comes to water, you're the expert, not I.'

'That Jurg is a bloody sham anyway,' bitched Hans Magic, looking at no one in particular. 'When there was water everywhere in the Devil's Valley he couldn't stop bragging about that rod of his. Pranced up and down like a billy goat smelling a nanny in rut. But now that we really need the water he's useless.'

'You old stinking turd,' Jurg hit back. 'I'll need just one blow to knock you down.' I could see it was no idle threat either. Truly strong men, I'd discovered long ago in bars and other joints where the boys are weeded out from the men, are not the ones with the broad shoulders and the six-pack bellies who become Mister Universe, but those with sloping shoulders and flat arses like Jurg Water. They're the ones to avoid.

'You lay a finger on me,' snapped Hans Magic like a mangy little cur facing an Alsatian, 'and I'll wither up your hand like Ben Owl's foot.'

Jurg Water, I noticed, took a small step back.

This Man

Then Lukas Death came forward, looking fucking uncomfortable as if he was there much against his will. After taking his time to clear his throat, he asked, 'Neef Flip, you were saying?'

'I said all I wanted to say, Lukas. I only came to find out whether Ben Owl could tell me more about Ouma Liesbet's empty coffin. He admitted that the two of them buried Maria after the stoning, but that he went back on his own later to dump the body in the Devils' Hole.'

'Why would he do a thing like that?' asked Jurg Water, still from a safe distance.

'He said it was the only place where even Hans Magic wouldn't find her.'

Lukas Death screwed up his eyes to peer through the billowing smoke. 'Where do you fit into the story then, Oom Hans?'

'Maria deserved better than she could find here among us,' growled Hans Magic. 'Ben Owl was the one who couldn't understand that. It was to keep him away from her that I struck him with my gift. I only tried to protect her.'

'You had your own dirty designs on her,' Dalena-of-Lukas said unexpectedly from the back. 'First on her, then on her daughter. But Maria wanted none of it, nor did Emma. Don't pretend it isn't true.'

'You're just saying that because you picked Emma for your Little-Lukas,' Hans Magic hit back.

'Keep Little-Lukas out of this,' barked Lukas Death in a rare flash of anger.

'And why should I?' demanded Hans, also losing his temper. 'He was the one who brought all this over us. He spread the story in the outside world and sent this man to us.' He was looking straight at me. 'And from then on everything has been turned into a heap of shit. Even the rain stays away.'

I didn't like this turn to the discussion. There was a barely subdued violence smouldering among the people, just waiting to break out.

'It was dry since long before I came, Oom Hans,' I said, trying to restrain my voice.

'That's true,' cried someone from the back. Other voices agreed. It was like a wind that came up and then died down again, but only for now.

Its Own Tail

Like so many times before, it struck me how shallow the fucking resentment and the rage lay under the surface, how ready the people were to growl and bare their teeth at the slightest provocation. But also how diffuse everything was: no conversation ever pursued to a conclusion, no accusation followed up. It was all bloody random and haphazard, as they kept snapping in all directions, going in for the attack at the slightest opportunity. But it lacked conviction; it had become habit, as if they just went through the motions without really knowing or even wondering why they were doing so. And all I could sense below it all was a kind of panic. But where did it come from, what was its target? Each fucking dog kept on chasing its own tail.

Lukas Death, from whom I'd have expected some direction, wasn't up to it either. Actually, I decided, he only wanted peace and quiet; and if anything could be swept under the carpet rather than solved, so much the better. Perhaps there *were* no solutions any more. The Devil's Valley was a fucking dead-end. I should never have come to it. And if it hadn't been for Emma, I'd have been on my way out by now.

'Lukas, will you take charge of the body?' I asked while he still dithered.

'There are more important things to do right now,' said Jurg Water. 'There's still yesterday's damage to clear up. And what I want to know is where are we going from here? It's clear that God has wiped His backside on us.'

'All we can do is once again to humble us before Him,' said Brother Holy. 'Sooner or later he will hearken unto us. Tomorrow is the day of the Lord. We shall dedicate the service to prayers again.'

'Your service is as much use as a pile without an arsehole,' said Hans Magic. 'It's time we started doing something on our own without bringing God into it.'

Collective Fears

The argument spilled through the front door into the road outside. Those in favour of leaving the matter to God turned out to be the minority — much to Brother Holy's apocalyptic indignation, as it meant that he was to be swept aside with God. What the people now demanded was a Plan of Action.

Right there in the road, between Ouma Liesbet's rickety little house and the church, and without constitution or chair or agenda, a meeting was held. Democracy in the Devil's Valley, I saw, meant fucking chaos. Those with the loudest voices soon shouted the others into cowering silence. But in the end it was Hans Magic who took control. For what he lacked in volume he made up by playing on their uncertainties, their collective fears, their superstition.

'Our ancestors had their own ways of bringing rain when nothing else helped,' he said slyly. 'It's time we returned to the example they set.' He glared at Brother Holy. 'Seeing that nobody else has been able to do anything.'

The crowd made more room for him. But whether it was out of respect or just to move further away from his smell, was difficult to say.

'The ancestors had many ways to make rain,' said Hans Magic. 'One remedy they often used . . .' He moved his eyes from one to the other until they appeared by accident to fall on me. But I was sure he'd long been planning it. 'I noticed that Neef Flip always carries a chameleon on his shoulder,' he said. 'Now that is just what we need.'

The crowd opened up around me. Like a lamb at the slaughtering block I stood where I was.

'Give it here,' said Hans Magic.

Suddenly there was a sharp cry from little Piet Snot. 'Not my chameleon, Oom. Please, Oom, not my chameleon.'

Jurg Water struck him a blow to the head which sent the child reeling.

This made me so fucking mad that I didn't think twice. 'Jurg, you lay another finger on that child . . .'

He gave a leisurely step in my direction. 'And then what?'

I'm not a fighter. If truth be told, I'm a bloody coward. There have been occasions, in a bar or at a rugby match, under serious provocation and in a state between medium and well-done, when I stood my ground and did my thing. Once or twice I came out of it not entirely without honour; on some of the other encounters I prefer not to dwell. But it's not my nature. And Jurg Water spelled shit. But I swore by my syphilitic soul that I wouldn't allow that child to be abused in front of me.

'You touch him and I'll fuck you up properly,' I said. All bluff.

And then, not a moment too soon, Tant Poppie stepped up beside me. 'If you've never been hit by a woman before, Jurg, then you got it coming to you today. You smack that child again and see what happens.' Before I could recover from my amazement, she turned to me: 'Now, Neef Flip, give that chameleon to Hans and let him make his rain. I won't believe it before I see it, but there's no time to waste.'

Meekly, I detached the little green creature from my shoulder, and she passed it to Hans Magic.

'Ag please, Oom, please,' whined Piet Snot.

'Piet,' said his father.

'Jurg,' said Tant Poppie.

Before everything could start again, a woman like a large bale of wool gently took the child aside and smothered him against her. It must be his mother, I thought, Hanna-of-Jurg.

With Plagues and With Pestilence

'Now I need a spade,' commanded Hans Magic.

As soon as somebody had brought one from the nearest backyard, Hans tripped off to the open space in front of the church, followed by the rest of us. He started digging. The earth sounded as solid as bedrock, but there was no need to go deep, a mere handwidth or so. He carefully place the chameleon on its back in the hole, held it in position with one forefinger, and quickly filled the hole up again.

In the distance I thought I could hear Piet Snot whining again, but it could have been my imagination.

'A chameleon draws rain like a tick sucks blood,' explained Hans Magic. 'As long as the clouds are right, of course. We'll soon find out.'

'The Lord shall preserve thy going out and thy coming in from this time forth, and even for evermore,' chanted Brother Holy.

But he was promptly interrupted by Hans Magic. 'You had your chance, Brother. Now shut up before you scare off the clouds. Today is my turn.'

'You can't make anything happen on your own,' snarled the preacher.

'If you didn't spend so much time fucking Bettie Teat, God might have taken you more seriously,' jeered Hans Magic.

'Slanderer!' fulminated Brother Holy, stretching out a trembling skeletal hand. 'Antichrist!' And then something just snapped in him. 'I curse you in the name of the Father, and the Son, and the Holy Ghost,' he boomed in a shaking voice. 'I curse you with plagues and pestilence, with locusts and worms and gravel and water in your intestines, with gout and arthritis and rheumatism and venereal disease, with lice in your groin and shit in your mouth, with boils and spitting of blood, I curse you and your house and your fields and your vegetables, and rust will slowly consume you and moths devour you, and you will return to your own vomit like a dog, and there shall be wailing and gnashing of teeth. I curse you . . .' He suddenly broke off just before the climax, his arm still stretched to the heavens. As we all stared, fucking flabbergasted, he turned round and ran into the church on his long spidery legs.

Nobody quite knew what was happening. Even Hans Magic was left gaping.

A minute later Brother Holy was back in our midst, clutching in his hands the little box Isak Smous had once shown me, the prize of their relics.

'. . . I curse you,' resumed Brother Holy exactly where he had left off and moving straight in for the kill, 'with the Darkness of Egypt.'

I heard Isak Smous exclaim under his breath, but it was too late. Brother Holy tore open the lid and remained standing in the grip of silent convulsions as he shook the box. A few unimpressive grains of dust and a dead moth flurried out, but that was all.

The crowd uttered a muted lament, but it kind of stuck in their throats.

This Feeling

And then Hans Magic asked flatly, 'Have you finished?'

'For the moment I have done,' said Brother Holy haughtily, but his voice didn't sound altogether firm to me. 'Why do you ask?'

'I'm just asking,' said Hans Magic, 'because all of a sudden there's this feeling coming over me.' He began to shake lightly.

'What sort of feeling?' asked Brother Holy, now openly apprehensive.

'A feeling that you are going to get an itch,' said Hans Magic, still shaking. 'And that you will start scratching and scratching and scratching until you have no nails left, but the itch will not leave you.'

Brother Holy was drooping visibly, like a candle melting in the sun.

'You will itch behind your eyeballs,' said Hans Magic in a high droning voice, like a castrated bee; and I could see the crowd slowly edging away from Brother Holy, 'and you will itch in your nostrils, and in your ears, and under your tongue, and on your palate. You will itch in your armpits and between your shoulder blades and up your arse. You will itch between your balls and behind your knees and under the soles of your feet. And then you will start itching inside, in your lungs and your liver and your kidneys and your intestines.' He stretched his neck forward like a chicken watching a worm. 'Prepare yourself to start scratching,' he concluded. 'The rest of us have enough to keep us busy until the rain comes. As soon as the clouds are right.'

And as the people started moving off in all directions, I noticed Brother Holy surreptitiously reaching a long cadaverous hand up between his shoulder blades to start scratching.

Old Hottentot Custom

THE CHAMELEON DIDN'T work. How could it? Yet Hans Magic lost no face in the process, as he blamed it on the clouds which came from the wrong direction. In the night there was another storm, possibly even worse than the previous ones – we were all too bloody shell-shocked to care – but once again without a sign of rain. Three houses were left in ruins. Tall-Fransina's shed was blown away, and her pot-still with it. It was something of a miracle that she hadn't been working at the time, otherwise she'd have gone too. Four people were killed; two died under a collapsed roof, the other two simply disappeared without a trace.

On the Sunday morning we all gathered outside the church after the morning service to watch Hans Magic opening the shallow grave in which he'd buried the chameleon. It was empty. I had a pretty strong suspicion about who might have spirited the little reptile away, but for obvious reasons I kept it to myself; and Piet Snot didn't look at me once. Somewhat to my surprise, no one else appeared to have jumped to the same conclusion; perhaps they were too fucking dismayed by the most recent disaster.

The church service had been unusually short. What should have been an ideal opportunity for Brother Holy to make up some lost ground was squandered in the damn St Vitus's dance he performed on the pulpit as he tried to scratch himself throughout the succession of prayers and hymns and sermon, so that no one paid much attention to his message. And afterwards, without murmur, they all accepted Hans Magic's latest proposal to conjure up rain.

This time the remedy was very simple. Someone born in a heavy rainstorm had to be stripped to the skin, covered in honey, subjected to a general laying-on of hands, and sent off into the mountains, to remain there until the rains came. This, Hans Magic assured us, should happen well before nightfall.

There were no sources I could consult, of course, but I was pretty sure that it was some version of yet another old Hottentot custom. And if my hunch was correct, Bilhah's legacy was indeed still running strong in the community. No matter how many little black sheep had been sacrificed over the years to exorcise her spirit, her hold on them was bloody permanent. But it was difficult to say whether the thought was comforting or distressing.

There was no long prelude to the new ceremony, due perhaps to the general sense of relief at discovering that there was still something they could do, on which to focus their much-distracted thoughts. And Jurg Water was the one who came forward, his huge hand closed like a vice over a cringing little Piet Snot's shoulder.

'Piet here is mos a storm-child,' he announced. 'We can send him off.'

'Pa,' the boy whimpered. But one look from Jurg smothered all protest in his throat.

Turbid Residue

As if summoned for the occasion, Henta and her flutter of finches came swooping down on us from behind the nearest house, raced past the gathered crowd and headed towards the bluegum wood. In less than a minute they were gone again, and only a cloud of grey dust remained as proof of their passage. Their brief appearance left a turbid residue among the assembled settlers – unless I was merely projecting on them the troubled state of my own mind. But I don't think so, for almost immediately a loud male voice shouted from the throng:

'What about Henta? Wasn't she born in a rainstorm too? She's just made to be dipped in honey.'

'You hold her, I'll do the daubing,' cried someone else.

More voices joined in. But there was an edge of hysteria to the false exuberance. Until Tant Poppie elbowed her way through the crowd and suddenly swung a blow with her fist which felled one of the men in the dust as if he'd been struck by epilepsy. It was Petrus Tatters. The jeering and tittering died away abruptly.

Jurg Water spoke up behind Tant Poppie: 'Leave him to me.'

He let go of Piet Snot, his two long arms like hyphens on either side of his massive frame. It took a great effort from Lukas Death and several others to hold him back while Petrus Tatters scuttled off, slobbering in fear and shame.

After the commotion had died down, Hans Magic took up his interrupted ceremony where he'd left off. Meekly, and without a squeak, Piet Snot allowed his father to drag him forward. He was twisting a bit in the big man's grip, but without uttering a squeak.

'Take off your clothes, Piet,' ordered Jurg Water. He turned to the crowd: 'Where's the honey?'

'Pa,' moaned the child, almost inaudibly.

Jurg Water raised his hand for a slap. I tensed up. God be my witness, I thought, if he . . . But he didn't. We all looked away energetically while the spindly little creature was peeled from his clothes. His body was as white as chalk, veined with blue. The criss-cross pattern of bruises and weals didn't bear looking at.

Someone approached with a tub of honey from one of the nearby homes. Like fucking bees the people converged on the child. For minutes on end they thronged and hummed and buzzed and bustled. Then Piet emerged from the writhing mass like a thin strip of sticky flypaper, his little monkey face smeared with snot and honey. He didn't cry. Only dry sobs racked his body from time to time. One by one the people filed past him and laid their hands on his sticky head, then moved on. I didn't want any part in it. Emma was standing beside me. I noticed Hans Magic leering at us, but just stared back.

'Now you go right up to the dry riverbed, Piet,' commanded Hans Magic. 'Make sure you go deep into the mountains and wait there. Before it's dark we'll come and fetch you. By that time, if all goes well, it will be raining.'

Miserable and sticky, the boy began to scuttle away. The two bony wings of his shoulder blades looked terribly vulnerable. Only once he stopped, as if he couldn't bear the idea of going on alone. He half-turned back to us. Among all the people his eyes singled me out.

'Isn't Oom going to help me?' he asked.

'It's just until tonight, Piet,' I stammered, too fucked-up to look him in the eye. I felt Emma's fingers on my arm. It was as if I'd just condemned him to death.

And for all I knew I had.

Threadbare Flour-Bag

THE NIGHTWALKERS were not visiting me any more. Perhaps they'd found out about Emma. Or perhaps the havoc in the settlement had simply become too much for them. Whatever the reason, it suited me. Emma and I needed, not days and nights, but months and years to catch up with all we had to talk about. Two lifetimes, hers and mine; everything we'd been saving up and which now had come out, a need as urgent as Brother Holy's fucking itch.

In her room, or mine; in what remained of Smith-the-Smith's rickety shed; under the deserted lean-to where bits and pieces of Tall-Fransina's broken still now lay abandoned; in the schoolroom Lukas Death had built on to the side of his house and which was now standing empty during the hectic days as the children toiled with their parents to repair the storm damage.

Only the mad and the feeble still came and went as always, slobbering and yawning and dribbling and pissing themselves. And of course Henta and her gaggle of girls who couldn't be contained by any natural or unnatural disaster: at unpredictable intervals they would still come hurtling past like a delinquent dust-devil, here one moment and gone the next, leaving behind only the improbable imprint of their bare feet and their smell of darkness and forbidden games.

Otherwise we met behind the windblown tatters where the ostrich pen had been, or in the bluegum wood, or up in the mountain at the Devils' Hole, the one spot where we felt truly secure and remote – until we discovered that more and more of the settlers were secretly visiting the place, in spite of all the public doubts and prohibitions, to fill their pails and barrels with water against the drought. And once, on the afternoon of the day little Piet had been sent off into the mountains, dripping with honey, tears and snot, we went back to the rock pool where I had first seen her in her dream. If it had been a dream, if it had been her. Emma brought a small threadbare flour-bag with her, stuffed with food: an apple, a few dried apricots, a handful or two of raisins, a small jar of lemon syrup. Only after we'd left the pool behind, well out of earshot of the houses, we started calling his name. But there was no answer.

'He's hiding,' I said, trying to convince myself. 'He won't come out, he's mad at me.'

Overhead there were once more clouds scurrying past, sending hurried, restless shadows across the narrow kloof; but I no longer set any store by them.

Emma called out again, then listened for a response, every muscle in her body tense, as if she wished to force an answer from the bloody mountains. Then again and again. But it was absolutely silent, that ancient unsettling silence of a birdless world.

'I'll leave it here for him,' she said at last. There was an obstinate set to her mouth. It was as vital for her as it was for me to believe that he was just hiding somewhere.

Talons and Claws

Where the dried-up bed curved in a wide, easy bend, she left the bag on a large flat rock where it could easily be seen. I took her hand. We went back to the dry pool, jumping from rock to rock. All around us trees blown over in the storms lay upended, large clusters of roots sticking up like hands with broken fingers. Here and there deep furrows had been gashed open as the roots were torn loose. Even their tips showed not the slightest sign of moisture. Curiously enough the ancient, half-charred wild figtree which had been split by lightning so long ago, Ouma Liesbet Prune's Paradise Tree, still stood intact, its long sinewy roots reaching across rocks and boulders, like the god-damn talons and claws of a huge animal that had burrowed in there, never to let go again.

'Just as pigheaded as the people in the settlement,' I said wryly.

'You're no different, Flip.' She took one of my hands in both of hers. 'I can't understand why you want to stay here. The rest of us have no choice. But you do.'

'There's nothing I'd love more than to get out of this place,' I said. 'But you know I can't bloody well leave you here.'

'I'm not holding you here.'

'That's not how I mean it. It is my own choice. I don't *want* to leave you here. I'm responsible for you now.'

'No, you're not. I'm still me, you are you.'

'It's no longer so simple.'

'Then it's you who are making it difficult. You've got to be sensible, Flip.'

It isn't easy to retrace all the meanderings of the conversation we had that afternoon. Because it wasn't only one conversation either. Every time we met, all the old arguments were taken up again. It was like some fucking kind of undergrowth in which we'd become entangled: and in what I'm trying to recall here of what was said that afternoon several other conversations are mixed up. It's like Gert Brush's paintings, with the ghosts of lost faces looming up through all those layers.

Pack of Hyenas

Almost every time – and that afternoon too, I'm sure – I'd end up saying something like, 'I can't throw you to a pack of hyenas.'

To which she would reply very calmly, but very firmly, 'I can manage. I always have.'

'It's too damn dangerous, Emma. You said that yourself, the very first time we spoke.'

'I said they wouldn't let me go. That's something else.'

'But now I've complicated things for you. There's nothing we can take for granted.'

'I know them, I'll survive. You're the one who doesn't know where to step. You're in danger, Flip. They told you their stories, and that gives you power over them. They can't allow it.'

'If we leave together, we have a chance. And the sooner the better.'

'No, they're counting on it that neither of us will leave without the other. As long as they see I'm still here they won't suspect anything. Flip, it's the only chance you have.'

'Then I stay here.'

'I want you to go.' Her eyes were fixed urgently on mine.

'Not without you.'

She changed her angle of attack: 'There's nothing for us outside. You just lost your head because . . .'

'Because I love you.'

'Don't ever say that. I don't want to hear it.'

'Once we're outside you'll soon see that it was a mistake. I'm too young for you, Flip, too stupid, too everything. Before we've been there for a month you'll get tired of me. And that will be worse than anything that could happen here.'

'Don't you believe me then?' I asked, stung.

'It makes no difference whether I believe you or not.' And with the kind of stillness which had so often surprised me in her, she said, 'Perhaps it would be even worse if I believed you. I couldn't bear the thought of waking up one day.'

'This isn't a dream, Emma.'

'Are you sure?' For a moment she pressed her forehead against mine, and gave a small laugh, but a bitter one; then leaned back, propped up on her arms. 'Don't you remember the day you first came here?'

'That was different,' I said.

She shook her head.

Without Warmth

Her hair had fallen forward, exposing the nape of her neck. I put my arms around her from behind.

'Emma.'

After a moment, with a slight but decisive movement, she freed herself. Not without warmth, but as if from far away, she said, 'It would be better to forget about me, Flip.'

'Then at least give me something to forget!' I stormed, unreasonable. 'I can't accept that my only memory of you must be the way you once looked like in a dream.'

'No one here can ever survive in the world you come from.'

'You're different, you spent time there. You told me yourself how much you miss it.'

'One only really misses what is impossible.' She took my face between her hands. 'I'm a freak,' she said with intensity. 'Like any of those poor creatures with waterheads or harelips or webbed toes that walk these streets. We're all marked. And that is why you must go back. One day you'll only remember me as a nightmare from which you woke up just in time.'

I pressed my face against her to reassure myself of the lean hard presence of her body. I could smell her, a smell of life and warmth and woman and desire, everything that was real and that mattered at that moment.

'*This* is the difference between dream and reality,' I said in a wave of fucking sentimentality. 'I can't go on without you.'

'You can. You must. And I without you. You can't allow this place to swallow you too. Don't you understand? My life is cut off already. It'll help me just to know you're *there*, your life is going on.' Adding more softly, an afterthought. 'And knowing perhaps that there'll be something you remember.'

'You can't give up like this.'

'It's not giving up. Don't you think I also want to live?' She moved away. 'We must go back. There's another storm brewing.'

I looked up. The clouds were billowing overhead as before. If only the blasted rains would come, I thought. That would change everything. The people would come to rest. There would be a semblance of bloody normality again.

Strange Contortions

THIS TIME THE storm wasn't quite as godawful as before, but perhaps we were becoming blunted. At any rate it didn't last for more than an hour or so. But the problem was that the damage done in the previous storms had not been repaired yet; the roofs, especially, had been so badly weakened that it didn't take much for several of them to cave in altogether. At least, thank God, this time round there were no casualties. And in the late afternoon, after the last fierce gusts had died down and the sky had cleared, people cautiously stepped outside again to inspect the ravages and to start, once again, clearing up the mounds of rubble that marked the passage of the hurricane.

The most important thing to do now was to bring little Piet Snot home. After the unsuccessful trip Emma and I had made up the dry riverbed in the early afternoon I was very worried. I would never forget that last look he'd given me, and his pleading, accusing words, *Isn't Oom going to help me?*

A few of us – Lukas Death, Isak Smous, Gert Brush and I – took the footpath to Hans Magic's hut. Incredibly, the rickety little structure had survived all the storms; even the thatch on the roof was undamaged. Perhaps the thicket surrounding it had protected it, but it didn't seem too far-fetched to guess that even the elements were taking no chances with the old devil.

He was in no hurry to come with us. First he insisted on stuffing his calabash pipe with dagga.

'Why are you pressing me?' he asked. 'There's more than enough time before dark.'

'It was a bad storm for a child to be in,' I told him angrily.

'There's enough shelter in the kloof, he'll be all right.'

'He didn't have a shred of clothing to protect him.'

'Children are used to running around bare-arsed.'

'It's easy for you to say.'

'Don't aggravate the man, Neef Flip,' Lukas Death stopped me with a look of concern. 'Hans knows his time.'

I took umbrage at that, but after what had happened to Brother Holy I was anxious not to bring another of Hans Magic's feelings over him; so I swallowed my irritation until his pipe was drawing to his satisfaction. Only then did he shut the door which hung unsteadily on leather hinges, and join us outside where we'd chosen to wait in the open air.

At first sight the settlement appeared to be going about its normal late-afternoon business: the old ravens in the cemetery, the afflicted in the streets, Bettie Teat in the doorway of the church, people in their backyards or chicken runs or parched orchards and vegetable gardens, poultry scratching in the dry earth, goats grazing among the scraggly bushes. But after three storms the place looked chewed to the bone.

Far in the background Brother Holy could be seen rolling about in strange contortions, blasting the valley with thundering curses from Jeremiah and Ezekiel. He aimed a hoarse shout in our direction as we passed below, but Hans Magic didn't even look up.

'Etch 'Ou

Along the way a few women joined our little procession: Hanna-of-Jurg, Annie-of-Alwyn, Dalena-of-Lukas, three or four others, and Emma. Hans Magic clearly resented their presence, but he said nothing openly, contenting himself with unsavoury remarks muttered under his stinking breath.

Some distance beyond the rock pool, high up along the course of the dried-up river, he stopped. 'He'll be somewhere here,' he announced.

That was just where Emma and I had earlier left the little bag of food on the flat rock. I was rather relieved, even touched, to see that the bag had disappeared. But of course, it could have blown away: the wind had torn a trench along the full length of the kloof as it came funnelling down from above. And how could we be sure that the child would have found a safe spot to shelter?

The women started calling, followed by the rest of us, first in single voices, then all in chorus.

'Piet! Piet, come out! We've come to fetch you!' we trumpeted among the cliffs, hearing our own voices echoing back from the distance: 'etch 'ou! . . . 'ou! . . . 'ou!

'The little shit is hiding from us,' grumbled Hans Magic. 'He's a stroppy one.'

We didn't bother to answer. Farther and farther we spread out, hollering his name.

Only the echoes replied.

'He could have fallen to his death,' said Hanna-of-Jurg, in a surprisingly high whining tone for such a voluminous person. She turned her vulnerable cow's eyes to Hans Magic: 'If anything happened to him, you'll be to blame.'

'I'm telling you he's just hiding away.'

'Then how come you can't find him? You always know everything.'

'He'll come out.'

Half an hour later we were back in the settlement, with empty hands. A small knot of people were awaiting us at the church. Children were dispatched with the tidings. Within minutes a large search party set out again along the dry riverbed. But when night fell they were forced to turn back.

'The dark will bring him home all right,' said Hans Magic, but his eyes were avoiding ours. 'He'll be back before morning.'

'And all for nothing,' Hanna-of-Jurg reminded him.

'I told you the clouds had to be right. They came from the wrong side again.'

'It's my child's life you're playing with.'

'You can always have another,' he said, and walked away.

Swollen Thick

It was Henta who brought the news in the morning. I was at home alone, Tant Poppie having been called out to help when a few people were injured by a wall that had collapsed in one of the stricken houses during the night. The moment I saw the girl I knew. I stood up very quickly from the breakfast table.

'Has something happened?'

'Yes, Oom.' She didn't cry, but her eyes were swollen thick. The normally blooming face looked very pale. There was a bloody weal across one cheek, and on the dusty legs under her dress. The dress itself was in shreds, the hem of it undone, one sleeve torn off, exposing the shoulder. Through the fresh smell of peaches she usually exuded wafted darker, more worrisome odours of the night, alluding to a kind of space she should not yet have knowledge of.

'Who did this to you?' I demanded.

She just shook her head, her knotted dark-red hair falling over her face.

'Henta, what happened?'

The she began to cry. 'It's Piet, Oom. Pa killed him.'

Shocking State

There are professions in which personal involvement in what happens around you is a sure recipe for a fuck-up. Objectivity is the golden rule. Any lawyer will tell you that. Any psychologist too, I'm sure. Be that as it may. But what I do know is that no crime reporter can afford to get emotionally involved in a case he's required to cover.

Ever since that day when little Piet Snot mistook me for God, he'd somehow become my damn responsibility, whether I'd wanted to or not; and even more so after he'd brought me the wretched chameleon. To bring me luck! To compound it all, there was Henta. From the first time in Jurg's shed (*What do you think I've come for?*), she'd been stirring up totally unbloodymanageable feelings in me. Her perverse innocence. And now, this morning, she turned up in that shocking state.

All of which spelled out quite clearly that I'd better stay out of it. But how could I? If *she* asked me? And if little Piet Snot was dead?

I couldn't believe it. In a way perhaps it was the worst that could have happened. Up to that moment, even when I'd become drawn into events like Ouma Liesbet's death or Hans Magic's rainmaking rituals or Ben Owl's suicide, it had been possible to keep to the sideline. But this time there was no fucking way I could stay out of it.

Any Cop

'Aren't you coming?' asked Henta. She looked like one of those cheap paintings of Spanish gypsy children who stare at you with their huge eyes and tear-stained cheeks, pure schmaltz. I didn't want to see it. Why couldn't she have gone to Lukas Death for help? He was the fucking judge. It had nothing to do with me.

Is Oom not going to help me?

'What can I do?' I asked helplessly, more to myself than to her.

'You want me to go back to that place alone?' she asked.

I took her by the shoulders. She winced, and I quickly let go again. 'What's wrong?'

She half-turned her back and pulled the dress down from her shoulder to show me the bloody weals. Jesus Christ.

'Do you want to see more?'

'I've seen enough,' I said quickly. 'Why did he do that to you?'

'I tried to stop him.'

Filled with bloody guilt and self-loathing I said, 'All right, I'm coming.'

Distraught, I looked round. I didn't like the idea of taking on Jurg Water with my bare hands, especially in the mood he would undoubtedly be in right now. But there was nothing in the voorhuis I could use as a weapon. I went to the kitchen and grabbed a long fire-iron from the hearth.

'Come.'

She cast a scared look at the fire-iron, but offered no protest. Shrugging her bare shoulder back into the torn dress she followed me. A few people on the road stopped when they saw us pass. They must have drawn their own conclusions, for they soon fell in behind us. By the time we reached Jurg Water's house there were a dozen or more on my heels.

The front door was closed. Like any cop in a film I kicked it open.

Foul Play

Confusion continues to surround events in the Devil's Valley where a young boy known as Piet Snot (9) was found dead on Monday morning after apparently getting lost in the mountains over the weekend. It is suspected that he lost his way in a violent windstorm. Although a search party was sent out on Sunday afternoon, its members were forced to suspend the search when night fell without any sign of the boy. However, it was reported that his father, Mr Jurg (Water) Lermiet, continued on his own to scour the mountains for his son until he found the child's body in a deep ravine in the early hours of Monday morning. Judging by the injuries to the body it would seem as if he had been attacked by a wild animal. According to a spokesman, Mr Lukas (Death) Lermiet, foul play is not suspected and rumours about dissension in the family are devoid of all foundation. The sister of the dead boy, Miss Henta Lermiet, was unwell and had been advised by her father not to speak to the press. Final funeral arrangements have not yet been made.

Wounded Buffalo

Everything suddenly got out of hand the moment I stepped into Jurg Water's house. The fire-iron had been meant only as a precaution, for self-defence. But when I saw the small broken body on the narrow bed in the corner, with a still-shocked Hanna beside it like a bundle of unwashed laundry and Jurg walking up and down in the background brandishing a sjambok, something in me gave way.

The moment he recognised me he came charging round the dining table, kicking a chair out of the way so violently that I heard the wood splinter.

'Get out of my house!' he shouted, his face looking more like a malignant tumour than ever.

'Pa,' said Henta behind me.

Jurg Water stared past me in disbelief. 'What are you doing with that bastard?' he demanded.

I glanced round at her. 'Henta, go and call Lukas Death. And Hans Magic.'

Like a frightened rabbit Henta just stood there. But some of the other people on the stoep scurried off. A handful of men came bundling through the doorway to stop us. But Jurg Water was like a fucking wounded buffalo. He shoved two or three of them out of the way and aimed a blow with the sjambok at me. I sidestepped and it only struck my shoulder, but I could feel it cutting through the skin under my shirt. Then I let rip with the fire-iron. Your Worship, it was he or I.

Jurg dropped to the floor on all fours, shaking his head as if he didn't know what had hit him. There was blood everywhere. The blow had struck him over the nose and forehead. It seemed as if the nose was broken. I hoped it was.

But that was that. Because the next moment a whole bunch of people burst past me to separate the two of us. In the struggle my watch was torn from my wrist, and as I stopped to pick it up someone crunched it underfoot. This made me even madder. But as I bundled up to hurl myself at them, I realised that Emma was there too.

If it hadn't been for her, I swear by the brass buckle on my father's belt, I'd have broken free from the hands pinning my arms to my back. I was man enough to kill Jurg, or anybody who tried to stop me. But not in front of her. Jurg was still carrying on like a bull brought down to be castrated. There were chairs and benches breaking all over the place as he wrestled with his tamers. The only unmoving objects in that voorhuis were the messy remains of Piet Snot on the bed, and Henta in the doorway, her hands pressed to her face.

By the time Lukas Death arrived everybody was talking at the same time. Those who'd come in last had the most to say. I couldn't make head or tail out of all their versions, but later in the day I was able to speak to Hanna and from Emma I learned what she'd been told by Henta; and from all those bits and pieces I managed to patch together a fuller picture.

Insult to Incest

It turned out that little Piet had never gone into the mountains after all. Just after Hans Magic had sent him up the dry riverbed, he'd made a detour back to the settlement. That must have happened during the Sunday dinner. Even in the heart of the drought there was the customary excess of goat's meat and samp and pumpkin and sweet potatoes and the rest. Piet must have avoided the loiterers and the stricken in body or mind, hiding behind his father's house where there was rubble enough lying about after all the storms. And during the heavy sleep that descended on the valley in the wake of the meal he'd slipped inside to ask help from Henta. For better or for worse she wiped the sticky mess from his body, fed him the remains of the Sunday meal, and hid him under her bed where she'd spread a few buckskins. The ample dassie-skin kaross on the bed hung down far enough to keep him out of sight. That, as it turned out later, was where he'd stowed the dead chameleon the night before, after scooping it up from its premature grave.

So far everything had gone well for him. But not for long. The main problem was Jurg Water's temper which had been building up towards an explosion for some time: the family, recognising the signs, had gone into a kind of catatonic state in anticipation. He was already fucked when the storm in the afternoon brought no rain. 'It's because that Piet is so bloody useless,' he ranted. And when Hanna tried to defend the boy he slapped her. Wanting to stay out of it, Henta had withdrawn to her bed in the voorhuis, but somehow that made him even angrier. And then the futile search in the mountains stirred up yet more bloody thunder inside him, which wasn't helped at all by Hanna's increasingly vocal reproaches. He hardly slept all night. My own guess is that he was already hatching schemes of revenge for the shame little Piet had brought on them.

What followed is still not clear. It would seem that Jurg's prostate sent him outside during the night. But it is also possible that darker designs drove him to Henta's bed in the voorhuis, because that was where the trouble came to a head. In the dark he either stumbled over little Piet's feet sticking out from under the bed, or the boy made a sound when his father's heavy body began to weigh down the mat of the bed on top of him. The particulars are not that important. All that matters is that Jurg plucked Piet from under bed and, to add insult to incest, discovered the dead chameleon in the boy's hand. That was all he needed, and Henta's attempts to interfere just about turned his arse-hairs grey.

Many Generations

It was in the church that the next chapter was played out. Which came as no surprise. There is no other public building in the settlement, and in the course of time the church has come to stand in for all kinds of functions, not all of them solemn or proper. I should have remembered what had happened to Alwyn Knees.

All that lived and moved in the Devil's Valley was there. Including Brother Holy, but he was scratching away so furiously that he couldn't have absorbed much of what was happening around him. Behind the communion table a few chairs had been set out for the members of the Council of Justice: Lukas Death in the centre, more pissed-upon than pissing; to his left, Isak Smous; to his right, Jos Joseph. Jurg Water and I were both in the front row, but with several other men in between. Just as at church services, the men and women were seated apart in two blocks, left and right.

Let me say immediately that it was the weirdest trial I have attended in my career as a crime reporter. Actually it wasn't a trial at all, and perhaps I'd been fucking naïve to expect anything of the kind. I should have taken to heart the way in which after the deaths of Ouma Liesbet and Ben Owl everything had simply petered out, but at least there was the excuse that his suicide had prematurely brought an end to both matters. But this time it was murder, loud and clear, and the perpetrator was at hand.

Even so, there was no accusation of any kind brought against Jurg Water. All that appeared to interest the three councillors was what weight could be attached to the fact that neither of Hans Magic's blasted rituals had been allowed to run its course. Did it mean that the whole process should start all over again, first with a new chameleon, then a new storm-child? Or should they attempt something different altogether? Because the situation, brothers and sisters, had now become critical.

I couldn't believe my fucking ears. Nor could I keep silent. I'd seen some pretty disgusting sights in my life; but the way Henta had appeared on my doorstep that morning, and the sight of little Piet's remains on that blood-spattered bed, would be screwing me for years to come. And after the first few opinions had been aired – including an intervention, so help me God, by Jurg Water himself, who proposed that Hans Magic should be locked up for the unrest he had caused – I jumped to my feet. My hands were trembling as they clutched the edge of the pew in front of me. From the murmuring voices around me it was soon clear that the audience didn't approve of my speaking at all. But fuck them.

'Lukas,' I said, 'while everything in front of my eyes began to waver, like a scene through a heatwave, 'please help me if I'm wrong. But a child was beaten to death in this settlement last night. We have all seen the body. Now isn't *that* what we're supposed to discuss? You're sitting here with a murderer in your midst and all you can talk about is chameleons.'

'It was *your* chameleon, Neef Flip,' Lukas Death quietly reminded me, as if that was the crux of the matter.

'I'm talking about murder. Doesn't it concern you?'

'Neef Flip.' Lukas Death's voice was infused with endless patience, which made me ever madder. 'Our customs go back a long way. They have been tried and tested over many generations. We appreciate your good intentions, but perhaps it would be better for you to stay out of this.'

'I don't understand . . .' I said.

'That is very obvious,' Jos Joseph cut in. 'Now please sit down.'

I was ready to boil over, although I still desperately tried to restrain myself: I mean, hell, this was no time for irresponsible speech or action. But how could I just let them carry on like that?

Parent and Child Inside

'When I arrived at Jurg Water's house this morning . . .' I began
again.

'How come that every time someone dies this man is on the
scene?' Jurg Water interrupted, his voice distorted by his mangled
and hugely swollen nose. 'First Ouma Liesbet, then Ben Owl, now
Piet. Ask him to explain that to us.'

A number of voices rumbled in support.

'Well, Neef Flip?' said Lukas Death, clearly uncomfortable.
'Entering another man's house with the clear purpose of assaulting
him with a fire-iron is not a very neighbourly thing to do, is it now?'

Sounds of approval from all sides. The farce was threatening to
get wholly out of control. All my resolve to restrain myself broke
down.

'You're speaking about assault?' I asked. 'I defended myself
when he attacked me with his sjambok. The same sjambok with
which he'd beaten his child to death. Isn't that what we're here for?'

Lukas stared at me in utter surprise. 'But Neef Flip,' he said,
'surely what happens between parent and child inside the four walls
of a house concerns no one outside? I've explained that to you
before.'

'We were talking about a thrashing at the time, Lukas. Are you
trying to tell me a father has the right to kill his son and get away with
it?'

'The father is the head of his house,' said Lukas Death, still in a
tone of great forbearance. 'As the Judge is the head of his people.
This authority comes from God, and it is not for us to question it.
How can we raise a hand against God himself?'

It was his mild way of speaking that made it just too fucking much
to take. And no one in the congregation – except Jurg Water, who
continued to glower at me with fire and brimstone in his eyes –
seemed upset or put out. Some of them even smiled indulgently in
my direction: this poor idiot in our midst who can't understand how
such things work, don't be too hard on him, he'll learn.

Conjugation of a Verb

In desperation I turned round in my pew to face the people behind me: 'Is there no one among you who has any question? Will you let a murderer get away with a crime like this? I don't believe it. I've come to know you as honourable and decent citizens . . .'

'You heard what Lukas Death said,' remarked one of the older men. 'We'll arrange a proper funeral for the child, we all liked him. Nice manners, well brought up. The rest is between his family and the Lord.'

'So it's out of sight, out of mind?' I asked, feeling like a lion in a den of Daniels. 'A man who steals a pail of water for his pregnant wife is flogged to death. But a father who kills his child can continue to sit on his big arse in church with you?'

'Drought affects the whole community, Neef Flip,' said Lukas Death, as if he were explaining the conjugation of a verb to a half-witted child. 'Don't you see . . .?'

'No, I don't!' I shouted back. This time I turned towards the female block for one last appeal: 'Is there not a single woman here who feels unhappy about what happened? Do you also go along with it?' I paused, realising very well how below-the-belt I was fighting, but this was my last resort. 'Hanna, you . . .?'

Hanna-of-Jurg half-rose to her feet, but sank back again.

'Neef Flip isn't familiar with our customs yet,' said Lukas Death from his chairman's seat. 'Women are not allowed to speak in church, except to address the Lord in prayer.'

I took the gap: 'Then perhaps one of them would like to raise this matter in prayer to God?'

But with a great show of long-suffering Lukas Death pointed out that this was a session of the Council of Justice, not a prayer-meeting. And then Isak Smous butted in:

'I think we've given enough time to one speaker,' he said, casting a smile of forgiveness in my direction. 'Can we return to more important matters now?'

'It's time we called another prayer-meeting,' proposed Brother Holy, executing a quick two-step as he tried to reach an itch in a difficult spot.

But most of the men immediately saw through the strategy, and the proposal was turned down flat. The congregation wasn't going to entrust anything to Brother Holy's itching hands again. With an overwhelming majority the Council of Justice was requested to co-opt Hans Magic in order to decide on the next step. In a surprisingly mellow mood the meeting was adjourned.

Weird shit. That is the Devil's Valley. Weird shit, in every sense of 'weird'. But also fucking dangerous shit.

Up To Here

I was the only one to remain behind in the church, shattered and empty, and still unable to grasp properly what had happened.

Which was why the transition caught me unawares. The others were still chatting in small groups when I emerged from the stale darkness inside the church into the bloody pitiless glare of the sun. I felt miserable; my only desire was to get away from them, back to my room. But Jurg Water must have been waiting for me, because the moment I stepped outside, past the stained door with the large mottled brass ring, he shouted from a distance:

'Don't think I've finished with you, you troublemaker!'

I stopped. My jaws felt tense. 'Are you talking to me?' I asked, 'Murderer.'

If this was the way to go, I thought, then so be it.

But the others must have been expecting something of the sort, because a buffer of bodies immediately formed between us. Some of the men pinned my arms behind me. For a moment I thought they were going to hand me over to Jurg Water, but then I noticed that he was being similarly restrained.

Afterwards it occurred to me how strange it was that the old Seer had not come down to call us all to order. But just as well, I suppose. He might have tipped the scales against me. That he hadn't bothered to come might in fact be a signal that I no longer had reason to fear anything from that quarter. Perhaps, having at last told me his story, he would now come to rest. I couldn't bank on it, of course, but the crisis might well be over. Jurg Water on his own I could take on. Just go for the nose, I decided.

Lukas Death moved quickly to stamp out the fires. But Jurg Water didn't even look at him. All his withering attention was focused on me.

'Look, you try to call me a murderer to my face again and see what happens,' he taunted me, struggling so furiously that the four or five men holding him back were swung this way and that like old rags. But for the moment they still had the upper hand.

'You can deny it till your face is bluer than your nose, Jurg, but you are a murderer,' I repeated. 'And there are enough people here who've got their arseholes plugged with the way you treat your family.' I mean, if he was playing to the gallery, right, then so could I. 'If you don't watch out you may wake up one morning with a peg through your head.'

'What's this shit you're talking?' he asked.

'You know what happened to Lukas Nimrod,' I said. 'When the men of the Devil's Valley were too scared to face him, his own wife killed him.'

'That's a lie. It was a porcupine that penned him. I told you myself.'

'That's why I don't believe it, Jurg.'

This stirred up even more shit. And in the bloody bedlam of talking and shouting I was relieved to hear women's voices joining in at last.

'No one here will dare to raise a hand against me,' he shouted through the noise.

All of a sudden it was his wife Hanna who broke from the crowd to come up to him. Her face was streaked with tears, like Henta's had been earlier, but her voice was fierce and unwavering.

'All these years I've let you have your way, Jurg Water,' she said. Silence fell on the crowd as if a huge kaross had been flung over them to quell all sound. It was very obvious that only one hell of an effort had brought her so far. But having made her move, nothing was going to stop her now. 'God knows, it was a sin, but I never interfered, even when I should have. For Pietie's sake. For Henta's. Because I always thought, no matter how terrible it was, you had the right. And at least you spared me. But last night you raised your hand against me too and then you killed Pietie. Don't think I'll ever forget that, even if I get to be as old as Ouma Liesbet Prune one day.'

Lukas Death cleared his throat as he tried to step between them. 'We understand your feelings, Hanna,' he said, as if he was pleading for help rather than offering it. 'But you must take comfort from the fact that one learns through suffering.'

'What do *you* know about it?' asked Hanna, even more provoked than before. 'The only thing that suffering has taught me is the uselessness of suffering. And now I've had enough.' She swung back to her husband. 'I'm telling you one thing, Jurg Water, and let these people be my witness: sooner or later I'm going to get you. I'm not saying when. It may be tonight or it may be next year. But it will happen one night when you don't expect it.'

'You think I'm scared of woman's talk?'

'We shall see what we shall see, Jurg. You've been warned. And you'd be wise not to sleep too deeply from now on.'

'Wait till I get my two hands on you.'

Legs Very Far Apart

And then it was Dalena-of-Lukas who came forward. There was something almost frightening about her look this time. 'If you touch so much as a single hair on Hanna's head, we women will take the law into our hands.'

'Dalena, now please!' a decidedly worried Lukas Death tried to intervene.

'You shut up, Lukas.' She came a step nearer to Jurg Water. 'If you can still walk after we've done with you, it'll be with your legs very far apart,' she said. 'And if you still haven't learned your lesson I shall personally push your forked stick up your backside.'

'And all this just because of the lies this man told?' asked Jurg, still smouldering, but with less defiance in his manner than before.

'They're not lies,' said Dalena. 'I told him myself what really happened to Lukas Nimrod.'

The men had let go of our arms, but they were clearly ready to jump in again if necessary.

'How can you turn against one of your own?' asked Jurg Water, deeply offended. He shook his head in my direction again. 'From the moment that man came here among us he's just been causing trouble, digging up all the sins of the past. Why? To blacken our name in the world outside? So that they can start sending in commandos and expeditions as in the old days to wipe us out?'

Unexpectedly Tant Poppie Fullmoon also came forward. In passing she elbowed Jurg Water in the wind. 'What do you know about the old days?' she jeered. 'You're only a second-generation settler, so watch your mouth.'

Jurg Water gawked at her, then turned towards his cronies. 'Now that we're on our knees in the drought this stranger wants to finish us off. It's high time *he* got hauled before the Council of Justice.'

'Not a bad idea,' commented Jos Joseph. 'He's been much too free in all his saying and doing among us.'

'You let him be.' This time it was Tall-Fransina. 'He's done no harm. Why don't you look into your own hearts for a change?'

'I agree,' said Gert Brush out of the blue, even if he did sound somewhat apologetic.

And then, to a hubbub of general surprise, Annie-of-Alwyn came forward to join the other women. She didn't speak, but it was as if a half-extinguished grey coal had miraculously begun to glow with new life.

The unexpected division in their ranks came to me like rain from heaven. But it was much too early to push my luck. The majority could all too easily turn against me. And so I chose, for the moment at least, to keep my own counsel.

Jurg must have felt much the same, but he kept on muttering, 'I haven't finished with him yet.'

'You just keep your knees together,' warned Dalena.

At that moment somebody took my arm from behind. Even

without looking I knew it was Emma. And I felt my body go numb. This she shouldn't have done. Not here, not now, whatever the provocation.

Witch

As I could have predicted it was like a rag to a bull.

'That one,' said Jurg, pointing a heavy arm at Emma, 'that's the one who turned him against us. She's always been cahoots with the Devil. First she drove Little-Lukas to his death. Now she's starting again. She's a witch, I tell you. We should have stoned her long ago.'

'You keep Emma out of this,' I snarled at him. 'She's had nothing to do with any of this.'

'Maybe Peet Flatfoot has something to tell us,' he said with open menace in his voice. 'He never misses anything.' He looked round. 'Peet, where are you?'

Prickhead came stumbling from the crowd, grinning sheepishly at me before he broke excitedly into an incomprehensible babble, one hand fidgeting furiously in his groin.

'Did you hear that?' should Jurg, triumphant. 'What did I tell you? In the bluegum wood, he said. At the rock pool, he said. At the Devils' Hole, he said. Right in Isak Smous's house, he said. They've been lying around all over the valley. He, a stranger from outside. Have you forgotten what happened to her mother then?'

No one dared answer.

'If justice must be done, then let it be done,' he shouted.

'Let us not be too hasty in our judgement, Jurg,' said Lukas Death, darting a quick glance at his wife.

'If the lot of you are too scared,' said the big man, 'then leave her to me. We can't allow this witch of Satan to bring even more shame over us.'

'For a man with blood on his hands you've already said too much,' Hanna interrupted him. For another minute she stood before him in eloquent silence, then came to us and put her arm through Emma's. Her eyes didn't leave him for a moment.

Even so we were a pretty small island in that sea of hostile faces.

Camel

WITH HER HEAVY body supported on the hams of her upper arms, Tant Poppie sat at the head of her large dining table. There was a pile of sewing in front of her, but she didn't seem to have been working. She was just sitting there, staring through the dusty panes of the small window in the wall opposite. Large cracks had appeared in the wall, but she didn't seem to notice. I'd never seen her idle before. Now she looked like a discarded bag from which some of the contents had spilled.

For a moment she tried to put up a front, but it was rather half-hearted. Then she held out her needle and a length of thread to me and said gruffly, 'Can you give me a hand? My eyes are not what they used to be. Here I've been trying to camel the thread through the needle but I keep missing it.'

I'm all thumbs when it comes to threading a needle, but after several attempts and much licking and aiming I managed to manoeuvre the fucking thread through the fucking eye and handed it back to her. 'What are you working on?'

'Just keeping out of mischief.'

'I still want to thank you for standing up for me.'

'That Jurg is asking for trouble,' she grumbled. 'He needs to be taught a lesson. But that doesn't mean you had the right to do what you did.'

'I couldn't let him get away with murder.'

'Ag, it's such a mess.' She shook her head; her bun had come undone and her hair looked tatty. 'I just don't know anything any more.'

'What's the matter then?'

She leaned back; the chair protested. 'On a day like this.' She shook her head again with a helplessness out of place in the woman I'd come to know. 'Everything we lived for, all our hopes, suddenly it's just all gone. Something has happened to us and I don't know where it's going to end. I feel like a stranger in a strange land. The Devil has been let loose among us, seeking whom he may devour.' She looked up. Light settled on her face like dust. 'Does that mean anything to you?'

Ostrich Egg

'Can it really be so bad?' I asked, against my better judgement.

'No,' she said tartly. 'It's worse. It's the limit.' Another shake of the head. 'And that's what I don't understand. All one's life one prepares oneself for the end, but when it comes you're still caught unprepared. That's not the way you expected it. So much sickness, so much anger.' A vague gesture towards the stuff on the floor. 'For the first time in my life my medicine doesn't help any more. It's all been in vain.'

'If only the rains would come . . .' I said automatically.

'That won't make any difference any more. We're too caught up in evil. We closed our eyes to it, we pretended it wasn't there.' There was no self-pity in her voice. The very matter-of-factness of her tone unnerved me.

I pulled out a chair and sat down opposite her. I didn't try to make conversation any more. Silence lay spilled across the space between us. There was something superfluous about words, or perhaps a lack. Same difference.

After a long time she spoke again, without looking at me, as if through the small window she could see something I couldn't. 'It used to be different, Neef Flip. Our people have always been quick to pick a fight, true. But we had good times too. Celebrations, like New Year's Day. We'd start preparing weeks before the time. Here in the middle of the valley, just opposite Ouma Liesbet's house, there used to be a stone dam. We'd fill that up to the brim with honey-beer, the people called it karie. A beer so strong, you can take my word for it, if you put an ostrich egg in it, it got dissolved overnight. And on New Year's Eve we'd all meet there, one lot from this side, the rest from the opposite end of the valley, each group with its own musicians. Fiddle, Christmas-worm, guitar. And then we'd dance and drink and have a roaring time. Even the dead would come from their graves to join in. You never saw such merrymaking. It went on until all the beer was done, sometimes it took a week or more. Then we'd just drop in our tracks and sleep it off. By the time we woke up again the dead would also be back where they belonged. And by next September a whole new generation of babies would be born. Make no mistake, Neef Flip: the people could quarrel and give one another hell, but deep down we were always united. When there was danger, or some kind of plague, we all stood together. In the time of the Great Flu, in times of drought or locusts. And in between there was always something to celebrate. Birth, marriage, death. Or when the bean-harvest came in, or the first witblits of the new vintage from Tall-Fransina's still, or from her father's before her. Or when Isak Smous brought in a new load from outside. But that was before the young ones started moving out, before our numbers went down, before Little-Lukas died, before the drought. Those days will never come round again. The Devil has come to claim his own.'

Welcome

Slowly, as if she didn't really want to, she turned her face to me.

'It would have been better if you never came, Neef Flip. Then you wouldn't have seen what you saw. And perhaps nothing would have gone wrong.'

'You can't blame me for it all.'

'I'm not blaming anybody. But you came here and woke up yesterdays that were better left alone.' A pause. 'Unless it's always been in store for us. I mean, the signs were there. We're all marked with them.'

'It depends on how one reads the signs.' With a touch of

provocation I added, 'If you hadn't believed right from the beginning that Emma had the mark of the Devil on her . . .' Without thinking I placed a hand on my breast.

'Ja, that mole on her left tit,' she said. 'Looks mos just like the footprint of a goat. So what else can it mean? It is the mole you're talking about, isn't it?' She made a long pause. I couldn't answer. She sighed. 'That's why I'm saying it's a pity we can't get away from our yesterdays, Neef Flip.' Her eyes scurried across my face. 'Now tell me honestly: if Emma never knew anything about her mother, don't you think she'd have been happier for it?'

'It's not for us to judge.'

She persisted: 'If we never knew about Grandpa Lukas and the things he did, wouldn't our lives have been easier?'

'It's the Seer himself who refused to go to rest.'

'You have an answer for everything. But we've come to the end of answers.' And then she said, in the same quiet voice, 'It will be better for you to take your things and leave this house, Neef Flip. I'm too old for the kind of thing that happened this morning.'

'Am I no longer welcome here then?' My mouth felt tight.

'It's not that I want to throw you out,' she said, unmoved. 'But it's just not working out any more.'

Twenty-Four of Them

As I left Tant Poppie's house with my rucksack on my back, I came past Tall-Fransina, wandering aimlessly about the broken lean-to where bits and pieces of her still lay scattered — part of the coil, the helmet, faggots, stones from the fireplace. Nervous cats were prowling around her, hissing when I approached.

'What are you going to do now?' I asked.

'What *can* I do?' Her short hair looked more grey and unkempt than usual. 'I could ask Isak Smous to bring me a new still. But I'm not sure. It's been a lifetime.' Followed by a bitter sigh. 'Just as well Little-Lukas left when he did, because now there's nothing left here for him.'

'You were very attached to him.'

'What could you understand about such things?' She kneeled down to stroke one of the cats. The animal stretched its neck back and closed its eyes, purring against her, licking her fingers with its rough, pink, pointed tongue. Fransina's eyes were closed too. I was fascinated by the scene, I couldn't keep my eyes off her. I tried to imagine twenty-four of them.

'Perhaps I understand better than you think.'

Tall-Fransina opened her eyes. 'Emma?' she asked.

I said nothing, but allowed her to look into me. She was the only one in this place, I thought, who needed no explanation.

'I noticed,' she said, continuing to stroke the cat. 'But there is no future in it.'

'There wasn't for you either.'

'No. And yet one keeps faith, against all the odds.'

'You and I are getting old,' I said.

'What will become of Emma?' she asked.

'I don't know. They're all against her. Especially Hans Magic. For reasons he'll know better than I do.'

'He's old too,' said Tall-Fransina. 'Perhaps he needs more forgiveness than you or I.' She stood up. The cat kept winding through her legs.

Stuck in the wheel

Rather unexpectedly I found lodging with Lukas Death. It was Annie-of-Alwyn who suggested it, when I ran into her on my way from Tall-Fransina; she was heading for Tant Poppie's to get medicine for a sick child. When she heard what had happened she invited me to move in with her, clearly without even thinking of the implications. But I was reluctant. 'You're living on your own, Annie, and the Devil's Valley is just looking for an excuse to get at me. It'll be much too risky for you. Especially after the stand you took this morning.' To my surprise she blushed, and I discovered that, haggard as she was and old before her time, she was more attractive than I'd thought. She wanted to protest, but she'd obviously realised herself that she couldn't afford the risk. That was when she referred me to

Lukas Death.

Dalena was quite amenable. The one who objected was Lukas. What would people say? But just as stubborn as she'd been in the morning Dalena nipped his arguments in the bud. 'Little-Lukas's room is empty,' she said. 'His bed is still made up. Neef Flip, you're welcome to move in there.'

In an uneasy way it rounded a circle. I wasn't sure how comfortable I'd feel in the dead boy's bed, but for the moment I was at least assured of a roof over my head.

But then an unexpected bloody spanner got stuck in the wheel when Emma also turned up on Dalena's doorstep looking for a place to stay. We were in the voorhuis when she appeared on the stoep, all embarrassed and apologetic. Seen from inside, it was as if the stark white light outside was eating away her silhouette like acid. Her story was brief and to the point: after the events of the morning Isak Smous's battle-axe wife and her two sisters had unceremoniously thrown her out. A woman accused of witchcraft was no longer welcome in their home, in case the taint was contagious. Isak hadn't been allowed any say in the matter.

What shook me was how small the bundle was she'd brought with her. After she'd unpacked, later, I saw it all: a church dress and a nightdress, a pair of shoes, a shawl and kappie, a small pile of books, a box of toiletries Isak Smous must have smuggled in for her. A whole life in such a paltry bundle. To be so rooted in a place, and yet so disposable, I found hard to grasp.

Your Reasons

I immediately offered to move elsewhere myself. Gert Brush was a possibility, he'd always seemed approachable, even more so after the stand-off at the church. If push came to shove I could even camp in the open air, in the dry riverbed or somewhere. But behind her jaded looks, as I'd already discovered, Dalena had a will of flint.

'The schoolroom is empty,' she said. 'With all the upheaval nowadays I'm sure it won't be needed again soon. So we have room enough.'

'But there's no bed, Dalena,' Lukas Death pointed out. I got the impression that he'd grasp at any pretext to be rid of his house guests – not necessarily because he resented our presence, but because as Judge he found it risky to be compromised in the eyes of his flock.

'Flip can stay, he was here first,' said Emma. 'I can find a place to sleep in Annie's house.'

'My yes is my yes,' Dalena cut her short.

Lukas Death tried another approach: 'Actually, it will be easier for her with Annie, Dalena. And she'll be a help for Annie too.'

With embarrassing directness Dalena asked, 'Do you have anything against Emma then?'

'It's not that I have anything against Emma, Dalena. But there are good reasons why she shouldn't stay with us.'

She looked him straight in the face. 'You may have your reasons, Lukas, and I know you've had them for a long time. But Klein-Lukas is dead and all I have to say is that if Isak threw Emma out then it's only right and proper for us to take her in.'

'She can have Little-Lukas's room,' I proposed. 'I'll sleep on the floor in the schoolroom.'

But there was no need for that, Dalena quickly pointed out. The outcome was that the unused coffin of Lukas Up-Above was prepared for me.

I'd have preferred the fucking floor any time, but Dalena wouldn't hear of it. And in a community where even bride and groom spent their first night in a coffin I suppose there was nothing offbeat about the proposal. Moreover, it turned out to be the biggest coffin I'd ever seen, almost the size of a double bed, and surprisingly soft inside. A bit dusty, if truth be told, but that was only to be expected after a hundred years.

Capital Offence

AND SO IT came that like two newly-weds in the Devil's Valley Emma and I spent the night in a coffin. Deep in the night she came to me, like one of my nightwalkers. I heard the door open, and sat up, startled. Although I knew it could only be her, it was unexpected all the same. It had been different in her room in Isak Smous's house; even in my room at Tant Poppie's it would not have been a problem. But here in the house of the Judge, it felt like a goddamn crime. A capital offence for all I knew.

She got into the coffin next to me. In a way I suppose it was funny. But more like macabre. And dangerous above all, for her more than for me.

'If Lukas Death finds out about this all hell will be loose, Emma.'

'He needn't find out.'

'He's already upset about your staying here.'

'That's his worry.'

'What has he got against you?'

'He never liked me. He tried everything he could to keep Little-Lukas and me apart.'

'But why?'

'I suppose I just wasn't good enough for his son. I'm rubbish, remember.'

'But Lukas Death is such a gormless soul, I'm sure he wouldn't hurt a fly. Have you ever tried to have it out with him? I'm sure he'll understand reason.'

'Don't underestimate the man, Flip. He's possessed by the same devil as all the Lermiets.'

'If that's so, then how on earth can you come here to sleep with me under his own roof?'

She held her breath. 'I just can't sleep in Little-Lukas's room.'

'What is there to be scared of?'

'You don't understand, Flip,' she said. 'Little-Lukas is in there. He wanted to get into bed with me all the time. He never pestered me like that when he was still alive, but he isn't shy any longer.'

I swallowed the sudden spurt of jealousy. In this fucked-up place nothing was too bloody outrageous to believe. And perhaps it was this very weird discovery of having a ghost for a rival that made it happen. In spite of all my good intentions, and after having struggled for so long to control my feelings, that night I fell for it. Hook, line and sinker.

My Hand Between

Even when she started caressing me with an urgency that caught me unawares, I still tried to resist: 'Emma, we're tempting fate. This is too bloody dangerous.'

'I know you want to.'

'As soon as we're out of the Devil's Valley, I promise you we'll make love. But not here, not now.'

To my consternation she said, 'You did it with the others who came to you.'

'How do you know that?' I stammered.

'I just know.'

'That was quite different,' I protested, 'I didn't even know them.'

'And if we never have another chance?'

'Don't say that, Emma.'

'Do you rather want me to go back to Little-Lukas?'

Quietly, as if it was the most obvious thing in the world to do, and in a way it was, she pulled up her dress to her waist and placed my hand between her legs.

Crime reporter forfeits last opportunity of redemption. Chooses hell with open eyes.

So yes, Your Worship, yes, we did. The earth didn't move, but when she came she cried. And as a matter of fact, so did I.

Not Alone

I was still inside her when, finding her invisible face in the dark, I said with an urgency I couldn't control, 'We cannot stay here after this.'

'I know,' she said, her hands entangled in the hair on my back. 'You will have to go.'

'You too, Emma.'

'We're not talking about me now.'

'You can't risk your life for nothing.'

'You call this nothing?' She briefly stirred, and with a contraction of subterranean muscles I did not expect in one so inexperienced, she clasped me and made me swell again.

'We're talking about life and death, Emma.'

'Don't talk,' she whispered.

We made love again, even though I never thought I'd be up to it again so soon. We were both exhausted. Perhaps we even fell asleep. But we were still joined when, sometime in the night, I said once more, 'You *must* go back with me, Emma.'

And after a very long pause she said, 'All right, I will. As soon as we can get away without anyone knowing.'

'We mustn't wait too long.'

But she had drifted off already, in the crook of my arm, in Lukas Up-Above's ample coffin. I couldn't sleep. Even the sense of fulfilment I felt about what had happened could not contain the many fears that beset me. And to make it worse there was the strange sensation – throughout the night, until just before dawn when she rose, and kissed me, and tiptoed out – that we were not alone. It wasn't just the sound of footsteps pacing through the house all night: that was probably Lukas Death wandering about, keeping watch. It was something else, and more unnerving in its way. It was too dark to see anything, but the stale smell of whisky in the room betrayed his presence. I'd recognise White Horse anywhere.

The Same Dress

FROM THE CONFUSION of those days, in which all bloody chronology was suspended, only two encounters remain vivid in my mind. With Henta, and with Gert Brush.

Henta in the bluegum wood, the day little Piet Snot was buried, a small interval between all the preparations for the Valley's next assault on God. I couldn't face going to the funeral. Nor could Henta, I suppose. But this meeting was different from the others. There was no provocation. Although she must have sensed how diffident I was, because with a bitchy edge I hadn't excepted of her she said:

'Oom needn't be afraid of me.'

'What makes you think I'm afraid?'

'You never liked me.'

'Henta, that's not true.'

'It is. Everything I do you think is dirty.'

'Please stop it.'

'Why didn't you go to the funeral?'

'Why didn't *you* go? He was your brother.'

Instead of answering she asked, 'Will you be going away now?'

'What makes you think such a thing?'

She just shrugged. The thin material of her torn dress — still the same dress — clung to her. She bore on her body the smell of the night as others do the smell of sex. Out of the blue she said, 'Won't you please take me with you?'

'If you go with me they'll immediately come after us to fetch us back.'

'Well, I'm not going to stay here any more.'

'You mustn't do anything rash, Henta.'

'What do you want me to do with this then?' she pressed her two palms to the curve of her lower belly. I remembered the prayer-meeting and I felt sick. I thought: *My God, she wasn't pretending after all.*

Her eyes stared at me, the once-beautiful eyes which had seen too much; nothing of which could now be effaced. *We're all marked.* Everything brings us closer to our death. (Little lesson from the crime reporter.)

I wanted to reply, but couldn't; she wasn't expecting anything more from me either. Without warning she turned round and ran off, effortless as a bird taking flight, leaving no scar. I stood bewitched. I wanted her to come back, but to which name would she respond? Henta? Talita? This time I didn't even have a bunch of bluegum leaves as an alibi. Who still remembered Talita Lightfoot? Who would remember Henta? For how long must the circles on the surface of this dark pool still go on? What price must still be paid, what sacrifices brought, before she would be redeemed? And all that remained in me after the girl had disappeared, forever, among the fragrant eucalyptus trees, was guilt. For something I still couldn't understand, but which felt like betrayal. Worse, much worse, than any other act of fucking betrayal I'd committed before, and God knows there were many.

Four Tits

GERT BRUSH. I didn't go to his place on purpose, but when in passing I saw him at work on a painting in his voorhuis I climbed up the few steps to the stoep. Like the previous time, I had the impression that I'd caught him unawares, and he quickly put out his hand to turn around the canvas he'd been working on, but then left it after all. His face was smudged with paint.

'Am I disturbing you, Gert?'

'Not really. I was just messing around.'

'I still meant to thank you for speaking up for me the other day.'

'This place is like a beehive,' he muttered. 'I don't know how long this can still go on.'

'Why did you do it?' I asked.

'Because I think you mean well.' He wiped his face with a much-used cloth, succeeding only in making a greater mess of it. 'But I think you have outstayed your welcome, if I may say so.'

'If it was only me I'd have gone long ago, Gert. But I'm worried about Emma. She deserves better.'

'We all deserve better.'

I came closer. The canvas on his easel was just a confusion of brush-strokes, yet it seemed vaguely familiar.

'Isn't this the one you were working on the last time I saw you?'

'Could be.'

'Why did you paint out Emma's face?'

'It wasn't Emma.'

'But I saw it myself.'

'Must have been a mistake.' He looked ill at ease. 'I was trying to do a portrait of Mooi-Janna. But it didn't work.'

'Strong-Lukas's daughter? The one who . . .?'

'Yes. It was the first time I tried to paint one of the women. The problem is no one can remember what she looked like. My father and grandfather also tried, I know, but it was no use. In the end we just paint the face we can call up most clearly.'

'But the black hair, the straight eyebrows . . .?'

He started to wipe the top layer of paint from the canvas with his cloth. 'All anybody knows about Mooi-Janna with any certainty,' he said, 'is that she had four tits.'

'Where did you hear that?'

'Everybody knows. That was why she could do what she did, you see. No man could resist that. And you must admit, it's not the sort of thing one sees every day. But of course I'd never dare to paint that, the people wouldn't allow it.'

Plaited Thongs

THROUGH ALL OF this, as in the days before Nagmaal, there was a sense of urgency building up. Its focus was the Final Solution proposed by the Council of Justice to solve the problem of drought. Pure sacrilege, boomed Brother Holy through his bouts of scratching, but no one was paying much attention to him any more. It had been Hans Magic's brainchild. And I must confess that even if the means were old-fashioned, the thought behind it was pretty up to date. The idea was to bombard the clouds when they showed themselves again: literally to shoot the rain from them.

'And if you hit God?' asked Brother Holy in righteous fury, tying himself into a most undignified knot to scratch his arse.

'Then He better duck,' sneered Hans Magic.

Not that there was much danger of that, the fucking technology was far too primitive. The plan was to select two sturdy saplings in the bluegum wood, close enough together to be used as props for the catapult they had devised, and then to tie a long loop of plaited thongs between them. Once this was done, all the men in the Devil's Valley – with the exception of a few conscientious objectors – would give a hand to pull the two saplings back as far as possible, fit a heavy boulder into the loop, and then to anchor the contraption in that position until the clouds came over. According to Lukas Death this was among the techniques first devised by Lukas Up-Above in his attempts at flying; and it had taken him six months to recover after a quite spectacular failure. It was after this event that he'd turned to birds.

All things considered, it was quite a feat. And in a way it restored to their ranks something of the unity that had been so sorely disrupted. To Emma and me it came as a bloody blessing as it gave the settlers something else to focus on.

The contraption was put to the test several times. With the first few attempts one of the trees, or both, snapped in the process, causing the rock to drop limply right in front of them. The fourth or fifth time round it hit Jos Joseph who was too slow in scampering out of the way, and shattered his spine. This caused several corrections to be made, and stronger trees were selected, but to play it safe it was agreed not to have another trial run: faith would do the necessary.

By the third or fourth day everything was ready. Only the clouds had to put in an appearance. And as it turned out, they proved to be surprisingly cooperative, because after the previous gales they'd more or less fallen into the habit of coming over in the afternoon. The wind sprang up. The first clouds came rolling through the mountains, white at first, but rapidly growing darker. The whole settlement was present, including the sceptics, the conscientious objectors, and even Brother Holy. A few of the oldest inhabitants, and some of the sick too weak to move, were transported to the bluegum wood on handmade stretchers or wooden wheelbarrows, as this promised to be a spectacle no one wanted to miss. The only absentee I was aware of, and a notable one at that, was the old Seer. Which confirmed my hunch that after spilling his black beans he'd finally chosen to go to rest.

Uninvited, and still scratching away, Brother Holy intoned a rambling prayer. But no one paid attention. Well before he'd finished a chorus of voices shouted, 'Watch out!' Whether it was meant for the crowd or for God, was not quite clear.

Requiescat in Pace

The plaited thongs were pulled loose from the anchor. The two elastic saplings swung up. But something in the calculations had gone wrong, because at the last moment the cocksucking Peet Flatfoot didn't let go in time with the rest of them, so that he was propelled into space with the rock. *Ejaculatio praecox*, in a manner of speaking.

For lack of velocity the projectile and its human pilot plunged to earth a mere thirty yards or so away. *Requiescat in pace*, Prickhead.

'I told you so,' exclaimed Brother Holy in a thundering voice before the next itch convulsed him into a ball.

Most of the spectators, shaken by the accident, gloomily prepared to return home. But Jurg Water was so inspired by the event and by the clouds which continued to churn overhead, that he had a rare moment of inspiration. 'If we all fire up into the clouds together,' he proposed, 'who knows, we could make the rain come down.'

There was very little discussion. Lukas Death was the only one with open reservations: this was a serious business, he argued, there was too much at stake to rush in blindly without weighing the consequences. But he was soon outshouted. Some might have felt that they owed it to the late Prickhead to succeed the second time round, so that his death would not have been in vain. Others were simply fired by the excitement they'd already worked up and which demanded an outlet.

From the bluegum wood the procession moved downhill to the settlement, where the men scattered among the houses to return within minutes bristling with the most unusual assortment of firearms I've ever seen. The latest models, as far as I could judge with my limited knowledge, were Lee-Metfords and Mausers. But there were ancient elephant guns too, which I remembered from history books, and impressive old flintlocks and blunderbusses and double- and triple-barrelled carbines.

Loading was a damn serious business. The men operating muzzle-loaders were allowed to start first, as it was one hell of an elaborate process first to pour a handful of gunpowder down the barrel, followed by a round bullet and a piece of greased cloth pressed into position with a ramrod, after which another handful of gunpowder had to be poured into the pan and the lid closed. Only then could the rifle be cocked, ready to take aim. It took careful planning to make sure that all the preparations would result in a single Big Bang. Lukas Death tried one last time to dissuade the trigger-happy men, but Jurg Water rudely brushed him aside. From a safe distance Petrus Tatters began the countdown. An earsplitting salvo thundered among the high cliffs.

'Got him!' shouted Jurg Water.

'Now you've gone too far,' cried Lukas Death. He was trembling, but whether in rage or fear was hard to judge.

A huge bank of thundercloud, hovering directly above the settlement, had begun to twist and writhe about in a most alarming manner, as if it had actually been wounded. The dark boiling mass threw out white scalloped edges as it began to fold into itself. And the wind which had been tugging at us sporadically, began very rapidly to work up a terrifying speed.

Even Hans Magic was beginning to show signs of alarm about the way things were going.

'This is bad,' said Lukas Death, now scared right out of his fucking wits. 'I warned you, but you wouldn't listen. God will not be mocked. We must get back to our houses. Make sure all the doors are bolted and secured.' In the absence of Brother Holy who was imitating the fucking convolutions of the thundercloud, Lukas stretched out his arm towards his distressed people. In a breaking voice he invoked the love of God, the mercy of our Lord Jesus Christ, and the powerful presence of the Holy Ghost to be with us all. Without bothering to say Amen he broke into a trot to get home before the storm broke.

All Over the Valley

IN THE BEGINNING all four of us sat in Lukas Death's voorhuis listening to the wind raging outside. From time to time large objects came hurtling and careening past the windows. Although it was no new experience any more, this time it was more terrifying than before. Nobody spoke. We were all huddled together, yet each was utterly alone.

The darker it became, and the wilder the storm raged outside, the warmer the scorched circle in the middle of the floor felt under our feet. In the deep dusk of the interior it was glowing an unearthly red, as if all the heat of the Seer's long-ago couplings on his enemy's grave had been rekindled.

When the thunder started, Dalena rose to cover the few mirrors in the house with cloths. After that she couldn't sit down again. The storm was growing steadily worse. The violence was unbelievable. It sounded as if the very mountains were falling. It must have been in a storm like this, in prehistoric times, that the earth was torn open and the deep gash of the valley ripped into it. Perhaps that first great battle between the Seer and the Devil was being fought again; for all we knew the whole fucking Book of Revelations was finally being thrown at us. Which would bloody well have served the Devil's Valley right, I thought: but why the hell should *I* be caught up in it? It was fucking unfair. If God wanted to have it out with this nest of vipers, then by all means, and with my blessing; but keep me out of it.

In the midst of all that noise Dalena suddenly went through to their bedroom, and when she came back she was holding something in her hands. At first I couldn't make out what it was. But when she opened the front door and it felt as though all the wind in the valley came gushing in to blow the lot of us away, I recognised it. By then it was too late to stop her.

'Dalena!' shouted Lukas Death. 'For God's sake, woman, come back!'

'You didn't want him back,' she called into the wind as she let go of the battered little box. The wind immediately tore it from her hands. 'There goes Little-Lukas,' she said quietly. 'Now he's all over the valley.'

Lukas Death ran after her to bring her back, but she was already inside. It took all four of us to push the door to again.

'Now one can at last be at peace again,' she said with a curious expression of relief on her drawn face.

'How could you do a thing like that?' He grabbed her by the front of her dress and started tugging with a kind of uncontrollable rage that left me dumbstruck.

But with surprising strength Dalena shoved him away. 'Let me be, Lukas,' she hissed. 'I've just about had it with you.'

'How can you humiliate me so in front of other people?' he shouted. 'Dalena, have you forgotten that I'm the appointed Judge of the Devil's Valley?'

She took a deep breath. 'Let's go to the bedroom, Lukas. We can talk there.'

Column of Fire

The two of them withdrew to their bedroom. We remained behind, too dismayed to speak for some time. From behind the closed bedroom door there was a long bout of angry, arguing voices, but at last it subsided. Emma went over to one of the two small windows in the voorhuis to look out.

I followed her. 'I'm not sure it's wise to stand here,' I said, 'with all this lightning.'

She shook her head. I should have known. This attraction of the violent and the dangerous. Together with her I stared at the near-continuous lightning. There was almost no interval between the flashes. The whole mountain, heaven and earth, everything, seemed to be going up in flames, alternating between sheet lightning in which whole clouds erupted into fire, and rapid blinding spiderwebs of light that made the sky look like a huge black egg cracking over us. And what would hatch from it, God alone knew. More than once a bolt was followed by a dull thud, a sure sign that something had been hit. But what – chimney, church tower, tree, or cliff?

The light coming from outside turned a strange, venomous green. Inside the deep dark red of the floor was glowing more and more ominously. I had no idea of how long the storm went on. I was too mesmerised by the violence of the spectacle to be conscious of time. If Ouma Liesbet had been right about the lightning-bird, even she could never have anticipated a winged monster quite like this. Forgetting all about our own safety we now stood squarely in front of the window. This time the earth was indeed moving, but not with love. If the lightning chose to strike us, at least we'd go together. It might be a solution for many people, including ourselves.

Somewhere during all that violence Emma suddenly half-turned towards me and caught my arm. I'd also seen it: high up on the slope behind the houses, where dark fingers of virgin forest reached down towards the bluegum wood, a column of fire had sprung up. The lightning must have struck a tree. As we watched, it began to spread at amazing speed, fanned by the wind, until the whole slope was ablaze. It wasn't surprising, the mountain was so dry, it had just been waiting to be ignited. There was a barren band between the wood and the houses where the goats had stripped the earth of all vegetation, but given the fierceness of the wind still raging in the kloofs, one couldn't be sure that the flames wouldn't jump the divide. And within minutes a second fire had started, then a third. We ran to the window opposite. The slopes on that side were burning too. The entire settlement was caught in a circle of fire. And as it became darker, the flames leaped ever higher.

But slowly, almost unnoticeably at first, the fury of the storm began to run out of steam. The thunder withdrew into the distance, down the valley, across the mountains, gone. There were still sporadic flickerings of lightning, like brief flaming afterthoughts, accompanied by the now almost inaudible rumble of thunder shuddering in one's bones. And then it was over. The wind also died down. But the mountains were still burning.

Greyish Ash

In the hissing silence following the storm we set out into the night. Like two ghosts we wandered through the emptiness of the dark settlement in its ring of fire. There was no light anywhere, as if the inhabitants were scared of attracting attention. No one else had ventured outside. Even in the dark the extent of the destruction was fearsome. The previous storms had been bad enough, but this combination of wind and lightning had been the fucking limit. Several of the houses had been razed to the ground. What had become of the inhabitants was anybody's guess. And all around us was that infernal circle of fire on the mountain slopes. Thank God it seemed to be working its way upward, not down to the houses. And the flames were slowly burning themselves out.

'Look, this is it,' I said. 'Tomorrow we must go. There's nothing left for us here.'

'If it isn't too late already,' said Emma.

'We're still alive.' I took her hands.

We were above the higher row of houses, behind Tant Poppie's place, which also lay in ruins. I went cold.

I stole nearer with a hollow feeling my guts, and shouted her name, but there was no sound from the remains of the house. In the dark it was impossible to make out anything. I could only hope that she'd been out on a call, or that someone else had offered her shelter.

In a way the discovery next door was even worse. It was the forlorn mewing of the cats that drew me closer. And on the front stoep, propped up against the door that had been torn from its hinges, I found Tall-Fransina, half-buried under the débris of a fallen pillar. We kneeled beside her and began to scrape away the rubble. What shocked me most was that her face was covered in ashes. Not the soot of the night's fires, but whitish, greyish ash that appeared eerily familiar even in the dark. Without saying anything to Emma, I gently wiped it from her face, then bent over to try mouth-to-mouth, but there was no life in her. Together we half-carried, half-dragged her inside and laid her on the big bed. Emma found a candle and lit it. In the dancing light cats approached from all sides to snuggle up against Tall-Fransina's body as they had done for God knows how many years.

We didn't speak. We went outside again, leaving the candle burning. I stacked some stones against the front door to prop it into position and keep out the night. For what must have been another hour we continued our speechless wandering among the ruins of the settlement.

Madman

'They'll all be working to clear up the damage tomorrow,' I said as we turned back to Lukas Death's house. 'They'll be much too busy to notice. I'll leave early and wait for you at the rock pool.'

'I'll help Dalena first,' she said. 'I don't want anyone to get suspicious, not even her.'

'I'll wait for you.'

'It could take a while, to make absolutely sure.'

'Of course. But don't be too late. It's a long way.'

She nodded against my shoulder. 'I promise. Before noon, at the latest.'

We turned back.

It was Emma who saw it first, clutching my hand in sudden fright: flames were shooting up from the thatched roof of Lukas Death's house. It was strange indeed, so long after the storm. And there was no wind any more to blow live coals from the distant mountain fires.

Then I noticed the black figure moving along the ridge of the roof towards the attic stairs. It was too dark to make out who it was.

'Hey!' I shouted. 'What the hell are you doing there?' I started running. Emma followed.

The arsonist had seen us. He broke into a huddled trot, scuttling away from the fire. But in his haste he lost his balance, stumbled, caught fire. I heard him shout. He came tumbling down the staircase, a spectacular ball of fire somersaulting in the dark, screaming like a pig.

When he reached the bottom he flung himself to the ground, rolling about to smother the flames. Emma came running past me, plucked the front door open and started shouting hysterically at Dalena and Lukas to wake up and come out. Already the fire in the dried-out thatch was leaping high into the night.

When I reached the madman who was still twisting and thrashing about on the ground, I began to kick at him, but whether to kill the flames or the man I honestly didn't know.

'Help me,' he groaned, 'help me, help me.'

'Jurg, you fucking bastard,' I hissed through my teeth.

True Colours

I've been sitting here at the rock pool since God knows when, waiting for Emma to come so that we can tackle the long climb out of the Devil's Valley. It must be past noon. I'm not sure I can risk going back to look for her, but I can't stay here either, doing nothing.

I'm tired to the bone. All kinds of memories are hurtling through the fucking tumble-dryer of my mind. The frantic attempts to help Lukas and Dalena save a few odds and ends of furniture, and sheets and pillows, and Lukas Death's two old rifles from the burning house before the roof fell in. By that time the flames had jumped to the house next door, and the next. Very soon the whole goddamn settlement was burning. Apart from trying to salvage whatever one could grab hold of, there was nothing to be done, not a drop of water to douse the flames. It was a sight, all those soot-stained faces in the wild firelight, the idiots jumping up and down like locusts, ululating and yodelling, laughing and dribbling, children screaming, old people crying, scenes from a pretty old-fashioned kind of hell. A few of the people had been injured, although none as desperately as Jurg Water. From somewhere in the night, to everybody's relief, Tant Poppie came waddling on to give a hand; but with all her remedies buried under the ruins of her house there wasn't much she could do. Several of Tall-Fransina's cats were flayed alive to apply the skins to the wounds of the injured, for what it might be worth. Duck-shit was used as well, and burnt peach-stones, and honey, and whatever came to hand as the night wore on.

Hanna squatted over the groaning, shivering Jurg, to pee on his burnt face where no skin was left. Henta was nowhere to be seen. I could only guess that she'd already run away as she'd threatened to; but where in that burning night could she have found shelter? I tried not to think of it, but it was — once again — like the remedy of the fucking woman's navel. *The slight curve, the deep inverted comma, and below. Throw it in the sea.*

Brother Holy was called upon to help Jurg when his wife's last desperate efforts failed, but he was caught in such a paroxysm of scratching than he was more of a hindrance than a help. Still, he tried.

I wasn't particularly keen to follow the stages of Jurg Water's painful death, but in a perverse way it fascinated me. *Crime reporter shows true colours.* Like a praying mantis Brother Holy bobbed up and down around him on his stick-legs, trying to the very last to snatch a lost soul back from death.

'Jurg, Jurg, can you hear me?' Hopping on his left leg in order to scratch under his right foot. 'Jurg, it is time to go.' Scratching under the left breast. 'Jurg, you must turn away from the Devil.' Scratching the old dry balls.

'This is not a time to make enemies, Brother,' groaned Jurg. And as far as I know those were his last words.

Fertile Rift

In small bewildered clusters the people huddled in the empty spaces between the houses as the last burning roofs subsided. From time to time a few hesitant flames would still spring up to flicker for a few minutes, but without much conviction. The air was heavy with soot. It was hard to keep away from Emma, but so near the end I didn't want to stir up even a hint of suspicion anywhere. With both the Peeping Tom and the prime culprit out of the way (so God didn't sleep after all, I thought with wry satisfaction) we could breathe somewhat more easily for a while, but it was prudent not to screw anything up unnecessarily.

Only at first light did people begin to stir again. There was a kind of morbid eagerness to see the full extent of the damage in the light of day. But there was fear too. No one knew exactly what to expect.

My own impression, as the dusty sun began to glow on the highest peaks, was that it was even worse that I'd feared. The mountains were black, the settlement a ruin. Even the heavy blunt tower of the church had collapsed. It was as if the lightning had struck from two directions simultaneously: the sky above and the earth below. And here where they met, in the once fertile rift of the Devil's Valley, there was devastation.

Once I'd shouldered my rucksack I tried as unobtrusively as possible to edge away from the dumbfounded crowd, winding my way through the houses, away from the church, first heading in the direction opposite to the one I meant to take; in passing, as if by accident, I brushed past Emma, and whispered:

'I'll be waiting.'

She nodded without looking at me, briefly touched my hand, and then accompanied Dalena back to the blackened remains of their house.

No Concern

At the far end of the settlement, where I meant to cut through to the patch of prickly pear on the opposite slope on a roundabout route to the dried-up riverbed, I came upon Hans Magic. His unlit calabash pipe clenched between his teeth, he sat slumped on Tall-Fransina's crumbled stoep, staring into the distance, deserted even by his cloud of flies. This was pure shit. He was just about the last person I could have wished to meet. But it was too late to turn back.

Without looking up at me he said, 'So, Neef Flip.'

My stomach turned as I desperately tried to think of a way out, but my thoughts were trapped. I felt like a meerkat facing a geelslang.

'Now Fransina is dead too,' he said unexpectedly. 'Brother Holy has struck me with the darkness of Egypt after all. I've now taken away his itch. But that won't bring Fransina back.'

'I found her on the stoep last night,' I said diffidently. 'The pillar fell on her. I don't know what she was doing outside in the storm.'

'She came to see me, that's what. I asked her to stay, but she wouldn't.'

'What could have been so urgent?'

'You,' he said. For the first time he raised his head to look at me. 'You and Emma.'

'I don't understand,' I said, aware only of a blankness inside me.

'She asked me to leave you alone. We're getting old, she said. We can't go on trying to hold on to life through others.' A pissed-off tone crept into his voice. 'I don't know what made her think the two of you matter one bit to me.' He sucked at his pipe as if he didn't realise it had gone out long ago. 'And now you're off?'

'I'm just checking on the damage.'

'With your rucksack on your back.' A dry snort. 'Do what you wish,' he said in a weary voice. 'Fransina is dead. I really can't care less about you. Just leave me alone with the feeling I got in me.'

For a moment I still lingered. Then I went on my way, unsure of whether I should feel relieved or concerned. Once before he'd asked me, *Do you believe me?* But this time I really had no idea what I believed any more.

More Gone

And here I am, waiting at the rock pool. Something must have happened, for there is still no sign of her. Without her I cannot even think of going on; but dare I go back to look for her?

I walk round the pool set deep in the barren rocks. How many times have I done so during the past few hours? Over there, right there, she was standing that first day, shaking the water from her hair. This was where I first saw her, as I've never seen her since, naked, with the light on her collarbones and her shoulders, and the four tips of her breasts. The way a painter would have seen her, someone like Gert Brush. Like a painter I recall the particulars of her body, as real and sure as these rocks. And yet she left no wet footprints, not a trace. She was and wasn't there. I still cannot explain it. All I know is that today she is even more gone than on that first day.

But she must come, for God's sake, she promised. That is, if I can believe her. I remember all her lies, her changing stories. But surely that was only in the beginning, wasn't it, when she was still unsure about me. It's different now. It must be different. I think I—

You Two

It's she, it's Emma. I can see her making her way very fast up the dry riverbed. It's one of the few thickets not touched by the fire. She is in such a hurry that she keeps on stumbling, even after she has stooped to lift the hem of her dress high above her knees. From a distance I can hear her panting.

'Emma, you've come!'

The long rectangle of the dried-up pool lies between us. She breaks into a run, along the left edge of the deep hole in the rocks. Watch out, I think, Jesus, watch your step, don't slip! And at last she falls into my arms. I feel her body shaking against mine.

'Emma, what's the matter? What happened?'

'They saw me. They're coming after us.'

'Don't worry. They'll never catch up with us.'

She keeps clinging to me. Is it my imagination or can I hear a crashing and breaking of branches approaching from a distance, rocks clattering, a sound of shouting voices? I press her hard against me. Over her shoulder I can see something moving. As he breaks through the brittle reeds I recognise Lukas Death. The crumpled black suit is in a fucking state. In his hands he has one of his two ancient, unwieldy guns. The moment he sees us he stops to raise the bloody thing to his shoulder.

'Lukas, wait!' I shout. 'What the hell are you doing?'

She tears herself away from me. 'Oom Lukas, don't!'

I can see him shaking with rage. 'You two . . .!' he stammers. 'You two, let loose among us by the Devil himself. If it hadn't been for you, Little-Lukas would still have been with us.'

Emma starts running back towards the man in black, her hands outstretched to stop him. Lukas Death drops down on one knee.

I can hear my own voice shouting, 'Emma, come back!'

And hers: 'Oom Lukas, don't!'

Then I hear the sound of the shot. She stumbles as she runs, and falls down. There is a great tangle of old dry branches and roots and underbrush at the farthest corner of the pool. She falls right through it all, down to the rock-floor below. It can't be true, it isn't possible. Someone must be dreaming again. Jesus Christ, when will I get into a dream of my own for a fucking change? I cannot move.

'Lukas, for God's sake, man . . .!'

Then comes the second shot. For a moment I don't understand what the hell is going on, I haven't seen Lukas reload. Only when he topples forward from his kneeling position and rolls over on his side do I realise that it wasn't he who fired.

Like a sleepwalker I begin to shuffle along the side of the hole, past the spot where Emma crashed through the branches, trying to get to Lukas Death. A pool of bright blood is spreading across the flat surface of the rock under him. Unbelievable how much blood there is in a person. It will never cease to amaze me.

Dalena appears among the withered trees and fynbos in the dry bed. She stops when she sees me. Her hair is plastered all over her sweaty face. She also carries a gun.

Half-Asleep

But why she? And why Lukas Death, such a harmless man, so pious, so insignificant? I'm still sitting down here on the floor of the pool, on my knees at Emma's side. The dress which in her fall was practically torn from her body, I have folded back to cover her. The left leg, which landed at an unnatural angle turned in under her, I've straightened out. One could almost think that she's only sleeping, dreaming, except if you look at what's left of her face.

The body I loved no longer moves. It was the events of this body, I think, which at long last turned me into the only historian I'll ever be, when my body wrote the chronicle of hers, and hers of mine. Now she is dead.

Was this, I wonder in a wave of nausea, what the motherfucking old Hans Magic meant when he said, 'Leave me alone with this feeling in me'?

Just leave me alone now. For fuck's sake, just leave me alone.

Above me, on the edge of the dry pool, stands Dalena. I'm trying very hard to follow what she says. Her breath, which came in deep gasps when I first saw her, is back to normal. She actually appears unnaturally calm.

Over and over again I hear myself asking the same questions. Why she? And why Lukas Death? And why Emma?

Dalena talks to me as if she's trying to soothe a child. I try to follow. It had to be done, she says, because Emma was Lukas Death's child. With the girl Maria, all those years ago. It happened when he went to fetch her back after she'd run away. His best friend, Ben Owl, had asked him to. But he cheated on Ben Owl. High up in the mountains he fell on Maria when she was half-asleep and didn't know before it was too late what was going on. After that she refused to have anything more to do with him. And when she found out that she was pregnant she agreed to marry Ben Owl, to spite Lukas. And Lukas married Dalena. Little-Lukas was born only a few months after Emma.

Now you'll understand, says Dalena, why Lukas Death's life became a living hell when the two children fell in love. He couldn't tell anybody why he was so dead against it. She herself had always had it wrong. Only last night he finally told her.

'Now it doesn't matter any more, I don't care if they all know,' she says, 'I have found peace in my mind. I have done what I had to do. But you must hurry up now, Neef Flip. The people down there will have heard the shots, they'll be coming up here any minute now. They mustn't find you here.'

'But Emma . . .'

'There's nothing more you or anyone else can do for Emma. She'd have wanted you to get out of this place. For her sake too.' A very brief pause, then she adds under her breath, 'And perhaps for mine, who knows?'

Dark Mole

I walk along the edge of the hole alone, over to the far side. Here is the spot where she stood that day. I stop. I go down on my haunches.

I touch the rock with one numb finger. For here are her footprints, clear as anything, pressed deep into the rock. Slowly I get up again. I stare across the empty pool. Dalena has gone back into the tangled underbrush. I can't see Emma's body from here either; but perhaps it is because I'm crying.

From down below, behind me, I can now clearly hear voices coming this way. Maybe Dalena will delay them, maybe not.

As if stoned out of my mind, my guts like a millstone weighing me down, I crouch down low and duck into the underbrush along the dry bed. God knows if I'll ever find my way again. But even if I don't find all the shortcuts Prickhead followed that first afternoon – and for all I know they may not have been shortcuts at all – I swear to God I'll get out of the valley sooner or later. How long did it take Mooi-Janna's pursuers to get to the top? At least they had her there waiting for them, with her dark hair undone, her straight eyebrows, her four nipples.

Today was the first time I'd seen Emma's body, when I kneeled beside her down there in the dried-up pool to fold the torn flaps of her dress over her. My hands were trembling, and I tried not to look. But there was time enough to see, and I know now that there were only two, not four. With a small dark mole like the footprint of a goat just below her left nipple, exactly as Tant Poppie had described it.

Memorise this, I thought, remember, hold on to it, against all the nights and days and delusions to come, when I might be tempted to distort and betray it, to lie about it. My body will not forget.

Nothing Happened

Once, when I have to stop to catch my breath – there is no sign of my pursuers any more – I look out over the long narrow valley stretching out far below, tranquil in the can't-care-less glare of the sun. There is an ungodly quiet over the mountains.

I have made unexpectedly good progress. Already it is difficult to believe what has happened down there. All I have, I the historian, I the crime reporter, in search of facts, facts, facts, is an impossible tangle of contradictory stories.

And yet she said, *It doesn't mean that nothing happened.* Don't ever forget that.

At the time I still thought that perhaps one day I could manage to put all the bits and pieces together and make sense of them. Now I'm no longer so sure. Not because there are so many stories I've not yet heard, but because I suspect that even if I were to know them all there would still not be a whole, just an endless gliding from one to another.

All I know is that I came here, that I tried to trace a history, and that I'm now on my way back, alone. Less than I was, or more.

Crude Capitals

This is the Bushman Krans. So I'm still on the right track after all. The colours of the rock paintings are surprisingly bright, as if they were done yesterday. The eland, the few elephant, the wildebeest, the small male figures with their silly little pricks. And chiselled right across them, the inscription in crude capitals: STRONG-LUKAS. The hero of his tribe, the one who wiped out the enemy commando. Somewhere below these very cliffs must lie the bones of the girl he shrugged from his back when they no longer needed her. To keep their honour and their pride intact, for all the generations to come. It is as if I can hear Ouma Liesbet Prune's little cricket-voice chirping again, 'Lukas Seer began Lukas Nimrod, and Lukas Nimrod begat Lukas Up-Above, and Lukas Up-Above begat Strong-Lukas, and Strong-Lukas begat Lukas Bigballs, and Lukas Bigballs begat Lukas Devil, and Lukas Devil begat Lukas Death, and Lukas Death begat Little-Lukas.'

All of it as improbable as the skeleton of a whale in the mountains. And yet I was there, I saw it, I crumbled a piece of bone to dust between my fingers. Does that mean anything? Or am I beginning to grow into my own story like a toenail? Would Tant Poppie have a remedy for that?

Is The Last

For the moment everything is focused on a single point. To get out of here. And I'm well on my way. The day is almost over. For how many hours I have been going I cannot calculate, but it's been a fucking long time. Just a short distance more. Our crime reporter is returning with a story after all. Perhaps this time he'll meet his deadline. It may not turn out to be publishable, but that is neither here nor there. What counts is that the rat will have been fed at last.

Here are the two grey boulders, speckled with lichen, with fire inside. One of them has been split in two and lies broken on its side. The light is fading. Dusk has fallen. A thin little breeze is rustling in the brittle grass. Summer is over. It is autumn now.

Less than a hundred yards to go and I'll be out.

Then something hits my burning breath right out of my fucking lungs.

In the distance, on a small outcrop of rocks, at the ridge of the rise, exactly where Mooi-Janna would have met the men, sits the almost transparent figure of the shrunken old patriarch, his piss-stained beard tangled in the breeze, the two crutches beside him. His flock of mottled goats are grazing in mock-tranquillity to one side. He is staring into the distance, away from me.

I can hear my heart thudding in my ears. All I still have to do is to get past him. This is the last ordeal.

And then I hear him say, without looking at me, 'I been sitting here waiting for you.'

Glossary

ag – oh well

agterryer – batman, (Coloured) aide

baas – master

bantom – quartz-like pebble, fool's diamond

bergie – Cape Town vagrant

biltong – strips of dried salted meat

blue-train – methylated spirits

boetie – sonny (literally: little brother)

bredie – stew

buchu – fragrant herb, often used for kidney complaints

bywoner – tenant farmer, usually poor-white

Cape Smoke – nineteenth-century husk brandy made in the Cape Colony, notorious for its potency and pungency

christmas-worm – accordion

Comrades – ANC-supporting activists in black townships in the 1980s

dagga – South African marijuana

dassie – rock-rabbit

doepa – medicine, usually with a connotation of a magic potion

droëwors – dried sausage

dwaal, in a – dazed (literally: to wander)

duiker – small antelope

eland – large antelope

fynbos – scrub, shrubbery, undergrowth

geelslang – yellow-snake, extremely poisonous species of cobra ja – yes

kappie – old-fashioned bonnet

karie – strong beer brewed from honey

kaross – blanket or bed-cover made of animal skins

Khoikhoi – indigenous inhabitants of South Africa, known (pejoratively) as 'Hottentots'

Khoisan – collective appellation of related indigenous peoples ('Hottentots' and 'Bushmen')

kierie – stick, cane

kist – large chest

klipspringer – small antelope in mountainous habitat (literally: rock-jumper)

kloof – ravine or narrow valley

koppie – rocky hill

krans – cliff

leguan – iguana

lobola – (African) bride-price

maar – but; just

mebos – sugared dried apricots

meerkat – ground squirrel

meid – (pejorative) black or 'Coloured' woman

mooi – pretty, beautiful

mos – indeed; as you should know

muti – witch-doctor's potion

naartjie – tangerine

nagmaal – holy communion

necklacing – lynching by burning tyres, often performed by anti-government activists on suspected pro-apartheid informers

neef – cousin or nephew; also familiar form of address for a man roughly the same age as the speaker, or younger

Newlands – rugby stadium in Cape Town

Ossewa-Brandwag – extremist right-wing Afrikaner movement which resisted the effort of the South African government under Prime Minister Jan Smuts in support of the Allied forces against Hitler in the Second World War (literally: Ox-wagon Guard)

oom – uncle; also familiar form of address for older man

ouma – grandmother

oribi – small antelope

padkos – traveller's provisions (literally: food-for-the-road)

pandoer – Khoikhoi or 'Coloured' soldier in nineteenth-century Cape Colony

predikant – Dutch Reformed preacher

Rebellion – 1914–1915 uprising of Afrikaners against the decision of the South African government to support Britain in the First World War

riem(pie) – leather strip, thong

riempiesbank – bench with thong seats

samp – stamped maize kernels

sjambok – horsewhip

skinder – gossip

smous – pedlar, itinerant trader

steenbok – small antelope

stoep – veranda

Swartberg – Black Mountain, a range in the Little Karoo

tant(e) – aunt; also familiar form of address for an older woman

veldskoen – rough handmade shoe

voorhuis – front room

wagon-tree – tree-protea, the hard wood of which was used to make the fellies of wagon wheels

witblits – home-distilled alcohol, moonshine (literally: white lightning)

witdoek – black vigilantes in cahoots with police during riots in the Cape Town area in the 1980s (literally: white-cloths, from the distinguishing scarfs they wore)

witgat (coffee) – acrid brew made from an indigenous root